WEAVERS

ALSO BY ARIC DAVIS

WEAVERS

ARIC DAVIS

 THOMAS & MERCER

Published by Thomas & Mercer, Seattle

www.apub.com

Amazon, the Amazon logo, and Thomas & Mercer are trademarks of Amazon.com, Inc., or its affiliates.

ISBN-13: 9781477849347
ISBN-10: 1477849343

Cover design by Mark Ecob

Library of Congress Control Number: 2014957296

Printed in the United States of America

For Megan, every single word

Chapter 1

1945

I do as I am told, and it is easy work, for there is not much I can do.
I help carry things that are handed to me, but often I trip in the snow.
I eat little, though everyone wants to share with me. My eyes see nothing. The world, for all of its supposed glory, is just a haze to me, a fog
through which the brightness of the sun and the darkness of night are
indistinguishable. Yet I suffer. I suffer as we all must in a war, and that
is all right, for I have known precious little else. I sweat and I starve,
and while the women around me falter and die, their souls leaving their
bodies like inconsequential things, I feel their deaths like knives in my
belly. I have never been struck in my life—even the men here won't
beat a blind girl—but this is just as bad.

I live in a long house with people from all over Europe. Strangers at
first, we are like sisters now, but I would trade all of that in an instant
for freedom with my family. When they die, it is not the pain I felt
when my mother or grandmother died. It is not me. They don't die
quickly enough, though, because God has forgotten us—I know that

now. We were supposed to be his chosen people, but that is not the case. We are fodder. We are the walking dead.

There is no food. Even the guards complain. They blame us (but never me). They blame the Americans. They curse the Russians under their breath. They who have been our hell are waiting to die themselves now. This is not good enough for me, not anymore. I want unholy things for them. I want the things in the Torah that my family never spoke of. I want hell for these men. I don't care if I die—all of us owe God a death—but I want the men who did this to us to die first. There are times that I think they might, but God is a comedian, not a butler. He ignores my prayers, but he keeps me alive. I know this happens so that I may suffer, but I do not know why that might be, nor do I care. We all owe a death.

We can hear the fighting sometimes, but there is no comfort in that. Artillery fire means that the smell of death is stronger, that more of us are yanked from the lines to die. But not little Ora. Never poor, blind little Ora—not her.

They whisper about me at night. I can hear them wondering why their own children, their healthy children, were chosen during the sorting, but the cripple has been spared yet again. I have no answer for them, because I am not God. I am just like them—a captive waiting to die—and my thoughts on the matter mean far less than a stick on the fire or a crust of bread. Far less than the ovens or the showers or the stacks of frozen dead that border the fences that I have never seen and will never see.

Every day here is death, and only the cold can convince me that we are not already in hell. I could even accept my death, but my turn never comes up, and even though the other women hate me, I never have my food stolen. I live. Either God is more of a jester than I ever could have imagined, or a crueler fate has been planned for me, but I always eat. I always wake, and I never am ordered from the line. They hate me for it, but no one says a cruel word to my face. My mother and grandmother have been murdered—everyone I care about dies here—but they never kill me. Never Ora. That is my burden: to live.

It could be worse. That is one thing you become aware of in the camps—that things can always be worse. There is no hope here, only mistrust and hunger. Some of the women believe there are those among us who report to the guards in return for special treatment, but even if there are, I don't think it matters. This isn't a game, every day is life and death, and who could blame someone for doing whatever she could to stay alive? This is a place where babies are clubbed to death, where women are dragged from their bunks and shot down like dogs. There is no cheating here, only scrabbling hands fighting for something to hold on to in the blackness. When there is no prayer left for a religious people like us, there is no hope. Still, we strive to live in this world that wants nothing from us but a final breath.

Chapter 2

1999

Cynthia Robinson stayed with her grandparents while Mom and Dad went to Vegas for a liquor store owner's convention. She was far too young, at the age of nine, to know exactly the nature of the products that their store sold—aside from snacks and slushies—but she did know that the trip to Vegas was very important and that it happened every year.

Typically, Cynthia didn't mind the time away from home. She loved her paternal grandparents dearly, and they loved her back, but this time was different. Cynthia had never been scared before when Mom and Dad would leave. She was homesick of course, but she was never scared, never filled with a dread that made the simple act of eating difficult.

Cynthia had heard the word "divorce" before. Kids on the playground used it sparingly, with the kind of reverence afforded only the foulest curse words. When Jimmy Keebler's folks had unexpectedly split last May—sending Jimmy to Lake Tahoe with his mother, his father to parts unknown—the word had for a while been heard more often and was as welcome as the recent arrival of June's mosquitoes and hot weather. Cynthia had been OK, however. She viewed the whole thing as more of a curiosity than anything else, something which could never happen to her.

On the third night in Nan and Pop's house in Lansing—a night that saw her snap awake, sweating and clammy—Cynthia knew differently. Mom and Dad were going to get divorce, and they were discussing it right now in their hotel room in Las Vegas as calmly as if they were talking about whether they wanted burgers or tacos for dinner on Wednesday. They had been fighting, though. The fight was terrible, unlike anything Cynthia could ever have imagined. She couldn't remember the awful things they'd said to each other—nothing beyond the words "affair" and "divorce," which were bad enough—and was glad she couldn't. The thoughts had twisted her dream into a horrible nightmare, and when she jolted out of sleep she knew none of it had been a dream at all. Cynthia was as sure of that as she was that Mom's eyes were red and puffy now and that Dad's voice had gone from angry to very sad. She walked to the bathroom, feeling sick but in a way she had never felt before, and knelt next to the toilet. She felt small, afraid, and alone, but there was a voice inside of her telling her she could not tell Nan and Pop about what she knew. Not because they would be upset—though of course she knew they would be; not even adults liked the "divorce" word—but because she couldn't imagine how to explain how she knew about the divorce at all.

Cynthia sat next to the toilet for the better part of an hour, listening to the noise of the old house and the ticking of the dining room clock, before finally returning to bed. She felt no better when she got there, but going back seemed a necessary thing, since she would have no idea how to explain why she was in the bathroom. She loved her grandparents very much, but even at her age she knew that things like divorce couldn't be discussed until Mom and Dad were back and told them in person. It would be wrong to know too soon—wrong and maybe even a little scary. Not as scary as the word "divorce," but almost as bad.

Cynthia could see it on Nan's and Pop's faces the next morning when she came down to breakfast. She wanted to ask them if they'd somehow overheard her parents' conversation in Las Vegas, like she had, but she knew it had probably just been a phone call that had shared the sad news from across the country. Cynthia took her place at the table, but no one spoke. Finally, Pop left, his exit punctuated by the opening and closing of the door that led to his workshop in the garage, and then Nan placed a bowl of cereal in front of her. Cynthia stared at the cereal, sure she didn't want to eat, but also knowing that she was a child and when a child is given food, she must eat. Cynthia stole glances at Nan while she ate, a Nan who suddenly looked older than she ever had—old and something worse. Nan looked defeated, as though her years on earth had finally caught up to her and the smiling woman who delighted in her granddaughter and gardening might never come back.

When Cynthia was done eating, she carried her bowl to the kitchen, dumped what was left into the sink, and then rinsed the bowl as she hit the switch for the garbage disposal. Nan jumped when the grinding started, but Cynthia could tell she wasn't too concerned, because she didn't turn to make sure Cynthia was OK. *Everyone is different*, thought Cynthia, but even worse was the idea that nothing might ever be the same again.

Cynthia left her bowl in the sink, then walked into the living room and pushed the button to turn the television on. It was Sunday, and there was a man talking about God on the box instead of the cartoons she would have preferred, but Cynthia found herself beyond caring. Nan was in the dining room; Pop was in the garage. Mom and Dad would be home soon, but everything was falling apart. Cynthia watched the churchman until another churchman took his place. Both of them reminded her of the videos she wasn't supposed to watch on

MTV. Both men craved the eyes upon them, just like the preening singers in the videos, rather than any real connection with their audience. Cynthia watched as the second churchman faded to football, and at some point she herself faded into the couch, honest sleep finally taking her away from the madness. There were no journeys to be had, no impossible truths. That would come later.

Cynthia awoke to the sounds of an Important Talk. The Important Talk was happening at the kitchen table, and she could hear Mom and Dad speaking with Nan and Pop. The adults were all trying to be quiet, but Cynthia could hear frustration in her grandparents, anger in her mother, and worst of all, fear in her father. Dad was never scared, not of anything. Dad had been in the army. Dad had flown on helicopters and one time beat up two bad men who tried to rob the store with guns and left with their tails between their legs.

"I want to fix it," Dad said, and Cynthia could tell without any effort that he was lying, just going through the motions. Dad knew he couldn't fix whatever the problem was, and she knew he didn't intend to try.

"Well, of course you can," replied his mother, but Cynthia knew Nan was lying as well.

Mom was not talking, but Cynthia had a feeling that hers was the only voice in the room that really mattered. This wasn't a problem Dad could chase away. It wasn't one that Pop could fix in the garage, nor one Nan could fix with her sewing machine. This was worse, and if Mom wasn't talking, then everyone else was just wasting air.

"No, you can't," Mom said to Dad, and Cynthia felt the tears begin to flow. *It's really happening.*

"Yes, he can," said Nan. "Be reasonable, Ruth. Think about what this will do to Cynthia."

"All I ever do is think about my daughter," said Mom, and Cynthia could hear the rage in her voice over the lie. Mom cared about her—she knew that—but Mom also cared a lot about shopping and having her hair just right. Mom liked things so neat that it was hard to know where Cynthia was even supposed to play, and though she knew her mother loved her, she was also well aware that Mom had other things on her mind than just the occasionally inconvenient child she was raising. "You need to share some of the blame in this, Nick. You know very well this is not just a decision I've made out of the blue sky. We can all have a nice long talk about that, assuming—"

"Not with Cynthia just a room away," said Pop, anger creeping into his voice, and Cynthia wanted to rush to him and throw her arms around his neck. She could hear the caring in his voice. She didn't know how she could know that, but she felt sure of a few other things. Dad didn't want divorce, because he didn't think that he was *supposed* to get it. Mom wanted it because she wanted to be right, no matter the consequences, and she was willing to suffer for it. Nan just wanted things to stay the same, no matter the reasons, but Pop was different.

"Dad, she's asleep—"

"No, now you hush," said Pop. "She was asleep when you two came in, and for all any of us knows now she's awake."

Cynthia could see the threads of their conversation in the air around her, beautiful and ugly swirls, the most vibrant of them the things that weren't being said. Pop's rage was a red ribbon. Pop cared—he cared a lot—but unlike Nan, he wasn't just sad; he was angry, too. Not at Cynthia but her parents. As best she could tell, Pop was mad at them for being quitters, for not having the guts to suffer through the affair, like he had. *What does that even mean?* This had to be a dream, but she knew better. Cynthia pulled a blanket around her and stuffed the ends in between couch cushions so that she was held in place like the stuffing in a ravioli.

"Dad," her father insisted, "she's asleep. We were just in there."

"It doesn't matter either way," said Mom. "If she's awake, then she'll figure it out that much sooner. It'll be better for everyone."

Nan started to cry—Cynthia could hear her. She could feel it in a way that she'd never felt before: Nan was dying in pieces. She was terrified that something she'd never considered was happening, her son succumbing to the same selfish urges she had suffered from.

"No," said Pop. "This is not how Cynthia is going to find out that her parents are too good for their wedding vows. If this is how you two think you want it, then she can stay here until you both have the common sense to either call this shit off or tell her in person. Cynthia deserves better than this."

"Don't you dare tell me what my daughter needs," said Mom, and then there was the noise of a chair sliding across the floor, and Mom was on the move.

Cynthia dove face-first into the couch, feigning sleep but knowing it wouldn't matter even before she felt Mom pulling her from the couch and to her feet. Cynthia stared at her mother. Somehow Mom was grinning, but the smile was cruel and false.

Pop and Dad burst into the room after her, and Mom said, "Looks like she is up, Tom. My daughter and I are going to go home, and then we're going to pack. Nick, please have the courtesy to wait until we're gone to come home. I'll leave the car in the driveway."

"Ruth, please," said Dad, a swirl of beautiful purple curling over his head, like a snake missing its head. "You two stay at the house, keep the car. I'll get a place. We'll figure this out. You don't need to make it like this. It doesn't need to be like this, not before we've had the chance to work on it, to fix—"

"You had ample opportunities to fix your zipper, but you were too selfish to bother trying," said Mom matter-of-factly, though from where Cynthia was sitting, Dad's zipper appeared to be working perfectly. "Cynthia and I will be as fine without you as we were with you—and let's face it, Nick, you don't really care."

Dad's face hung dejectedly as Mom spoke, and then Cynthia was ushered out of the house by her mother. The sun was low in the sky as they left, and she watched out of the window as Mom pulled away from Nan and Pop's house.

Dad was standing in the yard staring at them, and next to him were Nan and Pop. Cynthia could see the tears on the faces of both Dad and Nan, but Pop was just staring after them, looking more miserable than any of them, even with his dry cheeks. *He's sad because he knows about affair and divorce*, thought Cynthia, and then Mom rounded the corner and the thought was gone, as though a string between them had been snapped.

"We're going to figure this out, Cynth," said Mom. "We're going to figure it out, and we're going to show them all. Just wait."

Cynthia nodded and said, "OK." It was all she had, but it was enough for Mom.

Cynthia could see her nodding back to her in the front seat, and she wondered if this was how it had been for poor Jimmy Keebler last spring when he and his mom disappeared to Lake Tahoe.

Chapter 3

Darryl Livingston woke covered in cold sweat. He couldn't remem-ber where he was, and then his surroundings filled him in. He was in the apartment he shared with Terry, the crappy one in Austin, and he was sleeping off a pretty bad day drunk. *I'm in Terry's fucking bed to boot. What the hell?*

Darryl yawned, stood from the bed, then sighed into a balled-up fist. Terry kept the walls of their shitty little apartment covered in porno pictures, and that wallpaper alone should have been enough to immediately hammer home his location. *I didn't even have that much to drink*, thought Darryl, but he knew damn well that wasn't true.

Darryl left the bedroom, took a piss in the yellow bowl in the bath-room, and then wandered into Terry's unfortunate living room. The wallpaper here could be described as tame compared to the bedroom—just T & A, no penetration—but it was still unlikely to impress anyone with ten cents' worth of brains. Darryl sat down heavily on the couch, then flicked the TV on with the remote from the coffee table. He gave a look to Terry, but if his friend had noticed him, he was keeping it a secret. *He doesn't notice shit.* Terry had eyes for a keyboard, mouse, and screen but managed to avoid just about everything else.

Terry sat just a few feet away, at the dining room table. His ears were covered in a pair of massive headphones, his hands were draped over a stained keyboard and mouse, and his monitor was filled with dancing numbers. Darryl knew what Terry was listening to—metal on his Walkman, always metal—but he didn't even want to ask about the numbers. Terry liked his porno everywhere and his women stuffed like turkeys, but his computer shit was not to be trifled with. Terry was way too good at that for messing around, and he was usually good for a place to stay if Darryl was too drunk to walk.

Darryl contented himself with the TV as Terry let his fingers tap keys and click buttons, but the sound of the work was just background noise. Darryl managed to sit in the apartment for all of one hour before getting a beer from the fridge, drinking it in a few savage pulls that had once really impressed girls behind the Austin Drive-In, and then leaving the can on the counter and grabbing another one. Darryl's days of impressing girls with his beer-slamming abilities were long gone. In fact, his time spent attempting to impress girls or anyone else was long gone. Lately he'd come to consider effort itself overrated when things could be had so easily.

After three more beers and another hour of TV, Terry finally peeled the headphones off and turned to Darryl. "I knew you were up," he said, and Darryl just nodded in response. "I could hear you the whole time. I was just waiting for you to say something."

Darryl nodded again, saluted Terry with his beer, and then finished it in a single gulp.

"You looked busy, so I let you be busy," said Darryl. It was only partly true. The sooner Terry realized he was up, the sooner they would have to talk about work, and Darryl wasn't in the mood. Work was how the bender had started and why he was drinking at such an unreasonable pace, but the subject was unavoidable at this point. He owed Terry, and they both knew it.

"I was only busy because I was waiting for you to come to your senses," said Terry, and Darryl nodded. "And don't try and fucking read me, Darryl. I'm not in the mood, and you already know what I'm going to say."

"You want money," said Darryl.

He didn't need to go rooting around in Terry's topknot to know what his friend was thinking. They both had green on their minds. There was just no good way to score right now. *Of course, that's Terry's job*, thought Darryl, and they both knew that, too. While he slumbered off a drunk in the smut chamber, Terry was supposed to be hard at work on something. That was the deal, even if it was an unspoken one.

"You need money just like I do," said Terry. "You'd rather make this my fault, though, than try to work out a solution."

That made Darryl raise an eyebrow and cock his head. Terry couldn't be in his head, not like *that*. *Not like what I can do.*

"It's true," said Darryl. "I do sort of hold you responsible. You're the one who wanted to talk last night, and I figured you'd have developed a solution to our little problem. Instead, you're on your stupid computer with your fucking smut, and I'm sitting here dealing with the back end of a serious bender." Darryl hoisted his beer, found it empty, and stood to walk to the fridge. "And I'm about to throw another drunk on while I'm waiting—see if you like that. I can hear that kid crying a couple of doors down again, and I can't fucking stand it."

"I'm working on a solution," said Terry, ignoring the comments about drinking, porn, and the kid down the hall.

Let him change the subject, thought Darryl. They both knew, thanks to Darryl, that the kid would be dead soon if his dad couldn't lay off the pipe and the beatings.

Darryl took a beer from the fridge and walked back to the living room before opening it. The tab hissed foam, and Darryl smiled as he drank.

"I like solutions," said Darryl. "Tell me more."

"It's this web shit," said Terry. "I know I've explained it before, but in a nutshell it makes it so that I can talk to someone far away. Sort of like a telephone, but all anonymous, and almost always with strangers. Hell, for all I know it's all people who live here in the building—it's that out-there. You can talk to anyone, and it's only going to get bigger. Just wait until the new millennium rolls around."

"Doesn't do me any good," said Darryl. "I need to see them in person. I need to be able to be in range. We've been over this. We've tried the phone, lots of different remote stuff. It just doesn't work."

Darryl drank beer and turned to look reproachfully at his partner, but Terry just smiled.

"I know it's hard to believe, but just trust me. Take a few hours to get acquainted with it, and then tell me what you think."

"I'll look," said Darryl, though he knew it was pointless. He'd look at Terry's bullshit solution, and then he'd walk away like he always did. *Then a few petty jobs to get us by and that will be that, just like always. Until Terry gets another strike-it-rich plan.* Darryl was tired of it.

"One other thing," said Terry as he stood, a grin plastered across his face. "You'll know better than I do, but I'm pretty sure almost everyone in these virtual rooms is a kid."

Darryl stood, his beer forgotten, and crossed the room. "Show me," said Darryl, and Terry grinned like a child on Christmas morning.

All kids, Darryl thought. *Holy shit.*

Chapter 4

Jessica Hockstetter woke with one thought in her mind: *Frank.* She sat up slowly, letting the ugly memory of their session two days prior continue to burn off heat in her subconscious, and then gave the off button on the alarm a practiced snap, minutes before it was due to go off.

Yesterday had been hell, today was going to be hell all over again, and tomorrow? It was a safe bet tomorrow would be a shitty day, too. Jessica sighed as she rolled off the bed. She walked to the bathroom and stripped her clothes off into the hamper before turning the shower on and then sitting on the toilet as the water warmed up. It hadn't always been like this—crappy days and unsolvable problems—but now that felt like all it was ever going to be. A living nightmare.

Jessica stood from the toilet, flushed, and then, against her better judgment, gave herself a look in the mirror. Aside from the lack of makeup, Jessica felt good. Yes, she was a year shy of forty-nine years old, but she ran every day, watched what she ate, had never smoked, and rarely drank—all with a higher calling in mind, but for what? Just like her father, she had given her life to the Telekinetic Research Center—the TRC—and she had nothing to show for it.

Jessica was what people in her field called a reverse-mute, meaning she was unaffected by telekinetics—TKs for short. Reverse-mutes were quite rare, possibly even rarer than full-grown TKs. A reverse-mute was far less likely to be discovered, to be sure, and finding a TK was like finding a specific pebble in the ocean. Being a reverse-mute had helped her career almost as much as being the only child of Jason Hockstetter, who had been a hero in World War II and won the greatest honors the OSS was able to bestow on a man at the time.

Of course, even more importantly, Jason Hockstetter had been involved in some of the most dangerous battles of the war with a TK at his side. That the very same TK who had helped Jason in combat was the one giving Jessica so much grief was an irony that was not lost on her, but as she turned the shower off, she felt quite sure Frank delighted in it.

Frank Rosenbauer was an anomaly even by the standards of most TKs. He had abilities that made theirs seem like parlor tricks. Lately, however, the combination of a government that always wanted more, the lack of TKs in the system, and Frank's surliness had been making for less than happy times. *It's not his fault that he's miserable*, Jessica reasoned to herself as she toweled off, and at least part of that was true. Frank had been held in the TRC since the late 1940s, but after the escape attempt he'd been involved in back in the early 1980s, he'd been locked down as tightly as was humanly possible. Not that everything about Frank was bad—in fact, his bizarre skill set had forced precautions on them that might have taken decades to put together without the necessity of keeping Frank in a cage.

Jessica dressed quickly in an outfit comfortable enough for a twelve-hour shift but also presentable enough if someone from Washington were to drop by. It was bad enough living with the fear of their funding being pulled by some suit who didn't get the importance of their work, but it would be far worse for the man to do so because he didn't feel that her dress befitted her supposed station.

So many fucking games. Her job was supposed to be about research, but lately it was about making sure everyone was happy, and she knew that Howard Thompson, the director of the TRC, was as miserable over it as she was. They were in grave danger of losing everything, of being mothballed permanently, unless they could find a new way to wow Washington. Sure, they had Frank, and then another low-powered TK at the TRC, but neither Frank nor Gus was up for the sort of heavy lifting that was being hinted at. Between his rebelliousness and his age, Frank couldn't be allowed near anything that really mattered, and there wasn't a chance in hell he'd be allowed within a hundred miles of the president.

Dressed now, Jessica hopped downstairs and walked to the kitchen. She'd prepped the coffeemaker the night before and hit the button to make the magic happen, before crossing the room and grabbing a to-go mug from the cupboard and walking back to watch the machine work.

I could quit, thought Jessica, but the idea was unrealistic. People didn't quit the TRC; they retired. It was the sort of government work where you did not pass go, did not collect two hundred dollars if you left. There was no one in the current or former administrations on any level who would acknowledge the TRC as being anything more than an unfunded joke north of Hartford, and there were no credentials to be had from working there. Sure, maybe she could turn her experience into a career spent ghost hunting or looking for cryptids in the Pacific Northwest, but neither of those fit the bill. As she poured the steaming coffee, Jessica reminded herself that she'd known all of this going in and she'd promised herself that it wouldn't matter.

"Fuck," said Jessica quietly as she crossed the kitchen to get some cream from the fridge. She stirred it in with the spoon she'd left on the counter the day before. When she was young and following in Daddy's footsteps, the TRC had been a dream come true. Now it was a place where dreams came to die, where old TKs paced their rooms, like rats in a trap.

Jessica let the thought fade, like so many others she'd had in the eighteen months since the last of their leads on new blood had dried up, and then topped the coffee with its lid and grabbed her keys. She might not want to be there, but like it or not, the TRC was all she had.

• • •

The TRC's building looked nothing like a facility designed for the planning of the occasional multimillion-dollar black-ops operation. It looked more like a middle school that desperately needed refurbishment, but in this case looks were intentionally deceiving. The building had been designed to appear like the sort of underfunded crackpot enterprise it had been before the Second World War and the success of Jason Hockstetter. Despite its humble digs, the TRC was considered one of the crown jewels in US preparedness programs. Or at least it had been.

Jessica left her car and crossed the cracked pavement of the parking lot, then opened the unsecured and unguarded front door and strolled inside. The interior of the main floor of the TRC mirrored the outside of the building. The walls were painted in the sort of colors that were all the rage for science classrooms in the 1970s, shades of yellow and green that would have been combined into a camouflage pattern called "Vomit." Tess, the receptionist working the door to the public area of the TRC, gave her a wave as she walked through, and Jessica said, "No Howard yet?"

"Nope, not yet," said Tess, and Jessica frowned. It wasn't like Howard to arrive at the office after her. Had he finally had enough? It was possible. He'd always struck her as being the sort of man who would have won his battles as a boy by taking his ball home rather than playing a game in which he couldn't succeed.

Jessica passed through the halls of the TRC, ignoring rooms that hadn't been used for anything in years, before entering the Hall of

Wonders. The name was a joke—the hall was far from great, but it was the largest room on the main floor of the building, and it housed the collection of dioramas that the founder of the place had put together back when the research done here consisted more of shoddy guesswork than science. The dioramas showed great TK moments in history, almost all of them culled from the Bible and urban legend. The one closest to the door showed Jesus walking across a blue plastic body of water, his hands aloft to the sky. Just a few feet away was a glass box filled with what was supposed to be Daniel in the lions' den. The lions were falling apart, and Daniel's paint was fading terribly, but it was still clear from his exaggerated pose that he was meant to be controlling the beasts with his mind.

There were several other religious scenes, but Jessica's favorite was located next to a plain-looking door across the hall. Inside the case were a pair of ships nearly identical in build and size. The first was the doomed RMS *Titanic*, the famously unsinkable ship that had proven exactly the opposite, and the other was the fictional ship the *Titan*. The *Titan* was an anomaly and the closest thing to actual TK activity Jessica could see in the room. The story of the *Titan* was written by Morgan Robertson in 1898 and was published as *Futility*. In the book, published fourteen years before its fictitious ship's real-life sister was to sink, the *Titan*—also "unsinkable"—hit an iceberg in the North Atlantic and eventually went down with few survivors, as there were not enough lifeboats.

Jessica had no opinion on whether or not Robertson was actually a TK—after all, no TK she had ever met could see into the future—but it seemed to her the only logical solution to the mystery. Robertson had either gotten very lucky or channeled into something very special.

Taking her eyes from the diorama, Jessica placed her thumb on a biometric scanner that was next to the boring-looking door. A few seconds later the door opened with a hiss, and Jessica walked through into her least favorite part of the journey, a sally port known internally as the Killing Hall.

The Killing Hall would have been as boring as the door leading to it if she hadn't helped design and test it. The walls and ceiling were all stainless steel, and the men who controlled the defenses and access through the port were kept off-site at an address known only to Howard. TKs had limited range—a thing that was both good and bad—and by keeping off-site the men in control of who entered and exited, it was impossible for a TK to influence them.

The hall itself was only necessary because of an escape in the 1980s. Frank had put together the plan himself and over time had earned the faith of two compatriots who desired to escape as badly as he did. Despite the planning and the timing of the endeavor, Frank himself never made it outside, Joseph Yee was shot dead, and Katarina Kaufman had never been seen again. Thanks to this escape, the hallway was as deadly as a medieval torture device, and far more advanced. With the push of a button, the man in control of the space could fill it with incapacitating or, if need be, deadly gas, or he could flood it with water, or trigger one of many other less- or fully lethal methods of preventing an escape. So far, none of the techniques had needed to be employed, but, as someone who had been on staff during the 1983 breakout, Jessica was all too aware of how necessary these precautions were.

At the end of the sally port, Jessica leaned in to a retinal-scanning device and waited as the computer verified that she was in fact allowed access to the real TRC. Once in, Jessica walked through a small antechamber, hopped on an elevator, hit the button for the fourth floor, and then waited as it dropped. The elevator dinged as it arrived at the fourth, and Jessica stepped through the doors as they slid open. She waved at Pam, the receptionist on this main level of the TRC, and then passed a man wearing one of the Tesla Helmets that kept safe the workers here who were not lucky enough to be reverse-mutes.

The Teslas were ungainly and likely unnecessary inside the walls of the TRC, but they were still required. The helmets looked like a mix of a forward-facing toaster and a knight's basinet, with their edges flowing with red lights so that other people could verify they were activated. Since TKs could seize a normal's brainwaves and influence them, the Tesla provided a constantly flowing stream of interference, each thread of which appeared to be normal brain function. A really good TK like Frank might be able to grab onto one or two real threads of consciousness even through the screen, but he would be able to do little more than give the helmet's user a headache, much less control him. Despite the helmets and the other safety countermeasures inside of the TRC, firearms were forbidden past the first floor, and there were no exceptions to this rule.

Jessica walked past reception and headed straight to the conference room, where on a typical day Howard would be waiting for her. Today the room was empty and dark, and though the motion sensors handled the lights, Jessica felt a little weird sitting without being invited to by Howard. Staring at the rarely used drink cart across from her, Jessica realized that she wanted to be anywhere but here, that the job really was wearing her that thin, and this might be the time to hang things up. As she buried the thought into the pit of her stomach like some ugly marble, Howard strode through the door.

"Question," said Howard as he walked in, and Jessica raised her eyebrows to let him know she was listening. "If I said we had six months to either get Frank to play nice or we needed a new TK, what would you say?"

"That six months isn't a lot of time."

"That's true," said Howard, "but according to the vice president, we're going to lose funding in three if we don't figure something out. There's a big job coming down the pipe, and if the TRC can't be made to be useful in order to help, this office is closed."

Chapter 5

Cynthia had lived with her parents in the yellow house on Glenwood for as long as she could remember, and though she had heard her parents laugh on more than one occasion about their previous apartment, she didn't even own fleeting memories of the place. The yellow house was home, but as she watched Mom stuff their things into shopping bags and a battered suitcase, it began to dawn on her that the yellow house would be her home no more.

Sleeping in the motel the night prior had been odd, but Mom had said to think of it as a little vacation, and she had. Now that Dad was at work and they'd come back to the yellow house for their things—it had felt funny going there, like they were sneaking, breaking into their own house—the reality was hard to deal with. Mom had started with her own things, and Cynthia had been fine watching that happen—it was like Mom was just packing for another trip—but when they moved to Cynthia's room, that changed.

Watching Mom cram Cynthia's toys and clothes into a few grocery sacks gave Cynthia a sinking feeling in her belly. This was her room, but it was becoming less and less hers by the second. Cynthia didn't feel any connection with her mom that went beyond what she was used to, unlike the way she had at her grandparents' home, but the awful weight, like cement, in her belly stayed there. Mom was alternating between crying and shivering like she was cold. Cynthia wanted her to feel better, but she also knew that Mom was part of the reason why they were all sad and were going to stay that way.

Cynthia had no idea where the threads had come from at her grandparents' house—the threads that showed people's feelings in a way she had never experienced before—nor did she know how she had been so certain about divorce before her parents came out with it. She had been right about that, though, and the threads had been there. Cynthia could still feel the place where she'd seen them snap away from her, and it made her head hurt a little. Still, that was a minor pain compared to the one she felt in her belly as she watched Mom pack.

Why isn't Dad here? He always helps. They do everything together. Cynthia knew that divorce meant that moms and dads didn't live together anymore, but her parents were best friends. They said it all the time. Wouldn't friends help each other with heavy boxes?

The packing took forever, and then they were in the car and the yellow house on Glenwood was fading, and the packing felt like it had taken no time at all. Cynthia watched the house disappear behind her with a cold feeling in her stomach. There were no threads this time, even though she felt a lot more attachment to the yellow house than she ever had to the one her grandparents lived in. The house was gone in just one turn, and Cynthia spun to face the front of the car and the back of her mom's head.

"Where are we going, Mommy?"

Mom ran a hand over her tear-streaked face and then looked into the rearview mirror so that she could see Cynthia.

"We're going to get an apartment, a little place just for you and me," said Mom. "I've already found a nice one. It will be cozy and a little snug, but we'll have each other, and you'll have all of your toys."

Cynthia nodded. That wasn't all bad. And then a shot like red lightning raced through her mind. "Did you pack Sammy?"

Mom nodded. "How could I ever forget Sammy the squirrel? Of course I remembered Sammy. How else would you be able to sleep?"

"Good," said Cynthia. She'd had Sammy since she was a baby, and the thought of going without him was even worse than how she'd felt as they left the yellow house. "What are you going to do, Mom?" Mom's eyes appeared again in the rearview mirror, and Cynthia clarified. "I always sleep with Sammy, but you sleep with Daddy. Are you going to be able to sleep without him? Is he going to be able to sleep without you?"

Cynthia paused to let Mom respond, and when there was no answer, she said, "Is Dad moving to the apartment with us?"

"Dad and I are taking a break, Cynth," said Mom. "Maybe a little one, but I don't want to get your hopes up—I think we're going to be taking a long one, maybe even a forever one. Your dad and I just aren't seeing eye to eye on a few things, and I don't know that we ever will again. That doesn't mean we don't love you. It just means that you and I are going to go live somewhere else. You'll still see your dad, but not all the time like we're used to."

"I like how it used to be," said Cynthia. This was the sort of thing that she'd known not to say at Nan and Pop's house, but she wasn't there anymore, and the strings were gone. "I like living in the yellow house, and I like living with Daddy, and I like everything how it is! I don't want things to change, not even for a little while."

Mom was nodding in the front seat, tears streaming again. "I know," she said. "I know. This was the last thing that I wanted either, Cynthia. It's just what had to happen."

"Is this because of divorce or affair?" Cynthia asked, and Mom jerked the wheel hard enough that the car swerved and almost hit a parked van before she got it under control.

"Your Nan needs to learn some sense," said Mom. "She doesn't need to be giving you her opinion about anything like that." Mom shook her head. "She only has his side of the damn story, anyway."

Cynthia considered telling Mom that Nan hadn't given her opinion on anything and that the only things she knew for sure about Nan were that she was very sad and very worried, but she knew she couldn't. There were some things that even a mother couldn't understand, especially a mother still wearing warning signs of divorce and affair.

"I'm sorry, Mom," said Cynthia finally, and Mom smiled at her in the rearview mirror.

"It's all right, baby. You don't have anything to be sorry about, not ever. This is between your father and me. You're just caught in the middle."

Cynthia didn't say anything to that. There was nothing that would make a bit of difference. *Of course I'm caught in the middle!* She wanted to scream it. *You put me there!* Cynthia stayed mum, though, and after just a short drive, Mom was pulling into an apartment complex. It looked sort of like the hotel they stayed at near Disney World, but it was a lot bigger, and the people she saw milling around outside didn't look nearly as happy as the ones in Florida had.

Mom parked near a building that had a sign on it that said "Leasing," then shut the car off.

"Stay here, Cynthia," said Mom. "I just need to sign some papers and get a key." Cynthia nodded earnestly, and then Mom shut the door and left to go inside.

Cynthia watched her mom disappear into the building and, when she was gone, began to take stock of her surroundings. She didn't see any kids, but there were so many doors with numbers that there had to be some kids here. Still, it was a little odd—summer break was only halfway done and there should have been someone outside playing.

Cynthia let the lack of visible kids slide as another thought took over: What if she had to switch schools? Her best friends, Maryanne and Audrey, went to her school, but what if she had to switch? The thought of having to go without them was almost as bad as divorce or affair, and for the first time in her life Cynthia realized just how quickly everything could change around a person, whether they wanted it to or not. *Like with Mom and Dad*, inserted a voice in her head. *Neither of them seem very happy.* The voice was right: Mom and Dad weren't happy, not at all, and now they were going to live in different places. None of it made any sense.

Cynthia watched as a heavyset woman and two little kids emerged from one of the numbered doors. The woman had a pleasant look on her face and a laundry basket under each arm. Cynthia couldn't figure out what in the world the woman could be carrying, and as she got closer to the car, Cynthia realized there was nothing but laundry in the baskets. Cynthia couldn't think of a single reason why a person would want to bring their dirty laundry outside for everyone to see, and then the woman and the two kids disappeared into the same building that Mom had, and the mystery faded.

Cynthia watched as a pair of little brown wiener dogs were led on leashes, one blue and one pink, by a small woman who made Nan look young by comparison. Cynthia wanted to run and pet the dogs. She couldn't have explained why she wanted to so badly even if she'd been asked. They were just cute, and she wanted to touch them. Cynthia looked at the door handle and then at the door of the building Mom had entered. She unbuckled her seat belt, gave another look to the door and then back again at the dogs. They were closer now than before, and the woman walking them was smiling, with a long cigarette hanging from her lips. Cynthia took a deep breath, decided Mom couldn't get that mad at her for just wanting to pet a couple of wiener dogs, and opened the door.

Cynthia looked both ways for traffic before heading across the parking lot toward the woman and the dogs. The woman was moving toward her as well, almost as if she could somehow sense there was a little girl who wanted nothing more than her yellow house and a smiling mommy and daddy, but who was going to have to settle for a pair of little dogs in boy and girl leashes.

As Cynthia got closer, she extended her hand, prepping herself for the dogs to smell her in the way Dad had always told her to greet a pooch, and then the woman said, "Look at this. Someone wants to meet you two. Come here, young lady. They don't bite, not these two."

"Hi," said Cynthia as she knelt close to them so that the dogs could smell her outstretched fingers. The dogs were on her hand instantly, quickly going from an inspection to a lickfest on her palm, and Cynthia giggled despite the wound in her heart. "What are their names?" Cynthia asked as she alternated petting the little dogs.

"Stanley and Libby," said the woman, "and they are very happy to see you."

Cynthia took turns petting Stanley and Libby, switching between them as each dog became jealous of the attention their new friend was showing the other.

"My name is Cynthia, and I think I'm just as happy to see them."

It was true, and Cynthia was shocked to feel that part of the hurt she was feeling was gone.

"It's a pleasure to meet you, Cynthia," said the woman. "It looks like Stan and Lib agree. My name is Mrs. Martin. Are you moving in here? I know I'd remember seeing such a pretty little girl around before, and my pooches would remember, too. They never forget a good rubdown."

Cynthia nodded, still petting the dogs. "Mom and I are moving in, I think. We used to live in a yellow house with my dad, but now we're going to live here. Mom says it's maybe only going to be for a little while, but she also says it might wind up being for longer than that, maybe even a really long time."

"Well, that must be difficult, but I think you'll find North Harbor can be a pretty happy place, too," said Mrs. Martin. "Maybe not as happy as your old house, at least not at first, but still pretty happy on its own merits." Mrs. Martin smiled, and Cynthia smiled back at her—the real thing, not like in the car with Mom.

"I hope so," said Cynthia. "My mom is really sad, and if she could be happy here, that would be good." As the words fell from her mouth, Cynthia heard a door behind her, and she spun to see Mom walking out of it, looking first in the car and then wearing a panicked look on her face. "I'm over here, Mom," called Cynthia, and then Mom was walking toward them.

"Jesus, Cynthia, I told you to stay in the car," she said as she raced toward them. "Ma'am, thanks so much for finding her. She's not normally much for wandering off, but we're going through some family things right now, and she's probably just a little bit off." Mrs. Martin extended a hand, and Cynthia watched as Mom took it, thinking how odd it was that humans met a dog in the same way that they met one another.

Mrs. Martin took her hand back, then drew off of her cigarette and exhaled smoke. Normally Cynthia hated the smell—it was how Dad's store smelled most of the time, stale and gross—but this was different. Mrs. Martin's smoke smelled almost flowery, and the smell enveloped her like sheeny gauze.

"It's no trouble," said Mrs. Martin. "Cynthia and I were just getting acquainted, though I have a feeling she was a lot more excited about meeting the dogs than she was this old woman."

Mom nodded, looking as though she was noticing the dogs for the very first time, then turned back to Mrs. Martin. "I'm sorry," she said. "I'm Ruth Rob—Ruth Sherwood. It's a pleasure to meet you."

Cynthia looked up at her mother. She'd told Mrs. Martin the wrong name for some reason. They were Robinsons, all of them. What in the heck was a Sherwood?

"It's a pleasure, Ruth. My name is Henrietta Martin, and the two little moochers down there are Stanley and Libby. As you can see, they've taken quite a shine to your little girl. Maybe I've finally found the dog walker I've been looking for."

"Maybe," said Mom quickly, before Cynthia could get a word in edgewise. "It was very nice to meet you, Henrietta, but Cynthia and I need to get settled in. This day has been long enough already."

"Of course, dear, I completely understand. I live in apartment 1138, and if you need to borrow a cup of flour, you be sure to look me up." Mrs. Martin turned to look at Cynthia. "That goes for you, too, Cynthia. These dogs are spoiled, and you're just making things even worse for me. They'll be talking about you for days, so don't be a stranger."

"They don't really talk to you," Cynthia said, though she said it halfway like a question.

"Of course not, Cynthia," said Mom, shaking her head. "Thank you again, Henrietta. We'd stay to chat longer, but we need to go see our place."

"Of course," said Mrs. Martin with a smile, and Mom gave her a half smile back. "Cynthia, you come see me and these dogs, all right? They could use a young person like you around, especially when it comes to playing ball. They wear me out after just a few throws."

Cynthia smiled and nodded. She could tell Mom was unsure about Mrs. Martin, but Cynthia knew that she was going to do everything in her power to see the funny-smelling woman and her little dogs again. Mrs. Martin gave them a wave and then walked off in a plume of smoke, the two dogs leading the way out of the North Harbor Apartments parking lot.

"Come on, Cynthia," said Mom. "Honestly, I don't know why you couldn't just stay in the car."

Cynthia took Mom's hand and walked back to the car with her without a word. She wanted to tell her that Mrs. Martin and her dogs were the only good thing that she'd seen all day, and that once she'd seen them she knew she needed to meet them.

Mom won't understand, though, so don't even try. Cynthia listened to the voice. It was different than the one that had told her about divorce, but Cynthia knew it was correct. Flying under the radar was the best bet, especially for small children, but sometimes there were little dogs that just needed a good petting.

Chapter 6

Darryl was sweating when he finally turned away from the com-
puter. Austin could get hot, and the air conditioner in the window was
kicking out the cold air, but Darryl's perspiration had nothing to do
with climate. Terry bounced from the couch, ran to the kitchen, and
returned with a pair of beers. He set them on the desk by Darryl's left
arm, pulled the tabs on both, and then sat back down on the couch.
Terry stared at Darryl, forcing himself to be as patient as he could while
Darryl worked through the beers.

Finally, Darryl was ready.

"I can get in, I think," said Darryl. "Not in all of them and not
every time, but some of them and a lot of the time. It's not foolproof,
though. There's still a lot to be worked out."

"We've worked out hard things before," said Terry. Some of those
things were buried in shallow graves, small burn piles with the remains
of their ID and credit cards left next to them. "If we could make them
work, we can make this work, too, I know it."

Darryl shook his head. "It's going to be harder than you said. At
least I think it is. But it's not impossible, like with the phones. I already
know this is different than that. I can connect here."

"I knew it," said Terry. "I knew you were, I could tell. You got that look on your face. That's the only time you look like that—when you're in."

Darryl frowned. Terry was getting too excited. He was already looking for word that it was time to start doing jobs.

"This is different, like I just told you," said Darryl. There was a lot that he would never be able to explain to Terry, not because he didn't want to but because Terry would never understand, and this was at the top of the heap.

Even if I'm right, what will be left behind? That had always been their downfall before. It was hard to take what you wanted even once without getting caught, and this was a lot different than just suggesting things to a couple of girls at the bar. This was serious, and if it worked the way Darryl thought that it could, there was going to be some serious recoil when he was done. *Recoil? More like shrapnel.* They needed to figure that out first. It was risky enough to hide a body in the earth, but leaving one out in daylight at the other end of a computer line across town or, hell, across the whole damn country—that would require finesse he wasn't sure either of them had.

"I know, man," said Terry. "I just want to know if you can do it, if you can really get in there and push buttons."

"I can," said Darryl after a moment. "At least I think I can. This wasn't like on a phone or in a crowded building. I could home right in on the person I was talking to. I didn't try and suggest anything, but I was there. Once in a twelve-year-old boy named Russ Fredricks, and then again in a sixteen-year-old girl named Tara Hunter. I was there both times, but that was as far as it went. I didn't want to blow anything out. At least not yet, not until we figure it all out."

"Couldn't you make the chick itch her face, or make the boy type something?" Terry asked. "It'd just be a ripple, a nothing. Make sure they listened, check the delay, and then get out." Terry snapped his fingers. "Simple."

"Not simple," said Darryl. "Dangerous. Every suggestion from an adult leaves a footprint—that's one of the rules."

"But you're good," whined Terry. "And if it's like you're saying, it might be different. Maybe you don't need to worry about burning them out or leaving a footprint. I mean, you're not really there, so why—"

"You need to stow that shit," said Darryl. He was already thinking about another beer. Terry could have that effect on him. *If you want a beer now, wait until the drought. Wait until you're crusted on some of that Bolivian shit.* Darryl grimaced at the thought. Going without was the worst, and for all he knew this new way would mean an even longer period between drinks, a longer stretch of staring at his own topknot in the mirror, knowing every single day when he woke up that it might be purple. *Or black—wouldn't that be a kicker? Black like your liver. Black like your guts. Black like your prostate.* Darryl shook his head, then walked to the refrigerator and got a beer. He opened it, walked back to the room, and sat heavily on the couch next to Terry.

"I know it's tough," said Terry, and in answer Darryl drank beer. "But maybe this will be the last time. If you bend the right kids, we can do a couple of runs and then retire. Think about that, Darryl. We've been running a long, long time. Can you imagine stopping? All you need to do is your little trick, maybe even just once, and then we can go. We could live on an island, sand and bitches 24/7. Or Alaska, or wherever the hell we decide to."

"You just need to remember that it has to be clean," said Darryl, "and I have to be dry. Going in half-cocked wouldn't do me or the kid any good. Give me a few days to get well, and then we'll see what we can do."

"Three days?"

"A few," said Darryl. Terry was pushing it, but if Darryl wasn't drinking in the first place, then they wouldn't need to wait. *Let him try this. Let anyone try it without drinking.* "Maybe three, maybe more, but today doesn't count."

"Are you going to need any blow? You know, to—"

"I don't know," said Darryl. "I hope not."

Terry nodded. "We still have enough money. I'll get some just in case. Vic probably still has some. He pretty much always does."

Darryl nodded, already dreading everything that was to come. Shaking, being all the way there, even that odd euphoria that felt so good until it was gone. *Like true love, all good until it's gone.* The first place Darryl had heard those words was in juvenile hall, but it took him years to fully understand them. It was true, though: being in the bend was good until it was gone, but the disconnect was hell.

"You never know," said Terry. "This time could be different."

Darryl nodded. Terry was full of shit, but he'd let Terry have it. Terry was a good friend, and it would only be a few days of suffering. It would be worth it. *You won't think that when you look in the mirror and your topknot is black, when you're staring at the proof you're rotting from the inside out.* Darryl slammed his beer, then stood and walked to the fridge for another one.

As he pulled the tab, he called to Terry, "When I wake up, I want all of the booze out of here."

Terry said something in agreement, but Darryl didn't hear him. He slammed the can, grabbed another one, and dreamt about it all being done. No more living in this porn-covered flophouse. No more drying out to bend some poor kid. Just beaches, like Terry said.

Chapter 7

Cynthia and Mom were unpacked far faster than it had taken them to pack. Even in the small apartment, Cynthia couldn't believe how bare it was when they were done. Mom's room had just an air mattress, a closet with a few outfits that Cynthia had never seen before, and an alarm clock. Mom seemed happy enough as she unpacked, though. Cynthia had been scared that Mom might cry once they started to get settled, but she came to realize, as she watched her mother work, that perhaps what she had needed was less time with Dad. Mom was hurting. Cynthia didn't need weird dreams to let her know that, but she could also see that her mom was healing. Mom was looking to the future.

Cynthia's room wasn't much better than Mom's. She didn't have a bed, just a sleeping bag on the floor with a pillow, but she didn't really mind that. She had always been a good sleeper, something Mom and Dad had been quick to remind her of when they reminisced about her early years, and she figured a spot on the floor would be as good as any bed. What she did miss was the security that everything in the morning would be the same as it was when she went to bed. After all, Mom and Dad weren't even in Vegas a week before divorce and affair destroyed them, and for all Cynthia knew, she and Mom would have to leave the apartment in the morning.

A part of her was hoping for exactly that—for Mom to somehow forgive Dad and then take them back to the yellow house on Glenwood. Cynthia knew that wouldn't happen, not with how proud Mom seemed to be of moving her to this confusing apartment building, where nice old ladies smoked cigarettes that smelled like flowers and where strangers carried dirty clothes outside. It wasn't until bedtime that Cynthia even really took stock of how they were living now. Neither of them had beds, most of their clothes were still in the yellow house, and aside from Sammy, so were her toys. They had no TV, no radio, and there were no dishes in the kitchen. Mom, who never liked to get takeout, had settled on ordering in a pizza for them to share, and though Cynthia enjoyed the treat, she wanted to know if this was how the foreseeable future was going to be.

"What's on your mind, Cynth?" Mom asked. "I know you probably have a lot of questions, and I'd like to try to answer them if you want to shoot me a couple." Cynthia smiled at Mom, and Mom grinned back. It was a sad smile, though, not the toothy grin Cynthia was used to, the kind Mom used when she looked at Dad or was proud of Cynthia.

"Why did we have to move away from Daddy?" Cynthia asked, and Mom sighed and nodded.

"Because Dad and I were having some problems, and I couldn't forgive him. You'll understand better when you're older, Cynth. This will probably all make sense, unfortunately. What it boils down to is that Mommy decided she couldn't trust Daddy to tell her the truth about some things, and I decided that I'd had enough of people knowing my secrets and laughing behind my back."

"You said that Dad was the best dad in the whole world," said Cynthia. "If he's the best dad, why would you leave him? Why would you make me come with you? I already miss him, and I miss my house and I miss my toys." Cynthia sniffled. Knowing that Mom hated the sound of a child who needed to blow her nose, she blew snot into a napkin. When she looked at Mom, she could see the beginnings of tears welling in her eyes. *You asked the wrong thing*, Cynthia said to herself, *and now she's going to cry, and next she's going to leave you. That's how this works.*

"It's OK, Cynth," said Mom. "You aren't doing anything wrong, and those are very good questions. I do think that your dad is the best daddy in the world, especially for you. I just don't think he's the best husband in the world for me. Your dad would never lie to you, or do anything that he knew would make you sad just to do it, but I'm not sure that he feels the same way about me."

Cynthia gave Mom a quick once-over. Mom didn't look hurt, but . . . "Wait," she said. "You mean like Dad hurt you inside, like here?" Cynthia tapped her chest over where she imagined her heart was, and Mom nodded.

"Exactly right, Cynth," said Mom. "I don't think Dad even meant to—men can be funny about that sort of thing—but he hurt me all the same, and he left me with no choice but to leave and get all of this sorted out. I'm not sure what Dad will do with the store, but I'll need to find something else to do. I'll figure it out, though, and that's not something that you need to worry about."

"Why is Dad going to hire more people for the store?" Cynthia asked. "Is Linda still going to work there? I like her."

Mom started to cry again then, and Cynthia wished that whatever had happened at Nan and Pop's could happen again. The voice had known what to do, and though she was having a hard time remembering it, she was pretty sure the voice had told her how to read the threads. *Were there threads? What does that even mean?*

"Linda may well still work there, along with a lot of other people, but I won't be helping Dad at the store anymore," said Mom as she dried her eyes with a napkin, but there was a tone in her voice when she said the younger woman's name that Cynthia saw as anger. *Linda has something to do with this*, thought Cynthia, but she couldn't imagine what that could possibly have been. Linda was sweet, a college student, and she always made sure Cynthia got a piece of candy at the store and that her slushie cup was filled to the top.

"I'm sorry, Mom," said Cynthia, though she didn't know what exactly she should be sorry for.

"It's not your fault, Cynth, and you don't need to worry about me always being like this," said Mom. "I'll get my head on straight in the next few days, figure out what I'm going to do for work, and we'll go from there." Mom smiled, and Cynthia smiled back, but she knew that Mom was only smiling for her—there was nothing real there. "We'll figure this out, kid. It's just going to take some time."

"When do you think we'll get to see Dad?"

"I don't know, Cynthia. I think at the very least a few days. Believe it or not, even though we're the ones who moved, Dad might have even more to figure out than we do." Mom shook her head. "We're going to miss him and he's going to miss us, but everything is going to work out for the best, and you certainly don't need to worry about not seeing him, OK?"

Cynthia nodded. She wasn't worried about not seeing Dad; she was just confused as to why they all had to live separately if they were all sad about it. There had been nothing wrong with the yellow house, but now she was sleeping on the floor of an apartment, and Dad wasn't with them. *None of it makes any sense.*

Mom clapped her hands. "All right, bugaboo, time to do your teeth and get to bed. I'm exhausted, and we've got another long day tomorrow."

Cynthia just nodded. She was tired, too. She couldn't bring herself to ask Mom about the long day. All she wanted was to wake up, not have any dreams about what was going to happen, and to have everything turn out normal.

Chapter 8

1945

We were called into the yard today, and I felt certain that it was going to be another selection. I was ready to feel the hand on my shoulder, to hear my number called as one of the ones to be doomed to an early grave, but they weren't calling anyone. We just stood in front of our barracks as the wind battered us, waiting for these men to tell us what they wanted, or possibly for the roar of a machine gun to start up as they began to do away with those of us who are left. That would have been fine with me. I am young, but my years on this earth have been hard, and I am used to death. It is not a thing to fear, just an animal that hunts us. Not out of anger, but because the German people have decided we must be culled.

A man began speaking, telling us he was proud of the work that we had been doing and that work was going to be delayed for a few days. "There will be a new selection process, a new way for some lucky ones of you to find your freedom," he said, but we knew what he meant. They were picking which of us were to die, and all I could wonder about was whether my abilities would allow me to survive. So far they had seen me through everything, only to leave me as the last of my blood, and with the ghosts of my family begging me to join them. *I will*, I tell them, *but if I have a choice they will have to wait a little longer.* There will be great rewards for my people somewhere, but first one must survive so that the atrocities done to us may be shared with the world. I do not long to be that voice, for I am just a blind girl who knows little of the world, but I will live if that is what God chooses for me. Otherwise, why would I have my gift?

After the man was done speaking, there was a silence, and then I could hear someone clear their throat and begin to speak. To my surprise, it was a woman. *What in the world is a woman doing with the guards?* It made no sense. Our guards were soldiers, men doing what their country asked of them, and there had never been a woman in their ranks. *Would a woman be able to kill like a man?* In my heart I knew that a woman could.

I knew from my own experience that evil is not committed by a single sex, but if she was now in charge, would this woman continue to allow us to be killed like animals? I knew the truth, but hope can be as poisonous as hemlock, and the sound of her filled me to the brim with wistful joy. I had given up, but now I had hope again, and I knew that having it torn away was going to be painful. Still, I could not help myself. My skin became goose-bumped as she began to speak, and I couldn't help but wonder if the things she said were true.

"My name is Fräulein Kaufman. I am here to help Commandant Wolfe and Herr Grumman with the women here, and to begin that process I will be interviewing you one by one. Germany has decided that it may still have need for a few Jews, and I'm here to help the Fatherland find the right ones. I will not mince words: I am to save but a precious few of you from the hard labor that you endure. Please be honest with me when you speak so that no one is wasting any time, either mine or yours."

I could not see Fräulein Kaufman as she left the yard and walked back into the office next to the men's barracks, but over the chattering of the women around me I could hear something that I doubt anyone else could. Fräulein Kaufman wasn't just a Nazi or a soldier of some sort; she was also a woman who enjoyed fashion. Her feet clicked on the boards as she left the frozen earth, and it was obvious to me that she was wearing heels or heeled boots, and this in the dead of winter! Only a lady who truly cared for such things would dress in such a way, to put her appearance over function in a death camp. I should not have admired Fräulein Kaufman, but I did, despite what she was and represented. No one would ever put heels on a blind girl, but I still lusted after the fashions that I had never seen before and would certainly never see now. *I like this fräulein.*

No sooner did the thought cross my mind than I felt the churning feeling in my belly that meant I was out of myself. I could see colors here—not faces, but bright strands twirling above the women around me. Amongst the ladies of the camp, these were hurt and angry colors, hues I will never see save for in this way—reds, purples, blues, and blacks—colors that I have not seen since I was very small. Over Fräulein Kaufman, so far away as to make my sight even weaker, were the colors yellow, green, and pink. Never since the last bit of my sight was gone have I seen anything, and even here in this hell this was beauty beyond measure. The colors were so disorientating that I needed to be shoved back into my barracks—the commandant was already ordering the girls from Barracks 1 to line up in front of the office—and all I could think was that I was in Barracks 4 and I wouldn't wait long.

• • •

It was three days later before the women of Barracks 4 were ordered to line up before the office of the Fräulein, but already the camp is abuzz with stories of her. The biggest rumor is that she had only selected four girls from the first three barracks in her special selections, but since the process began, no one else has been chosen in the regular selections! I have a hard time believing that only three girls were chosen, but I know the second part is true, as no one could ever forget a selection.

The second rumor is that the Fräulein is a wicked, wicked woman, and that she is here to kill us all. This rumor I know to be untrue, because if she wanted us dead, then why should we be alive? Every one of us could be ordered to the showers, never to be seen again, if that is what she wants. I know that what she told us is true: the colors coming from the mind of Fräulein Kaufman mean inquisitiveness. She really is searching for something—or, as she says, someone. That part I know for sure, but I cannot tell anyone, of course. Threading the needle in this world is more dangerous every day, and the last thing I need is for the other women to think I am crazy.

The third rumor is that the Nazis in Berlin know the war is over and they will need Jews who will say positive things about the camps, perhaps to tell the courts of America and England that the ovens were for burning the dead who passed from sickness, and that the camps were a misguided attempt to save Israel's people from the fury evident in Germany since Kristallnacht. I find this hard to believe, but the fourth rumor is the one that truly terrifies me.

The fourth and final rumor I have heard is that the Fräulein is looking for magic—old magic that Hitler believes some of the Jews may still have. This rumor terrifies me, because what else fills my head but magic? When my mother died, I heard her screams. I felt her inability to catch her breath. I was there, but my mother was nowhere near my side. I know that if the Fräulein is looking for magic, she is looking for someone like me.

I am not vain enough to think that I am the only person in the world who sees like I do, but I do think that we are rare and that perhaps the Nazis have discovered our abilities and wish to use them. If that is true, I am torn between the urge for self-preservation and my desire to aid in no way whatsoever those who killed my family. It would be easy to convince the Fräulein that I could be special, but I would rather die than help these men. So my mission is simple, even if it finally sends me to the ovens: I must convince Fräulein Kaufman that I am nothing but a little blind girl, poor little useless Ora.

Chapter 9

1999

Cynthia woke alone. She was terrified, had no idea where she was, and then it all came back to her. The apartment, divorce, affair. All of the packing at the yellow house, and Mom's tears, and then a pretty tasty pizza dinner before being put to bed.

It wasn't morning yet. It was dark out. Cynthia heard someone yelling and then a group of people laughing in response. Everything about this apartment was different than the house on Glenwood, where Dad used to say that their street was so quiet you could hear a mouse fart. Thinking of Dad gave Cynthia a sick feeling in her stomach, like maybe she had betrayed him by coming with Mom, but it wasn't her fault. No one had even asked what she wanted.

That thought changed quickly to another one: Dad hadn't exactly been chasing after the car. Maybe he wanted her to go away. Maybe he never wanted to see her again. Cynthia loved her dad very much, but if that was true, how could she go the rest of her life without seeing him? Mom had said that she would always get to see both of her parents, but she didn't feel that either of them were particularly trustworthy at the moment.

Cynthia heard another noise outside—a dog barking—and then the sound of something metal being tipped over. Curious about what the dog might have been barking at and about the dog itself, Cynthia crawled from her bed and peeked over the windowsill and between the vertical blinds.

At first there was nothing visible but streetlights, but slowly the nighttime world of the North Harbor Apartments came to life as her eyes adjusted to the yellow glow. Unlike the suburbs, North Harbor appeared to come alive at night. Cynthia could see the fat woman with the laundry basket from earlier, now sans basket and kids, and she was drinking a bottle of beer and talking to a too-skinny woman. The two of them sat in a pair of old folding chairs and had a case of beer between them, but both looked as happy as could be.

Turning from the women, Cynthia could see a group of teenagers walking out of the parking lot and toward the road. It was late, but apparently not too late. Still, Cynthia felt sure the kids were just out and about, not up to anything in particular, and that thought made her wonder about the dream from the night prior. Cynthia let that thought slide from her mind—it was an ugly and sad thing, a bad memory she wanted to forget.

Cynthia heard the dog bark again, closer this time, and she stuck her forehead into the screen and looked down, where she saw Mrs. Martin. Cynthia gave her friend a wave—and Mrs. Martin was a friend, Cynthia was sure of that—even though she knew that the unseen wave wouldn't be returned.

Watching Mrs. Martin and her two dogs, Cynthia felt an itchy feeling on her arms, almost as if she were wearing a sweater that wasn't agreeing with her skin. Cynthia scratched at herself—not hard enough that Mom could have ever seen—and when she looked at Mrs. Martin again, she saw what had to have been there the whole time. Mrs.

Martin was sitting in an old lawn chair with the handles of Stanley's and Libby's color-coordinated leashes stuck through a chair leg, but that was nothing new to Cynthia. What were new were the strands of green thread that Cynthia could see ever so faintly stretching from Mrs. Martin to the dogs, leashes of another kind entirely.

Cynthia backed away from the window and rubbed her eyes, but when she returned to it the strings were still there. They were glowing a beautiful golf-course green, and to Cynthia they were both some of the scariest things she'd ever seen and the most wonderful. The strings at Nan and Pop's had been a deep red—not the color of blood, but close. These green strings were vibrant and electric, and while the red strings had made her feel scared, these made Cynthia's heart feel as if it were singing. Cynthia wanted to run out of the room, down the steps, and into Mrs. Martin's arms. Surely her new neighbor had to be seeing these things as well, but that was impossible. Cynthia sat at the window watching Mrs. Martin smoke her oddly floral cigarettes instead, smiling as the blue smoke permeated the screen in her window. All she could hope was for a chance to ask Mrs. Martin about where the dancing green strings had come from and what they meant.

Cynthia faded to sleep still propped on the windowsill, the world around her emptying even of its late-night critters and guests. As North Harbor finally grew quiet, Mrs. Martin went inside, Cynthia snored away the sleep of the just, and below her two dogs growled as a man with a red string trailing from his head crossed the parking lot.

Chapter 10

Jessica stared at Frank in his cell through the two-way glass that looked like a mirror inside of his room, and shook her head. Somehow, impossibly, Frank had gotten even bigger, and she'd only seen him a couple of days ago.

Frank Rosenbauer was a reluctant war hero of both theaters of combat in the Second World War. He was a dangerous TK, and he and his late wife, Edith, also a TK, had once sold the Soviet Union nuclear secrets that Frank had stolen from a four-star general's head. Ever since then, Frank had been a guest of the TRC, which was doubly beneficial for the government. Frank was too useful to be executed, and his bizarre powers made it impossible for other TKs to use their abilities when they were kept within a few hundred yards of the man. The most amazing part of this skill was that it wasn't something that Frank channeled to make happen; rather, it came off of him like an aura that couldn't be turned off. Looking at him today, Jessica felt sure that the last of Frank's days would be coming soon.

Frank had always been big, but in the years since his wife's death he'd grown to enormous proportions and despite his controlled diet was still increasing in mass. *Pretty soon it won't matter how disagreeable you are, you big lug*, Jessica thought to herself, and it was true. She didn't think it was possible for Frank to be ordering his cells to make him fatter, but it wasn't exactly impossible, either. Frank had spent his entire life proving people wrong.

Finally, having seen enough, Jessica opened the door to Frank's room and walked inside as the door closed after her. Frank regarded her with eyes that were both hungry and lazy and then grunted a greeting.

"Hi, Frank," said Jessica. "I need to talk to you about some stuff, so let's keep it friendly, all right?"

No response.

"Frank, I'm serious. We need to talk. I need your help."

No response.

"Frank, goddamnit," said Jessica. "Do you want me to cut off your food, maybe have somebody kill the electric in here?"

"No, of course not," said Frank finally, his voice a wet rasp that made it sound as if he had a mouthful of soup. "I need my electricity for the computer, and you know I need my food." Frank grinned—it was an awful mask of flesh and excess—then said again, "You know I need my food. You'd never take that from me."

"I wouldn't want to," said Jessica, "but I need your help right now. If it makes it any easier, just think of it as helping yourself instead of doing me a favor."

"Your dad asked me for help," said Frank. "I helped him, too, and look where that got me."

"Let's not play dumb. You came home a decorated war hero, and then a few years later you gave the Russians the bomb."

"I just wanted to see if you were paying attention."

"I am, Frank, always," said Jessica. "What I need is your cooperation, maybe a few parlor tricks for someone from Washington to verify that you've still got it, and then we can prove our worth. There might be more later, possibly even some time outside, but for now I just need my friend Frank to show off a little bit."

"I'm too old to do a mission—too old, fat, and weak."

"I'm not asking you for that right now," said Jessica. "All I need is for you to buy me some time. Everything else that might come later you can say no to. But I need this."

"No. I'm not your dog jumping through hoops, and I'm not going to waste what's left of my life trying to convince someone that there's more to this than there is. There are no more telekinetics out there to be found, Jessica. The ones who had the sight are on drugs, they're drunks, they don't see the magic, they see a shrink. I'm the last of my kind."

"Cut the bullshit. That's a bunch of crap, and we both know it. There are plenty of TKs out there left to find."

"I can't help you."

"You won't."

"The words don't matter."

"What if I made you a deal?"

"To release me?"

"To find Katarina," said Jessica. "To bring her back here."

"You can't make a deal like that. If you could find her, she already would be here."

"That's not true, but to try to locate her, I'm going to need time, and only you can give me that."

Frank sighed. "What kind of 'parlor tricks'?"

"The usual," said Jessica, feeling the lifting of a weight from her chest that had been threatening her for months. "A two-man, maybe some RC work. You know, the usual."

"How about I do the two-man and then have your government man start diddling himself for everyone? Better yet, I can have him yank his eyes out. Maybe slit his throat for an encore."

"No," said Jessica, doing her best not to sink to his level for once, to have a conversation with this evil piece of shit without letting it go to hell, like he wanted. "No, no need for any of that, Frank. I just want you to do some silly bullshit that will be as hard for you as tying my shoes is for me."

"Did I ever tell you how I met my wife?"

"You haven't," said Jessica, her interest piqued. As far as she knew, this was a story that no one at the TRC had ever heard.

"I was living in North Carolina then, grifting my way up and down the seaboard and having some wonderful times with the young women there," said Frank. "This was shortly after your father and my trip to Japan—a story in its own right—and I fancied myself quite the dashing young gentleman."

"Hard to believe."

Frank laughed. "Oh my, yes it is," he said, "but true all the same. Anyway, as I mentioned, I was having fun with the young women there, and after a few good times things got even better. The press was calling me the 'Ham and Egger' because I had killed a pair of waitresses from a diner, and even though I hated the name, I felt like I'd finally made it." Frank coughed—a wet, nasty sound, like someone shaking a fistful of change in a half-empty jug of water. "Every good killer had a name then, of course, just as they do now. Those murders are still unsolved, by the way. Of course, they never will be solved now. Will you look them up on your computer tonight, Jessica? When you can't sleep and you're thinking about how blessed you are that I can't reach into your head and make you my little marionette, will you read about my adventures?"

"No," said Jessica. "What does this have to do with your wife?"

"We'll get there, we'll get there," said Frank. "All in due time, my dear. You will read about this, though, won't you? You simply must. It was by no means my masterwork. That took place in Berlin—wish I'd known at the time that I was at my peak—but it was still very good work. Anyway, I had enjoyed several girls very much, including the two from the diner who made me so famous, when I saw Edith walking down the street. I was smitten instantly, I had to have her, and of course I did, but not in the way I was thinking."

"You couldn't bend her. I get it."

"No, of course I could," said Frank. "You had her here for years, God rest her soul, and you know as well as I do that I could bend her whenever I chose. Anyway, I decided right then and there to park the car and to make this girl come with me, damn the consequences and full speed ahead. So I parked and followed her into a store, and when I walked in I saw that there were three people there—Edith, the clerk, and an old biddy—and all of them were standing in place, their eyes locked straight ahead. The clerk was emptying the register into a flour sack, but no one was speaking, and then there was this voice in my head. I remember it like it was yesterday.

"'Hold still,' she said, and I about doubled over laughing. She had a strong bend to her—the strongest I'd encountered at that point besides my own—but I was just beyond amused. Who could plan on such good fortune? I told her to get the money and follow me, and that's exactly that—the rest is history. I will admit, however, that she did not agree with the idea to sell the plans to the Reds. It was one of the only things that we disagreed over, and of course she was right.

"Anyway, I insist that you look into the adventures of the Ham and Egger. Do it tonight when you're sleepless, just like I said, and then come back here and tell me what you think of my exploits. A portrait of a young man as a serial killer, if you will."

"Why, Frank?" Jessica asked after a pause that had grown into a third trimester. "Why would I want to do that to myself, to read the details, if I can even find them on the web? I know what you're capable of. I don't doubt any of this."

"I want to know if you can solve the riddle," said Frank slowly. "I want to know if, based solely on the evidence left when the Ham and Egger took on a partner, you can tell when Edith began to have fun with me."

"And what if I do?"

"If you do your homework and get me the answer I want, I will do your parlor tricks."

Chapter 11

The three days stretched to five. Five days of arguing and sweating, Darryl and Terry treating each other like a couple of dogs that know they don't like one another and know exactly why. Terry was as sweet as he could be, and then he was just as poisoned as Darryl. The mood was death, scabs being pulled off too slowly and too soon, but it was necessary. All Darryl could think about was booze, and when he dreamt, he had both a bottle in his hand and a strand of black and purple threads growing from the top of his head. On the fifth morning, he woke covered in sweat in the porno room. Darryl walked to the bathroom, pissed, and looked at himself in the mirror. Growing from the top of his head and fluttering in the wind from the air conditioner were strings.

They were red, yellow, and green, but there was no black to be found.

Now you know. No black yet. So maybe this time you stay dry. It was a good thought, a healthy one, but it wasn't going to happen. Darryl knew from experience that after a few days of staring at the threads in the mirror and poking through the heads of others he'd be more than thirsty. That was the cycle and had been ever since he'd been old enough to get alcohol. Darryl ran his fingers through his hair, thinking about the first time he'd seen the strings.

He'd been ten, and they'd been glowing bright red. Darryl saw them in the reflection from the school bus window, and he knew why. Some kids were being mean to his friend Terry again, beating on him in the back of the bus, and that was only going to get worse when the two of them got off at their stop. Darryl knew what would happen if he tried to stop it because he'd tried to stop it before—they'd beat on him, too. The last time he'd had a tooth loosened and his eyes blacked, and then three days later his old man had come back from an onion run, trucking in the South. Dad had a temper—that was never a secret in the Livingston household—and when he'd asked his son how the other guy looked, Darryl knew he was in for it.

Dad wouldn't care about Darryl's weak little fatboy best friend, just like he wouldn't care about how many guys there were, just like he didn't care about how many rotten onions were on the back of the truck as he fueled himself on white powder and CB static while driving across southern Florida. Dad would care about the beating his son had taken, and he would care about why his pussy-bitch boy couldn't defend himself. "I'm not raising you to be some faggot," Dad had said on more than one occasion, including a particularly memorable week where Mom had been visiting her sister and Darryl had been all but convinced that was exactly what his father wanted from him, and those words echoed in Darryl's mind on that school bus as he stared at himself and the odd red things in his reflection.

Helping Terry would mean a beating from the kids on the bus, and then it would mean a beating when he got home. Dad wasn't even off running onions or anything else. His old man had the week off and was probably working through a few bottles of Tropical Golden Ale at this very moment. As mad as Dad got when he'd seen Darryl a few days after that earlier beating, Darryl couldn't even imagine what his old man might have to say when his boy came home in a ripped shirt, dripping snot, blood, and tears. Darryl broke his gaze from the window, heard the sound of a boy yelping in pain, and left his bag and seat behind him.

"Let him go," called Darryl—not a yell yet, but close.

If the bus driver heard or cared, there was no indication, but the boys on the back most certainly did.

"You want some, too, faggot?" asked Tim Ostwich—Tim of the buckteeth, flannel shirts, and wicked right hand.

Darryl smiled while he made his way to the back of the bus, stealing a glance at himself in the reflection of the windows as he walked the rows. The tendrils were blaze red now, violent and awesome all at once, and even more incredibly, Darryl had no fear.

"Yes, I do, Tim," said Darryl. "I want you to give it to me. I want you to show me what a faggot I am. Like how your dad shows you sometimes."

Tim's mouth fell open like a trapdoor, and then the bigger boy was racing down the thin corridor between the green leather seats as fast as his hand-me-down Keds could carry him. Darryl watched this progress, watched as a red thread from his head leapt up and found purchase with a thread that was just as angry and pouring from Tim's noggin, and then leaned down and grabbed a second grader's metal G.I. Joe lunchbox.

"Here it comes, Livingston," said Tim, and then Darryl yanked the thread with his mind at the same time as he swung the lunchbox.

The corner of the box—one edge of a scene showing Cobra Commander aboard a H.I.S.S. Tank—crumpled as it collided with Tim's head, and the older boy staggered as his body dealt with the fact that his lights had been dimmed. Darryl leapt at the opportunity, feeling into Tim's concussed brain with a part of his own mind he barely understood, and then he made the bigger boy void his bowels onto the floor. The damage was worse than just that—far more than the nudge that Darryl had intended; more than the ruined lunchbox alone could ever have provided—but that was the lasting memory for those on the bus: Tim Ostwich writhing on the ground in his own filth, and the rest of the back of the bus screaming.

Tim died a few weeks later, and Darryl wound up in a state home for five years. It was infinitely better than living with his old man and his broken mother, but it was still jail, and jail sucks. When Darryl was released, there was one person waiting for him: Terry Huckland. Terry was no longer a fatboy, had earned a few of his own scars, and was the proud owner of a Ford Escort wagon. Darryl had learned a couple of tricks of his own while he was locked up: that he could own people, really *own* them through the bends in those little reeds coming from their scalps, and that the only way to shut that crap off was through booze.

Darryl learned one more secret on the day Terry picked him up, and it was a big one. Terry believed him—truly believed in what he could do. Darryl simply told his old friend what was going on in his mind, what had happened on that bus five years before, and what he needed now. Terry had enough money for a bottle, and before Darryl got it, he fried a man talking on the pay phone. They emptied his wallet, bought two bottles instead of the one, and disappeared. Off the grid was easier than on—that was another easy discovery—and soon enough they were doing what few could, exploiting a talent that almost always dies at puberty.

Now, at long last, Darryl emerged from the bathroom and said, "I'm ready."

Terry smiled and stood up from the computer desk. "I'll unplug the phone. Do you need the white, or should I—"

"Just get it," said Darryl. "This is going to be a long night. Put a pot on, too. We're both going to need some coffee. Did you open the bank accounts?" Terry nodded—he had—and Darryl walked past him to the computer and sat. "Christ, we are about to raise some hell." Darryl looked back across the room at his friend and really saw him, saw the threads connecting them, blue, yellow, and green. "I'm sorry, Terry," said Darryl. "You know how hard this is for me."

"Just make it worth it," said Terry. "If everything goes right, we'll never be broke again."

Chapter 12

Cynthia woke when Mom called to her. Her mom's words were a blur, but the message was easily interpreted: it was time to get up.

Cynthia rose on an elbow on the floor beneath the window. She'd never made it back to her sleeping bag. She dragged herself to her feet and yawned. She was no longer surprised to find herself in the apartment, not after last night. And though Cynthia would have preferred the yellow house, North Harbor seemed a lot more like home than it had when she lay down. Even being apart from Dad was starting to feel normal. Cynthia was used to him working all the time, so as long as she didn't think about it, this was just another long shift at the store.

Cynthia walked from the bedroom, stopping for a moment in the hall to stare at Mom, who was dressed up for some reason, and then walked into the bathroom. The toilet was grungy, but it was far too early in the day to worry about anything but making water, so that's what she did. Cynthia pissed, wiped, flushed, and washed, then wandered into the shared kitchen and dining area and sat at the table. Second grade didn't start until the fall, but this already felt like a school day, just maybe one happening to a different person.

#231   10-18-2017 12:07PM
Item(s) checked out to p11152473.

TITLE: The X-files : true reports of Wis
BARCODE: 36430000207547
DUE DATE: 11-08-17-14

TITLE: The daily feast : everyday meals
BARCODE: 36430000305943
DUE DATE: 11-08-17

TITLE: People.
VOLUME: Oct 23 2017
BARCODE: 36430000387784
DUE DATE: 11-01-17

TITLE: Smithsonian.
VOLUME: Oct 2017
BARCODE: 36430000387214
DUE DATE: 11-01-17

TITLE: Time,
VOLUME: Sep 4 2017
BARCODE: 36430000386521
DUE DATE: 11-01-17

TITLE: Time,
VOLUME: Aug 21 2017
BARCODE: 36430000386356
DUE DATE: 11-01-17

TITLE: Wisconsin natural resources.
VOLUME: Oct 2017
BARCODE: 36430000387511
DUE DATE: 11-01-17

Boyceville Public Library 715-643-2106
Renew or Request at www.more.lib.wi.us

Mom was wearing a suit at the table and staring out of the living room window. Cynthia followed her gaze and then turned back to her mother, as after last night she knew there was nothing worth seeing outside. Cynthia had seen her mom's suit before, but it had been a long time. She couldn't recall the occasion, only that she hadn't seen her mother in it since the last time she'd gone on a date with Dad.

There was no date this morning, however, just Mom in her suit and the empty apartment.

"I'm sure you're wondering what I'm doing today," said Mom, and Cynthia nodded to be polite. The truth was that she hadn't wondered about that for even a second. What she'd been curious about, until Mom had spoken, was what *the two of them* were going to be up to. "I need to get a job, Cynthia," said Mom with a sigh, and Cynthia nodded. It made sense. After all, Mom had always worked before, and she said she couldn't work at the store anymore.

"What kind of a job?"

"The kind that will hire me and that pays me something that I won't be ashamed of," said Mom. "I suppose we'll know pretty soon how it all shakes out regarding the store, but I don't plan to just sit back and wait for your father to do what's right before the court forces his hand." Mom shook her head, a disgusted look on her face, and just for a moment Cynthia could see a tuft of red string coming from her scalp. The only difference was that this time the thread didn't lead anywhere. It just hovered over Mom.

"Can I come with you?" Cynthia asked. She had a feeling that she already knew what the answer would be, but if Mom really did say no, then where was she supposed to go?

"No," said Mom flatly. "Your dad should be at the store by now. We'll run by and drop you off to him, just like we would on any other day when I had something going on. You can sit in the back and draw or read books, just like you have a bunch of other times."

"I don't want to go to the store." She knew as soon as she saw the bitter smile on her mother's face that Mom was happy she'd said this, and once again the threads over Mom's head were visible, only this time they were a cool blue instead of the angry red. *She's going to bring me there, but she doesn't want to, because she doesn't want me to be happy there.* This didn't make much more sense than the threads did, but Cynthia knew she was right, just as sure as she knew the stuff over Mom was blue. Mom might leave her there, but if Cynthia was smart, the last thing she should do afterward would be to brag about the amount of candy or fun she'd been allowed to have.

"Sorry, Cynth. It's our only option right now," said Mom. "Maybe we'll figure out something else later, but for now you need to go ahead and get dressed, do your teeth, and I'll get that rat's nest on your head brushed."

Cynthia nodded and then voiced a concern she immediately knew should've been left unvoiced: "I need to eat breakfast."

Mom scowled in response, the strands over her dancing from blue to red and then back again.

"All right," said Mom, "we'll get you something on the way." Though Mom didn't look sad, Cynthia knew she was. "It won't always be like this, Cynthia. Things are going to be weird for a little bit, but your dad and I will get this all figured out. No matter what happens, you're the most important thing in our lives."

"OK," said Cynthia, before turning to walk to her room to get dressed. She knew Mom was lying, and the sting of it was like a whip on her cheek. *If I mattered as much as she says I do, we'd still be in the house instead of this apartment, and she wouldn't be looking for a job.* Cynthia couldn't read Mom's thoughts the way she could a Berenstain Bears book, but she did know that, as important as words like "divorce" and "affair" were, all Mom cared about now was *showing him.*

Neither of them spoke as Mom drove from the McDonald's drive-thru to Dad's store. Cynthia wasn't talking because her mouth was full,

Weavers

but she figured Mom was being quiet because she was starting to have doubts about leaving her daughter with Dad and about looking for a job. Cynthia's parents had worked together for as long as she could remember, usually on opposing shifts, but never had they worked anywhere but the store. *It has to be so weird for Mom.* Cynthia was sure of that, just as sure as she was that of everyone involved in divorce, Mom had planned for it least of all.

Mom parked as Cynthia finished off her hash browns and orange juice, but when Cynthia unbuckled her seat belt, Mom said, "Go ahead and stay in the car for just a second, Cynth. I'm going to go inside and talk to Dad for a minute, and then I'll be back to get you."

"OK."

Mom took her keys from the ignition and left the car, locking the doors before walking inside. Cynthia watched her disappear and then took a drink of orange juice before looking to the lot to see who else was parked there. She could see Dad's truck, as well as Linda's little convertible, and something in Cynthia's stomach twisted as she realized that Mom, Dad, and Linda were all going to be in the same confined space. Cynthia was small, alone, and not well versed in the world of adults, but it was no mystery that the three of them together would be a bad combination.

Cynthia was staring at the store when two bearded men came out of it carrying their purchases, and as she watched them drive away in the last car in the lot, she knew what she needed to do. If her parents and Linda were going to argue, they were going to do it now, when there was no one else left in the building. Cynthia opened her door and as she left the vehicle could already hear Mom shouting from inside the store. She had to keep going, though. So Cynthia walked to the front door, took a deep breath, and pulled it open.

The store was exactly how she remembered it, only now it felt different, as if it were scarred somehow. Cynthia could hear Mom and Dad yelling louder, as well as another sound—Linda sobbing from the back of the store. Cynthia walked past the magazine racks, cigarette ads, and an impossibly tall shelf covered in glass bottles before walking to the coolers and taking a right through the open door into the stockroom. Farther back was Dad's office, but there would be no need to walk that far. Mom, Dad, and Linda were right around the corner from her, by all of the recycling bins.

Cynthia could see them as she poked her head around a stack of cases of bottled beer. Mom stood just a few feet from Dad, her careful makeup job already spoiled, though Cynthia doubted Mom was aware of anything besides Dad and Linda. Dad was red-faced and furious looking, but even with everything that was happening, Cynthia felt bad for him. Dad looked tired, angry, and weak all at once, but she could also see the man who loved to read with her shining through the aches on his face. Linda looked scared, like a mouse trapped by a pair of cats. Cynthia catalogued these emotions in seconds, in a hurry to get to something far more astounding in the room: all three adults had threads pouring from the crowns of their heads.

Mom's were once again red, a deep burgundy color that was several degrees darker than Cynthia had seen a few days before. Dad's were purple still, a dark color that shimmered red and blue, before leaping back to the thick violet shade that was dominating them. Linda's threads were different, a color that Cynthia had never seen before. The threads coming from Linda were corn-silk yellow, an iridescent shimmer as bright as the reflectors on the back of Cynthia's bicycle.

As fascinating as all of these threads were on their own, what was even more amazing was what they were doing.

The threads of all three adults had collided in the center of the storeroom, weaving in and out of one another as though they'd been clumsily bound on a loom. Mom's were red, Dad's were their purplish red, and Linda's were vibrant and yellow, but where they met above them the threads were knotted and an ugly, bruised color. Now that she could see the knot, Cynthia found it impossible to tear her eyes from it. She knelt next to the boxes of beer, staring into the impossibly writhing and twisting mass before her, and then Cynthia felt as if she were floating.

Cynthia knew she was still on the floor—she could even see herself there, next to the boxes of beer—but she was also above the arguing adults. She was *in* the threads. Here it was easier to see where the colors were muddled into darkness. The purple from Dad was the easiest to see in the knot, but where its red strands touched Mom's she could see a binding taking place. Linda's yellow was vibrant in the knot, but where it touched Dad's purple and Mom's red, the yellow faded and died, turning to the other colors immediately at the place of contact. Cynthia waved her hands at the threads, and she could see her fingers passing through them like a shark's dorsal fin cutting through water. The threads had no more weight than the air around them, but Cynthia could feel things in them. Bad things.

Dad's threads felt angry, just like the look on his face, but there was something more there, something worse. Dad had a darkness in him that Cynthia had never seen before, a darkness that she didn't think anyone had ever seen, not even Mom or Linda. Mom's strands were easy to read—pure anger at Dad and his selfishness—but where they meshed with Dad's red strings, Cynthia could see hope. As long as her parents could stay mad enough to yell at one another, there could be hope, but threatening the bond of rage was the purple, along with Linda's yellow.

Linda wanted them to be fighting. Cynthia knew it in her guts, and she hated her old friend for the betrayal. Linda had always been the one to listen to her when the other adults were too busy, the one who knew what Cynthia needed when she was sad. Linda had been a friend, but that was no longer true. Linda wanted Mom and Dad to keep fighting, and even though she was crying, the tears only came because Linda thought they were supposed to.

Linda wanted Mom's and Dad's threads to split once and for all, and she was willing to do anything to make that happen. As Cynthia stared at the threads that made up the knot, she could see that what she had first thought she was seeing was wrong. Linda's yellow strands weren't being attacked by Dad's purple and red; they were acquiescing to the other colors, assimilating with them. For every turned strand, Cynthia knew that one of the red strands connecting Mom and Dad would split. Linda had her own goals in the argument, and they were as black as the threads at the center of the knot.

Cynthia reached into the knot again, concentrating on the colors and the threads as she stretched out her arms, and then she began to tear the yellow strings from where they touched the purple and red ones. Electric pulses fluttered up her arms as she grabbed at them—strong enough to feel but not painful for her—and with concentration, Cynthia discovered they could be parted. Watching Linda as she worked, Cynthia could see the woman's face twitching slightly, even as nonsensical thoughts burned through Cynthia's mind. / *Get out, bitch / Just leave us here / We've got this figured out / He doesn't need you or the brat to be happy / He just needs me /*

Cynthia gasped. The thoughts in her head were poison, and the electricity on her hands now felt like thrumming tar. Cynthia tried to pull herself free, but it wasn't possible. She was stuck in the knot as sure as if it were a tangible thing, and then she began to scream. The knot turned pitch black, sending black threads toward all three of the adults, and then all of them were screaming together. Cynthia heard what sounded like static electricity and then a sound like a balloon popping. The threads fell away from her, even as the screams became louder, and then the knot roared toward her, and Cynthia fell into the black.

Chapter 13

Darryl laid his hands on the keyboard and took a deep breath. He felt alive, connected, and he hadn't even begun to reach out yet. Going without booze for a few days sucked, but this moment was always the same—he felt pure and alive—and though he knew the feeling would die, it made him wonder why he covered this with booze. This was his gift, what he was meant to do, and he willingly buried it under alcohol.

"Do you want me to help you get started?" Terry asked from across the room, but the words may as well have come from across Texas.

"No," said Darryl as he began to type. Terry had showed him how to enter live chat rooms, and Darryl found himself entering one that was supposed to offer conversation about a game called *Resident Evil*. Not that it mattered. Darryl couldn't have cared less about the game or what other users had to say about it.

It only took a few moments for Darryl to connect. There was a user in the chat room named JVTINE911, and Darryl let his mind wander until he could make a connection. He was used to seeing the threads and working amongst them, but this was different. He was with JVTINE911, but stuck inside of the teenage boy's head inside of his room. Darryl knew nothing about the boy and then everything in an instant. His name was Bryce Rucker, he was in tenth grade, and he loved his PlayStation. Bryce had never kissed a girl, was smoking the occasional cigarette, and had masturbated twice in the boys' locker room at school. Bryce's dad was a lawyer with the Crawford and Crawford firm in Phoenix, where their family lived, and Bryce's mother was a homemaker. Dad worked too much, Mom tried too hard, and Bryce was spoiled and lonely.

As disconnected as he felt from them, Bryce still knew a great deal about his mother and father. As he began to type on his keyboard, blood started to pour from his left nostril, but Bryce made no effort to wipe it away. Threads of pure amber spilled from his head and his fingertips, all of them brushing over the keyboard and screen of his computer, but the only things Bryce was moving were his fingertips. He was a zombie, a sight that would have made his mother scream and dial 911, but Bryce was hard at work. Despite the fact Bryce felt like he didn't know his parents very well, his father's online banking security information collapsed at his fingertips.

Darryl knew he was shitstomping the kid, but he didn't care; he couldn't care. Bryce was a victim of circumstance, nothing more and nothing less. He had no aura, no ability to protect himself from someone, like Darryl, who could bend him. It was perfect and couldn't have been any easier if Darryl had held a gun to his head. The kid knew everything that Darryl needed, and in just forty-five minutes the work was done.

Darryl gave Bryce one last push, a hard one, before leaving, and though he didn't hear the gunshot, he knew what he would see if he looked at a Phoenix newspaper the next day. Bryce Rucker had never fired a gun, but he knew where Dad kept his .357, always loaded, and as soon as Darryl was out of his head, Bryce was going to retrieve that gun, put it in his mouth, and pull the trigger.

"Shit, are you all right?" Terry asked when Darryl came back, the walls in the apartment swirling as his mind realized that he was no longer attached to Bryce.

"I'm fine," said Darryl, knowing that it was the farthest thing from the truth. He felt sick, dirty, and diseased, but he had only done what he had to. Darryl had no idea if there were other people like him who had kept their ability to bend past adolescence, but if there were, he had to imagine they would be doing the same things he was. "I need coffee," he said, knowing even as Terry scrambled to get him a cup of the black that it wouldn't be good enough.

Terry returned with the coffee. It was ice-cold and double brewed, and Darryl slammed it like the sludge was a cold beer at the end of a hard and hot day. The caffeine went to work immediately, making him feel alive again, as if there were springs under him.

"Again," said Darryl, and he handed the cup to Terry, who once again made the trek to the kitchen. Darryl slammed the second cup, set the mug down next to the keyboard, and sighed.

"Do you want me to get you a bump?" Terry asked, and Darryl shook his head as he looked for a new person to chat with.

"Not yet," said Darryl. "We need to save it, anyways. I'll be ripping through the stuff soon enough."

"Did you get anything?"

"Twenty-four grand," said Darryl. "It would have been more, but his dad just bought a boat. It had a big down payment, bigger than what he told his wife by almost triple, so he was a little lighter than I was hoping. The next one will be better."

"Twenty-four thousand dollars is a lot for one," said Terry. "That's a record."

Darryl nodded as he punched keys and entered another web-based chat, this one for lovers of the *Final Fantasy* games. "It won't be the record for long," he said. "This is going to be a hard night."

Terry said something else, but Darryl didn't hear him. He was racing through the wires and static into CAiT$iTH, known to her friends as Ericka Hurley. Ericka was seventeen, a big fan of *Final Fantasy VII*, and the daughter of two veterinarians. As Darryl took her, Ericka's cat, Thumper, leapt from her lap and began to hiss at her best friend and the yellow strings running from her scalp. No one else in the house heard anything, not until the tub ran over with pink water and began to flow down the stairs.

"That's two," said Darryl as he snapped back, and Terry came running from the kitchen with another cup of room-temperature coffee. Darryl took the coffee, drank, and then belched loudly. The caffeine was cutting through the fog, but he could already feel the shadows racing in. Darryl had made two teenagers kill themselves to cover his footsteps, but he harbored no guilt. They were casualties of war, a necessary mess while making an omelet. There was no guilt, but he could feel his aura fading and couldn't even imagine what a mirror might tell him about his current state. *Black and purple, black and purple—like your liver, like your guts, like everything inside of you, just waiting to die.*

"Cut me a line," said Darryl. "A big one. Cut me a fucking worm."

Terry nodded, then ran to the bathroom and grabbed the small mirror they kept for just such an occasion. Darryl watched his friend— no longer a fatboy but instead a man with a very unfortunate attitude toward women—and then took the offered mirror with its requested line. Darryl grabbed the glass straw that was next to the line of coke, which was fat enough to be a leech instead of a worm, and then hunkered down and got his Hoover on. He shut his eyes as he snuffled up the coke—the last thing he needed to see was his topknot when he was doing blow—and then he felt reborn.

"Take the mirror," said Darryl, and dutiful Terry did as he was told while Darryl dove back into the machine.

Darryl stole, committing acts of rape far worse than he ever could have with his dick and a gun, and then he was really steamrolling. He'd pop out, sniff coke and chug coffee, and then dive back in. Looking at the clock made him sick, so he stopped looking, and then, what turned out to be two days later, he wandered into a chat room based around the *Legend of Zelda* games and started a conversation with a boy named Vincent Taggio. Darryl sunk his teeth in like a vampire, but it wasn't until he was all in that Darryl realized his victim was himself a vampire.

Vincent wasn't like the rest. He was playing his own game, using his own skills. Vincent was a bender, too, and he'd already figured out the trick that Darryl was using, but he wasn't ready to be struck back. Darryl was on him like a hungry dog after a sack of Ol' Roy. Vincent asked him, "What the fuck are you?" and the voice was accompanied by a sizable jolt. The boy thought he was invincible. He fought back, and they never fought back—not in person, and so far, not over the wire, either. Vincent's defenses crumbled, of course—he was just a boy, after all—but a part of Darryl still wanted to get the hell out of him.

Darryl dove into Vincent's mind and took all the important things. It was quite a load. Mom and Dad were rich, Dad was connected with the Chicago Outfit, and he was a player, not a kickstand. Vincent knew all that, but even better, Vincent knew his dad's friends—goombahs with names like Ricky and Sal and Tony—and Vincent had done his own exploring into them. Instead of one bank account, Darryl had been given the keys to the vault, Cayman Islands keys, and he got to cleaning house while Vincent pissed himself and shuddered at his desktop.

When Darryl was done, he slid free from Vincent with a snail trail of shit dripping behind him. Darryl had never been inside another bender—he'd never even thought about it—but he'd cleared almost half a million dollars in under an hour. Vincent had been easy to shove, and Darryl hated that he couldn't use the boy again and was leaving him to a slow death at the end of a rope, but he came clean of Vincent with a sheen of sweat and a new knowledge.

"You'll never fucking believe this," said Darryl as Terry ran to him with a coffee and the mirror. Darryl could see light outside and didn't even want to think about what day it was.

"What?" Terry set the goods down in front of his friend, but Darryl shook his head at both the coke and the coffee.

"I need booze," said Darryl as Terry cocked an eyebrow, no doubt wondering how his friend could already be done. "I'm serious, Terry. I need a drink."

"All right," said Terry, a wounded tone in his voice. He'd only been trying to help.

"This last kid was like me, he was doing the same thing we are, and I was able to make him do things, everything. Half a million, Terry. Half a million because this kid was a bender like me. Can you believe it?"

"Holy shit." Terry could believe it as it turned out.

"If there's one, there's a million," said Darryl. "They're all kids— remember me telling you that? For whatever reason, there's just me and then all these kids that can do this, and the ones that can do it all have access to their whole worlds."

"Let's get a drink and talk about it," said Terry.

Darryl ran a hand through his hair. He could see that Terry thought he was crazy, and not for the first time.

"Yeah, let's get a drink. I can explain better, I think," said Darryl, but he didn't really care either way. Terry didn't need to understand for it to be true. *I've been wasting my time.*

• • •

Terry drove them back from the liquor store in the shitty car. Being in it now was just a reminder that they would have a better one soon, that soon Austin and the car and the porno apartment would all be in the rearview mirror. Freedom from all of that would carry its own weight, of course. The need to always be moving was rough, and some of Terry's tastes could be tough to deal with as well, but they'd finally have money to grease the wheels. Darryl didn't talk as his friend drove, didn't even want to think yet. There were three cases of beer in the trunk, along with a couple of handles of Johnnie Walker Black, and he didn't want to think about any of it until he could get a drink in his hand.

Darryl had only been bending over the computer for two days—an eternity in his mind, but nothing compared to the marathon sessions of his youth. Of course, with the computer they weren't just tricking guys into emptying bank accounts from strip club ATM machines. This new way was better, cleaner, though the kid—fucking Vincent with his gangster dad—had shown Darryl that he was still operating penny-ante scams when he could have been fishing for whales all along.

Terry finally parked at the apartment, and the two of them humped the booze up the stairs. The neighborhood was quiet, almost as if the psychic energy coming from his topknot was enough to warn the rest of the apartment dwellers to stay inside. Not that he cared, of course. Darryl wanted a drink in each hand. He wanted to shut it off. He wanted to walk past a mirror without squeezing his eyes shut.

They piled booze on the kitchen table, and then Darryl went to work on getting a scotch. By the time he got to the couch, Terry was already there with a beer and a lit cigarette, waiting to hear why Darryl had bowed out so quickly. Darryl sat down beside him and slammed the scotch, loving the burn as it curled through his chest and down into his belly.

"OK," said Darryl at last. "Like I said, the last kid was doing the same thing that I was, Terry. He wasn't stealing, but he was thinking about it. His dad is some mobbed-up guy, and the kid was making a list of his father's connections in his head."

"He couldn't just kick you out?"

Darryl shook his head, letting Terry keep rapid-firing questions.

"What made this kid so special but made him unable to eighty-six you from his head?"

"I don't know, not exactly," said Darryl. "I do have some guesses."

"Spill."

"I think he could have kicked me out—that is, if we'd been face-to-face," explained Darryl. "The thing is, he had no idea that someone could do what he was doing. This isn't exactly well-documented shit, you know? Point is, I pulled close to a half a million out of that kid, and all I had to do was let him do what he already knew. There was no discovery process, no rooting around in his head for maiden names or old addresses so that I could try and figure out a likely password. He'd already done all of the work. Do you know what this means?"

"That we got lucky?"

"All I need to do is find kids like Vincent, maybe even ones more powerful, both mentally and in terms of family. Can you imagine if the Clintons' kid was a bender and we could get to her? Or maybe the son of a stockbroker, or head of the FBI? As far as we know, I'm the only adult who can do this, but how many of these scammy little kids are out running the same kind of racket, but without the stones or smarts to set up offshore accounts and actually take? I mean, when I was a kid, just knowing I could do something was usually good enough, but that's what makes them so ripe."

"What if you didn't make them off themselves?"

"We've been over that, Terry," said Darryl. "I don't like that part any better than you do, but if they didn't die, the kids might be able to remember what happened. And without the deaths, the empty bank accounts are going to be noticed a lot faster. These kids might not deserve to die, but I don't deserve to be broke, not after what we've been through."

"Couldn't you, like, explain to one of these bent kids what you're doing?"

Darryl couldn't figure out what his friend was suggesting.

"Not permanently, of course," Terry went on, "but think how much shit one of these kids could gather up, but at no risk to us. What if you could trick them into getting access to all sorts of stuff for a week, and then came back?"

"It wouldn't work," said Darryl, but he was thinking, already considering that maybe it could. *That would make even this run look like a kid's game by comparison.* Darryl had long believed that there was a better place for him in this world, if only he would reach out and grasp it. He knew that this, finally, might be his chance to catch hold of the brass ring. "Even if it did work, it's going to be really hard to find any more of these kids."

"If all you're doing is scouting, you wouldn't need to stomp the kids. If you kept off of caffeine and cocaine, you could be careful."

"I'm not sure," said Darryl, but he knew he was lying. Already, thoughts of making it work were swirling in his head. He'd still need to stay off of the booze—he doubted he'd ever conquer that mountain—but he could be more surgical, and rather than bombarding a bent kid with commands, he could try and communicate with them. *Think about how you felt as a kid, how miserable you were. A voice in your head would have made all the sense in the world.*

Darryl's beer was empty, and there were three dead children in his wake, but he was smiling. Terry was on fire right now: first the idea of using the web to get at people, and then the idea of farming any bent kids he came across. Even better, now the two of them finally had enough of a nest egg to put some miles between themselves and the States. *Move first, and then hunt.* For the first time in years, Darryl was looking forward to going dry and putting the bend on someone.

Chapter 14

"Call fucking 911!" Dad screamed next to her, and Cynthia's eyes fluttered open. The smell of beer was ripe all around them, and even after what had happened it was a happy smell. Dad owned a liquor store but rarely drank more than enough to get silly, and the smell of malt and hops reminded Cynthia of summer days that seemed impossibly far away. Cynthia could see Mom fumbling with her phone, and as Mom tried to dial, Cynthia sat up and said, "I'm fine, it's OK. I just came inside because I wanted a drink of water and I got dizzy."

"Oh, thank God," cried Mom as she fell to Cynthia's side next to Dad, and then Linda appeared opposite her.

There was a truce in the air. Cynthia could feel it even if the threads were gone again, but it was only because they were worried about her. *Is Linda worried, or is it still an act?* Cynthia decided it didn't matter, not right now, and then Mom was pushing a bottle of water into her hands and splashing liquid all over both of them.

"Drink," said Mom, and Cynthia did, hoping as she swallowed that Mom would forget Cynthia had plenty to drink in the car.

"I got dizzy," said Cynthia again, and Mom and Dad nodded their heads.

"I know, Cynth," said Dad, "but you're OK now. Can we get you anything else?"

"I'll grab the poor thing some paper towels," said Linda. "She's covered in beer."

Cynthia smiled at that. It was true, and she wasn't sure how she'd even noticed the water that Mom had spilled. Cynthia was covered in the smelly drink, and though she figured Dad would be mad about the loss of product, he didn't seem to care in the slightest.

Cynthia let Mom and Dad help her off of the floor and onto a small stool that the bottle sorters used, and then Linda was wiping her down with paper towels from the roll in the bathroom. Cynthia felt good, but as the memory of what had happened came back to her, she found it hard to look at Linda. Linda was younger than Mom, with no family of her own, but she wanted Dad, wanted the liquor store, and wanted the money. Of the last part Cynthia was the most sure. And she was also quite sure that Dad intended to give her all she wanted. Cynthia wanted to warn him, to tell Linda she knew about the plan, and to tell Mom they needed to run from this place, but instead she allowed herself to be comforted by the three of them.

Cynthia managed to talk Mom out of taking her to the hospital, and by the time she and Mom left for the car she could tell that Dad was starting to finally think about the broken beer. After all, his daughter was fine, so why not worry about the cost to the store? Especially when / *They're going to bleed you bleed you bleed you dry* / The thought was ugly, but it only lasted for a moment, and then Dad was smiling again.

"Cynthia, can I trust you to stay in the car while I run inside?" Mom asked, and Cynthia nodded. It wasn't really a question. Adults always did that, asked things like, "How about hot dogs?" but would then get furious if you said anything but what they wanted to hear. Cynthia was used to that world. She found it almost a comfort after the strings and all of the things that just didn't make any sense.

Mom gave Cynthia another look, one that was supposed to tell her daughter how concerned she was, and then closed the door. Cynthia watched Mom talk to Dad in front of the store. She didn't want to see any threads, didn't want to go floating after them, and most of all, didn't want to see if Linda was connected with Dad even while he talked to Mom. She was thankful that none of that was there. It was just her Mom and her Dad talking.

Finally, Mom walked back to the car, opened the door, and hopped inside. "Looks like the great job hunt is going to wait until tomorrow, Cynth," said Mom with a smile, but even before Cynthia had seen the strands, she would have known the smile was a fake one. Mom knew she had to be at home in case Cynthia collapsed again, but there was a part of her that resented it, that needed to go find a job, and not just for money. *She wants to feel like she's worth something.*

"I could just stay home alone at the apartment," said Cynthia, a proposition that sounded worlds better than spending time at the store with Linda and her ugly yellow thread.

"No way." The tone in Mom's voice suggested she wasn't even going to think about something like that, especially not after what had happened, and maybe not ever at the apartment.

If you don't trust the people there, then why did we move? It was a question that would never get the answer it deserved, because Cynthia would never ask it. The truth was that Mom had moved them for the same reason that she needed a job: she wanted to prove she was worth something; so she could *show them.*

"I'd be fine," said Cynthia. "There's no TV, so you wouldn't have to worry about me watching too much of it, and I could just read until you came back."

Mom didn't say anything, and for a moment Cynthia thought that she might really be considering the idea. But then she said, "No, there's no way. You're too young, and you just fainted."

Cynthia smiled at Mom from the backseat, looking into the rearview mirror so that Mom could see her eyes. "Well, I could come along until we figure something else out."

"That's not going to work either, Cynth," said Mom. "Not when I'm applying for work, and especially not after what happened in the store. I can put this off for a day or two if that's what our family needs, and everything will be just fine."

Cynthia didn't say anything to that, just sat quietly in the back of the car as Mom drove them to the apartment building. She wanted to plead, to tell Mom she was fine, that it was her own fault for trying to get Linda's ugly yellow thread off of Daddy's confused purple one, but she knew that would raise more questions than she wanted to answer. Especially since most of those questions Cynthia knew there was no way she *could* answer.

Mom pulled the car into the apartment complex and parked in front of their building. Cynthia looked for Mrs. Martin and her little dogs, Libby and Stanley, but there was no sign of them outside.

"C'mon, Cynthia," called Mom as she got out of the car. Cynthia followed her mother from the vehicle and then plodded up the steps after her. When they got inside, Mom declared, "Right into the shower. You smell like a darned brewery, girl."

Cynthia smiled, then began to strip as she ran to the bathroom. She wanted the beer gone but also couldn't wait to wash the feeling of the threads off of her.

Just like the night before, by the time Cynthia was out of the shower, her memories of what had happened at the store felt more like a dream than reality. That feeling didn't last, though. Cynthia knew there had been threads coming from the adults, that she had been among them and it had been an ugly place to be. Still, the shower had been calming, a relief from the pressure, and even removed from it she felt better than she had in days.

As she walked into the living room, she saw Mom sitting at the kitchen table, but there was also a guest—Mrs. Martin.

"Go get dressed, and then come back out here," said Mom, and Cynthia smiled. Mrs. Martin grinned back at her, and though her mouth never opened, Cynthia could hear the older woman's voice in her head: / Do as your mother says / When she's gone I will explain everything / These words from Mrs. Martin were soft, not at all like the near barking she'd heard when she was looking into the knot of thoughts between her parents and Linda. These words were as calming as the shower, and Cynthia wanted to know how Mrs. Martin had done it and why the words before had been so poisonous.

Looking back over her shoulder at Mrs. Martin and her mother, the two of them already conversing and ignoring the departing nine-year-old, she couldn't help but notice that there were just the faintest threads coming from them. Mrs. Martin's were lustrous, amber and almost gold, while Mom's were a fading red that was swirling with the amber and making a cold blue aura in the space between them.

Cynthia had known enough not to respond to Mrs. Martin's words, but leaving the words hanging between them was still pretty weird. So Cynthia tried sending her own words to Mrs. Martin.

/ Can you hear me? /

There was a moment where nothing happened at all, and then Mrs. Martin's words came through as clearly as if they'd been standing next to one another: "Of course, dear. Now get dressed like your mother asked. We're not in any rush."

Cynthia nodded, as though somehow Mrs. Martin could see the gesture—though Cynthia wasn't willing to concede that Mrs. Martin couldn't have seen the gesture—and then quickly dressed. She gave her hair a quick dry that she knew her mother wouldn't approve of and then headed back out to the living room.

The threads between her mother and Mrs. Martin were all amber and cool blue now, and the two older women smiled at Cynthia as she walked back into the room.

Mom is smiling.

Mom was smiling—for-real smiling. It was hard to even believe.

"I have wonderful news," said Mom. "Mrs. Martin has volunteered to watch you while I go running around today. She used to be a nurse before she retired, so she'll be able to take even better care of you than I can if you get dizzy again. Does that sound all right?"

"Yes, of course," said Cynthia, trying to keep the joy from her voice, though she had a feeling that it wouldn't much matter. Mrs. Martin was using those strings to make Mom feel good, just like her parents' bad feelings had made that ugly knot build up in the liquor store, and that was just fine with Cynthia. "Can I see your dogs again, Mrs. Martin?"

"Absolutely, my dear," said Mrs. Martin, before turning to Mom to ask, "It is all right if we go down to my apartment, isn't it? We'll be just downstairs, and that way we can check on my mutts. They get along well enough with supervision, but without, they can be a dickens."

Mom looked like she was considering things for a second, and Cynthia watched as Mrs. Martin smiled at her, making Mom smile back.

"Yes, of course. That will be fine. You'll be right downstairs, after all."

"Perfect," said Mrs. Martin. "Cynthia, why don't you give your mother a hug and wish her luck, and we'll go see what those naughty little pups have gotten into?"

Cynthia nodded, then ran to Mom and hugged her. Mom squeezed her back, and then Cynthia slithered from her arms and headed to the door with Mrs. Martin.

"Are you sure you'll be fine, Cynth?" Mom asked as Cynthia made the door, and Cynthia turned back to her and smiled.

"I'll be fine, Mom. Good luck."

Cynthia followed Mrs. Martin down the steps to the lower floor of the building, watching the strands from her elderly neighbor's head trail behind her. They were the color of honey, the prettiest thing that Cynthia had ever seen.

When Mrs. Martin opened the door to her apartment and waved Cynthia inside, Libby and Stanley ran to greet her, and Cynthia knelt to meet them and dispense rubs and accept kisses. The apartment smelled like baked goods and Mrs. Martin's funny cigarettes and was filled with old furniture and framed photographs of smiling people.

"I'll get us some milk and cookies. We can talk at the table," said Mrs. Martin as she passed by Cynthia, but Cynthia was too busy petting to respond to the words. The dogs were wonderful, the living opposite of that awful knot or waking up covered in beer in the back of the store. Cynthia was happy, truly happy, and milk and cookies sounded just perfect.

With a wagging dog under each arm and Kelly-green strands stretching from her scalp to the tops of the dogs' heads, Cynthia walked into the kitchen and took a seat at Mrs. Martin's table.

Chapter 15

1945

The special selections stopped after the third barracks was inter-viewed by Fräulein Kaufman, and they remained stopped for over a week. The weather then was some of the worst I have ever seen, and though at first the guards joked about how much the Americans and Russians must have been enjoying the cold, those boasts turned bitter soon enough. A pair of oafish guards named Reinhold and Kahler died when an oil lamp fell and set their cabin alight. The two of them were dead by smoke inhalation long before the blaze was extinguished—and don't think there weren't smiling faces that day. After all, we were usually the ones leaving the earth amidst fire, but that day it was the Germans.

The fire was only the start of it, however. The winds blew so hard that the old and young still left were dying nightly, even while inside their barracks. Lucia Lowenstein and Felicia Gruber died in my barracks within hours of one another. We did what we had to, moved the bodies outside, and then divided up what they had left in this world. That may seem callous, but if a scrap of bread or piece of fabric was enough to keep one of us alive a little longer, then so be it. The dead have no need for such things in any case, at least if what the rabbi says is true. I doubt his teachings myself. If there were a God, none of this would be happening. In any event, I think that in times like this it's fine to borrow from the dead, at least as long as you remember not to mind when people borrow from you!

On the eighth morning since the storm came, I woke to the sound of songbirds. Sure that I must be dreaming, I sat up and hopped out of bed. The floor gave away the secret before I could sneak outside to feel the wind on my cheek. Spring had come a couple of weeks early. I felt like singing and dancing, but I did neither. Most of the women were still slumbering or pretending to be sleeping around me, and the last thing I needed was anyone complaining about me to the guards or the Fräulein. Instead of dancing, I hugged myself and then sat on the floor by the door. My happiness only lasted a few minutes, however, as I realized that my reprieve from facing the Fräulein was likely at an end, and I felt freshly ill by the prospect of being forced to help the Nazis.

Not that fear was the only emotion this prospect elicited in me. There was a part of me—a part I thought was long dead, that wonders at the unknown instead of the constant and bleak acceptance of death—that was curious about meeting this odd woman of power in the middle of this war between men. Fräulein Kaufman, regardless of her possibly ignorant views regarding my ethnicity, must have been a powerful woman to make her place amongst all these soldiers and needless deaths. That she could command my own extermination made me no less interested in meeting her, as that order would at least let me know what she was sent here to do. If all she wanted was more dead Jews, then she was just another monster. But what if she was like me? I had no illusions about being alone in my abilities, minor as they must seem when compared to my disability. To encounter, in this of all places, someone like me—it might sound mad, but I honestly think

I would have traded my life for a shared minute or two with such a person.

As we lined up in the warmth of the sun for the selection outside of the office, it was hard not to smile. Snow still littered the ground here and there, but compared to the week of waiting we'd endured, a little leftover snow was no problem. The line moved slowly, but that was all right, simply because of the weather. I was at the back of it, not because of my name, Rabban, but because of the number tattooed into my skin, another Nazi indignity that I think God will forgive us for.

My name in this world is 226160, and in the line of women I was stuck in, that meant I would be waiting for almost all of them to talk to the Fräulein before me. I did not speak while I waited. Instead, I absorbed information. That is another gift of being blind amongst these strangers. Few if any of them have lived around a blind person before, and they think my handicap makes me weak or stupid. It doesn't, but for once, that others would think so was a good thing. I might not have been able to see the line—and I was scared to use my second sight, in case the Fräulein was looking for that—but I still knew everything that was happening ahead of me.

"No one is being taken"—that was repeated over and over again in a hopeful voice by the woman ahead of me, a grouchy lady of former wealth named Edna Greenberg who still believes she will be returned to her deserved station someday. I like that she has this dream, despite her attitude toward others. Some of us must hope for the best. Otherwise, we will all wallow in the truth. I know that her stolen money has been long spent and that despite the Allies' impending victory, those she cares about are likely dead, and there's a fair chance she will be soon, too. What good would it do tell her? None. I would upset her for no reason, and I would let a small and ever-growing circle of people know that I am cruel and perhaps not as stupid as they assume.

The line moved slowly, but still one truth remained: no one was being taken by the Fräulein. I knew that this was no confirmation that the first rumor was true, but rather that it was unlikely. It was still possible that the rumored four were taken, but why did no one know a name for any of these mysterious girls? We don't all know each other in the camp, but collectively we work like the roots of a tree—you're never separated from another person by more than a few names. If there really were four girls selected, I would know about them. What was happening before me, in the ever-present void of my eyes, was exactly what I suspected: the selection had netted no one of worth to the Führer—at least not yet.

Finally, the ground under my feet changed from frozen earth to wood, and I reached out a hand to lean on the wall of the office for a moment. Any other day and I would have made sure that I wasn't watched before committing an easily punished offense like not standing to attention, but today felt different, and besides, I didn't want to give myself away. Today I was just poor little Ora, the blind girl whose family is dead, and if that got me killed, then so be it.

I could hear the door ahead of me opening and shutting, opening and shutting. Every time the door snapped closed, we shuffled forward a few meager steps, that much closer to the Fräulein and our fate. *Is she taking notes? Is it like a play—will there be callbacks for the prisoners she likes best?* Most important of all, *How far away are the Americans?* That last thought faded as the door closed again and I shuffled forward. Reaching my hand out, I could feel the door before me, and my heart began to race in my chest. I was next. For better or for worse, soon I would know what the Fräulein wanted with us—or at least with me. A few minutes passed, the door opened, and I walked inside, feeling along the wood and shuffling slowly so that I did not fall and make a fool of myself.

The squeak of a chair got my attention and I looked up, an instinct even for the blind. I heard heels on the wooden floor—the sound of Fräulein Kaufman coming to heave me from this building for being useless, no doubt—but then I felt a hand cup my elbow.

"Come sit, come sit," said Fräulein Kaufman as she slowly guided me to a chair and helped me settle into it.

Her hand left me—a hand that was small; she is no beer-hall wench—and then I heard her heels again crossing the room, the sound of metal against metal, and then more heels. Fräulein Kaufman was shoving something into my hands—a cup that was impossibly warm; the warmest thing I'd felt in forever.

"It's coffee," said Fräulein Kaufman, and I didn't need eyes to tell that she was smiling.

It could be a trick, I reminded myself, but it was like she was in my head.

"If I wanted to kill you, girl, I'd just do it. I don't need to trick you. The only things in there are coffee, sugar, and cream. You probably would have enjoyed it more a few days ago, but it should still warm your belly." She paused, and I sipped coffee. It was warm and wonderful, the most flavorful thing I'd had to eat or drink in years. "Now then, what is your name?"

"Two-two-six-one-six-zero," I said, doing my best not to drink the coffee too quickly or do anything else that would make me look like an animal to her.

"Your name, child," said Fräulein Kaufman. "What is your name?"

"Ora Rabban," I said quickly. This, I worried, was a trap. We were told that names are dead, that numbers are all we are now, and I told her as much. "I'm used to the number, though. That's what everyone calls me."

"I like Ora better, don't you?"

"I guess so, but the number is all right."

"You need to speak your mind, child. I need the truth," said Fräulein Kaufman, and I nodded.

"Yes, Fräulein, I'll do better."

"Katarina, child, Katarina."

"Katarina," I said, waiting for the back of her hand to strike me, for the chair to be ripped from underneath me, for the showers, for the ovens, all for the cost of a name.

"Much better," said Katarina, and again I knew she was smiling. "So now you know my name and I know yours. We both have cups of the best coffee available to us at this point in this war that Germany is losing, and we are out of the cold. Things could be worse, right?"

"Things can always be worse," I said, and then I knew I'd gone too far. Katarina Kaufman may have been treating me well, but I had to remind myself that she is still working in a death camp, and I am one of the soon-to-be-dead. She had disarmed me, made me feel even younger and stupider than I am, and I felt as if I had no control over what I was saying.

"How much worse could they be?" Katarina asked, and I shook my head. "You are here in Dachau, and our country is about to be spanked very hard by three angry parents. The only saving grace for Germany is if the Americans beat the Russians to Berlin." She sighed, sipped coffee, and said, "That is unlikely to happen. The Russians are furious, as they should be, and nothing will stop the bear."

"Aren't you worried that someone will hear you?"

"No, of course not," said Katarina, and I knew that she was telling the truth, and I even knew why: Who would I tell? "No worries, little Ora. We can speak freely here. Have you noticed how long we have already been speaking? No one else has lasted in this office as long as you, child. Do you know why? Because no one else has been nearly as much fun to talk to. In case you were wondering, that is a good thing. I know you cannot see my smile, nor can you see my uniform. I am just a voice, and there's nothing wrong with that." She paused then, waiting for something from me, but I was frozen. Finally, she said, "I do wonder, however, what can you see?"

"Nothing," I said, and it was true, at least as far as what I could explain. What would telling her of my visions do for either of us? She would either think me crazy and into the oven I would go or, worse, that I was the solution to some mad plan, and then it would be off to Berlin. It was better to be quiet Ora who never saw anything and rarely spoke.

"You see nothing, child?" Katarina asked, and for just a moment, a flurry that lasted but tenths of a second, the room erupted in color. Not just the strands that I could make myself see, but the ghosts of all the strands from that day. Every little contrail from the women who had come before me. It was magic, it was ours, and I could see it. Not as one of my own visions, not as true eyesight as I understood it, but something better. Something special. *She has my gift.*

"And you mine," said Katarina, and despite my fears, my desire for every Nazi to simply drop dead or surrender, I smiled back at her. I had no idea what else to do. Then it happened. */ Are we done being coy now, child? / Is it time to stop playing games? / I may wear the uniform of your enemy / But you must trust me / I am one of the only friends that you have left /*

I recoiled in my chair, nearly spilling coffee all over my lap, and then steadied myself. My breathing was hard and heavy—I feared I might even pass out—and I'm sure if I could see, my vision would have been blurry. There was the sound of a thousand insects in my ears, and then the most wonderful feeling in the world came over me.

It was the soothing of the womb, of mother's milk, of safety in a place where safety is the furthest thing from one's mind. I knew at once that it was the Fräulein, that somehow she was making me feel that everything was all right in the office, and it was wonderful. I hadn't felt like this since time out of mind, when I was too young to know that my people were hunted and that the wolves were everywhere. For as long as I could recall, death had been around every corner. I had learned to temper the fear of death, but now that fear had been lifted.

How can I describe such a feeling? I'm not sure there are words to explain how glorious it all felt. This wasn't the end of the war and the gift of freedom; this was something that was somehow better than that could ever be. I felt alive, like a bird in flight in the sky, and if I had died, then it would have been a happy death.

Instead of dying, I felt the sensation begin to fade, until I was just Ora in the office again. I was still seated across from the Fräulein, still holding my lovely coffee, and my feet were planted firmly on the floor.

"How do you feel?" Katarina whispered to me, and I smiled back at her.

"I felt wonderful," I said, knowing there was no longer any point in attempting to lie or deceive her. "I felt safe. It's not a feeling that I'm used to."

"It will be," said Katarina, and though I could not see her face, I knew she was grinning back at me. "You shall be my maid, for lack of a better word, Ora. You shall be safe from the selections, and together we will find a way to survive this war."

"I will be your maid, though I'm not sure how useful I will be," I said. "But what do you mean about finding a way to survive the war?"

"I mean that at some point we are going to need to leave this place, to make our way to safety," said Katarina. "The Russians will be raping and killing anyone in their path, but the Americans may pose a far greater danger. Their lines will be our refuge, but we will need to sneak across them."

"Why?" I asked plainly, and Katarina was silent.

Finally, she answered in my head: / *They will be hunting people like us* / *Just like the Nazis hunted people like you* / *They may not kill us but use us* / *But we will lose our freedom all the same* /

/ *I will escape with you* / was the message I sent her from inside of my mind, and I knew that she had received it when she began to clap across from me.

"I will teach you all of my tricks," said Katarina.

Chapter 16

1999

Jessica stood on the lawn outside of the TRC next to Howard and the CIA director, Herm Miller. All three wore Tesla Helmets so as to make Herm feel comfortable, and Jessica was already getting a headache from the constant humming of the machines in the helmet that kept the TKs from doing their damage. Three hundred or so yards away from them was Frank. It had taken four Tesla-clad TRC agents to get him from the floor of his cell and onto a gurney, and that was where he lay at the moment, five hundred pounds of flesh containing one of the most brilliant and diabolical minds the world had ever known.

Jessica had shocked Frank a week prior by telling him that the first victim of the Ham and Egger and his partner had been Miranda Walter. The poor woman was a young mother who had been widowed by the war, and the pair of them had stolen her from the broom factory where she worked. The body was found in a ditch a few days later, and though the papers of the time would likely have skipped over the extravagance of the brutality inflicted upon Miss Walter, Jessica's friend

Buddy Everts at Quantico hadn't exactly been limited to just what the reporters at the time knew.

Jessica had known immediately upon leaving Frank's room that too much rested upon her getting the answer right, so she'd called Buddy, a onetime lover and still good friend from years back, and once the pleasantries were exchanged, Jessica got down to the details. She'd left out the parts about Frank and his future wife being declared legally dead after their executions in a federal prison for being convicted traitors, just as she left out her current job at the TRC, and Buddy had been around classified files enough to know not to ask.

They'd settled on Miranda after two hours of comparing files after work. Although all of the Ham and Egger's victims had been stabbed and left to bleed to death, Miranda had been stabbed with two different knives. One of them was the same blade that had been used on the rest of the victims to that point, but the other had only been used on Miranda and the girls who had come after her. The wounds from this second knife varied in quality, as though the offender had been learning his limits as he cut, discovering a joy in his work as the blood poured from Miranda. Jessica had thanked Buddy for his help, promised to buy him dinner the next time they caught up—which was likely to never happen—and then hung up and breathed a sigh of relief.

Now, Frank was running a perfect two-man drill across the field. In the two-man, a TK controlled two separate volunteers at the same time but made them behave perfectly in sync, so that when one sprinted, the other did so next to him. The two-man was one of the surest gauges the TRC had found to determine a TK's prowess. A good two-man drill would infer that they were dealing with a skilled telekinetic. And a drill like the one Frank was performing was proof that the TK in question had godlike powers.

Frank's pair of men cavorted across the lawn, doing somersaults, sprinting, and managing synchronized back handsprings. At this last feat of acrobatics, Jessica had been able to hear Herm whoop with joy even over the hum of her helmet, and the sound of it made her grin with pleasure. Frank was doing the work, that was true, but she was the one who had made it happen when no one else could.

When the show was done, after the conclusion of the spirited two-man and another drill involving two volunteers wearing boxing gloves and headgear, Herm retired with Howard and Jessica to the TRC conference room. It was not his first time there, but it had been several years since his last visit, and he settled in comfortably at the table so few had ever seen.

"This is great coffee," said Herm once they were settled in, "and that was a hell of a display. My question and the president's question is, when can we expect to see new TKs in service? Frank has got to be about at the end of the useful period of his life, and even if he weren't, I can't imagine using a man his size on an operation, especially a covert one."

"Frank is the most talented TK we've ever seen," said Jessica. "I pray that someday we find someone even half as powerful. And frankly, I'm not sure I'd want to play with the grown-up version of one who was stronger than Frank. He already pushes the limits of what this facility can control."

"I think what Jessica means to say," said Howard, with a peacemaking smile across his face, "is that while Frank is a wonderful example of what a great TK can do, we too would like to see some new blood in this facility. And to do that, we need time, Herm, and the president needs to know that. We're as aware as everyone else in this line of work that big things are coming, and the TRC wants in. We just need the time to get our house in order."

"You've told me many times how difficult it is to find new subjects for this program," said Herm, "and you can be sure the president is well versed on that subject as well. What assurances can you give me that you aren't just looking for a Hail Mary in order to buy some time? I realize the impact the TRC has had on this country—especially the actions of your father, Jessica—but I need to bring the president something more, some sign that things are right in your house."

"Jessica has a few lines in the water currently," said Howard, "and though I would hate to speak out of turn, we both strongly suspect that we will have at least one more TK by the end of this calendar year, with perhaps even more to come."

"Oh well," said Herm, brightening, "that does change things. Can you share anything about this acquisition process with me? It must be fairly new."

"It is," said Howard. "We're still working out the kinks, in fact, but we have high hopes for what this will bring."

"My congratulations," said Herm as he stood. He walked to the cart with liquor and fine crystal—a staple of the room, but almost never used—and began pouring neat glasses of Lagavulin. "Jessica, I cannot wait to hear more about this when you can share more."

"I can't wait to tell you all about it, but like Howard said, I just need a little time," said Jessica as she took the glass from the CIA director, and this was certainly true. This was the first she'd heard of Howard's new program, and she was hoping against hope he really had come up with something for her to work with.

"That sounds perfect, and I'm sure the president will be delighted."

"Please send him our regards," said Howard, smiling magnanimously as he raised his glass.

• • •

Herm was gone, and empty glasses sat before Jessica and Howard in the TRC conference room. Neither of them was speaking, and neither had even looked at the other since they'd walked Herm to his waiting driver and security team upstairs.

Jessica was scared to ask what she wanted to ask, and the silence from Howard only made her more nervous. The booze had done nothing—not even the third glass of scotch, and that one had been poured to roughly a four-finger height by Howard.

When they finally spoke, it was at the same time:

"Howard, I need to know—"

"Jessica, I must confess—"

"You first," said Jessica. "I need to hear this confession before I waste any more wind on this shit."

"There is no plan."

"Goddamnit," said Jessica under her breath. It wasn't that she was concerned about cursing out her boss; it was that she wasn't sure she could even stay in her chair. She felt beyond dizzy, like someone had swatted her behind her ear. *He's hanging me out to dry, and I blew the only chance I had to make sure the director of the fucking CIA knew I was not in on this shit.* "Goddamnit."

"What I mean to say is that there is no plan in place as of now, but I know that between the two of us we will find one," said Howard. "I know what you're thinking, Jessica, but I'm not setting you up to take a fall. Rather, the TRC is going to be in your more than capable hands."

"I'm going to pretend I believe you," seethed Jessica. "Explain. Make me get this, because right now I see a big pit with my name on it, and I feel your hands on my back getting ready to give me a shove."

"Jessica, you know how much I respect you, and you know how I felt and continue to feel about your father. I could never do that to you, and I could never do that to him. This is not a setup."

"So what is it?"

"I'm taking you off of Frank immediately," said Howard. Jessica started to simultaneously open her mouth and stand, and then Howard waved a hand. "Stop. Let me finish." Jessica sat, staring at her glass and wishing there was more whiskey in it. "Like I said, you're off Frank, starting now. I know you had the breakthrough, and I appreciate that, but this is more important. You're going to find us those TKs, and I figure you have six months at most to do it."

"How am I going to do that? Are you bumping me down to Research? Those people don't even have clearance, Howard. They don't even know why they're looking for what they're looking for."

"Of course not. Jesus," said Howard as he shook his head. "You're going to do something that has never been done: a senior agent of the TRC is going to be putting her all into finding TKs, open and shut. You'll have my blessing to do whatever is necessary in order to accomplish these tasks, and you will be allowed as large of a budget as our coffers can allow. In short, Jessica, once again the fate of the TRC falls on the shoulders of a Hockstetter."

Jessica stared at him. "I'm not sure what to say," she mumbled at last.

Howard wasn't throwing her under the bus; he was telling her the train was coming at 12:15 and that it was her job to make sure the TRC was off of the tracks. *I'll be saving him, myself, and all of this.* She might even like this job again.

"Just say you'll do it, and make me believe that you can succeed."

"I know I can."

"Godspeed."

Chapter 17

Darryl was sober, and Darryl was fishing. It was harder work than they'd figured. Bending a kid or some drunk for pocket change was easy, but going in and acting like a scalpel was harder. It took finesse. Twice in the past week Darryl could tell the kids he was invading knew he was there, but it hadn't mattered: they weren't what he was looking for. He didn't need to find a perfect specimen, one as strong as him, but he did need a gifted child to work with. Finding some kid who was learning how special he was wouldn't be good enough. He needed a child who was already getting his hands dirty. Darryl needed a kid who could bend but also had a flair for the diabolical. Thus far, such a kid was proving hard to come by.

Which made Darryl freshly bemoan his discovery and quick disposal of Vincent. That kid had been perfect. He was smart, twisted, and loyal to no one. Had Darryl felt like looking for them, he was sure he would've found on the kid the sort of scars that predicted a sociopathic future. Darryl hadn't looked, though. He'd taken what he needed and settled for a half million when the kid could have been eyes and ears into tens of millions of dollars, maybe even more. Darryl was going to be carrying the regret for shoving Vincent into a noose for a very long time.

"Fucking nothing, man," said Darryl as he leaned away from the computer.

Terry nodded from the couch, then took a butt from the pack on the coffee table and lit it. The walls here weren't covered in porno, and the view out the window showed a beach covered in bikini-clad women instead of a punk club, but Darryl couldn't have cared less. Terry was kicked back, enjoying the spoils of war, while he was still struggling to find their next battle.

"It'll happen, Darryl," said Terry. "Just relax and let it come to you."

It was good advice, but Terry was still chapping Darryl's ass. While Darryl had been working constantly, Terry had been back up to his old tricks. Darryl knew that was the real reason his friend had wanted a spot on this Mexican beach. Life was cheap here. But the way Terry was playing his game, it could end up costing them a lot more than just a few pesos for a woman.

Darryl had been in Terry's head only a few times since they'd been kids, but he'd gone digging twice this week while Terry was sleeping, and for good reason. Terry had always liked to hurt women a little bit—no big deal, really; both their dads had that hobby, too—but he'd killed two girls this week. Barely teenaged girls. Worse, he thought he could hide it from Darryl. That Darryl wouldn't notice the normally teetotaling Terry was increasingly drunk, and that Terry had a longing in his eyes when he looked over those white Mexican beaches.

Terry knew Darryl could see into him, could see the lights go out in the eyes of those two girls as Terry flexed his fingers around their necks, and he even knew that Terry pictured his own ineffectual mother as he did it. Terry's mother had allowed him to be beaten so that she could avoid a few licks of her own on occasion, but really, he needed to move on. Terry was still revenge-killing the woman in his fantasies, even though she'd been in the ground for five years and counting.

None of this should have been Darryl's problem, but it was. If Terry got busted, they were both going down, and there would be some rough questions for Darryl to answer if the police dug into their finances.

"I'll get there, Terry," said Darryl, hating himself as he spoke for not being honest and just calling his friend out on his indiscretions. Terry thought he didn't know, and that even if he did, he wouldn't care. After all, Darryl killed people, too, and for whatever reason, Terry couldn't see the difference. *I'm killing as part of a solution so that a couple of lost lives can see a happy ending. He's just doing it to hurt women because his childhood sucked.* Darryl knew this was true yet couldn't imagine discussing the matter with Terry, whether the man was sober or drunk—or, for that matter, whether Darryl was sober or drunk.

Instead of facing it, Darryl ignored the problem, giving drunken Terry a wave before turning back to the computer. As he did, though, he gave Terry a little poke, one that he didn't think his drunk friend would recognize as anything at all, and what he found was even worse than what he'd imagined. Christ. Terry had taken another girl last night—the third one in a week—and this one hadn't been a native. Darryl could see the whole thing through Terry's eyes: his friend coercing the drunken teen away from her friends and then slowly raping and killing her on the beach, where he left her body to be discovered by whoever was unlucky enough to stumble across it. The bar he'd taken her from had been packed. Darryl and Terry were both regulars there, and there was no way he hadn't been noticed.

"Motherfucker," said Darryl as he stood and started across the room at Terry.

In response, Terry dropped his can of beer, sending suds flying into the air as the can bounced on the hardwood floor, and cowered behind his hands.

It was all Darryl could do to stop short of blowing the fucker up. "We need to go right now, asshole," he said, looming over him. "Do you realize what you've done? You didn't even have the nerve to tell me. You were going to just let me sit here with you until the police showed up!"

"You're not supposed to look in me," whined Terry. "We have a deal, Darryl, a deal we made a long time ago. You're not supposed to ever look in me. We both know that I'm poison, you more than anyone. After all—"

"Think very hard about what you're going to say," said Darryl. "I'm serious, Terry. This could be it, and we've got a pretty good thing going."

"I know, I know," moaned Terry. "And I ruined it. I fucked up, all right? I was going to tell you, but you know how hard that is, to admit what I did. I can't just say it, not when you're risking everything every single time you do your trick."

Darryl shook his head. It was already starting to ache, and he was beginning to wonder why he was even still in the apartment. For all he knew, the authorities could already be on their way with some serious questions about the men who had been living there. And if all Terry wanted to do was make excuses for himself, then maybe Darryl should just get on a plane without him and stop waiting for the other shoe to drop.

But no. He wasn't ready to do that.

"Terry," said Darryl finally, "this isn't about us, about me breaking our 'deal' and looking into you. I *have* to look into you, you fuck. This just proves that. And you can't just boohoo this away, say you're sorry. This is about you being sloppy and putting everything that we have at risk."

"How it went down with that girl wasn't how it was supposed to be," said Terry. "It was consensual, all of it. I just got rough, and then—"

"Not 'that' girl, Terry. Those *three* girls," said Darryl. "Get the story straight if you're going to lie. And while you're at it, try and remember that I know the rest. You didn't give me some half-cocked drunk confession where you tried to save me from the worst parts. I'm a thief, remember? I fucking know what you did, all of it, so just cut the shit."

"All right," said Terry. "All right, Darryl. I know it was wrong. I knew I could mess things up, and that this was a good place, but there will be other good places, right? You're not going to leave me here, right? I can't do that, Darryl. I can't go back to a regular life. I can't be what I am if—"

"You can't be what you are anywhere," hissed Darryl, and Terry waved his hands.

"I don't mean like that, seriously, I just meant—"

"No, Terry, shut up," said Darryl. "This situation is bad enough without you trying to explain. I know exactly what you mean, but there isn't a place in the world where you can take a girl like that from a crowded bar and just kill her. Fuck." Darryl walked away into his bedroom. He could hear Terry scurrying behind him, and Darryl called back to him, "Time to pack, Terry. I'm leaving on the next flight out of here that isn't heading stateside, and if you're not with me, you're never going to see me again."

"I'm coming to pack right now," called Terry.

Darryl could hear the desperation in his voice but didn't care. *You could blank him right now, make him forget everything he's ever known and just leave. He's never going to get better, and you know it.* Darryl swallowed thickly. It was true, but he knew why Terry was having those urges in the first place. He knew why, and he knew it wasn't just a bad childhood. The fact was he needed Terry.

"Just pack quickly," said Darryl. "You didn't leave us much time to work with." Darryl was throwing his own things into a pair of suitcases, pleased as he worked that he had so little to pack.

You'll need to be rid of him before it's too late, a voice screamed in his head, but it didn't matter.

"I still need him," Darryl said to himself. "At least for now."

• • •

Darryl and Terry sat in the backseat of the cab. The cabbie was a local and thankfully wanted no conversation after the word "airport" had been uttered. Cops were everywhere, especially for a sleepy Mexican coastal town, and Darryl knew why and that the cabbie had to at least be wondering about the two rough-looking foreigners. Darryl read the cabbie as they moved, letting his topknot meld with the cabbie's, but aside from irritation with his job, breakfast, and wife, the cabbie was doing pretty OK.

That is, he was doing pretty OK until they passed a cop car. / *Couple of fucking gringos* / *Probably fucking did it* / *So sick of them treating this country like a toilet* / Darryl took in the thoughts like poison, then leaned back in his seat and tried to have golden thoughts. He dug in the cabbie's head for memories of his wedding day, of his daughter's birth, of playing baseball with neighborhood kids. Darryl let these memories bubble to the surface one after another, and when he looked at the space between them he could see that the yellow from his topknot was bending the cabbie's to a calming blue.

The cabbie parked at the airport, helped them get the bags from the car, and was actually whistling as he got back in the driver's seat and pulled away from the curb.

Darryl led the way wordlessly as the two slipped into the airport amid a sea of other travelers. He tried to think positively—Mexico was still a borderline Third World country, and the chances of the police having much of a lead on Terry seemed low—but a very loud, angry, panicked part of him screamed that he would be better off just shutting Terry down on some airport bench and leaving while his friend slept.

But it was a quiet voice that he ended up heeding: *You need him just as much as he needs you.*

Darryl led the way to the ticket booth and parked his luggage two customers back from his turn to talk to a rep from Delta. Terry whispered something to him, and when Darryl turned to ask him to repeat himself, he saw a group of four cops working their way through the airport. *Fuck*, thought Darryl. The cops were stopping Americans, checking passports. He wanted to dive into Terry's brain right there so he could know if there was any reason to think the cops had Darryl's name, but he didn't really need to. They had a sketch of the two of them from the bar and they had Terry's name, he was sure of it—when you're chatting up a potential date for the abattoir, you pretty much have to give your name, and Terry wouldn't have had the sense to make one up. No, the cops had what they needed. It was just a matter of time until they found them.

The old couple in front of them parted, and as Darryl walked to the young woman working the counter, he hit her with a bend without even thinking of the consequences. He knew he'd have to work fast, could feel the cops on their necks. He settled in, doing his best to control both himself and the ticket agent, and reminding himself as he worked that this was practically running an old-school operation compared to the computer work.

Darryl laid his own hands atop the ticket counter, then set the woman's fingers to flying on the computer in front of her. He could feel her breaking, but it didn't matter. He punched in his name and then Terry's, not even checking where the flight was going, because that didn't matter right now. There were connections all over the world that they could take later, but right now all they needed was to be out of Mexico. Darryl made the woman take the tickets from the printer, her hands feeling like he was working with a pair of oven mitts, and then laid the boarding passes on the counter. This was the sloppiest he'd worked in years, but he could see the police through the woman's eyes working their way up the line behind them, and the mess he was making of the woman was the least of his worries.

Darryl grabbed the tickets with his own fingers as he slowly took back control of his own body, and as his hearing came back, he could hear the clerk next to the woman asking her rapid-fire questions in Spanish. "*Sí, sí,*" said Darryl through the woman's mouth, and that just made the other clerk look even more confused. Darryl grabbed his bags, leaving a connection to the woman still flowing behind him like a bridal train, and then took off from the counter with Terry at his heels.

"Go to bed," said Darryl to himself as he cut the woman off, and behind them he could hear panicked screaming.

"Hit the bathroom," said Darryl as he steamed ahead of Terry. "Leave the suitcases, get on the plane."

In the bathroom, Darryl led Terry to an empty stall and took his bag from him. He balanced both their bags atop the stall's toilet, then unzipped the top bag and pulled out a pair of pants and a pair of worn loafers. He set the shoes on the floor and the waist of the pants on the toilet seat with the suitcase atop them, then tucked the ankles of the pants into the shoes and shut the door. From the outside, it looked like someone was taking a shit.

"How are we going to get our stuff back?" Terry asked as Darryl led them from the bathroom toward the security checkpoint.

"We're not."

Darryl ignored his friend's protests as they closed in on the security station, pulling his ticket from his pants pocket to see where they were headed. *Shit.* They were on their way to Des Moines, Iowa, for some reason—back in the middle of the central United States. *We're going to need to stay there awhile, too. You know that.* The best thing to do—assuming they even made it through security—would be to hit Des Moines and lie low for a few weeks before getting the fuck out of Dodge.

Darryl winced as they hit the line for the checkpoint. He must have left something with the woman at the ticket counter. She'd just died, and his brain felt like it had been snapped with a rubber band the size of a fan belt.

"Are you OK?" Terry asked as they shuffled through the line, and Darryl turned at him and smiled for the benefit of the people around them.

"I'm just ready to get on this plane and get back to the US," said Darryl, turning back around and ignoring the confused look Terry gave him. *Jesus, it's bad enough I had to bend that woman in the fucking airport, but I'm going to have to euthanize Terry, too, if he can't start thinking straight.* Remembering that Terry had started this adventure drunk, Darryl took a deep breath and tried to calm down. The serious part of the checkpoint was coming up, and it was safe to assume that the guards were looking for a gringo who resembled Terry a great deal.

Darryl gave his passport and ticket to the man standing at a little podium in front of the X-ray machines. He was ready to fry him—to not even attempt to use the man, just send a blast into his brain and shut him off like a light switch—but there was no need. The man took his passport and ticket, grunted, and then handed them back, before doing the same for Terry. The two of them took their papers back, passed through the metal detector, and walked to their gate.

It was an hour later before they could board the packed plane and sit down. It would be hours until they could talk about what had happened, but Darryl was just fine with that. He had no idea if he was going to let Terry ever leave Des Moines, or if he even wanted to keep the charade going. Everything since Vincent had been a nightmare, and the setup in Mexico was going to cost them a significant sum of money. Darryl grabbed a magazine from the seat back and then opened it to read. He fell asleep moments later as the plane took off, and his dreams were awful.

Chapter 18

Cynthia took a sip of milk as Mrs. Martin returned to the table with a plate of delicious-looking chocolate-chip cookies. Mrs. Martin set the cookies down between them, then sat in the chair opposite Cynthia and took a drink of her own milk. Cynthia smiled at her, and Mrs. Martin smiled back, while the dogs ran around Cynthia's ankles, begging to be picked up again.

Mrs. Martin looked down at them and shook her head. "I can lock them up in the bedroom if you want, dear."

"No, I like them just fine where they are. They're so friendly."

"They are indeed, at least to the right person," said Mrs. Martin with a curt nod. "Do you know why they like you so much, Cynthia?"

"I guess because I'm not much bigger than they are, and because they like to be petted, and I like to pet them."

"Those are certainly very good reasons," said Mrs. Martin. "But I was looking for another answer, and it's kind of a scary one. I don't want you to be afraid, though. I want you to trust me, even though you have a hard time trusting any adult right now. I know that adults—"

"Lie," Cynthia finished for her. "They lie and they get divorce, and then you have to move. They get in really mean fights where no one says what they're thinking but everyone hates each other. They lie." Cynthia could feel the tears welling up in her eyes, and she leaned down to rub Libby between the ears and to dry her eyes in secrecy.

"They do lie," said Mrs. Martin. "That's one of the worst things about childhood, the discovery that adults make mistakes and are far more apt to lie, cheat, or steal than even the worst little child. Adults are cruel, and often with a purpose. At least when a child is cruel it is typically for reasons they don't understand." Mrs. Martin took a cookie from the plate, dunked it in her milk, and nibbled at the edge of it. She smiled and said, "But we both know that's not what I was asking you, not really. You've been seeing the threads of the Moirai."

"The what?"

"The strings, my dear," said Mrs. Martin. "You have been seeing them, haven't you?"

"It just started," said Cynthia. "I was at my Nan and Pop's house taking a nap, and when I woke up I knew my parents were going to get divorce because of affair. When my parents came home, I could see red lines coming from their heads and from Nan and Pop's heads. My dad's were a little purple, but the rest were bright red—so bright that I can't understand how no one else could see it."

"Are you sure they were purple?" Mrs. Martin asked in a small voice, and Cynthia nodded.

"Yes."

Mrs. Martin pursed her lips, set the cookie she was eating down, and took a pack of the funny-smelling cigarettes from her pocket and stood. She walked back into the kitchen and grabbed a glass ashtray from a drawer, then walked back to the table and set it down. Cynthia realized as the older woman went through the motions of removing and lighting a cigarette that she had been watching her head, as if she were expecting to see something there, but there were no threads betraying Mrs. Martin's emotions.

"Purple is never good," said Mrs. Martin between drags of her cigarette, and Cynthia looked at her with a terrified mask on her face. "Calm down, dear," said Mrs. Martin. "You haven't even touched a cookie. Let the dogs alone, and let's discuss this. I regret that I won't be able to answer every question that you have, but I should be able to help with a great many of them."

"You looked scared when I said that Daddy's strings were purple," whispered Cynthia. "They were purple yesterday, and they were purple again today when I went to the store and they were all fighting."

"You have crayons, don't you, Cynthia?"

"Yes, but they're still at the old yellow house, not here in the apartment."

"Well, you're going to need to get your mother to buy you a set," said Mrs. Martin as she tapped her cigarette on the glass ashtray. "I suppose I can if she won't, but it will make a lot more sense to her if they don't just happen to show up. Your mom trusts me, but only just so much, and I don't think a gift from me now, even a small one, would help build her trust in me."

"What will I do with the crayons?" Cynthia had no doubt that she could get her mother to buy her a set. Her mother knew she loved coloring and couldn't imagine not being able to draw.

"You're going to make a color chart," said Mrs. Martin as she stood again, leaving her cigarette in the ashtray and walking into the living room to get her purse. She took her wallet from it, walked back to the table, and sat before opening it, and then removed a sheet of worn and yellowed paper. "When my great-grandmother told me about the Moirai, she was close to dying, and she made me promise that I would remember every word she said. More specifically, she made me promise that if I could ever see, I would get a set of paints and make a chart so that I could remember them all."

"You were blind?"

"I was indeed, though my great-grandmother said I could see in other ways, and she was right," said Mrs. Martin. "I didn't know it at the time, but my second sight was the only thing keeping me alive."

Mrs. Martin rolled up her sleeve and pointed to a row of blue numbers, and Cynthia leaned over to get a better look.

"Is that a tattoo?"

"It is indeed," said Mrs. Martin. "I got that when I was just a little bigger than you, believe it or not, after I was put in a camp with my mother and great-grandmother."

"Like a summer camp?"

"No, honey, not like a summer camp at all," said Mrs. Martin with a sad look on her face. "Quite the opposite, in fact. It was a place where bad people were putting people like me. They made us work, but sometimes they killed us, too. Everyone there had their number tattooed on their arm because that was all that we were to them—just numbers."

"Where was the camp?"

"In Germany. It was called Dachau," said Mrs. Martin. "Someday you'll learn all of this in school, and if you remember this conversation it might strike you as a little odd that you knew someone who was there, but you do: your old friend Mrs. Martin almost died there. Of course, back then I was no Mrs. Martin, I was just little Ora Rabban, and I never should have survived the inspections on the first day. They were getting rid of handicapped people, you see."

"You mean, like, killing them?" Cynthia whispered.

"I do, regrettably," said Mrs. Martin. "I know that all of this probably sounds like some awful fairy tale, but it's all true, unfortunately. A bad man made a whole country angry, and they wanted a scapegoat, so that's what they found in me and others like me. Giving up your rights is like marrying a man, Cynthia. You need to make darn sure it's for the right reasons, or you're apt to carry a heavy load. Germany was like that back then. It was a heavy load for all, but especially for the Jews."

"Why were they killing people?" Cynthia asked. She believed Mrs. Martin, but killing someone was a serious thing. It was something that always made the news and always made Mom sad and Dad angry. *Why would a whole country just start killing people?*

"Because they needed someone to blame so that everyone else could stand strong," said Mrs. Martin. "That, however, is a lesson for another day. You should know this about me, young lady: I am a notorious rambler when the mood strikes me, and I am definitely struck. It's been a long time since I talked to a weaver."

"A weaver?"

"Yes, just like yourself and a great many other people as well," said Mrs. Martin. "Not many are as strong as me, and certainly not many are even close to you, but they are out there." Mrs. Martin dunked a cookie in milk, took a bite, and smiled. "A weaver is a person who can see those little threads you're getting accustomed to seeing, and weaving is the act of manipulating them." She smiled. "I'm getting ahead of myself again. Back to my story in Dachau: I had no idea I had this power, mostly because I was blind and I could not see the threads in the air around me. What I could do, however, was manipulate those threads to make people look at me not as someone to take pity on but as someone to love. The guards there had orders to find people like me and get rid of them, but they left me alone. Everyone loved little Ora back then, but I had no idea it was because I was altering the way they saw me. I was a prisoner, but they still loved me, even as they—I'm sorry, Cynthia. I get worked up talking about my mother and great-grandmother. I need to remember how young your ears are."

"It's OK," said Cynthia, not entirely sure if she really thought that it was. "Were they killed?"

"They were indeed. If I would have known how I was surviving the selections, I might have been able to help them, too, but I had no idea what I was doing. I was just a little girl, and at the end I was a little girl with nothing. What God gives he can take away, and though God saw it fit to take my family—all of my blood except for an aunt and her husband—I did find my sight just a few weeks after our camp was freed. It was a bitter prize."

"Why were you able to see?"

"I was never entirely blind," explained Mrs. Martin. "I couldn't see, not like I can now, but a couple of eye surgeries fixed me right up. You should have heard me screaming in the hospital. Not only could I see, but I could also see—"

"The threads, right?" Cynthia asked. "You went from seeing nothing to seeing everything, but also the threads. I didn't scream, but I thought about it, and I've always been able to see. It had to have been horrible."

"It was awful," said Mrs. Martin. "Awful and wonderful, all in one big lump. I was happy to see, but I would have happily traded it all to have my family back. I have had many happy times in my life—right now being one of them—and that should have been one of the happiest, but instead it was one of the saddest. I saw all different colors of thread, but you need to remember that I was in a hospital near the end of a war. I saw a great many of the bad colors, and there was nothing happy about that."

"You looked scared earlier when I said that my dad's were purple," said Cynthia. "Is that a bad color?"

"Any of them can be bad, Cynthia. That's just the nature of the situation. Humans are an odd lot, even the ones we care for a great deal, but yes, in my experience there is nothing good about purple, not when you see it like that."

"What does it mean?"

"Everything, my dear. Everything and nothing," said Mrs. Martin. "Do you have any other questions, or should I explain the colors?"

"Just one. What are the Mooreea?"

"The Moirai, sweetie. The sisters," said Mrs. Martin with a frown. "Let's talk about colors first, and if you still want to know, later we can talk about the Moirai."

Chapter 19

Jessica could have had as many as she wanted, but she only wanted
four. They were the four best computer geeks she could find, all culled
from the Hartford area, given security clearance—a necessity, as much
as it tested Howard's patience—and then told some small parts of some
very big secrets. The TRC had researchers who worked with computers, even some who could easily have been considered experts, but these
new nerds knew the ins and outs of the real final frontier, the gallery
of lost souls and hidden identities that made up current Internet users.
Jessica barely understood or used the web herself, but she knew that
for those who could navigate its landscape, it was a tool whose power
was beyond measure. The goal of Jessica's elite geek corps was simple:
use this tool—and anything else they could think to ask for—to flush
out TKs.

To that end, Jessica's analysts were combing both the black hole
of the web and all available records of modern events for anything
that might signal TK interference, either through a computer or from
across a room. There were a few incidentals found in the first couple of
days—occurrences that might possibly fit the profile, based on some of
this often less than legal probing—but so far nothing had panned out.

Still, Jessica's geeks—Geoff Miley, Rick Cambridge, Pat Evans, and Brinn Bobrovsky, all pulled off of Y2K prep squads and with impressive pedigrees that Jessica barely understood—were working hard, and that was all she felt she could ask of them. Rabid for results as Jessica was, putting too much weight on a person doing an impossible job seemed counterproductive.

About four days in, her approach began to bear fruit. Thanks to unlimited access to federal and local law-enforcement data, along with the fledgling Internet media, her four were getting leads.

Brinn was enamored of the case of two men suspected of a trio of murders in Mexico. The last time they'd been seen was boarding a plane to come stateside. They'd been spotted in the airport and actively pursued by security. Sure, the authorities south of the border could have done a better job—grounding all of the damn planes until they'd hunted down the pair, for starters—but after watching the videos, Jessica came to doubt any airport in the States would've had better luck holding them. Everything seemed to fall magically into place to allow the two Americans to escape—and Jessica didn't believe in magic.

There had been no news of the duo since they'd landed in Des Moines, and Jessica figured things were going to stay that way. If one of the two men really was a TK with homicidal tendencies helping his buddy jump country to country on some sort of murder tour, they'd pop back up with even more crimes under their belts. If they disappeared or got busted in the next week or two, they were just a couple of run-of-the-mill scumbags—still dangerous, but not worth the TRC's time, especially during the current manhunt.

There was another case in Wisconsin—some idiot who won a few million bucks in table games at a pair of Indian casinos over by Lake Michigan. The twist that made it interesting was that he'd left a dead wife at home before heading off on his spree. Geoff and Rick followed that one like a couple of ghouls, poring over FBI docs well above their security clearance but far below Jessica's, but the trail ended in a bloody puddle after a week when Mr. Lucky, the cops on his trail like a pack of Glock-toting bloodhounds, finally ate a bullet to put an end to the game.

The man was dead and so there was no way to be sure of his possible abilities, but Geoff still came away certain he had been the real deal, his double casino run too spectacularly lucky not to have been orchestrated by some TK puppet master tugging at the dealers' strings. Jessica wasn't having any of it, though. The guy may have been crazy as a homicidal bedbug, but his winning streak had been just that—or at least it hadn't been driven by a TK. A real TK with an ego big enough to kill would never be cornered like that for so long, she explained, and if he was, he'd go down fighting.

Pat found what he felt looked like his own bent-work as he pursued what started as a smattering of details surrounding the death of a young man named Vincent Taggio, a recent teen suicide from a well-respected St. Louis family. The more Pat worked the idea, the more tantalizing tidbits came out—and then, a couple of weeks after Vincent's death, his dad, Paulie, turned up dead, too.

And then all the shit came out.

Paulie wasn't just the well-regarded patriarch of his family but also a dues-paying member of *the* family—the Chicago Outfit, Our Thing, or whatever they were calling it these days. In what could hardly be a coincidence, it also came out that just before Paulie's death, someone had emptied La Cosa Nostra's coffers to the tune of half a million bucks. Judging by his untimely demise, Paulie himself—undone by grief in the days following his son's shocking death—was judged the prime suspect. But the reality proved to be that all of the money taken from the mob's very discreet Cayman accounts was removed *before* Vincent sent himself swinging. The simple fact of the matter, as Pat told Jessica, was that young Vincent had transferred the money from one account to another and then killed himself.

Why in the world would someone do that? Who would steal half a mill, dump it somewhere untraceable, and then do the one-footed dance?

No one had a good answer for that, but the two players involved were dead, and as Jessica had insisted from the start, TKs were survivors. They wouldn't accomplish a goal and then run from the victory, nor would they die a normal death. If Paulie were a TK, he'd have bent the men sent to kill him and then walked out singing "My Way." If Vincent were a TK, there might have been a rope, but it wouldn't have been around his neck.

Another dead end then, but Pat kept the file. He was no bender, but he knew a twist when he saw one, and despite Jessica's assurances, there was something broken there.

Chapter 20

Darryl and Terry walked out of the airport and into the brutal shock of Midwestern humidity. The rental car that Darryl had arranged for them was just outside of the terminal, in a parking garage across the road, and Darryl wanted nothing more than to be in it and gone. Mexico had been a place of mistakes, and it was time to be done with that. Having a dead bank account—even if they still had many others—was an ugly thing, and there was no reason to think that they wouldn't eventually be traced to Des Moines. *Don't think about that now. Get the car and go.* Try as he might, though, Darryl couldn't stop thinking about the mess they were in and just how much work it was going to take to get out of it.

They showed the Hertz attendant the receipt for their rental, and then Darryl and Terry were pulling free of the parking garage aboard a Ford F-150. Darryl hated driving trucks and hated that the cost was almost three times what a compact car would be, but he hated the idea of sliding off the road into a ditch and having to talk to the law about it even more. Making a quick stop for supplies was almost as nerve wracking as driving. As they purchased clothes, food, and a computer, he could feel eyes probing him, even though he never caught anyone actually staring at him.

Darryl was most nervous about checking into the hotel—if there was anyone who might be ahead of the news, it would be hotel managers and state troopers—but the sun was shining on them at the check-in desk. A large and loud troupe of grade school–aged cheerleaders and their parents were either on their way to a competition or had just returned from one, and they had clearly drawn the ire of the hotel staff. Darryl didn't even need to probe, much less bend the woman who checked them in. In minutes he was walking back to the car with a pair of key cards in his pocket.

When they finally made the room, Terry unlocked the door with one of the key cards, and then Darryl slid the luggage dolly in through the door. No one had seen them park, nor had anyone laid eyes on Terry. The situation could go bad at a moment's notice, but right now Darryl and Terry were as smooth as baby shit.

Terry unloaded the cart quickly, the only heavy items being the computer, and then Darryl walked the cart back to the elevator before heading back to the room. Terry was sitting on the bed watching the TV, and Darryl moved to see the screen.

"It's not good, not at all," said Terry.

Darryl sat next to Terry for a few moments, watching the talking heads on CNN discuss the murders in Mexico, flashing between pictures of the savaged and slain girls and an image of Terry that had been taken from a security camera at the last bar. Along with the airport security footage, there was a sketch of Terry that looked exactly like him. Darryl sighed, thankful they could at least stay in the Holiday Inn for a day or two, then walked to the computer and started unboxing it.

"What the hell are we going to do?" Terry asked as Darryl slid the heavy monitor free from the box and set it atop the table in the corner of the room.

"I told you before that there was going to need to be another trag-edy to get this thing out of the news," said Darryl. "I'm not sure what it's going to be just yet, but I'm going to get us a tragedy. Something big, something mean." Darryl swallowed thickly. "Like that Columbine thing this spring."

Terry nodded and stood, the TV forgotten, and together the two of them worked to assemble the computer.

Chapter 21

1945

A week has passed since I was moved into the room where Katarina sleeps, and though I hate to admit it, life has been wonderful. I feel at times like I am doing something wrong, that I am one of those Jews who is given special privileges for telling the secrets of my fellow prisoners to our captors, but I have done nothing of the sort.

And yet I have been rewarded far more richly than any of those traitors.

I have a bed—my own bed—and the bedding is clean and washed every few days. There is heat from a little stove in the room that I share with Katarina, along with books to read on a shelf. We are fed thrice a day the same food the commandant eats, and I feel like I am actually gaining weight. It's the most comfortable I've been in years, and it's hard not to enjoy it, even with the misery going on around me. I could smell the ovens today, and I know what that means, but I was alone in the room and I just buried my head in my pillow and tried not to think about it. Even all of that death couldn't chase away the thought of how lucky I am, how wonderful it is to be warm and fed.

Of course, none of that is as wonderful as the rest of it.

Katarina calls what we do "weaving" because of the threads that she can see coming from people's heads. I can see the threads, too, of course, just not the people beneath them. Not that that matters—all I need are the threads. We talk about all manner of things that deal with this weaving—what the colors mean, how to manipulate or ruin those threads, how to make someone align with your own thinking. Many of the things we talk about I've been doing for years without even knowing that I'm doing it! Katarina says that this is why I'm alive, and I believe that to be so. Without my abilities, why else would a blind girl be left to live when so many more fit people have been taken away and disposed of?

Every day there is a new lesson, and today was no different. Katarina has been teaching me about mapmaking. It's a hard concept for me to grasp, but the more she explains, the more I understand.

"Think of it like this, Ora," said Katarina, and I nodded, ready to try. "You can't picture the courtyard, but can you tell me where the fences are, where the guard towers are, where the showers are?"

"Yes, of course," I said.

Just because I cannot see doesn't mean I don't know how to get around the camp. I've been here for years, after all.

"Perfect," said Katarina as she clapped her hands together. "Take my hand. I want to try something."

I did as she said, but already I could feel my heart flutter. *Katarina has never needed to touch me to do her weaving before*, I was thinking, *so whatever she is planning must be either dangerous or—*

The second that our skin made contact I could feel myself racing through the air next to her, and then there was a flash of light like nothing I had ever experienced. I rubbed my eyes, rubbed them again, then pinched my skin. Turning to Katarina, I could see she was beaming. I could see it with my own two eyes, as if I'd always been able to see. Looking from her to the ground, I could see that we were several hundred feet above the camp, but there was no fear in my belly over being suspended like this above the ground, because I could see.

Below us was Dachau. I could see the barracks houses, women working, guards standing around and smoking, the area by the showers, workers earnestly removing ashes from the ovens in the forbidden brick building. The whole world inside of these fences was visible to me, yet outside of the fences the world faded to black. I stared at the house of ovens, then turned to Katarina. I want to ask her how she could be here amidst all of this evil when she is so sweet, so kind, but I forced the question from my mind.

"You want to know why you can see?" Katarina asked, and I nodded my head emphatically. I did want to know why I could see, almost as much as I wanted to know why she is here. "You can see because only Ora's eyes are damaged. Here you are not using Ora's eyes. Our bodies are below in our room, sitting comfortably right where we left them. Can you imagine the scare that would give one of the guards if he was to walk in there? He would think we'd gone mad."

"I still don't understand."

"I am showing you my map, Ora," explained Katarina. "Because of your affliction, your own maps would be much more stark. Still visible to you, of course, but plainer. No shingles on the roofs, for example. The guards with unpolished shoes—details such as that would be gone. Your view would still be serviceable, and very impressive when one takes into account your affliction, but different from mine. Do you understand?"

"Do you make a map like this for everywhere that you go?"

"I do for everywhere that I might get myself into trouble," explained Katarina. "By having a map, I can quickly bounce from person to person, manipulating them as I see fit, all the while leaving my body in a safe place." I nodded, and Katarina shook her head. "It's hard to grasp, but you'll get there. Do you see that guard tower there?" I nodded again. "Inside of that are a pair of men—Herr Henkel and Herr

Junkers. Go in there and convince one of them that he sees something in the trees. Pick whatever you like."

"Just go there?"

"Exactly," said Katarina. "Picture yourself diving there, and soon you will be. Trust me, Ora. Give those men a show."

Not sure what else to do, I did what she said. One second I was hovering in the sky below the clouds, and the next I was roaring toward the tower. My hands came up instinctively over my face, but I slipped through the guard tower as easily as if I were a ghost. In an odd way I suppose that may have been exactly what I was—just another ghost here in this place, which must surely be haunted with so very, very many.

Herr Henkel and Herr Junkers were playing cards and drinking schnapps from a flask, and I found myself frozen there, wondering how often they'd wiled away days doing this same thing. The number of women who could have escaped near the southwest tower due to the sloth of these men was incredible to contemplate, and I hoped I would have the chance to do this with Katarina again to see if this was a routine for the guards.

It took a few moments of watching them to remember that I had a job to do here. Katarina had been explicit about my purpose. She wanted me to make one of the guards see something in the woods that the tower looked over. I found myself wondering if it would be possible to make both of them react while I was at it. I could see their threads— mostly bored blue, with a few strands of limp and dead black. I took a deep breath, and then I was in them both at once, working their minds like I was walking down a crowded street, feeling my way to the right path. When I felt I had the reins of each of them, I made a simple observation: / *Sherman tank and American soldiers on the tree line* /

It was like watching a landmine explode under the two guards. They were out of their seats in an instant, bringing the MG-42 that had been pointing toward the inside of the camp to bear on the trees outside of the fence, and then Henkel was shouldering the machine gun while Junkers began to sound the alarm. Below us, guards and prisoners alike were scrambling and screaming, running to their positions or barracks. As Henkel began to fire, I leapt back toward Katarina, but when I arrived at our place in the sky, she was nowhere to be found. There was a time when that would have terrified me, but that was before I knew what to do.

Leaping toward Katarina's room was easy now that I'd gone to the guard tower, but I was disoriented as I hit my body, and my sight winked out. I sighed heavily. Tricking the men had been thrilling, but it was a relief to be back in my own head.

Katarina was walking behind me, and she said, "Coffee?"

"Of course. Thank you."

I could hear her going through the coffee ritual behind me, and the idea of a steaming cup filled me with even more happiness. Around us the alarm was still being raised, machine guns chattered like typewriters, and men could be heard screaming. One voice, which I was quite sure was the commandant's, was shouting at his men to cease fire, but they weren't yet following his command. Katarina set the coffee cup softly in my hands, like she always did, and I smelled the delicious treat, as though it might be my last.

"Those men are idiots," said Katarina, "but it is not the idiots that we need to fear."

"Who do we need to fear?"

"Everyone else," said Katarina. "The word from the front is the Americans will be here very soon, that the last of Hitler's winter gambit in the Ardennes has been destroyed. He cost the Americans some lives, but now the best troops in Germany are dead, and there is no one to replace them but old men and boys. We will need to run soon, my dear, but we will live. We have to."

"Where will we run?"

"Wherever we can be safe."

Chapter 22

1999

"Yellow is my favorite color," said Mrs. Martin, and Cynthia nodded in agreement. "Yellow can mean that someone is content, or that they are trying to comfort someone else. Yellow is not only friendly, however. You can control a mule with a stick or a carrot, and people aren't much different."

"There was yellow when you were talking to my mother," said Cynthia. "Why?"

"Because your mother was scared, Cynthia," explained Mrs. Martin. "My thoughts were woven yellow because I wanted her to be calm. I wanted her to know that everything was all right and that she would be fine to leave you with me."

"So you tricked her."

"That's a way of explaining it, but I prefer to see it another way," said Mrs. Martin. "I may have been tricking her, but it was all for her benefit. She was able to get rid of the sick feeling in her stomach, she stopped worrying about you, was able to go looking for a job, and you and I get to have this little talk."

"Wouldn't she be mad if she knew?"

"Of course, dear, but however would you explain it to her? You need to remember that I'm not pushing thoughts into your mother's head that she doesn't wish to have. I'm just nudging her toward what would be best for everyone involved. Plus, by weaving those pretty gold thoughts with her angry red ones, she was able to have a much better day."

"So red is mad but yellow is happy?"

"Yes and no," said Mrs. Martin. "They're both powerful colors, but they don't necessarily mean exactly what you'd think. Blue and green are much more passive—those just kind of happen. Red and yellow aren't just emotions a person or animal is feeling. They can indicate something that they want to change."

"I think I understand."

"There isn't going to be a test at the end, Cynthia," said Mrs. Martin. "My point, little one, is that someone who isn't a weaver can still try to influence another person through cruelty or kindness, and that is why those will be some of the most common colors."

"What about purple? What does that mean?"

"Purple can be bad, but it can mean a lot of different things," said Mrs. Martin, and for the first time Cynthia wondered if the older woman was being entirely truthful with her. "What purple usually means is unpredictability. They could be thinking of hurting themselves, or maybe even hurting someone else."

"So I should stay away from my dad?" Cynthia asked. "I already don't live with him anymore, and now I'm just supposed to stop seeing him? That's not fair."

Mrs. Martin shook her head, took another cigarette from her pack, and lit it. She looked at Cynthia, exhaled smoke, and said, "No, I don't suppose it is. It's not fair at all when you put it that way."

"I'm sorry. I didn't mean to make you sad."

"I should be the one apologizing," said Mrs. Martin. "It's been a great many years since I've spoken with a person who can do what we do, much less a child who can see so clearly. Still, fair or not, avoiding your father might not be a bad idea."

"He was worried about money. He thought we were going to take it all from him."

"Money is a problem that has everything to do with the world of adults and nothing to do with weaving," said Mrs. Martin with a wave of her cigarette. "If I had to guess, I'd say that your father has little to worry about in that regard, and I imagine spending his money will begin to feel like a mouthful of poison after a very short amount of time. I would say that his purple will have faded to a nasty bloodred the next time you see him, and then maybe just red the next time. It could be a while until he's blue or green again, but it will come, child, you just have to believe. Of course, trying to remind him how much he loves you might not be a bad idea when you do see him, and you needn't be a weaver to do that."

"I'll do it," said Cynthia, but as she spoke she could see that though Mrs. Martin had been mostly truthful, she was still leaving some of it out. Cynthia didn't know if she could jump into Mrs. Martin's mind the way she did over the knot, but she did have a feeling that Mrs. Martin might not want Cynthia poking around in her head.

Instead of invading her privacy, Cynthia asked another question. "How many weavers are there?"

"Not many, not many at all," said Mrs. Martin gravely. "I'll see a child every now and again that I can tell has a bit of a spark, but never anyone like you."

"How can you tell?"

"Trust me, you'll know," said Mrs. Martin, and Cynthia nodded, not sure she believed the older woman, but unsure of how else to phrase the question to get a new answer.

"Why are there so few of us?"

"That's a good question, and I'm not sure I have a good answer," said Mrs. Martin. "I think a long time ago, maybe even a few hundred years ago, there were a great deal more of us than there are now. Take the advances in art in Europe during the Renaissance, or the explosion of technology at the turn of the twentieth century. If you listen in history class over the next few years, you'll be able to put together some guesses as to who might have had some help."

"All right, I will," said Cynthia, "but that still doesn't explain why there are less of us now than there were before. Shouldn't there be more?"

"I don't know if there should be, but I do have a few guesses as to why there are not," said Mrs. Martin. "First and foremost, many of the children who are born with the ability to see drown it out with drugs or alcohol. Remember, ours is a world still in recovery from the death of magic, and a child who told a normal parent what she was seeing might make her mother think there was something wrong with her. For a very long time, many so-called crazy people were shamans or magicians or fortune-tellers. Nowadays, it's assumed that when someone can do something like that they're either mentally ill or fakers."

"So you think other weavers are in hiding?"

"Hiding in plain daylight like you or I," said Mrs. Martin with a smile. "Though I do find it much more likely that a lot of those poor people who discover their sight live on the fringes of society. Of those born with it who do live here, enough years of alcohol or drug abuse will either stop the visions, or make the so-called normal folks decide that someone who should develop into a powerful weaver is just a person prone to seeing things."

"That makes sense," said Cynthia, and Mrs. Martin nodded.

"I'm glad to hear that. There will be a time in your life—and I know this seems impossible—where you will be tempted by pills, a bottle, a needle, or maybe all three. There is nothing more important in that moment than saying no."

"I will," said Cynthia, and she meant it, but she could also see yellow threads spinning from Mrs. Martin's head. Cynthia didn't block the threads—she wasn't even sure she could—but she did wonder if that was a possibility.

"Are there any more questions, my dear? We need to get these pups fed, and we will have many more days this summer to discuss the colors, the rules, and weaving."

"The Moirai—what are they?"

"The sisters," said Mrs. Martin. "It's a Greek myth, but probably much older, in truth. The myth says that the sisters live alone, high on a mountain, and their names are Clotho, Lachesis, and Atropos."

"What do they do?"

"They measure the string that determines the length of a person's life. At a certain time, Atropos will cut that string and the person will die."

All at once, Cynthia understood. "Those are the strings—"

"Yes, exactly," said Mrs. Martin, a sad smile creasing her face. "I think it's more a case of the strings being the reason for the myth rather than the myth being the reason for the strings to exist at all, but the sisters, real or not, are all the proof I need to know that this is far from a new phenomenon."

"Phenome—"

"A new thing, honey," said Mrs. Martin. "It's so easy to forget, when we get to talking, just how young you are." Mrs. Martin stubbed out her cigarette and then clapped her hands. "Let's get these dishes cleaned up and then feed these two little piggies. There will be plenty of time to ask questions next time, all right?"

Chapter 23

Brinn hit first—a direct hit, because she had evidence. Jessica had approved the lead, and Brinn had taken it further than anyone else had managed to. Brinn was proud of that, almost too proud to imagine calling Jessica over when she came in, for fear that the whole thing would be dismissed and her moment in the sun would be over before it had really begun.

Brinn was a heavy woman in her early twenties with a pretty face and a worker-bee attitude. She had scars on her arms from a cutting hobby that had been nipped in the bud years earlier, and a tattoo of Darth Vader battling a velociraptor amidst the scars. From the look of things, Vader was finally getting the upper hand, despite his tattered armor.

"We've got tape from Mexico," Brinn blurted as soon as Jessica walked into the computer lab, and Jessica grinned and walked to her.

Brinn grinned back. She couldn't help herself—Jessica Hockstetter was the mother she never knew that she really wanted to impress—and then Jessica was standing next to her.

"Show me."

"All right, it's pretty straightforward, but I'll give you everything."

"That's what I want."

"I know, I'm sorry," said Brinn with a sheepish grin, and Jessica rolled her hand to tell the younger woman to get to it. "Anyways, I just got confirmation that they flew into Des Moines, got picked up by a pile of security cameras, then rented a truck and hit the bricks. That should be the end of it, right up until the impending arrests, but it's not. I have new shit from Mexico, just a few minutes before they boarded. Check this out."

Brinn grabbed a remote off of her desk, then pointed it at the VCR mounted under the TV at the far end of the room. After a blast of static, the thing started up and then began to show some blurry camera footage from what looked like an airport or bus terminal. Around her, Jessica could hear chairs turning and various types of tinny, abrasive music released as headsets were pulled away from heads, but she was too engrossed to care about the noise.

The video was from the airline terminal in Mexico, and it showed Darryl Livingston and Terry Johnson—both names presumed to be aliases—standing before the ticket counter. Everything looked normal, and then, right on camera, Jessica saw something incredible. There was no audio, but it was obvious that Darryl had heard something he didn't like. He stiffened, froze, and then the woman was frozen as well, except for her hands. As her fingers worked the keys, it would have looked normal to anyone untrained, but to Jessica it was obvious that he was running her, getting what he needed and preventing her from sounding an alarm. It was classic untempered power. The woman looked in rough shape—Jessica could see her weaving on the grainy video—but if all she came away with from her meeting with the pair of psychos was a headache, she was damn lucky.

"Holy shit," said one of the other researchers as Darryl and Terry walked off camera and the woman dropped from sight behind her counter.

"All right," said Jessica as the tape went to static, "this is exactly what we've been looking for. Excellent work, Brinn. Everybody else, you're a bunch of lazy shitheads." Jessica grinned. "Now, this is all we're going to be focusing on from here on out. Until we can get a conversation with these two assholes, no other work is to be done."

"Nothing else?" Pat asked.

Jessica nodded at him over his desktop. "Nothing," she confirmed. "Unless you're looking at a better lead than this one and have video proof to back it up, I want you doing whatever Brinn needs you to." Jessica turned back to Brinn. "I want to know everything, all right? No more waiting on a tape or getting confirmation, I want it all. We need to be boots-on-the-ground after these guys the second we get the chance. Pretty soon they're either going to disappear or end up backed into a corner, and that's when all the killing will start. We need them before they go to ground or end up ordering a double suicide by cop."

"I don't know where to start," called Geoff.

Jessica stood and yelled over to him. "Start in Des Moines. Work on cash purchases over a thousand dollars, and remember we have federal warrants. Rick, you start pulling surveillance footage from hotels. I want any video of two men checking in together over the last two days. Pat, I need you on crime—anything out of the ordinary. That means a bar that got cleaned out with no one seeing anything, rapes or robberies with no possible suspects—anything at all to confirm that they might still be in Des Moines."

"What are you going to be covering, Brinn?" Jessica asked, hoping her new researcher wasn't getting ahead of herself.

"All of that stuff, but in a donut around Des Moines," said Brinn. "I'm scared they already left, even though my gut tells me they stayed for a minute to cool off." She grinned. "I don't need sleep—we have coffee."

"We'll sleep when we're dead," called Geoff, and he and Rick high-fived. Jessica nodded, more pleased than she'd been in a long time, then took a seat next to Brinn. She understood little of what happened online aside from newsfeeds, but she could pretend she knew what the younger woman was doing as her fingers fed the hungry beast inside of the keyboard.

Chapter 24

Tom Nichols liked the porno rooms the best—he could normally knock out a stiff one or two playing in there—but the video game chats were useful, too. Like today: Tom needed to know how to unlock Tofu in *Resident Evil 2*, so he was set up in an AOL-based chat room called *RE 2*. Right where he needed to be, he knew. The only problem was that he was alone at the moment. Glancing up from his cursor to the clock on the monitor, he could see why: it was still two hours until school, and the whole world was practically asleep. Someone would come on eventually, though, and they'd know exactly what to do.

Tom yawned, tilting his head toward the ceiling, and when his eyes came back to the monitor he saw there was someone else in the room with him, a person named simply D. Score! Tom bent down to the keyboard. He still had enough time before school that if D could help him, he'd have a few minutes to fuck around on the PlayStation before he had to leave. But as Tom began to type a greeting his fingers grew numb, pounding on the keyboard instead of on individual keys, and the room began to fade around him, the walls spinning and the sound of a swarm of bees coming from deep in his ears.

/ Kill, Tom. You need to kill / Guns. The guns in Dad's room / Get the guns and go to the day care / Tom, you need to kill / Tom woke on his floor, not quite sure of what had just happened but not really caring, either. He walked down the steps to the first floor and then into the garage. The rest of the family was still asleep. Tom slipped quietly outside and grabbed his little brother Henry's aluminum T-ball bat. The bat was short and wore a few dents from being knocked around by Henry, but Tom liked the feeling of the weight in his hands. It felt solid; it felt right.

Tom walked back into the house and climbed back up the carpeted steps toward the rest of the family, still slumbering away in their beds. He walked past Henry's room, past his own room and the still-glowing screen, and finally made his way into his parents' room. Tom could feel something in the back of his mind telling him not to do what he was about to do, telling him he needed to hit himself in the head or just run away and keep running, but Tom ignored that voice. Instead, he did as he was told. */ Dad first. It has to be Dad first /* Tom raised the bat over his head, looked blankly at his sleeping father, and then brought it down on the center of his father's face as hard as he could.

It wasn't like in the movies. Instead of just dying, Dad reared up from the bed, blood pouring from his shattered mouth and nose, and Tom wound up like it was the World Series before driving the bat once more into his father's face.

Mom was wrestling with the blankets now, shrieking nonsensical gibberish at him, and Tom gave her a lick with the bat, too. Dad was quivering on the bed, his life draining from him in a bed-ruining mess, but Mom flopped out onto the floor after Tom hit her. He walked around the bed, stalking his mother as she butt-scooted away from him into the hall. Her jaw was shattered and hung off of her face like a ruined marionette's, and Tom began to swing the bat back and forth as he came for her. She left a bloody trail, a smear and handprints on the floor behind her, and Tom brought the bat down again. Mom had been starting to make sense before he hit her, and that wasn't going to stand, not today.

As Tom looked up from Mom's body, he saw his younger brother, Henry, staring at him from the other end of the hall.

"Henry, there's a robber in the house. He hurt Mom and Dad!"

Henry was frozen in place, staring at his big brother. He knew something was wrong but couldn't begin to guess what he should do about it.

Tom knelt next to Mom's still-shaking body and said, "Come on, Henry. We need to go in my room and call the police."

Tom grinned—Henry bought it. Tom dropped the bat as his brother approached him, and the two of them went to his room. Tom sat Henry down at his computer, amid his brother's sobbing protests, and then sat on his bed with his eyes closed. A few minutes later the boys walked with stone faces into their parents' bedroom and equipped themselves.

Neither boy spoke as Tom drove them to the day care. In the trunk of the car were two Glock semiauto pistols, a pair of preban AR-15 carbines, and a number of magazines for both weapon types. All Tom could hear was the crackling of static electricity as he parked in front of the facility, and the two of them walked inside with pistols in their waistbands and long guns in their hands. There was silence in the day care, and then a woman began to scream. Sure that he recognized her from his tenure there years earlier but unable to place her name, Tom stopped worrying about it and cut her down with rifle fire. More adults began to flood the hallway at the noise, and then it was time to get it on.

Tom and Henry moved from room to room, shooting random victims as they appeared and spraying bullets into cowering children. Tom felt flashes in his head, stark cuts to black-and-white messaging, which would then return him to his mission. *Kill, reload, kill.* Both boys worked at the task at hand for as long as they were able, and when the SWAT teams finally flooded into the carnage, the Nichols brothers sat down and fed each other bullets.

• • •

Darryl fell onto the floor of the hotel room and began to dry-heave. Terry just stared at his friend, unable and unwilling to help. Finally, after a few minutes of unsuccessful voiding, Darryl dragged himself back to the bed and lay down.

"Shut off the TV, Terry," he said, but Terry didn't respond, nor did he shut it off.

The talking heads on CNN had given up on the dead girls in Mexico. The death count in Santa Cruz was still rising, and they were expecting it to get much higher than the eighteen deaths originally reported. Darryl watched video footage of a daisy chain of children being led from the building like a morbid conga line, then stood and shut the TV off himself.

"I didn't have a choice," said Darryl. "It was too hot."

"Tell yourself whatever you have to," said Terry. "Blame whoever you want, do whatever you need to so that you can wake up tomorrow, but this isn't my fault. What happened in Mexico was on me, but this is on you, and you are going to need to live with it. Or not, I suppose. We've had a good run, but this planet would probably be better off without us."

Darryl left his sputtering friend in his dust, walked into the bathroom, and shut the door after him. He ran water over his face and then looked in the mirror, not even thinking about what he might see there in his dry state. Staring back at him was a man with sunken eyes and a purple topknot coming from his head. Darryl shook his head at his reflection. He knew he'd pushed it too hard with his possession of the brothers and their visit to the day care, but he also knew what he had to do.

Darryl left the bathroom and immediately went to work on Terry, who fell to his side on the bed as Darryl put the bend on him. Terry was shivering like the warm room was breath-foggingly frigid. Darryl forced himself to look at the ugly space between them, at Terry's vibrant and angry red and his own ugly purple, and then slowly did the work of pushing the purple into Terry. This was exactly how the murders in Mexico had happened: he'd filled his friend too high up with the bad stuff, and some of it spilled. Terry shook like he was in the throes of an awful dream, but Darryl knew that when he woke, his friend would remember none of this. Finally, the threads between them were blue, and Terry began to snore on the bed.

It's your fault that he is the way he is, and it's your fault that you had to fix it the way that you did. It was true, and there was nothing to do but accept what had happened.

Darryl flicked the TV back on as Terry snored on the other bed and then gave a look to the tube. The death toll was up to twenty-six, and the shot from the helicopter showed a triage set up in the day care parking lot. Darryl lay down on the bed, letting the newscasters tuck him in, and when he slept it was without dreams.

Chapter 25

Mom picked up Cynthia from Mrs. Martin's after a long day knock-ing on doors, and the two women exchanged pleasantries while Cynthia busied herself with Stanley and Libby. Cynthia listened to her mother thanking Mrs. Martin for the third or fourth time, and then her eyes caught on the happy green line extending from her own head to the bouncing Libby in front of her. Cynthia closed her eyes and reached out to the dog, not sure what she might find there. As her mind met Libby's, Cynthia found none of the ugliness that had plagued the knot or the humans beneath it. As far as Cynthia could tell in her brief sojourn into dog territory, Libby was happy about the smells around her, happy about dinnertime, and very happy about the little girl kneel-ing before her.

Cynthia broke the connection with the pooch as her mother said, "Cynth, you're going to give that poor dog a nervous breakdown. Let her get some air."

"All right," said Cynthia as she stood.

"You be good, dear, and I'll see you soon," said Mrs. Martin, but in Cynthia's mind, she heard / *Crayons. Get her to buy you crayons* / Cynthia smiled at the older woman, letting her know that she would do as she asked, without so much as a twitch from her lips, and Mom said, "Thanks again, Henrietta, we really do appreciate it."

"The pleasure was all mine," said Mrs. Martin. "Smart, polite little ladies like Cynthia will always have a place at my table."

"Well, I really appreciate it. You got me out of a heck of a bind."

"It really was no trouble," said Mrs. Martin, while above the pair of them Cynthia could see Mrs. Martin's yellow threads wrapping around Mom's red ones, slowly cooling them to blues and greens.

Cynthia kept petting the dog and watched as the women talked, wondering what might happen if she was to try and do what Mrs. Martin had called weaving. *You could find out exactly what Mrs. Martin is doing to her, exactly what Mom needs to hear and feel to be happy.* Cynthia let the thought die a quick death. She didn't want to spy on them, and besides, what if Mrs. Martin could tell what she was doing?

Cynthia knew that Mrs. Martin wasn't telling her the truth about everything but rather was only telling as much of the truth as she was comfortable telling a child. There was something disturbing about that, something Cynthia couldn't quite put her finger on, but she had done a lot of growing in the last few days, and she wasn't sure how much she trusted adults or the strange rules that they lived by. Adults get divorce and have affair, made you move on a whim, or see a black knot of pain in the back of the store. Worse, adults had thoughts about money instead of family.

Cynthia looked down at the dog by her knee. Little Libby was wagging her tail, staring at her with sad eyes, and the strings connecting them were no longer green. Instead, red was pouring from Cynthia's head, and Libby was sending trails of blue and green.

Cynthia wanted to burst into tears—even the dog wanted her to feel better. Instead of crying, Cynthia stood as her mother said, "Time to go, buttercup," and then waved at Mrs. Martin as she left the apartment.

"I'll see you soon," said Mrs. Martin, and Cynthia smiled as the door closed after them.

"I got us a pizza," said Mom as she led the way up the stairs. "Half cheese, half supreme, so we can both be happy."

"That sounds good," said Cynthia. "I'm superhungry." That spun Mom around from putting the key in their door to look at her, and Cynthia didn't need to see the red yarn to know what she was thinking. "I had plenty to eat, Mom. I'm just still hungry. Mrs. Martin wouldn't forget to feed me."

Mom smiled—a thin one—and Cynthia found it interesting how quickly the older woman's influence on Mom had worn off.

"I hope not," said Mom, "and I am glad that she could watch you, but you would tell me if things were bad there, right, Cynthia?"

"What do you mean?" Cynthia asked, not sure entirely of what her mother was asking but also knowing that her mother wasn't just asking if Mrs. Martin had told her to keep her mouth shut or to not drop as many crumbs on the floor. *She wants to know if Mrs. Martin hurt you, if she touched you.*

"I just want to make sure that she was nice."

"She was really nice, Mom. We had milk and cookies—homemade, I think." *She told me about the Moirai, too, Mom, and she looked scared when I told her about Dad. In fact, I think she even lied a little about that part.*

"That's good, Cynthia," said Mom, turning back to the door and unlocking it but then turning again to Cynthia before leading them inside. "But we can always work something else out if you'd prefer not to go back."

"I want to go back," said Cynthia. "I like her dogs, and Mrs. Martin said if I get my crayons that she can help me draw things."

Mom nodded and then led the way to the dining room table and opened the pizza box.

"We'll get you some new ones at the drugstore after dinner, honey. I'm not sure I have the energy to go see Dad right now."

"That would be great. I don't need a lot," said Cynthia, thinking to herself that the standard eight-pack would still have a few more shades than she needed.

"Well, if that's settled, let's go ahead and eat," said Mom.

Cynthia smiled and sat at the table as Mom passed her a paper plate with a piece of cheese pizza on it, and as she ate, Cynthia felt sure that things were finally going to be OK.

Chapter 26

When Darryl woke it was still night, and Terry was still sleeping.
Darryl looked at his slumbering friend, and then it all came back:
Mexico, the murders, the day care, the purple shit coming from his
head, and finally, passing that poison on to Terry. Darryl slipped from
the bed and walked to the bathroom, telling himself as he made his
way there that he was still going to be purple, or would maybe even
be black by now. *That would be fair, wouldn't it? You blame your friend
for what he does while you shit in his brain and kill a bunch of children so
you can stay free.*

Darryl turned to the mirror as he entered the bathroom, not just
ready but almost eager to see another premonition of his own death.
He didn't, though. His topknot was red, blue, and green. Darryl waved
his fingers through it as though the strands could be physically moved,
and he finally accepted there really was no purple or black to be seen.
He knew what he'd find if he looked at Terry—a deep shade of violet—
but in that moment he didn't care. *If you cared, you wouldn't put that
shit in him in the first place.*

After his shower, he found Terry sitting on the bed with a swirling
mess of purple atop his head, grinning at the carnage on CNN like a

child watching Saturday morning cartoons. Darryl suppressed the urge to get dressed, make up an excuse to leave, and never come back. *What would be the point? You'd just need to find someone else like him to inject your venom into.*

"Dude," said Terry without looking away from the screen, "you have to watch this."

He sounded like he was inviting Darryl to watch some gut-busting video of a guy getting accidentally whacked in the nuts.

"Any updates on the other thing?" Darryl asked as he took a seat on the bed, and Terry shook his head in answer and pointed at the TV.

The Nichols boys had stolen all of Terry's thunder. The anchors were talking about gun control and barking about how "something needs to be done." Darryl smiled at the chaos happening on the screen as an NRA rep was added to the fray via telephone. He had done this. He was influencing a national debate and possibly even driving the creation of some new laws.

"These assholes act like they can actually stop this from happening, Darryl," squealed Terry. "I mean, they really have no idea what happened, and they're trying to play Monday morning quarterback. Fucking hacks, man. Can you even imagine if they knew?"

Darryl shook his head. He couldn't imagine the scale of the witch hunt that would begin if anyone had even an inkling of what he and Terry were up to. That wasn't going to happen, though, not even if they got caught. Darryl wouldn't let it. He had no doubt that there was a lab in a cave somewhere with a couple of kids who could bend being treated like lab rats, but he doubted the CIA or whoever was working the project had any luck getting their pets to do any tricks. *At least not any tricks that matter.*

"They wouldn't know what to do with it," said Darryl. "It would be like reporting real information on ghosts or aliens—a huge scoop that would cause mass hysteria. They couldn't let it out. They'd lose their whole viewing audience in minutes while the rest of the country stocked up on canned goods and ammunition and everybody took cover in their basements. Can you imagine how fast ad revenue would dry up?"

Terry shook his head. "Like there's anything they *could* do. I mean, they couldn't even get to you, much less manage to say a bad word around you with you in the same room. You'd carve their heads out like pumpkins and walk away, dude. They wouldn't even know what hit them."

The thought hit Darryl like a jolt: *We've been playing this wrong the whole time.* The idea had always been to fly under the radar, to live off of the grid as much as possible, but this computer shit was a game changer. The days of bilking some drunk rube out of his bank account were long gone. Darryl hadn't had a failure yet on the computer. Even if he was having trouble finding another kid who could bend, he was certain there were plenty of other ways he could ply these newfound abilities.

"I don't think they'd know what to do with either one of us, Terry," said Darryl finally, his mind still racing. "Probably best that they never find out."

"That's all right by me," said Terry, his attention already wandering back to the ugliness on the television, but all Darryl could think about was finding another bent kid. *You've spent your whole life playing the short game, taking the money and running whenever you got two nickels to rub together. But what if the next time you found a kid like Vincent you used him for the long term?*

It was an interesting thought. Make the kid into some sort of remote-operating device. *You might still leave a footprint*, thought Darryl. But did that even matter? A bent kid, one who knew of his own abilities, would already be covering up for himself.

Darryl stood, walked to the computer, and fired it up. There was no reason to let this downtime spoil what could be a productive few weeks. *You thought you'd be drunk for a month*, thought Darryl, but that idea felt like it had come from another person. Right now he wanted an outlet, and if he had to search every kid out there, he was going to find it. Vincent was proof: there were still kids in the wild like him. Kids who were strong mentally, had the power to bend, and were born with criminal minds.

Darryl listened as the modem sang its screeching song, and then got to digging.

Chapter 27

"It's not exactly what we were looking for, but have any of you guys heard about this mass shooting in Santa Cruz?" Pat asked the room. He knew they were only supposed to be working on Des Moines, but the killings in Cali just smacked to him of something more, just like the thievery and then nonsensical suicide by Vincent Taggio had.

"Heard about it," said Jessica, "don't care. All I care about is Des Moines and crimes there."

"Hear me out just for a second," begged Pat. "This shit doesn't make any sense. Two kids are home with their folks, then decide to kill them for no reason—literally everyone who knew them says the family was very close—and then they go shoot up a day care that these boys had absolutely no gripe with."

"It happens," said Geoff. "These kids see all of these crime shows, think they'll just get caught if they go the 'normal' serial killer route. They want to be famous *now*. Want it so bad they don't care if they're both dead twenty minutes later. Being famous is worth it for them, like it's worth it for jihadists to blow themselves up just to get to those virgins waiting for them."

"No way. This isn't that," said Pat. "These kids were normal—completely normal—and they just go off their nuts? It doesn't make any sense."

"It doesn't need to," said Brinn. "We're looking for telekinetics, remember? Jessica said they don't commit suicide, that they have that god complex that makes them think they can always find a way out. Those two shot each other to death. TKs wouldn't do that, just like if your other kid had been a TK he wouldn't have jumped off of a chair." Brinn paused, typed furiously for a moment, then turned her gaze back to Pat. "Come back to us, Pat, back to the world of the living. There's enough bad stuff out there that we can't comb through it all. I need you on crimes in Des Moines."

"I'm on it," said Pat, "and I have been this whole time. I'm just suggesting that maybe there's more to that thing in California than any of us realize right now."

"Here's a thought," said Geoff. "What if one of these TKs made those kids off their parents and then go shoot up the day care?"

"Why in the hell would they do that?" Rick asked.

Geoff shrugged. "How the hell would I know? I'm just trying not to push a possibility away. We're supposed to look everywhere and at everything."

"Guys, come on," said Brinn. "Let's get back to work. I'm in charge, and we're working Des Moines. I don't think there's much room for debate."

The three men nodded and got back to their tasks involving the Greater Des Moines area, but Pat kept a thought to himself. Jessica never mentioned what they were supposed to be doing after work, and his home rig was nearly identical to the one before him now. He even had an idea of why the kids might have snapped: *What if Darryl or Terry got to them?*

Jessica had said that was impossible to do over the phone, but she'd been talking about via voice transmission. What if there was something different about data firing over a modem? Pat knew it was a long shot, but hell, so was everything. Nobody knew anything about this crazy shit when it came down to it. And God knew he didn't have anything else going on at home, anyways.

Chapter 28

Cynthia waited for Mom to hurry up and get dressed as she colored at the dining room table. She was being careful not to break the tips on the crayons her mother had bought her the day before—not that she really thought it mattered, but she wanted them to be in good condition when she saw Mrs. Martin again. Finally, Mom appeared from the bathroom, dressed just as fancy as the day before.

"Let's get that stuff picked up if you want to bring it," said Mom as she brushed past the table.

The words might have once stung Cynthia, but now she could read her mother so much better. Mom wasn't mad at her; she was mad at Dad and stressed out about trying to get a job. *Mom wants to show him still, whatever that means.*

Cynthia ignored Mom as she raced around the apartment, instead focusing on boxing up her crayons. Cynthia was excited to see Mrs. Martin again, but nowhere near as excited as she'd been the day before, now that so much of the mystery had been revealed. Cynthia knew that Mrs. Martin would tell her more about the secret little world that she'd happened upon, but also that it wouldn't be enough. Cynthia wanted to know how to keep her father safe, how to make the purple go away, and how to make her parents fall in love again, but she knew that they weren't going to discuss any of that.

"Are you ready?" Mom asked, but even without her gift, Cynthia wouldn't have recognized the query as an actual question. Mom wanted to hear that she was ready so that she could deposit her somewhere safe and be on her way.

"Yes," said Cynthia as she loaded the last of her crayons into the box and then stood.

"Well, let's go then, silly," said Mom, trying to be funny and not succeeding.

Cynthia followed her mother out the door and then watched as she locked it before the two of them made their way downstairs. Mom rapped twice on Mrs. Martin's door, and the two of them could hear the dogs long before the older woman appeared.

"I was starting to get a little anxious," said Mrs. Martin.

Cynthia just grinned and slid past her, bidden by a voice in her head that told her to take a seat at the table.

"Are you sure this will still work for you, Henrietta?"

"Of course it will," said Mrs. Martin, her voice glistening with honey. "Like I told you yesterday, having her here is a blessing for me. I don't get many visitors, and you can see how the dogs have taken to her."

"All right," said Mom, and Cynthia could hear the questions she wasn't saying in her voice, as well as see the threads in the air interacting between the two women. The strands were of varying thickness, gold, red, blue, and green.

Cynthia watched them talk and considered trying to see their conversation the way she had the knot at the store, but she didn't want to be a thief in their minds, and she knew that somehow Mrs. Martin would know. Finally, Mom was walking out the door, and Mrs. Martin latched it after her.

Cynthia leaned down from her seat to pet Stanley on his little brown-and-white head, and Mrs. Martin took the seat across from her.

"What are we going to do today?" Cynthia asked. "I brought my crayons in case you want to help me write down a color list."

"No, not right now," said Mrs. Martin. "Today we're going to weave. I can practically smell purple from where I'm sitting. Someone who lives nearby is going to need our help, and we're going to give it to him, whether he wants it or not."

Cynthia had to all but pick up her chin from her chest. This was the last thing she'd expected. Mrs. Martin wanted her to help get into the head of a stranger, and who knew what else she'd need her to do once that was done?

"Is it safe?" Cynthia asked, and Mrs. Martin shook her head.

"Very few things worth doing ever are, my dear, but it will be safe enough. I'll make sure of that." Mrs. Martin laid her arms down on the table, her palms up, and said, "Now, I want you to take my hands, and we're going to figure out who's aching. With the two of us, it ought to be like searching a shoebox with a flashlight. Just let me lead, Cynthia, and we'll be to the root of it soon enough."

Cynthia took Mrs. Martin's hands, her heart thumping in her chest. She could feel their breathing become as one, and then it was as though she were looking down on the apartment complex from the belly of a low-flying airplane. There were dots of color flecked over some apartments, and Cynthia realized with a start that the building she lived in had a star marked over it. / *I started adding color a few years ago* / *It helps me remember where my people are* / Mrs. Martin's voice was in her head, but when Cynthia whipped her head back and forth she could see no sign of her friend.

"Where are you?" Cynthia asked, but her voice had no sound.

/ *I'm right here with you, dear* / *Neither of us is above the North Harbor Apartments. We're both still in my little place with the dogs* / *Now, the purple man* / *Can you find him?* /

Cynthia accepted Mrs. Martin's words without argument, not because she didn't have any questions, but because she didn't even know where to begin. Instead, she began studying the dotted apartments, looking for any sign of what was happening inside. She wasn't sure what she was seeking, beyond purple. She was just hoping that she would recognize whatever she was supposed to be searching for when she found it. Cynthia started by concentrating on one of the apartments with a red dot on top of it—red was close to purple, she supposed—and in an eyeblink she was there, floating near its ceiling like she had in the liquor store.

A man sat in the apartment watching TV and drinking beer. He was drumming his hands on his knees and talking under his breath, and atop his head was a violent curl of writhing red and pink string.

The phone began to ring, and the man turned toward it and shouted, "Nobody home, Mick, so just leave me the hell alone!" The words were audible—a surprise to Cynthia—but when she thought about it, that made sense. Here, the man was actually speaking, but at her father's store the voices she heard were thoughts.

Cynthia knew the man was in trouble. She didn't know what kind of trouble but also had a feeling this wasn't the place she was looking for. She didn't know if Mrs. Martin would have spoken up if she was wrong, but Cynthia knew she wasn't. Cynthia pictured the apartments again, and once again found herself above them.

Next, Cynthia picked another red dot, this one at the far end of the complex, far from where she stayed with Mom. Cynthia barely focused on the dot this time, and she was inside. Here there was a woman instead of a man, but she looked just as miserable as the man had. Red curls poured from her head, rising high enough to brush the ceiling, and she was flitting about the apartment getting ready to leave, though Cynthia had a hard time imagining where she would need to go dressed like she was. The woman looked like a living version of one of the Barbie dolls Mom always griped about buying for Cynthia, and despite the woman's rage, the only thought blaring from her was / *Hope Reg is happy* / *Hope Reg is happy* / The words were like an assault, a constant siren in the building, and Cynthia jettisoned once again and found herself staring down at the North Harbor Apartments from somewhere in the sky.

"It's harder than I thought," said Cynthia to herself, and then Mrs. Martin's voice was in her head again: / *You're doing fine* / *Just keep looking* / *If you try, you should be able to feel it, to smell it* /

Cynthia tried that, tried to make herself feel anything besides fear over floating high above North Harbor, but there was nothing there. There was nothing to scent up in the sky, either. As far as Cynthia could tell, the air above the complex smelled a little like one of Mrs. Martin's cigarettes. / *Reach out* / *Reach out* / Cynthia had no idea what Mrs. Martin meant, but she concentrated on the top of the building next to the one she lived in, and all at once she understood what Mrs. Martin meant.

Cynthia was in all four of the building's apartments all at once, though she knew she was really in none of them. Looking at the building felt sort of like watching a television that had several different programs running on the screen. Two of the apartments were empty. In the third the heavyset woman she'd seen doing laundry that first day was whistling and making breakfast for her kids, and in the fourth a man sat at his kitchen table looking at a gun. Atop his head was a thick purple-and-black knot, and he was sitting and staring at the gun as if in a trance. Cynthia focused on him, and the split-screen view she had was gone, and she pushed herself so that she was floating above the man.

/ *Stop being a bitch. Just do it* / *Do it* / *Do it* / *DO IT* /

The words were a wall, and Cynthia knew that something bad was going to happen. She wanted to be home. She wanted to be back in Mrs. Martin's little apartment, petting the dogs. She wanted to forget any of this ever happened. She wanted to be home with her parents and have all of this be a dream. Instead, Cynthia stretched her arms out and, with fingers she could neither see nor feel, took hold of one of the purple strands. Cynthia felt electricity flowing through her, the same way she'd felt it when she took Mrs. Martin's hands, but this was different. She knew everything.

The man's name was Patrick Kettle, and he was sad because he'd always been sad. All he wanted was for the pain to end. He hated his work, he couldn't get a date, and he had no friends to confide in. He felt alone because he was alone, and the weight of it was killing him as sure as if it were a tangible thing. Patrick didn't know where he was supposed to fit. He felt like a puzzle with a matching picture but all of the wrong pieces. He was alone and unhappy, and he wanted to die.

Not sure of what to do but hating the way Patrick was looking at the gun, Cynthia gave the purple strand a tug. She could see where it was catching on another thread a foot or so below the ceiling, and she slowly pried the two apart, letting them swing freely. / *You have a lot to live for* / The voice was Mrs. Martin's, and Cynthia could see yellow strands grasping at the freed pieces she had just released from the stranglehold of the knot.

Cynthia went to work at another of the strings, a black one this time, and when she took hold of it she could see silhouettes of her fingers against the murky color of the thread. Cynthia could feel the black thread in a way that didn't make sense; she couldn't feel anything else here. Taking hold of it sent a memory like a lightning bolt through her, a young Patrick running from a group of children, bullies who always caught him. Cynthia tugged at the strand, ripping it free from the ones next to it, and then was shocked to see that it had torn free from Patrick entirely, like a dead branch on a tree. Cynthia stared at it in her there-but-not-there fist, and then the strand began to dissolve in her grip until it was a shadow, and then gone entirely.

/ *Now do the rest* / Cynthia could see yellow strands grabbing the broken piece, and she did as she had been told, reaching deep into the knot, then twisting and pulling to spread them apart. She could feel Mrs. Martin there with her, not in the same way that Cynthia was, but there all the same. Patrick was quiet, but Cynthia could see him, stone-faced, below them, paused like one of her DVDs as she worked. The threads came apart more easily the longer she pulled at them, the blackened and dead ones dropping off and dissipating, while the swirling purple ones were enveloped by the yellow threads from Cynthia and Mrs. Martin.

It was impossible to know how long the job took to do, but Cynthia felt a weird elation as she released the last of the threads from each other. She felt tired and exhilarated all at once, and as she looked through the threads, she was happy to see that a good many of them had changed from purple to blue, though there were several strands that had transformed to red. Cynthia felt her focus changing. Patrick's hands were moving, but he was ignoring the gun on the table. Cynthia felt the world blink out, and then there was darkness.

Chapter 29

While the world around us crumbles, Katarina and I train. The only shame of it is that we are forced to train only in the camp. Katarina is a powerful woman, and the guards respect and fear her, but I don't think even the Führer would be allowed to leave Dachau with a prisoner. Since the little joke I played on the two guards with my imaginary Sherman tank and American soldiers, the camp has been on edge, and the commandant has doubled the practice drills that the soldiers run through daily. All the guards do now is worry about the Americans, about what will happen when they come, and about what will happen to them after the war is over. Of course, I have come by these musings by being a bandit of their minds. No guard at Dachau would ever talk about his fears in front of a Jew.

Still, despite being confined to these walls, we train. Mostly, we work on my own map of Dachau. Like Katarina told me it would be, it is sparse compared to hers, the details are few, and what is there remains muddled. To me it looks like the world drawn by someone who has never seen it, and of course that is exactly the case. Yet I can see the world through my map, and slowly I fill the details in as I explore the camp. The only areas I avoid are the showers and the ovens, and this is at Katarina's request. "I know what is there and so do you," she says, "but to see it will only make you sick." I'm not sure if she's right. I think I could see it and it would have no effect. After all, I can still see the selections being made.

Because of their fear of the impending arrival of the Americans, the guards are working at an even faster pace than normal to eliminate the walking and talking evidence that stands before them in Dachau. The most recent selection took ten women from each barracks, all seemingly at random, and then they were gone. I know how they end up, of course—as smoke flowing from the chimney at the ovens, and ashes being scooped out with a shovel—but that just makes things worse. I don't weave with these condemned women, for there would be no point. I already know how they feel, and there is no reason to live it with them.

Sorrow is the emotion in my head as Katarina and I hover over the camp and stare at my map. Katarina can tell something is bothering me and has given me space, but as the whistle blows to summon the women to the area before the barracks and selection, I reveal what is upsetting me. / *Another selection? / Why? / There was just one yesterday* /

Katarina nods at me, and I know what she wants—for me to dive into the mind of a guard and get my answer. The Americans could be here any day—my little stunt in the guard tower has taught them this—and the men are paranoid. They know that there will be no short internment for those who worked at the camps. There will be a hangman's noose and a short drop, then a shallow grave. They mean to kill all of us and then make up their excuses later.

Staring at the line of women, I see so many familiar faces as the selection begins, but one leaps out at me. I have not seen Edna Greenburg since the day I first met Katarina, but now she is standing in the line. She is doomed.

What happens next is an accident. I do not mean to go to her the way that I went to the guards, but I do, racing toward her, dancing in the blackness of the threads over her, and then I see through her eyes. Her memories are mine in an instant—her children, her husband, everything. This didn't happen with the guards, perhaps because the guards' hearts hadn't been racing in their chests. It hits me like a shovel to the head: Edna's life is flashing back to her, and I've got a front-row seat for the show. This is worse than sharing a toilet with a thousand other women, worse than sharing a bed with total strangers. I am a thief, no better than a Nazi.

As Edna shuffles along, I see her Bat Mitzvah. I see her wedding night, I see stolen kisses from a man who is not her husband, and I see her looking down upon her smiling daughters. Edna has never spoken of her children—this thought strikes me like a slap, as does the reason. Her children are dead, just like so many other Jewish children, and she has never been the same since. Her children already stolen from her, she packs, gets dragged from her apartment by her husband, and then I watch with her—through her—as she sees a soldier pick up a little boy she has never seen before by the feet and smash him headfirst into a brick wall. *This is all she sees when she thinks of her daughters: Nazis holding them by their ankles and swinging the girls like sacks of flour.* Her babies—our babies now that I have stolen into her memories like the spy that I am. Though she is not sure of their deaths, she knows in her heart. A mother knows.

As the selection finishes, Edna and the rest of the doomed are marched across the camp's grounds toward the showers. At one time the guards acted as though all of this actually was just to end up in a shower, but they no longer bother. We know where we're going—all of us do. Finally, we march inside, where we are ordered to strip. I feel as though I'm watching a nightmare, but I'm loath to stop. This was my mother's fate, my grandmother's, and that of so many others. My father and brother could have died in this way, too—I don't even know if they're dead—but there are many other methods. Not that it matters: the end result is always the same. Just another dead Jew.

Next, Edna and the rest of these shaking, miserable women are led to the killing floor, a room that actually does look a great deal like a shower at a gymnasium. The difference here, of course, is that no one is getting clean. The sound of prayer fills the air, as though it matters. If there is a God, he is not in places like this. Once we are packed in too tightly to turn, I hear the giant door close behind us. Latches are shut, and the sound of prayer gets even louder. The amazing thing is that people are still hoping for a miracle, still hoping the Nazis will let them out. The gas comes next.

"Are you all right?" Katarina asks me, and I nod, though I am not sure if the answer is 100 percent correct. I can breathe—my lungs are not being destroyed by gas—but I am not all right, either. "Good, stay here."

I do as she says, listening to her boots on the wood floor as she leaves my side, and not for the first time I wish I had true sight. At least if I could really see I could purge my eyes of the last vision of Edna Greenburg and those other poor women dying. Instead, that is all I can see.

Katarina's boots are clicking on the floor again, then she stops near me, kneels down, and hands me a cup of water. I sip from it gratefully.

"Thank you."

"Do you understand now?"

"Understand?" I ask. "Who could ever understand the madness of this place?"

"Not about Dachau," says Katarina. "I know that you are educated when it comes to this place, educated far beyond your years. I mean about death. Did you understand that there was nothing you could do to help that woman?"

I could not answer.

"What could you have done?" Katarina persists, and I just shrug. "You could have tried to make her fight back, but the guards would have won. If you were a more skilled weaver, you could have made many of them attack the guards, but the end result would have been the same, or perhaps worse. A reprisal might have driven them to simply machine-gun the barracks. The guards are already on edge."

"So we do nothing."

"When we leave here, that is exactly what we are going to need to do," says Katarina. "There will be roads piled with the dead—Nazi, Jew, and American alike. We will see more dead than this camp could hold if the bodies were stacked like cordwood to the tops of the fences instead of burned, more dead in one war than this world has ever seen. But it is the dying we must fear."

"Why?"

"Because for the dead the pain is over," Katarina explains. "They cannot beg you for water or a kiss or a bullet. They just lie there, and no matter how ugly their condition, they can't harm you. The wounded, the ruined but still breathing, are different. You take a half-hanged man from a noose and hand him a sword and he'll hack his way to freedom, or die trying. You deny a gutshot man water and he'll shoot you in the back if he has half a chance. Now, imagine if they knew the gifts that you or I could give them. We could make them walk, like a puppet, to safety, take their pain away, and then see them off on their journey. But we cannot do any of these things. We have to let them die."

"That's cruel," I say. I know my mother's thoughts as the gas poured from the showerheads, just as I know Edna Greenberg's. Those were bad deaths—evil and unnecessary deaths—lives stolen from women who were years and years from meeting a natural end. All I can think of is the things I cannot see but yet I know are there. Katarina's uniform, with all of its ugliness. The smoke from the ovens, just as sooty, black, and thick as I'd always imagined. The sound of those women praying. *The noise of a thousand death rattles occurring at the same time.*

Mrs. Greenberg's memory of the little boy being held by his feet and his skull being crushed like an egg against the bricks. / *How can I ever ignore such things? / How can I walk away from pain? /*

"You do what you must to survive," says Katarina. "Do you think I like my uniform? Do you think I like what my country has become? Do you think I like any of this? You know what I can feel, what I can see. I am trying to survive, and I'm doing my damndest to help you survive as well, child. Listen to me. If this race is to survive—our very small, precious race, yours and mine—we need to be selfish. I have been a demon to get in this position, a sinner who pretended to love my baths in blood, but it has all been for one reason: to find you. To find people like us. My mission has been largely a failure, I can admit that, but I did find you."

"So all that matters is that we live?" I ask her. I have never been a selfish person—never—but I understand that sometimes selfishness is all that can keep you alive.

"Child, the Nazis know what I am and what I can do, on a very small scale," says Katarina, "but they keep their secrets close. The Americans will steal everything they can from Germany, but they can never steal us. The Nazis will ensure this, as they will kill the only men who know we exist. In order to survive, we must make our own way. Does that make sense?"

/ *It does* /

Chapter 30

1999

Darryl and Terry left Des Moines a week after they'd arrived. There had been no new leads on the web, and Darryl was frustrated by that, but a quick peek into Terry's mind the night before had told him everything he needed to know to make his decision to blow town. Terry was hungry, and Darryl didn't think there was going to be anything at Denny's that was going to sate him, at least nothing that was on the menu. Best to keep him on the move, where if the worst came to pass and he did break loose, they'd already be set up to leave the carnage behind them.

Darryl watched Terry staring at every gas station and late-night restaurant they passed while they traveled east, feeling like he was watching a lion sizing up his prey. Terry wasn't begging him to set him loose, but he didn't need to. It was in his eyes, in the air between them in the truck, and pouring from the top of his head.

Finally, Darryl had enough. Even though she was a good number of years older than what he normally went for, Terry was all but drooling at the cashier reading alone in the Texaco gas station while Darryl was gassing up.

"Oh, for Christ's sake, go," said Darryl, and Terry did, steaming on into the gas station like he'd been holding a piss too long.

Darryl turned his back on the store and finished filling the tank, and when he was done and turned back to look at the store, there was a flailing arm smacking the window and Terry above it, looking like he was trying to tear something loose from the wall.

Then everything went wrong.

Darryl caught the light out of the corner of his eyes and turned to see the Iowa State Patrol car. *Please just pass us*, thought Darryl, but it wasn't to be. The car slowed, the driver flipping on the blinker, and then it pulled into the lot behind them. Darryl already knew he had only seconds to react when the woman inside the gas station shrieked. The cop must've had his window open, because there was no question he heard her. He was out of his car with his gun in his hand, covering the ground in front of him and ignoring Darryl, when Darryl jumped in his head.

The cop reacted as if he'd been smacked with a board. He flew off of his feet, landing on his back with a groan ten feet from the door, and Darryl dove back into his head as the woman began to scream again. Darryl wanted the cop to just shoot himself, to make all of this end, but he couldn't do it. Making an adult off himself was a lot different than forcing a kid to do it, and if the man had a happy family at home, it could be nearly impossible. *You've been wasting too much time on drunks and teenagers*, said a hateful little voice in his head to Darryl.

The woman would *not* stop screaming inside the gas station, Terry was still ecstatically working her over, and the cop was trying to sit up. Darryl sent another blast at the cop, the sort that would maim rather than bend him, and the state trooper dropped back to the ground to do his fish dance. Darryl walked to the prone cop, grabbed his gun off the ground, and shot him in the chest. The connection Darryl had with him faded and went dark, the threads between their heads falling to nightshade and then dropping to the ground like dead snakes. Just as abruptly, the woman in the gas station went silent, and maybe another minute later Terry came waddling out as he buttoned his pants.

"Shit, the cops showed up?" Terry asked.

Darryl thought he would be too angry to speak, but he managed. "Yeah, and you can bet this is all on about seven video cameras around this station, so now it's time to go."

There were no sirens in the night, no brigades of uniformed police flooding their position, but both men knew this was bad—and not just because of the bloodbath itself, which was bad enough. Closed-circuit footage here was sure to get matched with film of the fiasco in Mexico. They were leaving a bloody video trail a mile wide.

Darryl drove the car until the tank was nearly dry, then fueled up again and kept moving. The sun was breaking the horizon when he finally pulled off at a small roadside hotel and got out to get them a room.

"Help you?" said the clerk as Darryl walked in, but Darryl already had the bend in him and knew everything. There were three other guests, and the man working the desk was a recovering drunk with five months on the wagon.

"Get a drink," said Darryl as he walked out of the office with a pair of key rings on his finger, leaving the man shivering behind him. All that the clerk was going to remember was that Room 12, on the far end, had been rented out by a single female, and that he was very, very thirsty.

Darryl got back in the truck, pulled down to 12 without a word, and then walked into the room with Terry at his heels.

"What now?" Terry asked.

Darryl could tell Terry needed a level of compassion that he just wasn't going to be able to muster without some help. *You may just have really broken him this time*, thought Darryl as he set blasts of yellow light into his friend.

"Now we sleep," said Darryl, "and in a day or two we're going to hit the road again."

Terry nodded and lay down on the bed, his body only taking a few moments to shut down. Darryl was tempted to turn on the TV so he could see for himself just how fucked they were, but he decided to follow Terry's lead and catch some winks.

The dead cop wouldn't let him do it, though. *Distractions like the day care made for a cool parlor trick, but do you really see the cops backing down from this?*

Darryl knew the truth. While the day care had taken public eyes off of them, the law had never stopped looking for them. And now they were going to be looking for two cop killers who looked just like them, in a truck that had been caught by half a dozen video camera eyes back at that gas station.

"We'll sit here for a few days, and then we're getting the hell out of this state, and then out of this country," said Darryl to no one at all.

We're fucked, and you know it. Kill Terry and duck out of here right now, you still have a chance. Darryl put the thought to bed, then closed his eyes and lay back. *Do you really think that you can just get away with this?* There had been a time where Darryl would have believed exactly that, but a lot of years had passed since then. He was stuck in the middle of Iowa with a maniac, and the pair of them had a few murders under the belt, and now they'd given the cops a special motivation to come after them. What they needed was a miracle, but Darryl didn't think there was much chance of that with what they'd been up to. The deck was stacked against them, and he didn't even feel like he and Darryl had any cards at all, aside from the ability to go out in a spree of violence.

We just need some space, thought Darryl, but he couldn't think of a single way for them to get it. Daryl and Terry were stuck between Des

Moines and Cedar Rapids, and unless Darryl came up with something big, that was going to be the end of the line.

Chapter 31

Cynthia went from flying, to black, to Mrs. Martin's apartment, all in what felt like a blink of an eye. Mrs. Martin stood as Cynthia came to, then walked to the kitchen and poured them each a glass of water. Cynthia looked to the dogs. Both were slumbering on the couch, but Libby woke up long enough to bare her teeth in the sort of lazy yawn that only small dogs and house cats seem able to muster. Mrs. Martin set a glass of water down in front of Cynthia and then retook her seat. Cynthia snatched the glass from the table, realizing as the cold cup touched her fingers that she was absolutely parched. Cynthia took a long drink, then set the glass back on the table and wiped her mouth with the back of her hand.

"I always get thirsty afterwards," said Mrs. Martin. "I never had anyone tell me that they did, too, but I had a feeling that it wasn't something that only I was experiencing. Watching you take after that, I can tell that I wasn't."

"Is Patrick going to be OK?" Cynthia asked. "He was so sad."

"He should be," said Mrs. Martin, "though it might not be a bad idea to drop in on him periodically to make sure that he remains so. I have a feeling, however, that a lot of the bad that was bothering him is all gone now. That doesn't mean he won't remember it, in most cases, but the parts of it that were the most awful, the most vivid, are gone." Mrs. Martin tipped her cup to Cynthia and said, "He has you to thank for that, you know."

"I didn't even know what I was doing," admitted Cynthia. "It was just like at the store, but worse, and I didn't know what to do there either."

Mrs. Martin smiled at Cynthia, then made a cigarette appear in her hands and lit it. "You learned quickly," she said. "I gave you a little push, but you already knew what to do. I can't even imagine how many things you've accidentally influenced around your house without even knowing it."

"I never even knew about this stuff until a few days ago," said Cynthia. "There's no way I was doing anything like that before then."

"You don't know that," said Mrs. Martin. "I was blind when I was in my camp, remember? Yet everyone loved little Ora Rabban, because I was in their heads without even knowing that I was doing anything at all. God and the world work in mysterious ways, my dear. Do you remember what I was telling you about the Moirai?" Cynthia nodded, and Mrs. Martin smiled. "You're a good listener." Mrs. Martin took a long drag from her cigarette and said, "Do you know what a fable is?"

"I think so," said Cynthia. "Like an old story?"

"Sort of," said Mrs. Martin. "There are certainly a lot of old fables, and many of them have stories of even older origin, but the idea of a lot of fables was that they were meant to teach a lesson. I think the lesson of the fable of Moirai was one to help us understand that they are real. Not real in the way that the stories portray—three lonely sisters on a mountaintop measuring the life-strings of every man, woman, and child—but real in another way. I think the Moirai were people just like you and me, people with powers that most do not possess and who deal with these life-strings that fables tell of. Do you understand what any of this has to do with you?"

Cynthia shook her head.

"I am telling you this because you have been given a gift, an ancient gift," said Mrs. Martin. "What you choose to do with it is up to you, but that is a decision for much later in life. Now, you are going to do what you are on this earth to do."

"What's that?"

"To help me keep the North Harbor Apartments safe, my dear," said Mrs. Martin. "It was no coincidence that you fell in my lap the way that you did. I will not leave you untrained. Today was just the first of the real lessons, but there will be many more. Keeping North Harbor balanced can be a full-time job."

"Are we going to help anyone else today?"

"No, dear," said Mrs. Martin. "You brought your crayons, so we'll go over the colors using them, and later I'll make us some sandwiches."

Cynthia nodded, her stomach rumbling at the mention of food.

"I have questions," said Cynthia, "lots of them. Like, why did we go so high above the apartments? Why were some of them marked? Have you helped Patrick before?"

"All in good time, Cynthia," said Mrs. Martin. "I'll get some paper, and you can get your crayons. The coloring first, and if we have time before your mother comes back, maybe we can get to some of the other questions."

Cynthia nodded, her curiosity nowhere near sated, but her child-like need to please overriding her burning desire for answers. She took her crayons from the bag by the door and walked back to the table. She could hear Mrs. Martin singing in the kitchen, and she smiled as she sat down and set the crayons before her. Mrs. Martin was her friend, and there had to be a reason that she couldn't tell her everything all at once, but what Cynthia most wanted was to be there the next time her parents fought.

They won't argue for long.

Chapter 32

"Oh fuck," said Pat, and around him was the noise of headphones hitting tables and seats being left. Pat was back at work now after a night busy at home exploring leads on the possibility of a TK using a modem. He knew he'd need a federal warrant to take it any further and that he couldn't exactly ask Jessica or Brinn for help with one. This new development squashed that frustration in an instant.

"Brinn," said Pat, "get on the phone with the FBI. We need all information pertaining to the gas station killings outside of Des Moines from last night. Geoff, call Jessica down here and tell her we need her to get on the horn with whoever suppresses leaks about this stuff and tell them to get to work."

Brinn being the lead no longer mattered. Both she and Geoff were on their headsets in an instant and then walking to opposite sides of the room so that they wouldn't be too loud for one another.

"Tell me what I can do," said Rick as he walked to Pat, and Pat shook his head.

"Nothing. We're landlocked until we can confirm via video that it was even them. Suppression matters more than apprehension right now."

"Bullshit. Jessica never even mentioned suppression, she said that—"

"They killed a cop, Rick. A state cop with a family is dead, and that's not even mentioning the woman who was raped and murdered." Pat stopped, took a deep breath, then drank deeply from the twenty-ounce of Mountain Dew on his desk, wishing as he did so that the plastic bottle were full of something much stronger.

"We need it suppressed," he went on, "because every cop and his mother is going to want to see that tape, and every news outlet is going to want to break it. I don't know how they suppress something like this, but I know the people we're working for don't fuck around. Remember our NDAs? They'll come up with something—or they'd better. Remember that video from Mexico? Now picture a cop being thrown to the ground by a harder version of what those assholes did to that girl at the ticket counter and then shooting him in the fucking heart."

"Jesus," said Rick. "Some pretty fucked-up questions would be asked. We'd probably be out of a job, and this is the only time I've ever been paid to do something I liked that was actually legal."

Pat wasn't sure how to respond to that, and then Jessica burst into the room.

"Are you sure?" she shouted. A cellular phone was pressed against her head, but she was shouting at Pat. "I mean absolutely, positively sure?"

"Yes. I mean, not until I see the video, but yes," Pat said. "I'm doing the best I can, Jessica. I just can't say with absolute certainty, and—"

"Yes, get the tape and fix things over there," said Jessica into the phone, turning away from Pat and making the younger man throw his hands to the sky in exasperation. "No, I don't know how. You figure it out." Jessica paused from her phone conversation as Brinn crossed the room to her.

"FBI will have a hard copy of the video to us by morning," said Brinn, "but we can set up for a videoconference with them to watch it in fifteen if you want."

Jessica gave her a thumbs-up, then walked out of the computer lab with the phone pressed to her ear. Brinn bolted from the room to get the videoconference set up.

From the hallway the remaining researchers could hear Jessica screaming expletives into the phone, and then there was silence.

"Yes, thank you," said Jessica from what felt like a world away, and then she was back in the room, tucking the cell phone into its place on her belt and grinning from ear to ear now.

"So this was your find, Pat?"

"Yep."

"Good boy," said Jessica, rubbing the top of his head as if he were a prized dog. "Now, should we go watch a video? If we hurry, we might get there in time so I can introduce you to what should be some very tired Fibbies."

"Sounds good to me," said Pat with a smile, and then Jessica waved them from the room.

• • •

The video was done, the FBI office in Des Moines had been thanked for their help, but no one was talking, not even Jessica or Brinn. The five of them just sat in silence, as though they were waiting for something else to happen, some sign that things were going to be OK. It wasn't coming.

Finally, Jessica stood, clapped her hands together, and said, "Pat, that's some great work, and I really appreciate how you handled the situation after discovery."

"It was just dumb luck," said Pat. "I've been following a watchdog newsgroup that updates police scanner information as it comes in. I don't watch it all the time, though, so I could have missed it." He shrugged. "It just worked out, I guess."

"Don't be so quick to discount yourself," said Jessica, and Pat saw the rest of the group nodding in agreement. He blushed, the red flush vivid against his pale skin. "You saw it. That's all that matters." Jessica clapped her hands together, a sign that praising the team was done, then said, "Now that we know they're still out there in the wild, what are we going to need to do to get closer?"

"Keep doing what we're doing," said Brinn. "Watch everything, but move our search east. We know they were headed that way."

"We have no way of knowing they're headed east," said Geoff. "I mean, other than them driving off that way in the video, and that's no proof. They turn north a block away, we have nothing."

"So what do you suggest?" Jessica asked, and Geoff shook his head.

"I don't know," he said. "Wish I did, but I have no idea how we could be possibly know which way they're heading. Not to mention they killed a cop, so there are going to be police everywhere. This could get really bad."

"It will get really bad," said Jessica, her voice hard and flat. "What we need to do is figure out how to track them."

There was silence, no one offering anything, and then Pat slowly raised his hand as if he were still in primary school. All eyes turned to him and he spoke.

"What if they use the web?"

"How do you mean?" Jessica asked.

"Well, it's possible that one or both of them use the Internet as much as we do. Given the sexual violence that went on in Mexico and again at the gas station, I think it's a lock that at least one of them is an extreme porn junkie. And if they are, they'll be like gamers and every other heavy net user. They'll end up going to the same set of sites every time. Right?"

The rest of the research nerds nodded and voiced their assent. All of them visited the same places on a daily basis. The sites they'd added since launching the hunt for Darryl and Terry marked the only significant changes in their routines in recent memory.

"So what does that mean for us?" Jessica asked, though she had an inkling. For one of the first times in her career, she was genuinely without any answers for the problem before her, and she had to admit this had some promise. But she was way out of her depth. Wrangling TKs or brokering deals with three-letter agencies? No problem. But the Internet was a whole new jungle, as she was rapidly learning. "Is it likely that one of you can just randomly come across one of them on one of those sites?"

"Not possible," said Brinn. "Maybe five or six years ago, but right now being online is like Indian country back in the Wild West. Even narrowed down to extreme porn sites, there's just too much turf."

"Well," said Pat, "except that right now these guys are in rural Iowa, theoretically heading east, right? Well, this isn't exactly New York City out there. It should be pretty sparse as far as net users go. All we need to do is find an IP address that is consistently visiting the sort of site that these two might like." Pat paused. "Assuming they continue on their path east, what is the next big city that they're going to be near?"

"Cedar Rapids and then Chicago," said Rick.

"All right, so we have until Cedar Rapids to find them, and then when they leave, we have until Chicago. After that they could head anywhere."

"What if they stay in one of the big cities?" Jessica asked. "What if they stay there as a way of hiding this IP address thingy from us?"

"Not going to happen," said Brinn. "First off, they don't know that we're going to try and track their IP address. Remember what I was saying about the Wild West? This would be like going to space back when guys were still jousting. It's highly unlikely these guys are web experts. It's just a tool to them. Secondly, they're going to try and avoid big cities as much as possible because that's where they're most likely to be spotted."

"All right," said Jessica. "Just so I can wrap my head around this, let me go over a few things. They're going to need to keep moving east, they're going to need to use the web frequently, and we're going to need to be lucky to find them. Does that about cover it?"

"Yes," said Brinn, and Jessica grimaced as the rest of them nodded in agreement.

Pat bobbled his head like the rest of them, but he had a secret, something he'd left out. He still wanted to find out if there was a connection between those deaths that didn't make sense—the day care shooters in Santa Cruz, and poor Vinnie at the end of his rope. It would have been hard to find out what, if any, websites those kids were visiting, but if there was any common ground between them, he would have a leg up. This could have been just as hard as finding the two runaway TKs, but thanks to the federal warrants they had access to, checking out what the boys were up to online before they died would be a snap. *Not to mention, I'll have been right all along about them being able to do things to people over a modem.*

Pat had never played sports, had been bullied most of his life, so had never realized he had a competitive streak that was a mile wide. Now it was coming to life, and in the search for Darryl and Terry, he was playing in his first big game.

Chapter 33

The first tornado touched down an hour so east of Des Moines, less than fifty miles from where Darryl and Terry were sleeping, with subsequent ones getting closer by the second. Darryl wanted to wait as long as possible to leave, and Terry just wanted to hide in the room, but when the air raid siren could be heard over the whipping wind, Darryl decided that it was time to be done with Iowa. He gave Terry a nudge with his foot at the same time that he did with his mind, and minutes later the pair of them walked to the door.

Outside, they could hear the wind rattling everything that wasn't nailed down. When Terry turned the doorknob, the door slammed into him as though someone enormous had heaved his shoulder into it from the other side.

The truck was bouncing on its suspension in its parking spot just outside the door as the wind buffeted it up and down, and when Darryl started running to it without thinking, as he cleared the building's edge the wind threw him into the air and dropped him onto the hood of the truck. Darryl could feel the wind grabbing him like it full intended to toss him again, and then heavy hands were yanking his shirt and pulling him to the ground. Darryl rolled over to see Terry screaming something into his face, and though it was impossible to hear the words, Darryl knew what he was saying: if they were really going to do this, it was time to leave.

Darryl stood, and the two of them fought with the door of the truck, before both piling into the passenger side. Darryl sneezed a mixture of blood and dirt, spattering the windshield, and then stuck the key in the ignition and gave it a twist.

"Where are we going?" Terry asked as Darryl threw the truck into reverse and stomped the gas pedal.

"East," said Darryl. He had no destination in mind, but their first inclination when leaving Des Moines had been to go east, and he liked the idea of sticking with that.

"How do we know the storm isn't worse there?"

"We don't," said Darryl. "Besides, as best I can tell, the storm has been with us ever since we got to Mexico."

Terry grunted in agreement as Darryl pulled onto the road and gunned the gas. The storm was all around them now, pulling and twisting the truck.

After maybe half a dozen blocks, Terry pointed out the passenger window and screamed, "Dude! Over there!"

Darryl knew what he'd see. He didn't want to look, but he did anyway. Sure enough, there was a black funnel cloud tearing its way north through a field. Cows dotted the ground, and the wind was throwing them about like a spoiled child that had grown tired of "Old MacDonald." Darryl shuddered as he turned his attention back to the road, knowing nothing could be done to avoid something like that.

"We're just going to get some miles under us, and we're going to leave this fucking state in the dust," said Darryl. "We'll hit Chicago or somewhere over east, somewhere big and quiet. We'll lie low for a while, and then we'll leave the country."

Terry nodded, his eyes wide. The purple that had made up the majority of Terry's topknot had been used up on that woman at the gas station, and that wasn't a bad thing.

"I think when we get to wherever it is we're going, I might get some help," said Terry.

Darryl grunted his assent, but thought, *You don't need a doctor, Terry. You need a friend who doesn't fill your head with poison until it all but bursts.*

"We'll figure it out, Terry," said Darryl, feeling like the world's biggest piece of shit. Not only did Darryl have no intention of helping Terry figure out his problem, he had every intention of continuing to use him as a walking wastebin. *Only for a little bit longer. Only until we get somewhere we can hole up*, thought Darryl, but he didn't give himself the luxury of believing the lie.

"I'm serious, Darryl," said Terry. "I'm going to figure this out, even if that means turning myself in."

Darryl just nodded, but his mind whirled in a panic. Terry would break under questioning in an instant. The poor guy had been scrambled for years, and without Darryl to keep his shit together, he'd be about as tough as wet Kleenex.

The sky was dark over the deserted road before them as the storm raged, but the scenery was nowhere near as bleak as Darryl felt in the cab of the truck. Then the wind somehow picked up even more, rocking the truck briefly up onto two wheels, and his knuckles went white on the steering wheel. Something flew across the road, an object both big and black, and when Terry began to scream, Darryl gave him a push. It was more of a twist than a bend, and as Terry began to snore, the only sounds were the wind and his sleep.

Chapter 34

"I got a job," announced Mom as she walked into Mrs. Martin's, and they shrieked and shouted for her.

Mom was beaming as she questioned Mrs. Martin about how her daughter had been, and though Cynthia could have easily eavesdropped, she chose not to. There had been too much to learn that afternoon, too much to process to listen to the boring patter of chatty adults.

All Cynthia could think about was what Mrs. Martin had explained about her map, and about how Cynthia could make her own maps with enough experience.

"Scientists call the flying part an 'out-of-body experience,'" Mrs. Martin had explained, and she made it sound like a pretty common thing. What made weavers different, though, was that they could initiate such a feeling and then use it in concert with their other skills. Mrs. Martin had been able to mark her own map of the North Harbor Apartments after a great deal of practice.

"It cannot be rushed, dear," she said. "It's absolutely essential to mark your map correctly. There's no point in having any information on a map if it isn't correct. Entering an improperly marked space can be even more dangerous than walking in blindly."

Cynthia let the last parts of the lesson run through her mind as she gathered her things and the two chatting women wound their conversation down. She stuffed her color chart into a bag. All of those mysteries had been revealed at least, even if Mrs. Martin had avoided most of the rest of her questions. In fact, the only thing Mrs. Martin had cleared up aside from mapmaking and the colors was when Cynthia asked her if there are any bad weavers. "No," Mrs. Martin had assured her with a shake of her head, "there's no one out there like that," and Cynthia had sighed in relief.

When she and Mom had said their good-byes and opened the apartment door to leave, Cynthia could hear the sound of a guitar. Across the parking lot, she could see a smiling Patrick plucking away at a battered six-string. */ You did that / You saved him /* Mrs. Martin said in her head, and Cynthia just smiled to herself as she took the steps two at a time after her mother. Patrick definitely did look happy. Maybe Mrs. Martin was right. *Maybe I did fix him.*

If Cynthia could fix Patrick with a little help from Mrs. Martin, why couldn't she fix Dad? She had her doubts that she could convince her parents to reconcile, but if she could make it so they were both happier, that would be better for everyone involved. *I could do it, maybe even without Mrs. Martin.* Though the work would be hard, she truly believed she could. Patrick's purple lines had been a lot darker than Dad's, and he had a lot of black in there, too. Dad was in great shape by comparison. He just needed someone like her to help him. He needed a weaver.

"Don't you want to hear about my job?" Mom asked as she locked the door behind Cynthia.

"Yes," replied Cynthia dutifully. "What are you going to be doing?"

"Well, it's not the most exciting thing in the world," said Mom, but Cynthia could tell by her mannerisms and the glowing green strands coming from her head that Mom was fibbing. *She thinks it's exciting, but she knows that I'll think it sounds boring.* "I met with an old friend of mine, from high school, and she's managing a clothing store downtown. I'll start on the floor, helping ladies look for clothes, but she says the company she works for is thinking of opening another location, so there could be lots of opportunities to move up soon, assuming I can handle working with a bunch of catty women."

"It should be a lot different than the store," said Cynthia, and she knew just seconds later that it had been the wrong thing to say. Mom didn't want to think about the store or Dad, or about the little yellow house. Mom wanted the new life they had to be so good that they forgot all of those things had ever happened.

"It will be different," said Mom a few pregnant moments later. "In this case, however, different will be good. I was tired of having to deal with all of those gross guys smelling like beer all of the time."

Cynthia set her bag on the table—still the only piece of furniture in the apartment—and then walked into the bathroom and closed the door after her. She wanted to tell Mom about Patrick, to explain to her that the reason that man could play guitar was because of her, but she knew she couldn't. Cynthia flushed the toilet without going, glad for the quick break from Mom's fragility, and then washed her hands and left the bathroom.

"What do you want for dinner, Cyn?"

"You can pick. It doesn't matter to me."

Mom nodded, the same sad look on her face. "All right, I'll pick, but you're going to have to help one of these days." Cynthia had sat at the table, and Mom joined her. "It won't always be like this, Cynthia," she said. "I'll talk to Dad soon, and we'll work out a schedule. I'm sure you miss him like crazy."

Cynthia nodded, as she knew she was expected to do, but she was thinking something else entirely: *If Mom makes me go, then I might have to help him. That wouldn't be my fault.*

"Well, I can tell by the smile that sounds good to you," said Mom, "or is there something else that I'm missing? If it's a joke and it's not about me, you better share. I could use a good laugh after two days in heels."

Cynthia shook her head. "Not a joke, Mrs. Martin's dogs. They look really funny when they sleep—funny and cute."

Mom smiled. "That Mrs. Martin is a wonder. We're lucky to have such a good new friend. You make sure you listen to her, Cynthia."

Cynthia nodded. Mom had no idea.

Chapter 35

Lem Stimson leaned a cheek off of his stool and farted loudly. He let the stink ease out of his jeans and off of the plastic seat and then said to himself with some satisfaction, "That's sauerkraut and beer right there."

That Lem knew the contents of his dinner made the detection no less impressive. He would have known that smell from a stranger. His mom had been Polish and his dad German, and sauerkraut and beer were staples in the Stimson household.

While he was almost up, Lem leaned over the counter and grabbed a copy of *Guns & Ammo* off of the rack and plopped back down to give it another look. The TV was still down, the gas station was as dead as could be, and the radio had said that the storms out on the west side of the state had finally let up.

Lem didn't see the headlights pull up—he was too busy reading some quotes from Jeff Cooper and chuckling to himself—but he did hear the door ding as someone walked into the station. Lem gave the man the sort of annoyed glance he'd perfected over ten years of holding down a stool at the Amoco, but the man didn't notice, just headed straight for the pop coolers.

Lem turned back to the magazine. Pretty soon the guy would come to the counter, buy some soda and maybe some food, and then possibly make some small talk. Lem had done the dance enough to know the particulars, and if the guy wanted more than that, Lem had a .357 tucked under the counter. It had been two years since he'd pulled it, but that didn't mean he wasn't looking forward to doing it again.

The man didn't seem like he harbored any ill intentions, however, and it looked like Lem was going to have to wait for another customer before he could fulfill his wish of becoming a gas station hero all over again. Lem watched over the magazine as the guy gathered sodas in his arms, and finally a case of Miller Lite. Lem gave him another glance as the guy hesitated by the coffee machine, thinking as the man goggled at it, *Come on, man, your arms are full. If you want some joe, just set that shit down up here and let's get this over with.*

The man didn't set anything down, though. He just kept staring at the coffee, until Lem shook his head and started looking at pictures again.

When Lem looked up again to check on his customer's progress, he was startled to find the man clattering his sodas onto the counter.

"Sorry," said the man at Lem's reflexive shudder.

"No problem. Just caught me a little off guard is all. You need any gas?"

The man nodded as he threw the case of beer on the counter. "Yeah, twenty dollars on pump one."

"All right," said Lem as he turned to the machine to access the pump. The man had brown hair, average build, and looked plain as the day is long but for some reason seemed eminently familiar to Lem. "Do I know you?" Lem asked as he turned back from the pump controls.

The man shrugged and said, "I don't know, it's possible. Did you grow up in Florida?"

Lem shook his head. *Hell no, I didn't grow up in Florida.* What he said, though, was, "No, I grew up right here in the asshole between

Cedar Rapids and Illinois. I do think I know you, though. You look damn famil—" Lem nearly choked on his own spit as his eyes fell on the stack of newspapers next to the stranger's Cokes.

The picture on the front of the paper was in black and white and a little blurry, but Lem knew exactly where the resemblance came from now. The headline above the photo read, "Cop Killer."

"Just a case of mistaken identity, I suppose," said Lem, his fingers finding the gun under the counter. "Cop Killer Brought to Justice by Hero" seemed like a good fit for tomorrow's headline.

"No, I don't think so, Lem," said the customer identified in the paper as Darryl Livingston. "I think you know exactly where you know me from."

"I don't know you." Lem's fingers were wrapped around the butt of the .357, but the gun felt like it weighed a few thousand pounds. Lem was no stranger to this in a dream—the gun that just couldn't be fired—but this was a new variation. Even in his sleep the gun had never been so damn heavy.

"Sure you know me," said Darryl. "I'm the man on that newspaper. I have to admit, though, that I'm not much of a fan of that headline. It's a bit loud for the circumstances, in my opinion. I was simply trying to help a friend, and things went a little sideways." Darryl cocked his head. "Is there a problem, Lem?"

"No, and I don't know you," said Lem, still struggling to bring his damn two-ton gun to bear on the fucker. "Why don't you just gas up and get the fuck out of here? Take all that soda and beer and shit, too. Take the whole store—I don't give a fuck."

Darryl shook his head, and then Lem felt his own hand rising from under the counter, the revolver gripped in it. "Careful," said Darryl as he lifted his hands palms-up between them, laughing as he pretended to be scared. "You don't want to shoot me, do you, Lem?"

"No," said Lem, perhaps the biggest lie he'd ever told. He wanted to shoot this customer more than anything he'd ever wanted in his entire life, but he could no more point his weapon at him than fly to the moon. Worse than that, as Lem rolled his eyes down toward the gun—for some reason he couldn't turn his head now, even an inch—his hand was turning the barrel toward him. As he watched in horror, his arm rose with the pistol until it slipped out of sight at the side of his head, which was still locked in place on his neck. Lem could feel the muzzle denting his temple, but no one else was holding the gun. He was shoving it into his own head.

"Please just . . . please leave."

"I can't do that, Lem," said Darryl. "You recognized me, and besides, that truck outside is about as hot as a car can get right now. Give me your keys." Lem felt his other hand go into his pocket, pull the keys free, and then lay them on the counter. "Thanks," said Darryl as he took them off the counter. "Now make a mess."

• • •

Lem's truck was filthy with food trash and cigarette packs, reeked of body odor and tobacco, and would be easier to scrap than clean, but it wasn't connected with the death of an Iowa State Trooper. After unloading their truck into Lem's and then stashing the rental behind the service station, Darryl and Terry pulled out of the gas station and got back to moving east.

All the folks on the radio wanted to talk about was the storm. Having driven through it, Terry and Darryl couldn't blame them a bit. The death toll stood at just over a hundred, and more than three hundred homes had been destroyed. It was odd. Hearing this put a lump in Darryl's throat. Even though the storm had nothing to do with him—his powers didn't rise to *that* level—he felt a little guilty over it. After all, they never could have gotten away without the insane weather.

Darryl was smiling as they crossed the state border into Illinois, and when he looked at Terry he could see that his friend was grinning ear to ear.

"Not out of the fire just yet," said Darryl, "but a good sight better off than we were two days ago."

Terry nodded. Des Moines had been bad, and leaving had been worse, but there was no disputing that getting free of Iowa felt fucking fantastic.

"What are we going to do now?" Terry asked, and Darryl took a moment to answer him.

"I've been thinking we might head to Chicago, but now I wonder if that's just what they'll expect us to do," said Darryl. "So instead, I'd like to head north of the city and get into Wisconsin. I read about this years earlier. I have no clue if it even still runs, but there's supposed to be a big-ass car ferry that motors across Lake Michigan. We can hit that, cross the lake, and then be in Canada a few hours earlier than we would be otherwise. Worst case, the ferry's closed and we just keep working north. It'll take longer, but the same eventual end."

"What about when we get to Canada?"

"We ditch the truck and go to ground," said Darryl, "though hopefully not for long. I have no intention of spending any more time there than I need to in order to bleed off some of this heat. As soon as we can, we're going to a sunny, warm island or something. Somewhere with beaches, white sand visible in the window, you know?"

"I won't fuck it up this time," said Terry, and Darryl nodded, knowing in his heart that it was true. *I know you won't*, thought Darryl, *but either way I'm going to have to kill you.* He didn't like killing and liked the idea of killing Terry even less, but his patience had been worn thin. Killing that cop might not have been Terry's fault, not exactly, but there was no denying the man had an itch, and when it didn't get scratched it was impossible to know what might happen.

"I know you won't fuck it up," said Darryl, aloud this time. "It's going to be smooth sailing from here on out. I'll drive until dusk, we'll get a hotel room, and then we'll do it all over again tomorrow. Does that sound good to you?"

"Yeah, it sounds great," said Terry as he turned to the window.

Glancing at his friend, Darryl felt his eyes drawn to Terry's topknot. Terry was all green, blue, and yellow now. No signs of any impending violence. But Darryl knew that was just a matter of time, just like it had always been ever since he'd begun using his friend like a psychic garbage can.

Sorry, Terry, but we're only going to be buying one plane ticket this time.

Darryl flipped on the radio, and "Livin' la Vida Loca" roared up. Twisting the dial with a grimace, Darryl smiled as the familiar sounds of Bob Seger came pouring through the speakers. He began to drum his thumbs on the wheel, the smile sticking. None of it had gone perfectly, but they were still alive and free.

Chapter 36

"I need a word," said Pat, and Jessica turned toward him in the hallway. Pat felt stuck, his tongue lodged against the bottom of his mouth as though it had been glued there, and he felt certain he was going to stand in the hall staring at her until she eventually walked away. But Jessica just smiled at him warmly, and Pat was able to swallow and say, "I have a hunch that I need to play out."

"I'm all for a hunch, as long as it's low risk for the TRC and has at least a chance of getting us somewhere," said Jessica. "Does this have to do with your IP thing?"

"IP address search—and yes," said Pat. "There have been two cases in the last little bit that have stuck out to me. The first one was a teenager from St. Louis named Vincent Taggio who liquidated his dad's and his dad's mob buddies' Grand Cayman bank accounts, and the other is a pair of brothers named Tom and Henry Nichols. They shot up—"

"A day care in Santa Cruz. Am I right?"

"Yes, they killed a bunch of people in Santa Cruz after offing their parents," said Pat. "No motive, at least not from what I could find. The press went nuts over the shooting—no surprise there. But I wonder if there wasn't more to it."

"More meaning a TK?"

"Yes, exactly."

"Here's the thing, Pat," said Jessica. "You've got a great lead on these two guys, and I need you focused on that. It would be great to bring this thing down and solve some collateral stuff at the same time, but I think you might be overreaching. It will be a very big deal if we can bring Darryl and Terry in unharmed, OK?"

"If I'm right, it's going to make it a lot easier to get them."

"How so? Make me understand."

"All right, I'll try," said Pat. "First off, this is about as unscientific as it gets. Since that's out of the way, the baseline is that I think these guys have been accosting kids on the Internet, using them and then destroying them so there's no evidence."

"Keep going."

"The Taggio kid made half a million disappear, but half a million bucks fell off the face of the earth, and I really doubt it's coming back anytime soon. I think Darryl or Terry or both of them met him online in a chat room, did their TK shit, and told him exactly what to do and how to do it, then put him down like a sick dog."

"There's a problem with that," said Jessica. "TK stuff doesn't work over a phone line. No exceptions, even with really powerful folks."

"Yes, I know. You told us that," said Pat, "and I believe you, but what if an Internet connection is somehow different? I hate talking on the phone—like, hate it, even when someone I want to talk to calls. On the Internet, though, it's different. I can talk to complete strangers for hours at a time and feel like we could go hang out in real life without a hitch. What if it's not the physical connection that stops TKs from working over the phone, but the—I don't know . . . the *emotional* connection? Because I swear, the connection in the wall may be the same as with a phone, but it's way more personal online, even with all of the anonymity."

Jessica clearly wasn't happy about what she was hearing, but she really did appear to be listening to him. After just staring at him for a minute, she said, "I'm not saying I'm buying any of this, but OK, I do want to see where you're going. Let's say you're right. Why does he send those two kids on a rampage?"

"Look at the dates," said Pat. "Those kids killed all of those people the day after Darryl and Terry flew into Des Moines. My theory is that our two runaways wanted a distraction, and they figured that one in Des Moines itself might just bring more heat down, so they thought outside of the box. Assuming I'm right, we even know the idea worked. They are out of Des Moines, after all."

Jessica wasn't buying. "They are, but that doesn't prove anything. There are a lot of other ways they could have bought some time, and even just a little bit of face-to-face manipulation can pay huge dividends for guys like this."

"Agreed. This is a stretch, but like I said, a hunch," said Pat, tapping the side of his head.

"A stretch is an understatement," said Jessica. "Tell me what you'd need to follow up on this."

"I need a warrant served so that I can see if those kids were online before they died, and if they were, the very last public communications space that they were using."

And like that, he was back in the game. He'd gone from feeling like he was just trying to stay afloat, fighting to convince this woman that his idea had merit, to feeling right back in the thick of it. He was pitching a no-hitter in those stupid baseball games Dad had insisted on, scoring a hat trick in hockey, running back a kickoff for a touchdown, but all in his world.

But then she took another step back. "You really think this could happen through a modem?"

"I don't know, and neither do you," said Pat. "What I do know is that if I can prove that those boys were chatting in the same place, I should be able to get a lockdown on Darryl and Terry. Not an IP address, but something almost as good. If they're feeding on children and we can figure out where they're doing it, we can set them up."

"Done," said Jessica. "I'll put in the order. Now get back to work."

Pat couldn't suppress a grin as he shook her hand before returning to the rest of the researchers, but the surprising part was that Jessica was grinning, too.

Chapter 37

Cynthia floated over North Harbor Apartments with Mrs. Martin.
They were studying the map, and though there were no plans to go
anywhere or try to help any of the other residents, Cynthia still found
the bizarre place in the clouds to be incredibly invigorating. / *Any place
can be like this with enough practice / Any place, Cynthia* / Cynthia felt
a ripple across her face that would have been a smile if she were in her
skin. She didn't know how she could make a map like this, but she
certainly liked the idea of it.

The school first and then Dad's store. Cynthia wasn't sure what she
would do with maps of those two places, but she had some ideas, like
influencing teachers to skip tests, or making Mom and Dad push past
their petty differences. Her mind was drifting on in this direction when
she felt the air run through her hair and then locked onto an unfamiliar
car as it pulled into the lot. Cynthia had no intention of seeing who
was in it, not at first, and then she noticed a red cloud dragging just
after it. / *NO* / said Mrs. Martin in Cynthia's head, but Cynthia was
already there, locked on to the car before dragging herself inside of it.

Three young men sat in the aging sedan as it rolled into the North
Harbor parking lot—two in the front and one in the back—and on

the floor of the backseat there were three baseball bats and a shotgun. Along with the crowd of red strands, there were also a number of purple and pink. Mrs. Martin had been clear about the colors and their meanings: red was anger but did not mean violence; purple was unpredictability, the fight-or-flight instinct tearing at the person it was attached to; and pink was fear, cold, ugly, and inescapable for a person caught in its throes. Cynthia didn't have the years or cynicism to predict what the men in the car were up to, but she knew instinctively that nothing good was going to happen when they got to their destination.

Cynthia stayed with the car as it drove through the lot and parked. The men inside of it were nervous but trying to act tough and brave. The man in the back handed up ball bats from the floor at his feet to the others, then grabbed one for himself. Then the one behind the wheel said, "Grab that shotgun."

The one sitting next to him shook his head as the man in the backseat grabbed it. "No, don't be getting that into this shit. We've got a bad enough situation as it is. Adding a gun won't be doing any of us any favors."

The driver looked frustrated, but Cynthia could see the pink strands in his hair fluttering, and she could read his thoughts as clearly as a book: / *No guns, good* / *Last thing I need is to go to prison* / *The kids need me* /

Cynthia watched as the three of them left the car, and then she drifted through after them, the car's steel frame no more a barrier than the air outside. She watched them walk up to an apartment door, number 217, and she watched as the kid from the backseat rapped on the door with gloved knuckles. The three of them stood there like that for an eternity, bats held behind their backs as they waited for the door to open, but finally it cracked and a face appeared in the slit.

"Can I help you?" the man behind the door asked, and then the three of them barged in, throwing the door open and knocking the man to the ground.

"We need to have a talk about your loan," said the driver, but then Cynthia was seized by another voice.

/ *Now. Take them now / Take the driver and the man who lives here / Take them now /*

Cynthia did as she was told, and all four of the men froze as if they'd been paused by some cosmic remote. Mrs. Martin was nowhere to be seen, but Cynthia could feel her in the room, could see the threads she was sending filling the room. As instructed, Cynthia had her hooks in the driver and the man who lived in the apartment, and now she sent yellow threads to intertwine with their pink and red plumes. Mrs. Martin was doing the same with the other two men, and Cynthia watched as three bats fell to the floor next to their terrified neighbor.

Cynthia could read everything from the man from North Harbor. He owed money from gambling and bad loans, he was a thief, he was depressed, and he had no one and nothing keeping him in Grand Rapids. *Go*, Cynthia implored him. *Go and never look back.* The man did as he was told just like that, never even pausing to marvel at what was happening in his apartment. The other three remained frozen, and Cynthia could hear a humming noise as Mrs. Martin told them to stay still, that soon this would be over, and they could tell the man they worked for that the person who owed him a debt was gone. Cynthia shared the same thing with her captive, too, but she also soothed him with thoughts of his children, telling him, *You need to be careful for them. No one else is.*

Finally, Cynthia and Mrs. Martin let go of the men and then winked out of the apartment. The last thing Cynthia saw of them was the third man reaching for his fallen bat and then tumbling to the floor in a heap, then all of them falling like puppets who had their strings cut. Cynthia's next sight was of Mrs. Martin sitting across from her in Mrs. Martin's apartment. One of the dogs was barking, and Cynthia yawned.

"I'll get us some water."

Cynthia stood, and Mrs. Martin smiled as she walked to the kitchen, then returned with two full glasses of water for them.

"That was very brave of you," said Mrs. Martin after she'd taken a sip from her glass. "Very brave, but perhaps not very smart."

Cynthia frowned as she drank from her own water, then set the tumbler in front of her on the table. "They were going to hurt that man," she said. "They were going to hurt him, and they thought that was the right thing to do. That's not OK at all."

Mrs. Martin shook her head sadly. "No, it's not, is it? Still, that was their job, nothing more, and tomorrow they'll catch a little sparrow that won't be lucky enough to have us on hand to help him out." Mrs. Martin smiled a sad smile. "Perhaps they won't even wait until tomorrow. Scared young men are more apt to do something dangerous than just about any other fool, in my opinion, regardless of how scared they may be."

"Well, even if they do hurt someone else, at least we could help that guy," said Cynthia. "He was so scared, and he has no one."

"He had very little," agreed Mrs. Martin, "but now he has even less. Whatever price he might have paid today, he still would have been himself. Now, the rest of his life will be spent looking over his shoulder to make sure those men aren't after him, angrier than ever from all of the searching."

Cynthia felt her face flush. "I was just trying to help so that he wouldn't get hurt."

"And that is a very noble thing to want to do, my dear," said Mrs. Martin. "Eventually you will learn to pick your battles. We have neither the time nor right to save everyone in need of help, and by helping people who wouldn't help themselves we miss out on the chance to help those who need our help the most. Do you understand what I mean?"

Cynthia nodded. She did understand. "It would be like helping someone who could swim get out of the water while someone else drowns, right?"

"Exactly," said Mrs. Martin with a curt nod. "Now, your mother will be here soon. I want you to tell me in detail why you decided you needed to do something about that particular car, all right?"

"I'll try."

Chapter 38

1945

The world is telling me that Katarina's words about needing to run and hide are prophetic. The Allied planes bomb everywhere except within the walls of the camp. There is no way to know if this is a coincidence or if they have some knowledge that we're down here praying for rescue, but it could end up not mattering either way. One errant bomb might do in an instant what takes the Nazis a week, and maybe that would be the best for all of us.

Edna Greenberg's last moments have left me haunted. The final images she saw are what I see when I go to bed at night, and they are there when I wake. Only Katarina can help with this, but even her touch can only do so much, and I am left to suffer through most of these memories by myself. I was never the type of girl to believe in ghosts or spirits before my time in the camp, but now I know they are real. There is far too much evidence, far too much pain just hanging in the wind here. Ghosts may not exist as they did in old pictures, but they are very, very real. About that I have no doubt.

Katarina is gone all the time these days. Her work in the camp—whatever it is—has been stealing her freedom. I check in on her while she's busy from time to time, looping into the sky over my much-improved map and then spying on her and watching what she does from afar. I've considered getting closer, jumping in behind the eyes of the commandant, who's usually with her, but I'm too afraid to actually take that step. If I find out what Katarina's real job at the camp is or she catches me spying on her, she might throw me in the showers herself.

One thing in the camp is as sure as the fact that the bombers will be back tomorrow, and that is the selections will happen every day. I'm not sure when they started, not precisely, but I can hear the explosions through the walls of this little room. What I haven't done is take to the sky when the selection itself is taking place, for fear of being sucked into someone the way I was into Edna Greenberg. The last thing I need is another ghost haunting my thoughts, and I know that's all that will happen if I go into one of them. Some secrets need to stay that way, but there are so many stories that are going to be lost in the rubble of this war. No one who lives through this will know what the final moments were like for people like Edna, just like how no one who isn't here will ever understand what these camps are really like.

Not that I have any right to complain. If anything, I'm part of the problem. I could be the curator of all of these memories, and if I do manage to escape and survive, could write a book detailing all of the things that people shared with the blind girl. Writing about all of this would be the brave thing to do, the good thing, and the book would serve as another reminder to the world of why this should never be allowed to happen again, but I cannot do it. It would be too much like stealing, like another betrayal of my people, but of course there's a more selfish reason. I can't bear the thought of what I might see.

Crossing the room to pour myself a cup of coffee, I jump at the sound of an explosion. Diving under the table—a useless safety measure, but one that I cannot help—I realize that I cannot hear the airplanes. The planes are always audible before an air raid, but today there was no warning. How could that be?

There is no noise of planes because there are no planes. The thought is a slap in the face, and then there is another explosion, just as close as the last one, and that noise is followed by machine-gun fire. The shooting is a much quieter noise than the roaring thunder of the artillery that I have only just realized I'm hearing, and it is now that I understand that the greatest fear of the guards has come true. The fighting has come to Dachau. Soon we will be free, and that means Katarina and I must leave this place.

Chapter 39

1999

Both Terry and Darryl were shocked into silence by their first sight of the SS *Badger*. The thing was enormous, her back half-open to accept cars into her gaping maw. Built to continue US Route 10 across Lake Michigan, she looked her age. The *Badger* had been finished in 1953, originally for use as a railcar ferry, then converted to carry cars and their owners. Now she was a massive hybrid of old and new, her old steamship lines interrupted by the radar and radio gear piled atop her tower.

There was no issue with boarding the *Badger*. Darryl had initially balked at the nearly five hundred dollars to get them across the lake, and then he took money from a roll of cash and paid the man at the ticket window. They left the truck with a valet and then boarded the ship with a group of other passengers. Darryl and Terry exchanged a sideways glance as they made their way to the upper decks. The ship was huge, and neither of them was sure of where they wanted to go.

"There's a movie theater according to that sign," said Terry. "There's a bar, too." He grinned at Darryl. "Might be nice to knock a couple off and relax, don't you think?"

Darryl did think so. It had been days since he'd had so much as a beer, and they'd been some of the most stressful times of his entire life. A cocktail or three didn't just sound good, it sounded perfect, but it was not to be—not yet.

"Let's go watch a movie and maybe catch a couple winks."

"You don't want to hit the bar? Come on, man," pleaded Terry.

"A movie," said Darryl. "We'll watch a movie and maybe fall asleep." He didn't want to tell Terry that he agreed, a drink sounded perfect. It had been well earned, and there would be precious few moments for him to relax when they hit the shore and found a place to live. That was the biggest problem with needing to bend at a moment's notice. He had to always be on, and there was no middle ground.

"Fine," said Terry in a wounded tone. "Let's go watch your movie."

The hours on the boat burned by slowly. Even with all of the amenities on the SS *Badger*, Darryl and Terry were bored. They were road weary and had no bed to look forward to, no home to pine for. There would be a hotel and then another one and probably others after that before they eventually found a permanent place to stay. That wouldn't be stateside, though. It could take months to get the paperwork together and to let a few new faces fill the top of the "Wanted" flyers that littered police stations.

Cheers erupting from the upper deck called Terry and Darryl to the top of the ship, where a group of twentysomethings were shouting and drinking beer. Terry pointed past the kids to where the shore was visible and growing by the second.

"Thank fucking God," said Darryl. "Let me off this bucket and into a hotel room."

"You and me both, brother." The pair watched the line on the horizon grow thicker and blacker and then begin to be filled with details.

Voices over the loudspeaker told guests to prepare to disembark and where to find their cars, but Darryl was ignoring all of it. There was a man on the deck with them, standing by the door about twenty feet away, and from the look of him he was a cop or at least ex–law enforcement of some stripe. Even with the hard lumps visible at his waist, though, the man was but one concern as the ship neared shore.

"Oh fuck," said Terry, and Darryl just grinned in the sunlight. The dock was littered with police, and there was going to be no way to get through it without some contact. "Do you think—" Terry began, but Darryl cut him off with a wave of his hand. Before Darryl could speak, though, the man behind him spoke up.

"Just have a seat," he said.

Darryl turned to see a gun in his hand, pointed their way. "Just have a seat. No one wants anyone to get hurt."

Darryl grimaced as Terry took a seat, all but admitting his guilt to this asshole. *So fucking close.*

"Is there a problem?" Darryl asked, and the man grinned at him.

"You bet your fucking ass there is. Now sit, before I make you."

Chapter 40

Pat's hands were shaking as he opened the e-mail. It wasn't his first eyes-only document, though the thrill of seeing what would have been forbidden goods was still fresh for him. It was especially intense at this moment, as he knew this was something special, the linchpin of his scheme to catch Darryl and Terry. The e-mail was going to confirm what sort of websites the dead boys from California and St. Louis had been hooked into. Pat knew in his gut that he was right, but still he couldn't bring himself to open the electronic document. Around him he could hear his friends—some of the best friends he'd ever had—but they were competitors, too. This was his chance to separate himself. If he was wrong about this, he'd tumble back into the background, and one of them would be the one who figured out where Darryl and Terry were headed next.

When Pat finally opened the stupid thing, the words were sparse but gave him at least hints of the news he craved. They confirmed that computers in both homes had recently posted on video game chat rooms, the dead boys no doubt looking for hints for popular games— likely some of the same games Pat enjoyed and the same chat rooms he himself had used to decipher their mysteries. The boys had both used

AOL chat to talk to Darryl or Terry—Pat was sure of that—but the rest of the details were muddled.

With time and resources, Pat could probably comb the site until he unearthed the name Darryl or Terry used in the chat rooms, but he had neither. And besides, Pat needed the men themselves, live online, not merely the name. *We need a sting.* Get someone who could safely be used by Darryl or Terry and then track down the pair of criminals via their IP address. It would be easy enough to pull off. These guys would be drawn back to the chats like crack addicts, if Pat was right about their MO, and he was more and more certain he was. But could a TK ever be fooled by such a ruse?

That was a problem above his pay grade, he knew. He could crunch data and troll websites, looking for footprints left by people who fit the parameters given to them by Jessica, but he couldn't be expected to orchestrate a sting operation against a pair of jet-setting telekinetic murderers. Pat stood, garnering a look from Brinn next to him, and then walked to the phone on the far wall to call Jessica. Ten minutes later she was downstairs and the five of them gathered amongst the desks and computers.

"Spit it out," said Jessica, and Pat nodded.

"My hunch paid off."

"What does that mean?" Brinn asked.

"I had Jessica get me a federal warrant to track the final web activity of those kids—the suicide and the day care shooters," said Pat, feeling his face flush. Brinn nodded, but he could tell she was frustrated that the lead she'd told him to ignore had paid off in some way or another. "The warrant revealed that at least one of the boys that shot up that day care was in a video game chat room just before the cops say he went off his nut, and Vinnie was doing the same thing, right up until he decided to rip off his dad."

"Holy shit," said Geoff.

"That's still not proof of anything, though," said Brinn. "Young boys like video games—hell, I like video games—but that doesn't mean some TK has been in my head."

"And there's still no proof it's even possible for one to do so," said Jessica. "What do you think we should do with this information, Pat?"

Pat was having a hard time breathing. His anxiety was reaching levels he hadn't felt since spilling his milk down the front of his shirt in high school, but he knew he was right.

"We need a sting," he said. This was met with skeptical looks all around, but he didn't care. It wasn't just a hunch anymore. This was the way in. "We need a presence in these forums, some kid flashing money around like an idiot. We need a kid who can fool Darryl or Terry. A special kid. If they're really controlling people over wires, we need someone who can feed them this shit back and make them believe it. Once we get an IP location, we can nail down their real location and send in whatever cops you call for a job like this."

"Not cops," said Jessica. "Cops can only manage the fringe for something like this." She shook her head. "I know a person we can use to work them, a TK, but I'll need you to be the face of the op, Pat. This TK knows nothing about the Internet. He can do all of the head bending we need to fool these guys, but the Internet stuff won't be possible for him."

"So you want me to let a TK into my head?" Pat asked, the idea horrifying beyond measure.

"No, man," said Rick, flashing an evil grin. "She wants to let *two* TKs in."

"Possibly three," said Geoff. He was enjoying himself, too.

"Holy shit," said Pat, the whole weight of what Jessica was asking crashing down on him. *She wants to let them go to war in my head, and if anything goes wrong I'll be a vegetable or worse.* "I don't know—"

"You'll be fine," said Jessica. "I just need to make this OK with the TK, set up a lab for you a few floors lower, and then we can start fishing. It shouldn't take more than a day or two to put into place. We just need to get the TK to say that he'll help, and the rest of it will fall in line."

"I seriously want to help," said Pat, "but I'm not sure I'm cut out for this. I'm just a computer guy. There has to be some badass cop who knows about computers that could do it, or maybe we could just teach the TK the basics of computer stuff. It's not that hard—I mean, we all learned it, and so have a lot of other people."

"The TK we're going to use has been in service for almost fifty years," said Jessica, "and if I had badass officers who knew as much about computers as you guys do, then I never would have had to get the four of you security clearance and a paycheck. No, Pat. This is your baby, and unless someone else wants to volunteer, you're going to need to own it."

"Just accept it, dude," said Geoff. "We've all got your back. It's going to be fine."

"Truly," said Rick, and Brinn nodded. "It's all good."

Pat didn't know where in the fuck they got all their confidence, but he couldn't figure out any other way to push back. This was going to happen.

"Excellent," said Jessica, getting to her feet. "You three keep up the therapy session, and I'll be back in an hour or two." As she made the doorway, the phone on her belt began to buzz. Jessica grabbed it, checked the number, then stuck it to her ear. "Hockstetter." She paused. "You're shitting me. Is this confirmed? One hundred percent?"

Pat felt the lump in his throat rising as he and the other specialists exchanged *What the fuck?* looks. Whatever this was was big—maybe big enough to make Pat's chat room sleuthing beside the point.

"No one moves until I say the word," said Jessica. "No, I am serious. I don't care! Listen to me, I'll be in a bird in fifteen minutes, and I should be there right when they're pulling in. No, make them wait. This is my gig now. This is federal." She paused again, mimicked throwing the phone, then stuck it back to her ear, shouted, "So get your balls out and handle this!" and hung up the phone.

"What's going on?" Brinn asked.

Jessica called back to them as she ran from the room. "They're being held by an undercover officer on some Wisconsin-to-Michigan ferry," said Jessica. "I need to be there when they disembark so the shit doesn't hit the fan."

Jessica was gone then, her fingers punching at the phone in her hand.

"Looks like you got lucky, dude," said Rick as he smacked Pat in the arm, but Pat didn't notice the punch or the comment. Freaked out as he'd been by his planned role in their scheme, now that it had been yanked away from him he understood how missing the biggest game of your life would feel.

• • •

Jessica had been right. Only fifteen minutes after hanging up the phone with the Grand Rapids, Michigan, FBI office, she was in the air and on the way to Ludington, Michigan, where the SS *Badger* was to dock. Aside from the flight crew, she was alone in the plane, and she was shaking with anticipation. This was the real deal, the first capture in a very long time, and she was heading the operation. She was going to save the TRC.

Don't get ahead of yourself. The fish isn't in the boat yet, Jessica warned herself, but it was hard not to be optimistic. She was flying, inside and out, even though after all she'd done—heading the operation from the start, putting all the machinery in place, prepping to perform one of the most spectacularly audacious stunts in TRC history to see the capture through—none of it had mattered. The old policy of sitting and waiting had yielded better results than her team of hackers and hundreds of thousands of dollars, but none of that mattered. This was still her success, and besides, what her team had learned could only help apprehending TKs in the future. *Especially if Pat's theories are right,* thought Jessica, which, the more she thought about it, seemed pretty likely.

Jessica felt the gun in her jacket. A weapon was a no-no for a normal agent looking to catch a TK, who was certain to turn both it and the agent carrying it to his own uses, but it was a perfectly acceptable risk for a reverse-mute like her. Still, she doubted she'd need it. With no room to run, Terry and Darryl would see the combined police force waiting for them and fold right up. All the officers needed to do was hold their fire, maintain good cover until the arrival of trained TK handlers, and make sure all the civilians ashore were removed in case of a firefight. Should events spin in that direction, time was all that would be needed: Darryl and Terry would run out of ammo and be caught by Jessica and her team, and that would be that.

The cop who called this in was dead, or would be soon. That the cop would die, along with most everyone on the boat, was a foregone conclusion with a TK who hadn't been isolated and contained. If Jessica could magically cuff the men and slap Tesla Helmets on them for transport to the TRC, she would. In a slightly less magical world, she would have them drugged and on a plane. In this case, though, according to her FBI contact, she had Darryl and Terry on a boat with a single cop's gun at their heads. Had the cop been trained, he would have called them in and done nothing, let a team that knew how to deal with this wait until the two men were in the middle of nowhere. None of this was the case, however. What she needed to concentrate on was retrieving a living TK. *All you need is one of them to survive long enough to get patched up.* Still, staring out the window, Jessica couldn't help but feel a little bad that things were going to come crashing down for so many people.

Jessica forced her eyes from the window and down to her watch. They'd be hitting the tarmac in Ludington in less than two hours, and she was already going over what she was going to say to the two men, how she was going to begin the process of breaking them. These might be the flyover states beneath her, but what she made happen down there would impact the whole country. TKs were among the most important resources in the entire world, and right now the United States government was the only one that could verify that TKs even existed. Already looking past the death and destruction the next few hours were sure to bring, Jessica smiled to herself. She had done it.

Chapter 41

Cynthia colored while her mother talked on the phone. Mom was talking to Aunt Laura, who lived in Texas, and from the sound of it, they were both pretty fired up about divorce. Cynthia did what she could to ignore most of it, though. If she wanted to know what secrets Mom was holding, she could easily poke around and just find out. Cynthia didn't want to know, however. She still wanted Mom and Dad to make things right, and she wanted to move back into the yellow house. She hadn't seen Dad in over a week, and she missed her friends as well. Aside from Mrs. Martin, North Harbor wasn't much fun, and even her time with Mrs. Martin had begun to feel more like school than just playing.

Cynthia sketched a little girl with a rainbow flowing from the top of her head. The girl in the drawing had far more colors than were listed on Cynthia's chart and a much busier root of threads than she'd seen on a real person, but she was connected to at least fifty stick figures, which were surrounding her. After Cynthia had taken over the two men, she hadn't told Mrs. Martin just how easy it had been. She was quite sure she could have easily handled all four of them on her own and maybe even more. Even though she was very young, Cynthia knew what a great power that must be. Mrs. Martin had needed her to take two of them, because two was the most her teacher had wanted to handle at one time.

Cynthia drew a full spectrum of colors coming from the girl on the page, with different color sequences connecting to the heads of the little people in her drawing. Mrs. Martin had told her about red, purple, blue, green, pink, and yellow. She hadn't told her young student about black, not exactly, but Cynthia knew what black meant without being told. That was obvious from what happened when she tried to manipulate the black threads over Patrick. They were too ruined to fix. Once they were black, they were dead. Cynthia had a feeling that if she was to see a dead body, like when she'd gone to her great-grandmother's funeral and there was an open casket, she would see a smattering of black threads coming from it.

"I didn't want to at first," said Mom from the kitchen, still ranting to her sister. "Yeah, I know. Now I get it. I do. When you told me about Nick, I said I thought it was ridiculous, but now I know better." Mom paused, listening to Aunt Laura, and then replied, "Exactly. Exactly. I was wrong, and we both know it. I was a judgmental bitch, and I should have listened to my sister."

Cynthia drew another stick figure, but this one she connected with just black threads to the girl at the center of the page.

"Well," said Mom, getting louder now, "that's what I'm going to do. He wanted to have fun, and now I'm going to take him to the goddamn cleaners. Eye for an eye, if you ask me. I mean, we bought that business together! If I'm going to be fighting for scraps in the world, then I'm going to get what I worked half my life for." Mom paused, and Cynthia picked another stick figure at random and colored over its lines, switching them from pink and blue to black. She smiled at her work and then heard Mom say, "He'll figure it out, you know? That's what men do—they figure stuff out, like how to keep a piece of ass on the side. Now I'll give him something else to figure out. It's called,

'Give me all of your money.' If I'm lucky, he'll talk to a lawyer, realize he doesn't have a leg to stand on, and we can just work everything out in family court." Mom sighed. "That would be the best for everyone involved. I mean, think of Cynthia. If he cares about her at all, he'll agree that this is what's best."

Cynthia slowly slid her crayons back into the box, then slid the black one halfway out. She knew that neither Mom nor Dad had her abilities, knew they weren't weavers in the same way that Mrs. Martin had known she was the second they met. She stared at the box of crayons, stared at her drawing, and then took the black crayon the rest of the way out of the box and got to drawing. When she was done, all of the little stick figures were connected to the girl in the middle, but now all of their threads were black. She understood things she never should have, and she knew if she looked at Mom she'd see threads of blue, red, yellow, and purple. Cynthia drew and drew and drew, and when she was done, the only color on the page was black.

Chapter 42

"I said take a fucking seat," said the man with the gun, the badge at his waist now visible, and it took only a glance around the deck for Darryl to see that everyone but him and the cop were sitting. "I'm serious, asshole. Take a fucking seat, and get your fucking hands in thggggnnnnnnnhhh—"

The cop dropped like he'd been hit in the head with a hammer, the gun clattering to the ship's upper deck and away from him, and then the cop was shaking like an unmedicated epileptic moments after smelling sour oranges. Darryl hit him again, hard, before walking to the pistol and picking it up.

"Come on, Terry," said Darryl as he stepped over the prone cop. Darryl considered the gun, his finger flexing on the semiauto's trigger, then tossed it back to the deck and hit the cop again.

"Holy shit," said one of the kids behind them.

"I said fucking come on."

Terry stood—Darryl knew it without looking back at him—and the pair of them walked to the door and slid down the steps to the next deck. Here, people were milling about and preparing to dock, oblivious to the mess above them, while Darryl and Terry were gliding through the crowd like a hot knife through butter.

"What the fuck are we going to do, Darryl?" Terry asked as they moved to the next staircase.

"Whatever we have to."

They moved past a large window. Inside, this floor was packed with young kids and their tired parents, and Darryl focused on a young mother near the back of the boat, sitting next to a sleeping baby in a stroller. He hit her as hard as he'd hit the cop, as hard as he'd ever bent anyone, and then grabbed the stroller. Terry shook his head while he and Darryl slipped away with the baby and the mother fell from her seat.

"What the fuck are you doing?" Terry asked as they moved back to the stairs they'd just come down, but Darryl said nothing in return. Terry already knew, and there was no reason to waste his breath on the words. Darryl hauled stroller and baby both up the stairs.

The voice over the loudspeaker returned as Darryl hurriedly pushed the stroller toward the bow of the boat. He handed off the stroller to Terry by shoving it in front of him and letting go. As Terry scrambled after it, Darryl could hear a humming noise as the ship approached the dock and could see police stationed by their cars, ready for them. Darryl took a deep breath and then was in the air above the ship, then descending to hover over the cop he'd left twitching on the deck. The man had settled down, was lying peaceably with a small crowd around him, and Darryl dove into him. One of his eyes was closed, most likely to never open again, and the cop was breathing harder than Darryl would have liked. Touching the wounded man with every bit of his skill, Darryl made the cop sit up.

The younger people gave the cop a wide berth as he stood up, the closest of them saying, "You better stay down, man. You don't look so good."

In answer, Darryl lurched the cop forward and used him to retrieve the pistol from the deck. The young man who had spoken gave him a puzzled look, and then Darryl made the cop raise the gun, point it at the kid, and pull the trigger. Darryl watched through the cop's working eye as the kid dropped and the rest of the people on the top deck began to scream. Darryl made the cop lurch forward, then raise the gun again and shoot a pretty woman in the chest. This time Darryl didn't watch her drop. He picked the next target, a man wearing a "Big Johnson" shirt with his arms outstretched as though to fend off the suddenly murderous zombie-cop. Darryl pulled the trigger again and shot the man just below the obnoxious design on his shirt, and he folded like an accordion as he fell.

Letting the rest of them run around him, Darryl made the cop walk to the end of the bow and then had him empty the pistol into the cops waiting on the dock. Darryl wasn't even making the cop aim, just emptying the gun as fast as possible, and it had the desired effect. The boat was full of screaming and running passengers, and the cops on the dock had their heads down. Darryl checked the cop's waist for extra magazines and found two in a discreet leather holster on the left side of his body. Darryl fumbled with one of the magazines when the *Badger* bumped into the dock, and then he stumbled backwards as a rifle round punched a hole in the cop's left shoulder.

Darryl could hear Terry yelling while he worked one-handed to reload the gun, but he was forced to flush his friend's voice from his mind. The cop was going to die soon—Darryl could feel it, even without the blood running down his side—and as he slid the new magazine in he stood and fired on the closest police officers. The cops ducked again, and then another pair of rifle shots cracked by him, both of them missing. Darryl felt a tug, almost as if Terry were trying to knock him loose from the cop, and he could feel his actual body moving on the boat.

Looking through the battered and bloodied cop's eyes, Darryl could see a flood of people on the boat running past the police barricade that had been erected to control the situation. Not seeing Terry or himself, Darryl fired into the crowd of people rushing from the *Badger*, fighting their way off the boat in a frenzy. Darryl dropped the new magazine from the gun and was reaching across the cop's body for the last spare when he was hit by a deluge of gunfire. Darryl fell backwards onto the *Badger*'s deck, then roared up above the boat, before plunging into his body.

"Fuck, thank God," said Terry as Darryl's wits came back, and Darryl saw that they were off of the boat and Terry had him pinned between himself and the stroller.

Cops were everywhere, but no one was paying much attention to the people flooding the streets. Most of the *Badger*'s passengers were corralling themselves just past the barricade, waiting for their cars most likely, but Darryl didn't care if they ever saw Lee's old truck ever again. He looked sideways as they ran past a couple of geared-up police readying themselves to board the boat, and he fell into Terry as he leapt into the closest cop. Darryl pushed the cop hard, took control, and then raised the M4 the man was holding on to and shot into the chests of the two police officers closest to him. Both of them collapsed, and Darryl turned to the crowd still streaming from the boat and sent bullets there as well. He wasn't aiming, just firing from the hip, and then it was over.

Darryl fell back into his body, once again having been carried on between Terry and the stroller. He looked over his shoulder and saw his cop lying next to the two he'd shot. The back of his head was blown out. *Somebody figured that out quick*, thought Darryl, vowing that if he survived this he was going to be sure to watch the evening news.

"Ditch the baby," said Darryl to Terry as they ran through the crowd, and Terry did, letting go of the stroller and then falling in next to Darryl as they sprinted away from the docks and into downtown Ludington, Michigan.

Darryl wanted a bar, and for the first time in his life, not just because he wanted a drink. They found one a few blocks from the dock and ran inside as the sirens of emergency vehicles shook the windows. There were three men sitting at the bar, no bartender in sight, and Darryl pushed the two closest to the bar. They were drunk and it was easy, and a few seconds later the pair of them were sawing logs with their faces on the bar. Darryl gave the third man a shove, and then he and Terry followed the old man out of the bar to his truck.

The old man laid his keys on the hood and then said, "Got to pay my tab," and went to walk back inside.

Darryl gave him one more little shove and sent the man behind the bar to make his own drinks for a change.

"Let's go," said Darryl as he grabbed the keys and clambered into the truck just as an ambulance went screaming past them down the road. Terry hopped in the passenger side, Darryl turned the key, and they got moving.

The only traffic was emergency vehicles going the other way, and Darryl couldn't imagine what a mess the docks were going to be to sort out.

"They're going to blame us for that, Darryl," said Terry, a little stupidly.

"Well, that's probably fair enough. Let them blame all they want. We're getting out of town, and we're going to figure this out."

Terry didn't say anything, just kept staring out the window, and Darryl rubbed his left temple with the palm of his hand.

You're going to need to let all of that out soon, Darryl thought, and the idea was sickening. He had a whole load of poison to throw into Terry, but he could tell by looking at him that the man was close to his own breaking point. Terry's topknot was a sick mixture of half purple and half pink, and Darryl watched for a moment as it swayed with the motion of the truck. *I need to figure out something, and fast.* The idea of getting rid of Terry was dead in the water, at least for now. Darryl needed him as a receptacle for all of that bad juju, but first he needed to figure out how to control him after shooting him full of the rotten stuff.

"We'll figure it out, Terry," said Darryl as another ambulance ripped down the road, headed in the opposite direction. "We'll get over the border, or drive south and get a flight. We can do this, man. It's going to be good." Terry nodded, not saying anything in response. The world rushed by them, but all Darryl could think about was how much longer they could possibly keep going. *We've been burning bridges from Mexico to Michigan, and we're about out of highway.* Darryl's hands tightened on the wheel as two sheriff's cars drove past them.

"They're going to be so pissed off," said Terry, his words slow, his voice hitching. "When they figure out what was wrong with those cops, we're fucked."

"They can't know that, not even if they filmed the whole thing."

"You really think you're so special?" Terry asked. "You think you're the only person to hang on to this shit past puberty? I guarantee you the FBI or ATF or CIA or somebody has a lab full of you creeps, and when they figure out what happened back there, they're going to go apeshit. Your little trick has gotten us out of a lot of shit, but I think the house might be coming down. All they need to do is find some bender stronger than you, and we can kiss our asses good-bye."

"That's not going to happen," said Darryl after a moment of silence. "There's no lab like that, no think tank of assholes in coats studying people like me. There's us and the road and a whole lot of pissed-off folks. Trust me, Terry, we're going to get out of this, one way or the other." Terry nodded, staring out the window and watching the trees zip by on the other side of it. Three more cruisers whipped past them, and Darryl said, "We just need a little bit of luck, and we'll be fine."

Chapter 43

"Just put the fucking thing down!" Jessica screamed into the cockpit at the two pilots. They'd already missed the landing the first time due to wind, and she wanted off of the plane. Darryl and Terry were loose somewhere in Michigan, and if the FBI reports that she'd been given in transit were even half-correct, they'd killed a lot of people to stay that way. She blamed herself for not being there, though she'd done everything she could to try and see the capture through. *They're out there, though, and now bringing them in is going to be impossible.*

"At least three dead cops," was what the FBI agent had told her, and Jessica expected the number to rise. Darryl and Terry were in pure survival mode, just like the story Dad had told her years earlier when Frank had tried to kill him, even though that meant Frank was likely to die, too. The way Dad had told it, Frank would have happily risked his own life for just the slimmest chance of escape. *Frank was right, too,* thought Jessica bitterly. *Look at what happened to him after he was caught.* The man had been locked up ever since, through president after president, through three directors and nearly fifty years.

The thought hit her like a brick to the head: *Frank.* She needed Frank. He had been the key to Pat's plan before any of this shit had ever gotten stirred up, and he still could be. She needed to go back to the TRC, convince Frank by whatever means necessary to help with the sting, and then put things into play. Looking through the windshield in the cockpit of the Learjet, Jessica could see green fields as the plane finished the wide turn needed to right itself for the approach to the little airfield. The wind had died enough for them to land, now that it was too fucking late.

"How much fuel do we have?" Jessica asked no one in particular, and the copilot responded.

"About three-quarters of a tank."

"We're going back to Hartford immediately," said Jessica. "Radio the tower."

Neither member of the flight crew said anything. They just began to follow orders, both of them well aware of the ridiculous power this woman's station afforded her, even when it came to the FAA.

"When you're done with that, get on the horn with the tower there. I want the company chopper ready to get me to the TRC."

The copilot nodded as the captain swore under his breath. Jessica didn't begrudge the man his frustration. The two pilots had been mustered at a moment's notice, been forced to scramble a jet in an impossibly brief time, and then had attempted to land at an airport so small that both of them had tried to talk Jessica out of the maneuver.

All of that was moot now, and she didn't care, she couldn't care. Frank was all that mattered.

• • •

Jessica walked off of the helicopter on the lawn of the TRC feeling like she'd been put in a bottle and shaken up. The trip had been a blur, a waking nightmare that was still going. She walked into the TRC, saw Westley working the desk at the front, and casually said, "Gun," before drawing the Glock and dropping it in the lockbox that he made appear on the counter. Jessica left before the box was even closed, passed the dioramas without a glance, and ran her fingertip on the scanner. It wouldn't be long now.

She collected herself as she walked through the steel hallway, used the retinal scanner, and took the elevator to the TK floor. Time was of the essence for them, and Frank would know it and want to take advantage of it. He couldn't read her like he could anyone else, but he was a genius, and he'd know from the most basic body language cues that she needed him more than he needed her.

Jessica swallowed thickly, wishing she had a glass of water but not wanting to waste even a minute before seeing him. The elevator dropped, plunging her past the floor that housed her research team and then finally stopping at the TK floor. She slid through the doors as they opened, waved at the receptionist as she passed the desk, and then ran to Frank's room.

She was breathing hard when she got there, decided it didn't matter, then used another retinal scanner and punched the keys to get inside.

"Well, there you are," said Frank as she entered, her prediction of his ability to read her becoming true in an instant. "What took you so long?"

"I've been busy."

"Of course you have," said Frank. Was it possible he was bigger yet since the last time that she'd been to see him? "Why are you so flushed?"

"I need your help."

"That goes without saying," said Frank in his thick, wet rasp. "Why else spend time with the freak?"

"Frank, I don't think you're a freak. I'm sorry that it's been so long, but I've honestly been busy, and—"

"You've finally found one?"

Jessica raised an eyebrow. *He's just guessing. He can't get to you like that, you know this. Don't let him throw you.*

"Yes and no," said Jessica. "We've been hunting two men—two bad men—but they managed to get away." She paused and then said, "That's where you come in. I need you to help me catch them."

"Where am I going?"

"Nowhere, Frank," said Jessica slowly. "I need you to help me catch them from here."

"Not possible," said Frank after a moment. He almost looked as though he was affirming that Jessica wasn't making fun of him. "I am very powerful, but I cannot reach someone from down here. Even if you shut off all of your little tricks—your walls and hats and everything else—I would have a hard time seeing aboveground, much less to wherever your little runner is."

"There's a young man here with an idea about that," said Jessica. "He's a computer expert, and he has a theory that someone like you could connect with a person through the lines that electronically connect computers."

"We tried phones, tried that trick forever ago—Edith and I both did," said Frank. "It didn't amount to a hill of beans. Tell your boy that he's wrong, it won't work. He needs a new tree to bark up."

"It will work," said Jessica, knowing it didn't matter, because if they failed then there wouldn't even be a TRC. "We've done the testing, Frank, but we need a high-level TK to make this work. We need you."

Frank just looked at her for a long moment, then said, "Say I believe you, what's the point? Why do you want to get in someone's head through a wire?"

"As I've said, there are two very bad men on the loose," said Jessica. "Neither is as powerful as you, and what they've been up to is nowhere near as smooth as your Ham and Egger routine, but they're young TKs, and I need them."

"The last time you needed a favor, you promised me Katarina," said Frank. "You promised that you were going to catch her and bring her to me."

"I still am, Frank. This is the start of bringing in a lot more TKs. I just need your help to get the program rolling. Katarina is the next step, but I can't get there without this."

"And what if I'm a fool and say that I'll help? How does your computer expert think this will work?"

"It will work," said Jessica. "It's really pretty simple. Our expert goes into a chat room—a place on the Internet where people can speak to strangers—and you go in with him. You lie back, leave him the ability to do his thing. He'll be making a spectacle of himself, making himself a big, fat worm on our hook. He'll be a blowhard kid, maybe the son of a banker or the son of a CFO. When our targets start working the kid to access daddy's cash, you'll save Pat—my computer expert—from any push that tells him to commit suicide to cover up the illegal acts, or anything else of that nature. While you do that, we trace the account that our marks are using to talk to the pair of you."

"What if I say I'll help but instead I warn your fish away?"

"Then I lose, Frank," said Jessica, feeling the same triumph she had moments before the rug was yanked from beneath her in the skies above Michigan. "I lose, and Darryl and Terry—our marks—win. But you lose, too."

"How do I lose?" Frank asked. "I get to pull the wool over your eyes, I get to enjoy a nice belly laugh for throwing a monkey wrench into the system that keeps me in a cage, and I get the satisfaction of a job well done."

"Trust me, Frank, you would lose," said Jessica. "I'll do whatever I can to ensure that whoever has been feeding you is fired before I am, and I guarantee that whoever takes this place over after Howard and I are forced out will be given a pretty simple mandate. And I doubt that order will involve keeping any of the lions alive."

Frank nodded, a grotesque maneuver that sent ripples shifting down the loose skin that covered his face and neck. "All right," he said. "I'm in. When do we start?"

"Today," said Jessica, and Frank nodded. If he was surprised, it wasn't showing. "One more thing," she said. "We're going to get you out of this room for a day or two, get you on up to the unsecured floor. Can you play nice?"

"Just so long as I can play," said Frank with a smile.

Chapter 44

Cynthia sat at the table in Mrs. Martin's apartment. The two dogs slept on the couch, having already received their ration of pets.

"Ready?" Mrs. Martin asked, and Cynthia nodded, and the two of them linked hands.

Cynthia closed her eyes, and when she opened them a fraction of a second later, she was above North Harbor again. The colors were exactly as they'd been before, and Cynthia would have smiled at the familiar sight if she'd been able to. Instead, she zipped down to street level and began to take in the world around her.

When she was weaving, Cynthia felt like she was as strong as any adult and just as smart. This was her world, even though she wasn't even really here at all. Next, Cynthia did as Mrs. Martin had said and zipped back out into the sky. All it took was a little push, the desire to be there, and she was. Cynthia had only ever sparingly played video games, but couldn't help but compare the two things. She was tethered to that odd version of her in the sky, only it was her mind and not her fingers on a controller that were providing the instructions.

Cynthia dove back down to the blacktop and then winked back up a second later. It would have been disorienting if she'd actually been moving, but there was no flying involved. "You start in one place and then wind up in another," Mrs. Martin had said, and there really was nothing more to it than that.

Cynthia blinked herself back to the sky and the overview of the apartment complex, then shot back to ground level before returning once more to the sky. Could other aspects of weaving be this simple? She doubted it, and yet, amazing as all of this was, Cynthia still felt like she was playing at a level far below her actual abilities.

She counted the apartments marked with color. Just over half of the complex's apartments were occupied, assuming that the dots left by Mrs. Martin were only visible when their occupants were actually home. Cynthia winked back to the ground, then back to the sky, and then fired herself into an apartment. Mrs. Martin had told her that this was just practice and not to engage people, but all Cynthia could think about was her drawing. She wanted to be the girl she'd drawn, minus all of the black lines, of course. Mrs. Martin had needed her help to deal with four people at once, but Cynthia hadn't felt the reins strain even once as she wove her thoughts into those two men.

Cynthia went from apartment to apartment, weaving for just seconds in each of them before moving on again, weaving in and then winking back out to the sky. Cynthia could feel Mrs. Martin trying to keep up, trying to figure out what she was doing, but her teacher's stride was simply too short. Cynthia blasted herself back and forth from the sky to the various abodes of the North Harbor residents, weaving herself into all of them, and when she was done she threw herself back to the earth.

Feeling out of breath even though she wasn't breathing, Cynthia tugged against the strings of her neighbors, an act for her that was no more difficult than blinking her eyes. Without exception, the people of North Harbor opened their doors simultaneously and at the same time all said, "Hi, Cynthia," before closing their doors. Cynthia released them at the same time, firing back to the sky and yanking her threads cleanly from theirs. Cynthia knew reflexively that she hadn't hurt any of them. She'd been careful with her weaving, hadn't bludgeoned her way through it.

Cynthia gazed down at North Harbor, pleased and more than a little proud of herself—and then there was a sound like nothing she had ever heard, and the world went black.

When Cynthia opened her eyes, she was sitting across from Mrs. Martin. Both of the dogs were barking, and Cynthia could hear the mad wail of multiple car alarms going off outside. Mrs. Martin slammed her fists onto the tabletop, making the dogs go from barking to diving for hiding places. Cynthia could see Mrs. Martin's threads, and they were glowing red and pink.

"What were you thinking?" Mrs. Martin asked, and Cynthia burst into tears. She hadn't been thinking; she'd been having fun. All she wanted to do was see how far she could push her new talent, and even the most difficult thing that she could think of had come easily.

"I was just trying—" sobbed Cynthia, but Mrs. Martin cut her off with a violent shake of her head.

"No, no more trying," said Mrs. Martin. "No more anything like that, not unless I tell you it's OK, do you understand?"

Cynthia nodded, but she still didn't know why. All she'd been trying to do was to see how far she could push herself, not to make Mrs. Martin upset.

"You could have hurt those people," said Mrs. Martin as Cynthia got her sobbing under control. "I know you don't see how, but you could have hurt them very badly."

Cynthia nodded again, though she knew Mrs. Martin was wrong. Just because her teacher couldn't do what Cynthia could didn't make it dangerous, and Cynthia knew beyond a shadow of a doubt that she'd been in control the entire time.

"I won't do it again, I promise," lied Cynthia. She wanted to tell the truth, and she wanted Mrs. Martin to be happy, just like she wanted her parents to be happy, but there was too much joy in weaving. At that moment, Cynthia realized that, as much as she could learn from Mrs. Martin, she was going to need to be her own teacher as well.

"Good," said Mrs. Martin. "I'll get us some sandwiches. Does that sound good?"

Cynthia nodded, then leaned over to pet the dogs as they sauntered back to the table. Food did sound good, but not as good as every person in North Harbor greeting her had sounded. Stanley and Libby ran around her hands and chair while Mrs. Martin hummed in the kitchen, and Cynthia silently told the dogs to sit in front of her. The pair did it at once, sitting with wagging tails before her, and Cynthia sent them yellow warmth in thanks for their obedience.

Chapter 45

Darryl and Terry sat on either side of a couch in a hunting cabin that they'd broken into a few miles off of the highway. There was no air conditioning, and the place was sweltering in the August heat, but it hadn't seen a visitor in some time, and it had two beds and a working TV with rabbit ears. The TV had only taken a moment to lock onto one of the local channels, and before long the programming was exactly as they had known it would be: pictures of them; security footage of them leaving Des Moines; shots of Darryl at the gas station, the cop blurred out; and finally, video of the mess at the docks and the two of them dashing through the crowd with that baby stroller. Darryl watched it all with a lump of panic in his throat. This was far worse than the distraction they'd used to take heat off in Des Moines. This was being twisted to bring all the heat in seven states down onto their heads. Not a single mention of the two trigger-happy cops Darryl had bent in their escape. According to the woman on the TV, Darryl and Terry had shot their way off of the boat.

"The TV station might not have the whole story yet," said Terry in an odd moment of prescience. "I mean, people did see the cop trying to hold us, and they did see us borrow that baby in its stroller. They knew we had *something* to do with what was going on, and it probably makes more sense that we shot those cops, so that's what they're going with. Not to mention they probably can't talk about cops going crazy on a raid and killing each other. People would be scared shitless."

"The media doesn't know what I am," said Darryl. "But the cops there do, and they were told to suppress information by some fucking black-suited government official and—"

"No," said Terry. "You're back to that conspiracy shit. You don't know how many people like you there are out there, and you don't know that the government is studying any of them, and you sure as hell don't know they're orchestrating some kind of black-ops nationwide dragnet for us."

Darryl waved him off and stood, reeling from the onset of what was going to be a dinger of a headache. He couldn't stagger into the bathroom, though, because there was a mirror there, and he knew what he'd see if he looked in it. *You need to unload this shit on him, and the sooner you do it, the better.*

Darryl walked into the rudimentary kitchen in the cabin, grabbed a towel from a drawer, and then turned on the water. Nothing happened.

"Fuck," said Darryl.

"I'm sure if we look we can find out where the hookup for that is," said Terry. He'd trailed him into the kitchen. "It's probably not far from here."

"Yeah, so some asshole birdwatcher can see us and call the law," Darryl spat, unable to keep the spite out of his voice. He felt himself bending under the weight he was carrying. He needed to be smart, play this all the right way, because it wouldn't take much for Terry to tear away toward civilization, find some honky-tonk and start drinking, killing, and skull-fucking everything with a heartbeat and without the sense to get the fuck out of his way.

You could play it that way. Send him off on a rampage and then head the other way. It was true: Terry was already packed with rotten shit, and after Darryl dumped off the rest of the crud into him, he was going to be one very loose cannon.

"I'm just saying, man," whined Terry, stung by Darryl snapping at him. "We could turn the water on. Hell, at least we have electricity."

Darryl shook his head. "I'm not sure that box is doing me much good. I have a seriously bad feeling about all of this, Terry. Whoever the hell's after us knew we were on that boat, and I guarantee you they know that some of those cops were shooting at other police. And so does the media. Too many people saw it. That would make for a hell of a news story, wouldn't you say? I don't see any reporter suppressing that just because some Podunk chief said please. I'm telling you, it's the feds—"

"Maybe it's the feds, maybe it's not," said Terry. "Does it really matter? There are hundreds, if not thousands, of cops looking for us right now, and the chances of this having a happy ending are just getting slimmer and slimmer. You need to come up with something, Darryl. That's what you do: you get us out of messes—and this is a pretty bad mess. We need to get out of this state, get you back in front of a computer so you can raise some hell, and then leave the country, in that order. I can't make any of that happen, Darryl. I can be your friend, and I can help you do things, but I can't get us out of this by myself."

"All right," said Darryl. He needed to focus, though that was hard when there was a woman on the television describing how Darryl and Terry tried to take over the boat, and when that didn't work, tried to take hostages. He turned away from the TV and grabbed the sides of his head. "They want to catch me and throw me in some lab, man. I don't want to get my brain dissected while I look at inkblot drawings and try and make someone piss across town. I'm not doing it. I'd rather just be dead."

"So we don't get caught," said Terry. "You can get us out of this, I know it."

Darryl sighed. Christ, what kind of trouble were they in if *Terry* was the fucking voice of reason?

"All right," said Darryl after a moment of silence. "We'll catch some winks, then hit the road at peak, right around eight. We'll get to Grand Rapids—it's the biggest city that's both south and close to here—and we'll get a room with a phone. I'll land us a couple of kids, make us some money, and then I'll get us another distraction. After that I'm not sure, but we'll probably need more than passports and hair dye to get out of here. Terry, I honestly don't know what's worse."

"What do you mean?"

"I mean that if there is some secret squirrel group collecting people like me, they're never going to stop looking for us," said Darryl. "But if there isn't, we're still going to have a hell of a time getting out of here. We're on the hook for three dead cops, and there's no way that's going to go away anytime soon."

He shook his head and smiled a black smile. "Hell, if there's some black-ops types coming after us, we might have a better chance of getting away. They'll keep the police presence at a minimum. They know we need space, and they'd be more apt to give it to us so they can get us alive. If it's just the cops, they won't care if they get us alive or dead."

"You're just spinning yourself into the ground," said Terry. "None of this matters. We'll leave in the morning and do what you said, and it will either work or it won't. I'm sorry I got us caught up in all of this."

Darryl shook his head. "We both knew the game we're playing at is for keeps, Terry. But I'll tell you something else: if they think they can just catch us, they're wrong. I'll paint the streets red first."

Chapter 46

It was like waking up to a dream. One minute Pat was logging on to the net, and the next thing he knew he was in his old room. Only, it wasn't really his old room at all. It was decorated with posters for popular current-day video games, he had a late-model TV with a PlayStation and VCR hooked to it, and a top-of-the-line desktop computer sat on the desk between the TV and his bed. Pat held up a hand to look at it. The scar from when he broke a glass washing dishes when he was twelve was there but still in its full, red, gory kid-era glory, running the entire length of the top of his hand instead of reduced to the pale, barely noticeable seam that marked his adult skin.

Pat walked to the desk, wondering if he was the one who'd decided to do it or it had been that man who was helping them, and then wondering if Frank could hear him wondering that. *It's OK. You knew this was how it would be, remember?*

Pat did remember, but that had been before he was here, thrust into this only half-familiar world. Pat sat at the desk, fired up the computer, then waited as it warmed up. It really was his room he realized as he looked around, just as a modern-era version of his kid self would decorate it. Instead of posters torn from *Nintendo Power*, the wall was decorated with images from *Fallout 2* and *Age of Empires II*, a pair of awesome games that Pat had logged way too much time with before Jessica had come along offering money to play a real game.

When the computer finished its boot sequence and the home screen flared up, Pat double-clicked the AOL button and then watched as the all-too-familiar logo appeared on the screen. Pat hadn't used AOL in years, but this was the pool that Darryl and Terry had been fishing in, so that's what he was diving into. Pat scrolled through the usual mess, slowly reacclimating himself with the system as he made his way to the chat rooms that featured video game chat.

Pat already knew the rooms Vincent and Tom had been messing around in—*Zelda* and *Resident Evil*, respectively—and he went to *Resident Evil* first and logged in as his old gaming handle, OICU812. Reminding himself that this was going to take some time, Pat eased in, making conversation, taking care to mention the spanking new NVIDIA graphics card that Pat's new daddy had just picked up for him, an item that had recently earned slobbering reviews in several prominent PC gaming magazines. Not surprisingly, this honey drew flies. New young Pat was soon receiving all kinds of advice for other ways to spend Daddy's money.

Pat was cautious, though. He made sure not to be too braggy, acting a little bored by all the toys his father's money could buy if he desired them, and soon he and his new pals were diverted into a spirited discussion of frame rates and what would improve them. As the conversation turned to video games again, Pat eased out of the forum and picked a new one. The second chat room was centered on *The Legend of Zelda: Ocarina of Time*, and Pat got to work planting seeds. Just as in the last forum, he and his father's bank account made friends quickly. It was going to be a long night.

Chapter 47

Mom picked up Cynthia after work, and now they sat on a park bench together. Cynthia had always been close with Mom, but she felt funny sitting next to her. She felt an odd disconnect from her parent. *It isn't because she's working*, thought Cynthia as she watched a dog catch a Frisbee across the lawn. Mom had always worked, and the separation Cynthia felt had nothing to do with Mom working more often now. The problem was the connection Cynthia had with Mrs. Martin, the connection she had with the rest of the world.

Cynthia knew that she could easily read the thoughts of the man playing Frisbee if she wanted to or could even make him chuck the red disc into the nearby river. Just looking at the man, Cynthia got a clear sense of how he was feeling. The man had pink and green threads pouring from his head. He was nervous about something, and though Cynthia had a feeling the man wouldn't be pleased to know how easily she could read his thoughts, she did think he might find it interesting that his canine companion was sharing his worries.

As wonderful and interesting as this window into a stranger was, Cynthia found she hated knowing what Mom was feeling. She was doing her best not to look at her mother's threads, and of course she wouldn't even consider searching her mind. That would have been the worst sort of betrayal. And besides, what if she looked and saw something she couldn't forgive? Being in the mind of someone who wants to do bad things was ugly—Cynthia had seen that with Patrick and his gun, and with the men who had come to collect a debt with their baseball bats. She didn't want to think of her mom being anything like those men, but Cynthia had heard the glee in her voice when Mom told Aunt Laura that she intended to take all of Dad's money—which, to make it even worse, Cynthia happened to know was Dad's biggest fear.

Mom would only do that to hurt Dad, but she didn't know how badly Dad was already hurting. *He was purple the last time I saw him*, thought Cynthia, and she was terrified to imagine what his threads might tell her now, a little over a week later. She shivered despite the heat.

Then she was thinking of Dad and Linda, which made her feel queasy, like she was looking down from a really tall place. She knew Dad needed to get away from Linda, that just that one little thing would make Mom less angry. Cynthia liked Linda, or at least she had, but she didn't like what Linda had done to Dad. And she didn't like what divorce had done to either of her parents.

Cynthia hadn't been able to see into their most private thoughts before, but she knew that they hadn't wanted to one-up each other before all of this. They had cared about one another, laughing and smiling daily, and they never would have put money before their daughter.

"You all right, Cynth?" Mom asked, and Cynthia turned to her.

"I'm fine, I guess."

Mom's threads were red, pink, and just a little purple in places. She was stressed out, felt like she was doing everything wrong, yet was still willing to stay the course just to show Dad she didn't need him. Cynthia knew all this without raiding Mom's head like a teenager hitting a cupboard for a midnight snack. The evidence was on her face and in the threads atop her head.

"If you weren't fine, you'd tell me though, right?"

"What do you mean?"

"I mean, if you weren't doing well, or if you needed to talk, that I'm here to listen," said Mom slowly, enunciating each word just so. "Is everything OK with Mrs. Martin?" Mom asked this question even more slowly, as if it were difficult for her to even speak about the older woman.

Is that something Mrs. Martin did? Something she'd left inside Mom to make it hard for Mom to talk about her? Cynthia wondered this, but only for a moment. Mom might have a hard time thinking ill of Mrs. Martin due to the light nudges Mrs. Martin had given her, not to mention the free babysitting, but Cynthia didn't think Mrs. Martin would have had a trick like that up her sleeve and not told Cynthia about it.

"Mrs. Martin is fine, too," said Cynthia. "She's always nice, and we have fun together."

Cynthia could see the relief on Mom's face. If it weren't for Mrs. Martin, Mom would have to lean on Dad a little bit, and Cynthia knew Mom wanted to avoid that for as long as possible.

"Do you miss your friends?" Mom asked. "I could set up a play-date if you wanted. I don't really want anyone else at the apartment yet, but I'm sure that if I explained the circumstances to your friends' parents, then—"

"No, Mom," said Cynthia with a grin. "I don't want to see them right now." Cynthia wanted to tell Mom exactly why—that she didn't want to have to tell them about divorce—but she knew the information would just hurt her. "Besides, school will be here soon, and Maryanne's birthday party ought to be coming up."

"Crap, I need to call your father and see if she sent you an invitation," said Mom, a screwed-up smile on her face that was more of a frown. "I'd hate for you to miss it."

"I know, Mom, but I won't. You'll get the invitation if she sent one, and then we'll see when it is." Looking up as she spoke, Cynthia could see goldenrod threads pouring from her and weaving in and out with Mom's damaged ones.

"Sure," said Mom, a real smile crossing her face. "I'll call Dad when we get home and see if the invitation has come."

"OK," said Cynthia, smiling herself as she watched the dog make another leaping Frisbee catch. The sun was shining, Mom was smiling, and there was nothing wrong at that moment.

Chapter 48

1945

We have waited three days in the camp after the fighting first came to us. These three days have been hell, but no one has enjoyed an easier time of it than me. Katarina is still doing whatever her job is in the camp itself, the guards are nervous as kittens, and my people are still being marched to the showers and then carried to the ovens. The selections come twice a day now, and I can hear screams of pain coming from behind the little room as well. Those screams have nothing to do with showers or anything else. I know these are the sounds of someone being tortured.

It has been hard to push all of that aside, but that's exactly what I have done. I need to wait for Katarina to tell me what to do, to tell me that the Americans are here and it is time to leave, but it seems as if that moment will never come. We are stuck, like a pair of flies in a drop of honey. If we leave too early, the guards will kill us, and if we wait too long, Katarina will be captured by the Americans and my fate will be uncertain. I do consider, however, Katarina's claims that I cannot find guaranteed refuge with the Americans. Would I not be safe with them?

Would that be better than staying with my mentor, the only person in this world I feel like I can trust?

Either way there's nothing for me to do now but cower at the sounds of fighting and to ignore the screaming from other prisoners and the barking of the guards. To just sit here in my little room and wait for something to happen is terrible, yet I know it is far better than what awaits those women who remain. The smell of smoke is all the proof I need of that—smoke and ash, as the Nazis kill as many of us as possible before their inevitable capture.

At last the door crashes open across the room, and I leap to my feet, spilling coffee down the front of my dress. I can hear her words in my head before I even feel the sting of the hot liquid / *We need to go / Now / Now / Now /* I set the cup down and lay my palms on the table so that I don't pass out. I know Katarina didn't mean to hurt me, but the words blasting in my mind feel as deadly as the guards' bullets.

As I stand I hear crashing noises from around the room and finally the sound of a gun being cocked. I wait to hear the blast, the noise of Katarina deciding that she can see no way to escape, nor avoid capture by the Americans, and then force the idea from my head. I'm relieved when I feel Katarina is next to me, grabbing me by the arm and placing my hand on her own arm. The sleeve of her jacket feels rough, not like the clean uniform she normally wears, and I realize she is dressed in camp clothes just like me. There is a burst of machine-gun fire from nearby, likely the tower, and then Katarina is pulling me from the room and back onto the grounds of the camp, a place I have only been while using my map since coming to live with Katarina.

I am glad that I am blind for the first time in my life as we leave Dachau. Women and men are screaming everywhere, and the noise of shooting brings back a fear that I no longer knew I was capable of feeling. The noise of the machine guns is a beast from hell brought to life, and in spite of that fury I can hear a male voice shouting *"Nein!"* over and over again in a garble that sounds increasingly like he is screaming while drinking water. The world is noise, a hell of fire, explosions, and screaming lead, but I am literally blind to the destruction.

Except that I can hear all of it. I can feel the heat, I can see it all in my mind's eye, and everywhere, whether I look for them or not, I can see the threads. These are the threads of madness, and I don't need Katarina to tell me about these colors. Everywhere the world is writhing black, blue, and red. Colors are fading on the ground as the bodies pile up, and the noise of death is in tune with the ebb and flow of the threads. I hear the sound of a pistol fired twice ahead of me, then a third time, and Katarina's voice appears in my head over the din. / *Quickly, with me / The fence is down just ahead /*

"Stop right there!" shouts a voice ahead of us in German, and I can see the source of it, threads standing erect like a bouquet of flowers, all of them red and blue. Gripping Katarina's arm tighter, I know what I must do.

I'm in the air above the map, and as I dive toward the man I see that he is next to a truck. I take in the rest of the camp as I roar toward the ground. Everywhere is chaos. Male prisoners have broken into our camp, and, alongside some of the girls and the Americans, they are slaughtering the Nazis. I should love this sight—it is just and fair—but all I see is another impediment. *How many of them would turn on me for feeling that I am a pet of Katarina? How many would put me to the slaughter?*

There is no time to ponder these questions, for a hair of a second later I am in the soldier. I shove the man with my mind, telling him to run back into the camp as fast as possible, and then I leapfrog from him, soar above my map, and fly back into myself just in time to watch the soldier hurl his gun to the ground and go running past us, toward Dachau.

Katarina is dragging me across the bare ground between the camp and the tree line, and someone else behind us begins to scream. This is the symphony of my escape from Dachau, the noise of the dead and dying as Jew and American soldier alike turn on the Nazis and unleash upon them the same brutality they had so wanted to share with the world.

Chapter 49

1999

Thunder rumbled in the sky as Darryl drove, the early-afternoon sky dark, reminding him of bad memories and worse weather. This storm was nothing like the one in Iowa, though. That had been hell, and this was just an inconvenience.

Terry slept on the other side of the bench seat, his face pressed against the glass in a way that Darryl was hoping at least partially obscured his more identifiable features. The truck was doing well enough on the road, but Darryl had his doubts that they'd be heading too much farther south in the thing. Once they crossed the border, its out-of-state plates would begin to stand out, and besides, the beast just *looked* like an outlaw's rig.

Darryl had always found driving to be relaxing, and that was the case now, even with the cloud of danger swirling around them. He felt different when he woke up that morning, more self-assured and positive once again that things would work out for him, because he was the star of the show. Darryl had always thought of the world as being his to play in, even before he was aware of his abilities, and still thought that his was the story that future generations would hear. That was why capture was so impossible, why he knew that they were going to get away.

Terry began to snore as the rain finally started to fall, and Darryl turned on the radio to cut through the noise. Classic rock filled the car. Springsteen was still alive and well in central Michigan, it seemed. Darryl smiled as the truck roared past a sign that said, "Grand Rapids, 100 Miles." They just needed to get there, get a hotel room with a phone line, and begin to fish. They were going to be all over the news for weeks even if nothing else happened, but if he bent a few people and they played it cool, they should be able to hunker down and hide in plain sight.

The truck bounced off of a pothole, lifting Darryl's ass off the seat and smacking Terry's head into the passenger window. Terry stirred but didn't wake. Good. Darryl looked at himself in the rearview mirror. His topknot was purple still, just like he knew it would be, and Darryl opened his mind and his mouth and sent all of that bad shit over to the still-slumbering Terry. If Terry minded the dinner he was being fed, he didn't act like it. His snoozing continued until it was done, and then Darryl smiled and let out a deep breath. *Now you're good, and he just needs to keep it together.* They couldn't afford any more mistakes just because Terry had needs.

"We could get an apartment," said Darryl to no one in particular.

It wasn't a bad idea. Cops or government men were going to look at hotels first and everything else second. Neither he nor Terry had a friend to speak of in Grand Rapids, but that was a good thing. They didn't need an excuse to go to one place or another. It would be far better to choose at random and live quietly. Darryl knew he could do it, especially after the months on the road, months running from the US and then back to it, and then the slapdash marathon that had put them on the *Badger* and now here and heading south.

Thunder roared again in the sky, and Darryl looked at the sleeping Terry, his topknot a glowing purple. "We'll figure this out," said Darryl to his deeply toxic, slumbering friend. "Get an apartment, hide out, and then disappear again. We can do this, Terry."

The man never moved, but that was OK. Darryl felt horrible for the time that he had spent thinking he needed to get rid of his friend. He needed Terry as much as Terry needed him, and unless he was forced to sacrifice him, there was no reason to kill him. Assuming the man could keep his pants on.

Chapter 50

If going in was waking up clean and refreshed, then coming out was like waking up after a drunken blackout. All that was missing was the hangover.

It had been three days since Pat had gone into the wind and gotten to work, but they were no closer to Darryl and Terry. Pat knew that he could have talked to them dozens of times under a dozen different aliases, but if they weren't going to bite, there was nothing he could do. As Pat was quickly discovering, owning a pole and a worm did not give a man the right to a good day of fishing.

Even though all of this plagued Pat when he emerged from his TK-induced fugue, it couldn't have mattered less when he was in no-man's-land with Frank. Everything there was perfect, the childhood that no one is lucky enough to actually have. He never saw his parents when he was in his head, but he knew they were there, his mother's cooking and father's aftershave two constant, comforting stimuli in the bizarre but really damned impressive simulation. Of course the real treat was in the computer itself. The PC in that world was years ahead of its time, the sort of impossible machine even a rich kid couldn't have dreamed of laying his fingers upon. It didn't matter that none of it was real. It was real enough to be seen, felt, and enjoyed—and what else is there?

After, though, was different. Coming out meant a severe power-down in thinking, as his doubled-up mind slowed to a snail's pace and he craved going back inside, like an addict craves a fix. Pat had expected to miss reality but had discovered the opposite to be the case. Life in this perfect version of his own history was impossible to beat. Still, Pat stayed focused in there, knowing that everything could change in an instant.

Blinking and aching in the real world, Pat drank water, choked down a pair of McDonald's cheeseburgers, and then set his hands back on the keyboard, the sign to Frank that he was ready to start. In the time before it began again, Pat had his first inkling that maybe this ride would, or anyway should, soon be over. Being inside was a joy, but it now struck him as a numb joy, a false one, but with the possible baggage of a real addiction. Just like that, Pat found himself looking forward to real life when this was all behind him. He had a few ideas for websites to start, and it was about time to grow some balls when it came to talking to women.

Then he felt it coming. Pat took a deep breath, and when he let it out he was back in the room.

The routine was just like every other time. He logged in to one chat and then another as OICU812, poking around, always alluding to money, always hoping there would be a bite. Pat was recognizing names by now, beginning to make conversation with people from the past few days, and even got a couple of good tips on *Counter-Strike*. It was almost like he was just there for fun—everything was so relaxed, the room so comfortable, the conversations ones he would have had willingly even without the TRC. It was easy to lose focus, and of course that was exactly what Jessica had told him needed to happen. Pat was no longer playing a role. He was becoming the perfect decoy to get

Terry and Darryl's attention. *My name is Robert Roberts, my dad is rich, and I love video games.* Pat was halfway to believing it himself.

Chapter 51

Cynthia watched Mrs. Martin shuffling cards. She had no idea what game they were going to play, only that Mrs. Martin wanted to teach her something, and that was very exciting. Mrs. Martin had been avoiding the subject of weaving as much as possible ever since Cynthia had made the neighbors greet her as one. Cynthia still didn't see what the deal was. Even if they remembered doing it—and she doubted they did—it would just be a weird memory, like one of a dream.

"Here's how this is going to work," said Mrs. Martin as she laid the deck down on the table. "I'm going to draw a card from the center of the deck, and I want you to tell me what card I'm holding."

Cynthia smiled and nodded. This was going to be easy.

Mrs. Martin grinned back at her. "Are you ready?"

"Yes," said Cynthia, and Mrs. Martin did as she had said she would. She cut the deck in half, took the top card from the middle, and held it in her hands.

"It's the eight with hearts," said Cynthia, and Mrs. Martin nodded her head and turned the card over on the table.

"It is indeed, and that was very fast. Want to play again?"

Cynthia nodded, and Mrs. Martin stacked the cards again, then cut the deck. She took a card just as she had the last time, but before she said anything, Cynthia was already calling it. "I think it's a king with a little red sideways square."

"It's called a diamond," said Mrs. Martin, "but yes, it's a king of diamonds. Very impressive once again. Shall we go one more time?"

Cynthia nodded again, and Mrs. Martin took another card from the restacked deck, and once again Cynthia beat her to the punch. "Two with a tree."

Mrs. Martin chuckled to herself. "Right again, dear. Now let's try a little variation. This time I want you to name any card that isn't the one that I'm holding."

"Won't that be really easy?"

"I suppose we'll see," said Mrs. Martin, her hands working to reshuffle the deck, before cutting it again and taking a card from the top of the bottom half.

"Three with a heart?" Cynthia asked, and Mrs. Martin laid the card faceup on the table.

"Three of hearts is correct, but we're trying to guess which card I'm *not* holding, remember?"

Cynthia nodded, flushing and staring bullet holes into the faceup card on the table. "Let's do it again," said Cynthia, and Mrs. Martin nodded and repeated the action, once again cutting the deck before palming a card.

"It's the ace of diamonds," said Cynthia, her voice full of confidence, and Mrs. Martin laid the card down. It was the ace of spades.

"Better," said Mrs. Martin, "but still very similar. Let's try and be more wrong next time, all right?"

Cynthia nodded in frustration. She had thought she was guessing very differently from the card her teacher and caretaker had been holding. Mrs. Martin restacked and cut the deck again, and once again removed a card. Cynthia was less trigger-happy this time, taking a moment to gather her thoughts after she realized Mrs. Martin was holding the jack of clubs.

"Two of hearts," said Cynthia slowly, and she was rewarded as Mrs. Martin flipped the jack onto the table.

"Want to know why that's so hard?" Mrs. Martin asked, and Cynthia bobbed her head up and down. "You are a very gifted child, Cynthia, and even though I have a few special abilities myself, your skills are far more potent than my own, especially at this point in my life. What you don't have yet, however, is patience. When you see the card that I'm holding, your mind still has to process what it is, and in this last test, what it isn't. Weaving does not come easily to anyone, even the most gifted of children, but someone like you is able to work so quickly that your mind sort of gets ahead of itself. Do you have your crayons?"

"Yes," said Cynthia, and she hopped off of her chair, grabbed the crayons from her bag on the floor, and set them on the table, before looking at Mrs. Martin expectantly.

"Pass them over, please, along with a sheet of paper."

Cynthia did as she was told, then began quizzically watching Mrs. Martin drawing on the blank sheet. When she was done, Mrs. Martin held the paper aloft. There were three words written on it.

"Read this to me, please," said Mrs. Martin.

"Red, green, and purple."

"One out of three isn't bad," said Mrs. Martin with a grin as she set down the paper, then ran a finger over it. "But this time I want you to actually read the words."

Cynthia grimaced at the paper. She had read the words, and there was no way she had read them wrong. She had known how to write her colors since before kindergarten, but when she looked again, she saw that Mrs. Martin somehow was right.

"You tricked me," she said.

Mrs. Martin shook her head. "You tricked yourself."

Looking at the paper, Cynthia could see that the word "red" had been written in green, "yellow" had been written in purple, and "purple"—the only one she'd gotten right—in black.

"What your mind did here is the same thing it did when you were reading the right card back to me when I was asking you for the wrong one. Again, when you slow down and don't just feast upon what repetition presents to you, you'll easily find the correct answer. It's just not always easy to go against some of our base ideas."

"So it's hard to think about another card when I saw the real one that you were looking at?" Cynthia asked, and Mrs. Martin nodded.

"Weaving comes so easily to you that you expend precious little effort when you do it. However, when you're trying to tell me something different than what you see, your brain gets confused, just like with the words written in the wrong colors. Do you want to try the cards again?"

Cynthia nodded, and Mrs. Martin pushed aside the crayons and paper and took up the cards again. She shuffled, cut the deck, and then slid a card from it.

"Six of clubs," said Cynthia, and Mrs. Martin smiled as she turned over the ten of hearts.

"Very impressive. Almost as fast as when I was only looking for the right answer and you managed to change the suit, number, and color. That's about as good as it can get."

Cynthia grinned, watching as Mrs. Martin cut the deck again and took another card. "Two with hearts," said Cynthia, and Mrs. Martin laid down the king of spades.

"Impressive again," said Mrs. Martin. "Do you want to keep playing?"

Cynthia did, even if she wasn't entirely sure what the purpose of the exercise was. Guessing the cards was fun, and the second game, with its trick, was even more fun.

"I'll call it out from here on," said Mrs. Martin, "so make sure you listen to whether I want you to tell me what I'm holding, or anything but the card that I'm holding."

. . .

Cynthia and Mrs. Martin finally put the cards away a little over two hours after they had started. Cynthia had the beginnings of a headache, and though she didn't complain about it to Mrs. Martin, she had felt a small relief when her teacher called for a break.

After Mrs. Martin returned to the table, she asked if Cynthia would like to take the dogs for a walk with her. "I could use the exercise, and I bet Stanley and Libby would like to stretch their legs as well."

"Sure," said Cynthia, and Mrs. Martin nodded and went to get the leashes for the dogs, then readied the leaping animals by attaching the leashes to their collars.

"We can walk North Harbor for a little bit," said Mrs. Martin. "May as well get out and walk while I still can."

Cynthia followed Mrs. Martin out of the apartment, the two dogs straining at their leashes and making Cynthia giggle with joy.

Once the dogs had done their business on the lawn out front and Mrs. Martin had gathered the mess in a small bag, the four of them walked past the leasing office and away from their familiar section of North Harbor.

Cynthia loved the feeling of the sun on her face, the wind in her hair, and the way that Libby pulled at her lead. Looking back at Mrs. Martin, Cynthia could see she was smiling as well. The weather was perfect for a little walk, finally not too hot.

The rumble of a truck with an exhaust issue turned them both toward the leasing office, where the truck in question found a space to park and a man got out. Cynthia could see another man in the truck, but he was boring, while the man walking was not. He looked familiar in a way that she couldn't place, and when Cynthia turned to Mrs. Martin she could see that she had been staring at the truck as well.

"Come on," said Mrs. Martin, as though Cynthia had been the only one who had been momentarily distracted by the truck. "Do you think they're going to move in?" Cynthia asked. When she looked to Mrs. Martin, she saw that her friend had an odd expression on her face.

"I don't know," said Mrs. Martin, "but I suppose we shall see."

Chapter 52

Darryl gave the fat prick in the leasing office of the shitty-looking apartment complex a shove, reminding him that his porno collection wasn't seeing a whole lot of love at the moment and he'd better hustle through this leasing process and attend to it, then decided it probably wasn't even necessary. There might be a multistate manhunt for them, they might've left a growing pile of dead civilians and police in their wake, but still the workaday world was utterly oblivious to them. That would change over time, but by then Darryl had no intention of letting it happen without doing something to avoid it.

A beard and a new wardrobe won't hurt things either, thought Darryl as he left the leasing office and climbed back in the truck. As he entered, a nervous-looking Terry asked, "Did it go OK?"

Darryl nodded and threw the truck in reverse, pulled out, and then drove down to the far end of the lot, past a little girl and an old lady walking a pair of dachshunds.

"About as good as it possibly could have," said Darryl. "I gave the greasy fuck running the place a little shove, but all he really needed was a credit card. I think I probably could have used my real name and still gotten a place."

"Thank fucking God," said Terry. "We could use a little bit of good luck for once."

Darryl and Terry had spent more than four thousand dollars at a Meijer outside of town, purchasing a computer, modem, hair dye, toiletries, two platform beds, bedding, clothing, and food, but it still only took about fifteen minutes to unload the truck. Terry had the computer set up on the cheap-looking kitchen table that came with the apartment within fifteen minutes of locking the door behind them, then moved down the hall to start assembling the beds while Darryl got to work.

It was the same deal—trolling chat rooms for kids on the other side of the wire who betrayed any sort of a bent angle. The work was tedious and exhausting, and not only did they have no access to cocaine, they had forgotten to even buy a coffeemaker in their trip to the store. Darryl tried not to think about it. After all, they'd been through hell and back to get to where they currently sat. He was lucky to still be free to look.

Darryl cruised through a *Castlevania* chat room, slowly working his way around the lame names and engaging just long enough with each to check them off as worthless goods. He was engaged in the work, but the thought of some secret government agency looking for him still weighed heavily on his mind. The news hadn't gotten the story right, sticking with the idea that two fugitives suspected of killing in Mexico had been involved in a crime spree in the US involving the deaths of four police officers and two civilians. He had to admit that the letter of the reporting was right—Terry and he had been at the root of those crimes—but the story from the *Badger* docks was still miles from the truth.

The only reason for them to hold to that is if they're being told to, thought Darryl as he entered a chat room focused on *The Simpsons*. No reporter would ever let go of a story of two cops helping them shoot their way off the docks—not now and not ever. It was too damned titillating. Darryl didn't have the sort of power to have turned all the cops at the dock upon one another, but even if that's what had happened, he had a feeling the news would have just told the story of him and Terry killing a legion of police officers. Thinking about it made Darryl feel sick. He had no idea what would happen if he was interned by a group powerful enough to make that happen, and he had no desire to find out. *They'll crack your head open when they're done with you,* thought Darryl. *There's no point in trying to fool yourself otherwise.*

Darryl found a teen on *The Simpsons* chat who at first seemed like a good candidate, but he quickly came to feel that she'd likely brushed aside most of her bend with weed and psychedelics. It was a lost cause in any case, regardless of the reason. There was nothing for it but to just keep looking.

Noise behind him made Darryl swivel in his seat, but it was just Terry dragging the second boxed bed into the other bedroom, grunting as he lugged the awkwardly shaped thing. Darryl turned back to the screen and the task at hand. Only five minutes later he had another lead, a kid with the handle of OICU812. Darryl was into him like a magician, seizing control in seconds and then worming his way with increasing excitement through twelve-year-old Robert Roberts.

As Darryl quickly discovered, young Robert had been up to some very naughty things. Robert's father was a regional manager for State Farm, and Robert had been taking his sweet time going through his father's accounts, figuring out just how much his old man was worth—which, it turned out, was a surprisingly great deal. Who knew insurance agents pulled in that kind of green? In addition to discovering the depths of his own father's wealth, clever Robert had found a way to bleed a single dollar off of every single direct deposit customer his father was connected to—which was every State Farm customer in nearly half the Midwest. Not only that, Robert knew that simply taking the dollar wouldn't cover his tracks sufficiently—his father was obsessive over math and money—so he had first increased each of these direct deposits to be billed an extra dollar on their monthly premium, a dollar that eventually wound up in his account. So far Robert had only amassed a sum of about twelve thousand dollars, but by the time he graduated high school, it would amount to a very considerable pile of seed money.

Darryl played in Robert the way a concert violinist would handle a Stradivarius—he was cautious but determined to push his chosen instrument to its full, wondrous potential. Darryl plucked at Robert both carefully and violently, twisting and poking his way through the boy but never damaging him. Darryl had never concocted a scheme even close to the one the boy had set up, and the kid was only twelve. There was a lot to learn from Robert Roberts, and Darryl planned to glean as much as he could before helping himself to any money or placing Robert at too much risk. Darryl had blown it with Vincent but would not make that sort of mistake again. Robert was special, and Darryl was going to handle him with kid gloves.

Chapter 53

"He's on," said Pat as he snapped back to his place in the TRC. "Did you get it? Do we have the IP address?"

Pat swiveled his head around the ring of waiting faces, his focus slowing on Jessica and then stopping on Brinn.

"No IP yet," said Brinn. "You were only on there with him for a few minutes tops, and you know how chat rooms are. Once the text scrolls offscreen, it's gone. If he's not e-mailing you or registering to some forum, there's a limited window for us to follow his footprints. Do you think you can get him to talk to you again?"

"What the fuck? We were on there forever, or at least that's how it felt, and the whole time he was going through me and into all of this shit that I didn't even know was in my head!"

"It wasn't in your head," said Jessica. "That was all Frank. He's your muscle, remember? He had a plan in place for when Darryl or Terry got into you, and you followed along perfectly. I know it's tough to think about doing it again, but that's what has to happen."

"This isn't just some little 'plan,'" said Pat as he stood. He sort of wished he'd been wearing special gear or a headset or something that he could strip off, toss to the ground, and further separate himself from the situation, but he was just standing there dressed normally, just plain old Pat. "He stole a bunch of money—like, a *shitload* from a bunch of accounts hooked into what was supposed to my dad's bank. It was easy to do, but did I really just help him steal all of that cash?"

"It was really stolen, but it was all money from the TRC," said Jessica. "We'll get it back once we catch these two, which is just another reason why I need you to be in those chat rooms as much as possible. He will be back, he'll be more trusting, and we'll get this figured out." She flashed a smile, the sort of look Pat was starting to think meant, *Fuck you very much.*

Ignoring his exasperation, Jessica just maintained the grin, then grabbed the fast-food trash from his desk, and pitched it into the can under it. "How long do you need, Pat?"

"Before I go back in? I just got out!"

"You need to change your mind-set, man," said Geoff. "That dude on the other side of the monitor doesn't know there's anything wrong with you. Think how often you're online, and then imagine that you're a fucking twelve-year-old kid with endless time on his hands. You wouldn't be taking anything more than the occasional bathroom break, and that would be if you weren't pissing in a jug."

"God, men are disgusting," said Brinn, shaking her head, clearly more amused than grossed out.

"Hey, if you could you would, and you know it," said Rick, and the three burst into peals of laughter.

Jessica let them carry on for a moment as Pat stared at the other researchers as if they'd gone insane, and then raised a hand to gather their attention.

"Let's not get offtrack," said Jessica. "Pat, how long?" When Pat only shook his head, she pressed. "Serious answer, Pat. How long until you can go back in?"

Her eyes were boring into him like a pair of drills. Pat knew she wasn't a TK, but she was also a woman who was used to giving an order and having it followed. He was feeling like he was arguing with a five-star general or a middle school teacher. It didn't matter what he said. What she wanted was what was going to happen, and any delays would be remembered, ruminated upon, and punished.

"Fifteen minutes," said Pat finally, and Jessica smiled.

"Fifteen minutes would be perfect. You should go stretch your legs. It could be a while until we get a handle on these guys."

Chapter 54

Mom drove Cynthia to Maryanne Fisher's birthday party, Maryanne's gift of a pair of Barbie dolls wrapped and sitting on Cynthia's lap. It was Mom's first day off since taking her new job, and though Cynthia was a little sad that she was going to be with her friends instead of her mother, she knew her Mom would be around the house with some of the other parents. Cynthia had heard her talking to Mrs. Fisher on the phone two nights prior, and both Mom and Mrs. Fisher seemed very excited to have some wine and catch up on the divorce proceedings and to talk about that "cheating bastard." Cynthia had been floating in and out of the space over the apartments on her own, something she knew she wasn't supposed to do, but it was an attraction impossible to resist. Still, she'd managed to catch most of the conversation.

Mom parked in front of the Fishers' mailbox, and Cynthia smiled sadly as she looked at Maryanne's house. It was smaller than the yellow house where she used to live, but it was much bigger than the apartment, and Cynthia guiltily felt a little jealous of her friend. *Her parents are still together, too,* thought Cynthia. *Don't forget that.* And the ugliness of this fact made her want to heave the present into the bushes and get back in the car.

Cynthia didn't throw the present, of course. Instead, she followed Mom up the path to the house and then waited with Mom for Mrs. Fisher to answer the doorbell.

"Ruth and Cynthia, what a treat," said Mrs. Fisher as she opened the door.

Mom and Mrs. Fisher hugged and didn't let go of each other when they were done. There was something weird about how excited they were to get together.

"Cynthia, the girls are out back," said Mrs. Fisher. "Warren is out there with them, Ruth," she said to Mom, "so we can get to the important stuff. I've got a bottle of chardonnay that is just begging for a friend and a pair of glasses."

Mom and Mrs. Fisher walked behind Cynthia through the house and into the kitchen, and then Cynthia left them there, walking on through the open sliding door into the backyard. Cynthia could hear Mom and Mrs. Fisher laughing behind her, but she didn't care. Maryanne's parents had gone all out.

The invitation Mom had picked up from Dad had a circus theme, and Mom had liked it enough to throw it on the fridge with a magnet, but it didn't begin to do justice to the setup for the party. Maryanne's parents had refashioned their entire fenced-in backyard like it actually was a circus. Paper elephants lined the back of the fence, while a row of great cats covered the right side, and a cadre of paper clowns decorated the left. Carnival-style games were set up all over the backyard. There was Skee-Ball, a plinko board, water guns used to shoot pop cans off of a rail, pin the tail on the lion, and several other games that Cynthia didn't recognize.

Cynthia set her gift on a table that was about half-full with other similarly wrapped packages and ran over to where Maryanne and a number of other little girls Cynthia recognized were sitting in front of Mr. Fisher.

"Cynthia's here," cried Maryanne as Cynthia began walking over to her with a grin plastered across her face.

"Well, that means we're only waiting on two more," said Mr. Fisher. "Cynthia, go ahead and have a seat. I was just showing these kids a few of my magic tricks."

Cynthia sat on the lawn front and center next to Maryanne.

"This one is good," said Mr. Fisher as he pulled a wand and an ancient-looking hat from the black trunk next to him.

• • •

It may just have been that Cynthia missed her friends so much, but the party was fantastic. The games were great, the Fishers even had tickets to be won and a prize table at which to spend them, and even Mr. Fisher's cheesy magic show had been pretty entertaining. Cynthia hadn't seen Mom except for a fleeting moment when she and Mrs. Fisher had stepped out onto the back patio, wine glasses in hand. Mr. Fisher and Maryanne's older brother and his friends ran the games, and Cynthia wound up with a stuffed dog and sack of candy, but she still was a little sad that she'd lost the day with Mom.

Cynthia was standing by the prize table, watching other little girls pick out what they wanted, when she heard something from inside the house. Mr. Fisher heard it, too. Cynthia could tell by the quizzical look on his face when he turned to the noise and the swirl of pink that threaded its way amongst the blue and green that had been flowing from his head before. No one else seemed to notice the sound, and Mr. Fisher lost interest, returned to his job as prize master. A few seconds later, though, there was another noise, and someone from inside—it sounded like Mrs. Fisher—shouted, "You need to leave right now!"

Mr. Fisher stood at that and started toward the house, the threads on his head instantly divided between red and pink, and Cynthia broke from her friends and began to follow him.

"Nick, no!" screamed Mom from inside the house, and then there was a crash of noise, and Mr. Fisher began to run.

Cynthia's heart fell when she heard her father's name, though she already knew it was Dad—she'd known since she'd heard the first noise. He was going to embarrass her in front of her friends, and there was nothing she could do about it.

As Dad burst through the back door, a screaming Mrs. Fisher all but hanging from his back, Cynthia's fear of being merely embarrassed died inside of her. The threads coming from Dad were purple and black, all of them swirling like sea anemone feelers in the wind.

"Where is she?" Dad yelled. "Where is my daughter? Where's Cynthia?"

Mr. Fisher held up his hands in a warding-off gesture as he walked up to Dad. Mrs. Fisher had backed off and was standing in the doorway holding a phone to her ear. Cynthia didn't see Dad cross the lawn and deck Mr. Fisher because she was gone, floating over the Fisher house as time hung like dew on a thread, and then dove into Dad.

Cynthia saw through his eyes as Mr. Fisher fell to the ground, and Cynthia could hear the screams of Mom and Mrs. Fisher behind him. / Get up, you bastard / She's kept me from my daughter for weeks / Ruining this family / Ruining everything / Cynthia let go of Dad and left him, working on his threads from the outside as Mrs. Martin had taught her. She knew that she could make him leave, but if she did he might just hurt someone else, because he was still so angry and confused. Cynthia began to tear at the black threads, but it wasn't like with Patrick. These were rooted, not yet dead but still dying. Cynthia felt the yellow surrounding her, yellow she tried to mate with Dad's angry purple, but Dad's threads blackened as swiftly as she took hold of them. Cynthia could feel a coldness coming over, something she'd never felt before while weaving, and when she pulled back at one of her threads, it was frozen and linked with Dad's.

Cynthia took hold of the closest braided threads connecting the pair of them and spun the threads apart, but as they split she could see that the black was still on the tip of her yellow strand, like some Gothic highlight. Ignoring the black, Cynthia began to part the rest of them, tearing herself free from Dad. The strands broke, and pieces fell and disappeared. Cynthia could feel Dad screaming inside as surely as if he really were screaming. *Just go, just leave*, Cynthia urged him, and then Dad took off running. Cynthia felt tossed around as if she were in a pinball machine, and then she dove into the sky and screamed back into herself. Dad was shoving Mom out of the way as the two women ran into the backyard, Mrs. Fisher headed for her husband, now propped up on one knee, and Mom to Cynthia.

"Oh my God, Cynthia, are you OK?" Mom asked in almost a whimper.

Mom had a cut over her eye and smelled like wine, but Cynthia had never been happier to see someone in her life. She wrapped her arms around her as both of them fell into tears, though Cynthia was upset for entirely different reasons than Mom. She'd tried to help Dad, but she hadn't been able to—it was too late. *He's lost, and you'll never see him again, unless he decides to hurt you and Mom.* The thought brought pain boiling to the forefront of Cynthia's mind, and her tears turned into a racking cough. Mom hoisted her up and began to cross the yard, the sound of emergency sirens in the distance, and Cynthia's eyes closed.

Chapter 55

Darryl was working on Robert's mind like an archaeologist slowly brushing the dirt off of an ancient fossil. The trick was to learn everything about Robert's scam, to learn the kid's limitations, and to never let Robert suspect the thoughts he was having were anyone's but his. It was hard work and slow going, but Robert was special. Darryl had bludgeoned himself over and over about just how much money and time had been wasted by the way he'd burned through Vincent, and it wasn't a mistake he intended to make twice. Robert was going to be the perfect project, one that would see them to a massive pot of gold at the end of the rainbow.

Darryl was so involved with the work that he no longer felt frustrated with their small apartment or bleak circumstances. The cops were looking for them, but Robert was going to lead the way to salvation. There might be a top-secret government task force headed their way, but Robert was the key that could lock all of those problems away, never to be seen again. Darryl knew he was leaning too hard on the possibilities presented by the faraway boy and his magic brain, but he didn't care. The sands of Mexican beaches still called to him in a way that no place on earth ever had, and now he knew that someday he would live in such a place again.

It had been weeks since Darryl had taken a drink, enough time that he was starting to wonder what the appeal had been in the first place. Terry had been clean, too, though his friend mostly stayed in his room and just sat quietly. Darryl thought he knew why. Terry was coming down from a mean bender of hatred and probably had a lot to think about. Darryl had filled him about to the brim with ugly medicine, and Terry had to have been reeling from the hangover.

Still, quiet or not, at least Darryl knew that Terry wasn't out killing. Neither had left the apartment alone, and Darryl made sure that even their dual supply runs happened as rarely and quickly as possible. Darryl had certainly never wanted to live in a place like North Harbor, but it had just felt right. And so far the instincts he had grown to trust had delivered once again: the apartment complex was proving to be a fine place to put their feet up and go incognito.

Currently, Darryl was a few hundred miles away and watching as his new recruit checked in on his scam, Darryl frankly a bit jealous of the kid's ingenuity. The kid was grifting on a far grander scale and at a far younger age than Darryl ever had, and he was even proud of him in a weird way. Of course, Darryl wasn't visiting Robert to steal a password or to admire the boy from afar; he was there to begin making inroads of suggestion that would allow him to work the boy like a puppet when the time came. Darryl had never been in someone else's mind so frequently or for such long stretches of time, and it was fascinating to be in so deep. He watched through Robert's eyes as the boy checked his pilfered deposits for the day and then closed down the browser before leaving his room.

With Robert untethered from his machine, Darryl slipped back into himself before his own computer and considered again his endgame for the Robert project. It was pretty simple. When he was ready, he was going to order Robert to do something, and he was going to order it in such a way that it felt to Robert like his own wild idea, not one thrown into his mind by someone like Darryl. If that worked, Darryl figured he and Robert would have a lengthy working relationship. Worst-case scenario, however, Darryl had prepared himself for the possibility that he might have to content himself with a slash-and-burn sort of plan. Some horses aren't meant to be broken, and Robert could very well be one of them.

If that proved to be the case, though, Darryl wouldn't be happy with the pittance he'd extracted from Vincent. No, Darryl would make the boy gather all of the money from his parents' accounts, along with those of the insurance company clients his dad was even tangentially connected to, and then have all of that money wired to an offshore account. This would amount to a payday of satisfying, if not staggering proportions—enough to ease the pain of having to dispose of the kid.

Still, Darryl preferred not to dwell on such a dark contingency. Though it was much harder to work with a scalpel than a club, Darryl was already discovering that using the blade offered a whole new sort of reward.

Chapter 56

"I'm never going to do it again," said Cynthia, and Mrs. Martin only nodded in answer.

Cynthia had been dying for the past two days to see the older woman—two days spent in the hospital, at the police station, and finally, at a firearms store, where Mom had looked into buying a gun and settled on pepper spray due to the cost. There were a million questions Cynthia had wanted to ask her mother, but she had asked none of them. Mom was heartbroken—Cynthia could see it in her eyes—and Cynthia knew that Mom thought it might have been her fault as well as Dad's. Right now, Cynthia didn't care about fault or anything else. She needed to find out from Mrs. Martin why she hadn't been able to make Dad calm down.

When Mrs. Martin didn't respond the first time, Cynthia repeated herself. "I won't," she insisted. "I won't do it again."

"Maybe you will and maybe you won't," said Mrs. Martin. "If I had to guess, I'd say there are a great many young people who choose to stop weaving at a young age and never take up the mantle again."

"Why?"

"Because they decide what they are doing is wrong or just a weird game of make-believe," said Mrs. Martin. "Most of them wind up drinking too much, or taking pills, or going to the hospital over it, but I'm sure there are some perfectly happy people out there who know what they are and simply choose to ignore it."

Mrs. Martin took a drag on her cigarette, then fixed her eyes on Cynthia's. "Did I tell you that something similar to what happened with your father happened to me once?"

"No," said Cynthia, her mouth twisting in confusion. Cynthia knew that she could do things that Mrs. Martin could not, but she had still never considered the idea of her teacher being beaten back like she had been. "I couldn't do anything," said Cynthia, hating the whine in her voice. "I couldn't do anything at all at first, and then when he ran at Mr. Fisher, I knew I had to do something, but nothing that you taught me worked. He was so angry, so mean, and when I tried to weave him, it hurt. It made me feel sad inside, like there was something wrong with me."

"Doing bad things can make you hurt, and sometimes doing good things for a person who is very sick can make you hurt as well. Your father was very angry, so he was not, I'm sure, considering the consequences of his actions. It would have been hard for anyone to rein in."

Cynthia nodded but was barely listening after the word "consequences." Mom had said the same thing on the phone and at the police station: Dad was still out there somewhere, likely more mad than ever about the loss of his house and family.

"He didn't mean to hurt me," said Cynthia. "That part was my fault. I think he meant to hurt Mr. Fisher and anyone else who got in his way, but I don't think he wanted to."

"I'm sure he didn't mean to hurt you, dear, but he hurt you all the same," said Mrs. Martin. "Your threads will lose the black soon enough—you're young—though I think it will be best to leave it where it is and keep the memory of what happened fresh in your mind. The scars you wear will be a good reminder that we are not comic book heroes."

"Then what are we?"

"We are Moirai, just like I've told you since the beginning," said Mrs. Martin. "We control what we can when we can, but we can cut whoever we like. Do you understand what I mean, Cynthia?"

Cynthia nodded, not sure that she did, but not sure she wanted Mrs. Martin to explain. She did, anyway.

"We can cut the threads of any man or woman we choose," continued Mrs. Martin, "but we are the ones who bear those consequences, and sometimes we can be wounded, even if we cut for the wrong reasons. There is more to it all, of course—there are things that you will only understand later—but for now, just remember: to keep yourself safe, you can be a blade. I can't even imagine how easy it would be for someone with your powers to reap."

"I can't do that," said Cynthia. She liked Mrs. Martin, cared for her intensely now that she was one of the only people Cynthia interacted with, but this was too much. *She's telling me to kill Dad*, thought Cynthia, and not only was the suggestion repellant, it was impossible. Cynthia didn't even like to step on ants. She couldn't hurt her dad, could hardly imagine doing something worse than that.

Seeing the distress on her face, Mrs. Martin said, "Cynthia, you mistake what I'm saying. I am telling you what you can do, dear, not something that you must do. You have great powers in your young mind and a great heart, and the last thing I would want is for you to be corrupted, but—"

"But if I need to protect myself, I can," said Cynthia slowly. She still couldn't imagine doing it, but Mrs. Martin was right. It was good to know she could if she needed to.

"Remember the old story," said Mrs. Martin. "There were three sisters—the spinner, the drawer, and the cutter—all tasked with different parts of controlling how long a person should live. But I think the reality is different. I think the real Moirai were all just cutters and that the other two jobs were invented long after the Moirai themselves were dead. There are powerful people in this world who would hurt you because of what you are, Cynthia, and when I speak of using your abilities to cut, I'm talking about them."

"Why would anyone want to hurt me?"

"Because they are scared of you, my child," said Mrs. Martin quietly. "Do you think that what you said earlier is still true—that you will never do it again? Or have you learned another lesson?"

Cynthia thought about that. "I won't stop being what I am, but I won't mess around anymore, not if I can really hurt people."

Mrs. Martin smiled and then bent across the table to pat the top of Cynthia's hand. "There is still time for fun, but being a weaver and being safe is hard work. You must be careful, with both yourself and others."

Chapter 57

Jessica walked into the conference room, where Howard waited for her. The bravado she kept on display for her net-researching kids was gone. Now she felt like the tired little old lady who she was so scared of becoming. This wasn't a bad hair day; this felt like the dissolution of her as a person.

When she had sat heavily across the table from Howard, he said, "So, do you want to tell me why you brought me here?"

"I need to clarify some things," said Jessica. "My project isn't off-track yet, but it could get that way, and fast. I need your assurance that you still have faith in me."

Howard nodded, stood, then walked to the drink cart and stared at it for a moment before removing a bottle of Pappy Van Winkle bourbon. "Do you know who keeps us supplied with this stuff?"

"I've never really thought about it."

"We have a budget, set by your father, of ten thousand dollars a month for liquor," said Howard. He scanned the room. "Don't you ever wish these walls could talk? I was in Research back then, you were only a field agent, so we missed those big decisions by those old Knights of the Round Table."

She hadn't called him here for a stroll down memory lane, but he was right, of course. Presidents had sat at this very table and brokered deals. Her father sat here and negotiated the Gulf of Tonkin Resolution just four months before he dropped dead of a heart attack.

"Those were men of action," said Howard, returning the bottle to the cart and then walking back to his seat. "Now, with all of the regulations we're forced to operate under and the very justified fear of having our efforts laid bare for the world to see, we're constantly hamstrung. That was the golden age."

"I have a million dollars in the wind right now," said Jessica. "Is that playing fast and loose enough for you?"

"I guess I should mention that I knew that," said Howard with a sigh. "And I suppose I should have poured us a pair of drinks when I was at the cart."

"No need. I can take my licks sober."

"No punishment—not in the TRC, not for a Hockstetter. What do you think the world is coming to?"

"Knock it off. Can we get to it?"

Howard stood and returned to the cart anyway and this time poured them each a few fingers, neat. He placed her glass before her, set his own in front of his place at the table, and then sat. "All right. The money." He took a drink, appeared to enjoy the bourbon's trip down his throat, and then looked at her. "Is it still something we can get back, or have they transferred it offshore?"

"It's not gone," said Jessica, her own drink untouched. "Right now it's in a Grand Cayman account that we can access, but that could change at any minute."

"Assuming it hasn't exited yet, could you call your geeks and have them retrieve the money?"

"Of course. In a matter of minutes. But then the game would be up," said Jessica. "We are making some headway."

"We'll come back to the money. I like headway. Tell me about headway."

"Well," she said, "headway might be overselling it, but we can absolutely verify that at least one of these men is still in the lower peninsula of Michigan and that he's been active on the web."

Howard nodded, then made a show of taking a drink and another of slowly placing the glass on the desk between them before looking up at her. "Including the girls they killed in Mexico, these two are responsible for eleven deaths in the past few months," said Howard. "Eleven. Eleven is enough that we might have been called in regardless of a TK being involved or not. We need these men captured, Jessica."

Parched from his little speech, Howard drank again, then shook his head and continued. "Another thing. I want these men brought in, but I don't want them for the TRC. I want them here so I can have them exterminated."

Jessica had to tell herself to close her mouth. She'd let her jaw drop open. "Howard," she said, "we can't do that. You heard Herm. This whole program is predicated on our success. Unless you're planning on executing these men yourself out back by the Dumpster, they're not going to sign off on anything like that." Jessica grabbed her glass, drained half of its contents, and then set it back on the table. "I'm willing to let this play out, but I will call a board meeting, Howard."

"We haven't had a true board meeting since the Mogadishu conflict," said Howard. "Do you really think they'd even agree to gather over something so obvious? Take off the blinders."

"Christ, is this ever ass backwards?" said Jessica. "I came here to beg you to let this thing go on and to give me the room that I need to run my operation. You tell me that's fine but that when I succeed, you're going to execute the people that I bring in. Howard, is that the only bottle you've been drinking from?"

"I don't care about the money, and you can call whatever meeting that you want. I already know the answer. I just want you to know that

I back every single part of this mission, but I will fight you when it comes to bringing these men in as TKs. They're not that special. Not every dog gets adopted, Jessica. There are a lot of strays that get put down. These are two of them."

"Board meeting, Howard," said Jessica.

"Best of luck," said Howard.

Jessica wanted to tell him that the joke was on him. They weren't even close to finding these men and nailing this thing down.

Chapter 58

Robert was up and running. Darryl had the kid functioning like an investment banker, using Robert's already impressive computing skills as deftly as he could. Robert was stealing like a career criminal, snuffling out and snatching little bits and pieces from everywhere he could gain access. On top of that, there was no sign that the work he'd done was attracting the slightest attention. Darryl could feel the kid's excitement as the numbers in his personal bank account grew from five figures to six. Robert was off of the leash and loving every second of it. Best of all, he had no idea that he'd been bent. The boy thought that every move he was making was of his own invention.

"It sounds perfect," said Terry, and Darryl smiled in answer. It sounded perfect because it was perfect. The kid was turning out exactly like Darryl knew that he could, how Vincent should have turned out. Before he'd unearthed him and set him to work, Darryl had envisioned running a few kids like Robert, but the more he thought about it now, the more that seemed like a mistake. As it was, he already wasn't in Robert as much as he would have liked. The boy could go off the rails so easily. All he'd need to do was get a little too greedy too fast and he'd get caught. Darryl wouldn't be in any legal crosshairs, of course, but the money would still be lost. At the rate Robert was paying out, that number would be in the millions in just another month or two, and Darryl had no intention of giving that up.

The plan the kid had invented to steal from his dad's clients was blisteringly simple: steal so little that no one would notice, and even if they did notice they wouldn't care very much. After all, who monitored the amount of spare change in their bank account? Darryl certainly never had, and he had a feeling that the bigger the dollar column number got, the more invisible the pennies became. Not that they stayed pennies for long, of course. A million of the copper disks were worth ten thousand paper dollars. Ten million pennies? A hundred thousand, and that was still just the beginning.

Darryl was chuckling to himself as he ran these happy little calculations when he became aware of the sounds coming from Terry's room. Terry had been hiding out more and more lately, leaving only for food and to use the bathroom, but Darryl didn't mind as long as he stayed in the apartment. It was troubling to think of what was happening just a wall away, but Darryl knew it was a lot better than if Terry decided to wander into the world to work out the purple on his own. *He's just doing what he has to*, thought Darryl, just like Darryl was doing what he thought he had to. Darryl had no illusions about the dark parallels between what he was doing to Robert and had already done to Terry, but there was just no other way to play it. If he was going to live the life he wanted, some backs were going to bend, and some were going to break.

Darryl stood, walked to the coffeemaker they'd finally purchased, and poured himself a cup of coffee. Terry had quieted down in the bedroom, and that usually meant about an hour or so of peace. Darryl brought the coffee back to the dining room table, smiling at the memory of cocaine benders and pounded coffees full of ice. There was no reason to work that hard. This time he was working much smarter. He knew there would be a point where he had to take the money and cut off Robert, but that was nothing to worry about at the moment. Right now Robert was going to keep earning, and that was all that there was to it.

Chapter 59

Cynthia's vow to never weave again lasted only until that evening.
Mom was on the phone with her sister again, and Cynthia found it easier to leave the apartment for a little bit than listen to the two of them
talk. Mom said things to Aunt Laura that Cynthia had a hard time
believing she would ever follow through with, but they scared Cynthia
just the same, especially since she could tell from the way Aunt Laura
was apparently agreeing with her on the other end that these ideas were
being encouraged. Dad was still missing, still wanted by police, but
Mom was still mad and wanted more. Cynthia had a feeling that was
going to go on forever—Mom wanting to hurt Dad, to punish him for
whatever he had done—and didn't know where she could possibly fit
into any of Mom's plans. As far as she could tell, Mom was giving that
issue no thought at all.

Once outside, Cynthia took to the sky without even thinking
about it. Looking down over North Harbor from an impossible place
above the trees, she eyed the apartment complex as a bird would and
then glanced to the apartment where the new men in the truck had
moved. Cynthia had been to their place only once and found it lacking
in anything of interest. One of the men did nothing, and the other just

sat at his computer. *What if you marked it?* The thought made her skin feel itchy. She knew that she could do it, and the two men seemed like the perfect candidates because they were so boring.

All Cynthia would need to do was go in, look at their threads, and then leave. She could get in their heads if she wanted, but Cynthia couldn't imagine a reason to do so. What would be in there? Numbers and blank walls? There weren't even any books in the apartment.

Cynthia went from thinking about her new idea to zipping into the apartment. She hovered over the computer man as he worked, and she could see the threads coming from him were green and yellow, with a few of them even crossing over a white box on the table. *He must really like computers.* She loved her toys but had never considered trying to weave with them. What would be the point?

Already bored with the computer man, Cynthia went to the other room. The plan was pretty simple: verify that this man was boring as well and then color a blue dot onto the map above the apartment. But the instant Cynthia entered the next room, she regretted doing so. The man in there was sitting and doing nothing, just like she'd suspected, but his threads were nothing but black and purple. Cynthia might once have tried to help him, but all she could think of was Dad and how she had been hurt when she tried to help. The man in the room was worse than Dad—he looked like he was going crazy, just sitting in there by himself. She left the room quickly, not wanting to know any more about the man than she already did.

Cynthia paused as she came back to the little apartment's living space, taking just a moment to look in on the computer man again, and what she saw there was just as shocking as the stalk of purple and black atop the man's roommate. The man at the computer sat slack-jawed before the desktop, his hands rigid on its keyboard. *He's weaving.* There was nothing else the man could be doing, but his threads were connected only to the computer. It took Cynthia a moment to realize what that meant. He was weaving with someone *through the computer*, through the wire that connected it to the wall.

Cynthia knew that she had to leave, had to get out, somehow sleep through the night, and then tell Mrs. Martin what she'd seen the next day, but she couldn't. She could only stare raptly at this strange man, seeing in him for the first time what she must look like when she went out of her own head. It was incredible to see, but there was more to it than that. There was something not right with what he was doing, something that Cynthia couldn't quite put her finger on. She moved closer to look at the screen he was staring at, but there was nothing there but a few sentences of conversation. *You have to find out what he's doing*, thought Cynthia, but she could also hear Mrs. Martin begging her to be smart at the same time. Cynthia stared at the man for a while longer and then dove in.

The man at the computer was looking through the eyes of someone else, and Cynthia could see what he was seeing. The person on the other end of the wire was furiously clicking and typing on his own keyboard, golden threads spewing from him and over the keys. It took Cynthia just a few moments to see that he was working with money, and then only another moment to realize that he probably wasn't working at all but stealing.

Cynthia wanted to run screaming from the man's mind like she would have wanted to run from a haunted house, but she knew instinctively that slamming the door on her way out would just let the monster know where she was going.

Cynthia pictured the room in the apartment where the man sat slack-jawed, then the scenic map over North Harbor, and then finally her bedroom—flashing in and out of each point—and when she opened her eyes in her room she realized that she had been tucked into her sleeping bag by Mom. *She must have found me lying down and just assumed I was sleeping.* Of course Mom would think she was sleeping, but it was another close call.

Cynthia shivered as she gathered the covers to her chin. She was scared to tell Mrs. Martin what she had seen, but even more frightened of what the man had been doing. Up until that moment, it had never occurred to her that Mrs. Martin might not have been telling the truth about bad people being able to weave. *If he is bad, then he can probably do whatever he wants.*

And so could she.

Couldn't she?

Yes. And this was for some reason more frightening still, the knowledge that she could easily cajole Mom into letting her stay up later, or into buying her a new doll, no matter how tight money might be. The apprehension of this power should have excited her—and it did, a little—but mainly it scared her. She wasn't sure she *wanted* it.

But she was quite sure that that man at the computer shouldn't have it. What was she supposed to do about it, though?

Mrs. Martin will know what to do. Cynthia felt sure of it. But then in the next instant, a new, even colder fear gripped her: *But what if she doesn't?*

Chapter 60

1945

"This is far enough," says Katarina, **"at least for now."**

I'm not sure that I agree with her. The sounds of war surround us still, but I'm glad that she has finally stopped dragging me along beside her. My legs, weakened from years of disuse in the camp, are on fire from our run through the woods. Then Katarina is abruptly sitting, tugging me down next to her, and her voice is in my head. */ Be quiet / So quiet /*

I worry about the sound of my labored breathing, but I feel Katarina begin to soothe me. My heart rate drops, my breathing slows, and I feel safe. There is gunfire to the left of us, then to the right. Men are shouting in German—I can tell they're surrendering—but the sound of them is quickly drowned out by more chattering gunfire and screaming. *It is the Americans executing the guards from Dachau.* But my heart still clings to Katarina's warnings about the American troops and how desperately we needed to avoid capture. I have no idea what to believe, but I know that after such a long internment that has cost me so dearly, I have no desire to be caged again.

The gunfire slows after just a few minutes, though sporadic shots can still be heard. I can feel ribbons of sunlight through the canopy of trees above us and realize that it must be midday. My throat begs for water, my stomach rumbles, but these are problems to be dealt with later. Katarina is on my arm, and she hisses at me, "There are troops just ahead of us—Americans. Stay down."

Katarina pulls my arm to drag me closer to the floor of the forest, and I follow her lead, pressing against a fallen tree and feeling the cold ground against my skin. It's not a bad feeling after all of the running, but I have been cold too many times in the last few years to really enjoy it, so cold that I may never enjoy the cold again. For the second time in my life I'm glad that I cannot see, that I'm blind to how close they are, nor can I see a watch and fret over how slowly time is passing.

Finally, Katarina pulls me to my feet, and the two of us begin to move again. My legs are still sore, my breath short, and the sounds of battle have picked up again when it at last comes crashing down on me: *I'm free.* There's guilt with that thought, too, but also an immense joy in doing what so many could not. Despite my blindness, I survived one of the worst places in the entire world, a hell for the Jewish people. There might be time to sit and think of this later, to realize my fate and to know that the best path for me is to be like Katarina, to seek out young people with this gift and help them the same way she has helped me, but first I must survive.

There are so many ways to die in a war. An errant bullet could be my undoing, a bombing, artillery. We could run into a German patrol and be cut down immediately. The same thing could happen with any troops we might encounter, really. If this war has proven anything, it is that there are no rules anymore.

The rising light and then the sun on my cheeks are the first indicators that the woods are thinning, and the ground changes. No longer am I stumbling over broken timber and across gullies and over low hills. Now the ground is flat. Katarina's grip is as tight as always on my arm, like an aggressive schoolteacher's, but I can't help feeling relieved. If she feels that we can leave the woods, even for a moment, then things must be getting better. My feet cross pavement as we sprint across a road, and then we're pushing our way through spring wheat in a farmer's field. We must be visible for miles, but of course I have no choice but to allow Katarina to gauge how safe we really are.

Finally, after what feels like forever in the open as the war rages around us, we are in the woods once more. I let out a sigh of relief and hear Katarina do the same thing.

"We can slow down now," says Katarina. "We should be able to cross the American lines soon."

Katarina would know this if anyone would, I tell myself. After all, she talked to the commandant on a daily basis. She had access to news and maps, even while she was stuck in the camp. In any event, where she goes I must go, and I just hope that when we get to safety we can find some food and water. It feels so good to be free, so magical, but the thought of real butter and bread without maggots—such a meager thing to wish for, but impossible in Dachau—is so good as to be almost nauseating.

"We'll find food soon," says Katarina, possibly reading my thoughts, but possibly only giving voice to her own hunger pangs.

"That sounds wonderful."

"Soon," says Katarina again. "We'll rest here, then get moving again and try to find a farmer who might agree to share a quick meal with us. And if he won't, we can use our tricks to make him see our way of thinking. That wouldn't be so bad, would it?"

"No, of course not," I say. "That seems a minor crime in the middle of all of this."

As if to punctuate my words, the rattle of gunfire can be heard, the noise terrifyingly close to our position.

"First we need to travel farther from the fighting," says Katarina, and for this I have no argument. The machine gun has settled the discussion for us.

Chapter 61

1999

Darryl fell away from the computer in a heap. His head was pound-ing and his ears were ringing. He stood, grunting at the pain in his legs and then nearly toppling over—one of them had fallen asleep while he was off bending Robert. Terry hadn't checked in on him to make sure that he wasn't gone too long. Darryl stole a glance at the clock on the computer and saw that four hours had passed since he'd logged in. The bastard.

Aching and hollowed out as he was, Darryl nonetheless put off bitching out Terry for later and plopped himself back into the chair and went right back to the chat. He didn't know who had been in his head or how they'd done it. He just hoped that his connection to Robert hadn't been spoiled.

Darryl found Robert floating in the same chat that he'd been in before, and he concentrated and found himself there. The boy seemed fine, wasn't trying to reject Darryl or doing anything out of whack, but Darryl was unnerved. As talented and deeply bent as the kid was, in the time Darryl was out of action he could have killed his family and emptied the coffers of the New York Stock Exchange into his bank account. There were no bloodstains on the floor or the walls, though, and Robert was staring at the same screen he had been before, the only difference being that the numbers were a little bigger.

Darryl eased out of him. He wanted to stay and watch him work, but his headache was bad enough, and he couldn't even imagine what a few more hours might do to him. Darryl came to at his computer and began to massage his right calf as the pain there intensified. When he felt like he could walk, he began a journey into the kitchen. Darryl drank from under the tap for a few minutes, then shut the water off and walked to Terry's room. Darryl pounded three times on the door, heard no answer, and walked inside. For the second time in one night, Darryl was truly shocked. The window to Terry's second-floor room was open, and Terry was gone.

"Fuck," said Darryl to the empty room. "Oh fuck, oh fuck."

He slammed the door behind him and then slid into his shoes and ran out of the apartment. Terry could have been anywhere, and there were hunters afoot after them. If Terry fucked up the way that Darryl expected he would, heads were going to roll, and a large police and federal presence was going to descend upon them. *Maybe your bogeymen, too*, thought Darryl, but that was too miserable a thought to let linger. Darryl hopped down the steps to the ground floor and ran to the flattened bushes under Terry's window. There were footprints in the lawn running south, so that was where Darryl went.

Darryl moved quickly, scanning the shadows with his mind along with his more normal senses. If Terry was nearby, Darryl would find him soon, but he was worried about what he might find with him. *You thought he was getting better, but he was just waiting for a chance to run away.* It was a sobering thought: If Terry could do that, what else had he been up to? Worse, how much did he really know? Darryl walked quickly through the night, avoiding streetlights as he pounded the blacktop, the glow of North Harbor fading behind him. If Terry was still in the building, then there was no way Darryl could come back, because there was going to be a room full of bodies there with him. Darryl's only chance was to find him still on the prowl, take him by pleading or with a good shove, and then bring him back to the apartment.

This is the time to get rid of him, thought Darryl, but that wasn't true. If there was a time to get rid of Terry, it would have been after Darryl had used up Robert. He'd need him then. The dose Darryl gave Terry after that would probably be enough to kill him, and if it wasn't, it would certainly make him too dangerous to keep around. Darryl felt like a man debating whether or not the latest incident from the dog was enough to justify putting it down. *Either way, you need to find him first*, and the thought propelled Darryl back into a sprint. The streets were deserted and there was no sign of Terry, but Darryl knew that his friend would find someone soon, assuming that he hadn't already.

Darryl saw the neon lights from half a mile away and felt like he could smell the spilled beer and ashtrays already. Where else would he be but a bar? Darryl slowed to a walk, cursing Terry with every step for making him do this instead of trying to figure out how in the fuck someone had gotten into his head. *You can worry about that later. Right now you need to find Terry before it's too late.* Though Darryl couldn't help but think that Terry was already gone from the scene ahead of him and that the trail left by whoever had been in his head back at the apartment was disappearing by the second.

The bar was called the Shipwreck and was of the blue-collar variety, and the smells were exactly as Darryl had known they would be. He had spent enough time in bars just like this, drinking and waking up drenched in those odors like he'd been dunked in a tank of Chanel Number Shit. There was no sign of Terry, but Darryl could feel and see eyes on him in the half-full bar. Of course, they would be on him— everyone else in this hole surely knew one another. This kind of attention was never comfortable, and even less so when one was a fugitive from the law. Darryl ignored the stares, and interest faded to boredom as he strode to the bar and sat.

The bartender, a heavyset woman with a blown-out nose and a yellow haze in her eyes, asked what she could get him. Nothing sounded worse to Darryl at that moment than a drink—he needed his wits about him if he was going to find and retrieve his psychotic friend and figure out who was sneaking around within his own skull—but he could hardly sit here without one.

"Miller Lite," said Darryl.

The woman grunted and walked to the cooler, and Darryl dove into her. The bartender, name of Mary Reynolds, would have been easy to pick apart—her whole life was laid bare before him, thanks to the booze and pills she was currently sweating out—but Darryl didn't have time and didn't care. *Another sterling member of the got-fucked-by-your-dad club,* thought Darryl as he wormed his way into her more recent memories, all of them murky. He found Terry a few seconds later—his friend ordering a drink and then walking into the bathroom with a butter-faced biker chick in a leather miniskirt. Mary's sole thought that accompanied this was, *Big Rick comes back, he's going to kill that man,* but Darryl had enough. He let her go, and Mary staggered as she knelt to get the longneck from the cooler but didn't go down.

Darryl slapped three bills on the bar. "Be right back. Just need to hit the head," he said as he slid from his barstool, and Mary recovered from her wooziness—she had a lot of experience with that—enough to give him a half smile and a nod.

Darryl saw more of those same smiles as he forced himself to walk without urgency to the restroom. They all knew what he was going to find, and he imagined it was a common enough sight: Big Rick's old lady bent over a sink getting the business. Only Darryl knew that tonight he would find a much worse show taking place in the Shipwreck's bathroom. Darryl drew a deep breath and then bumped the door with his shoulder, loath to leave a fingerprint on the entrance to a certain crime scene if he could help it.

"Ah shit," said Darryl as he stepped inside.

Big Rick's old lady was indeed getting the business from Terry, but she was quite visibly dead. Terry, lustily pounding away at the woman's still-twitching body, hadn't even noticed that he had gained an audience.

"Jesus Christ, Terry," said Darryl, and Terry's slit eyes winked open, first in anger and then in shock.

Terry let go of the woman, and she dropped to the floor of the bar's bathroom, landing with a wet thud and rolling, allowing Darryl to see her ruined throat.

"I don't know," said Terry, and Darryl just shook his head at this insightful comment.

Terry was covered in blood and so was the bathroom. The bar beyond the door was at least half-full, and even this crackerjack crowd seemed likely to note the gore slathering his friend. *Not to mention the return of Big Rick.*

As though summoned forth by this unhappy thought, a bellowing man could be heard from the bar. "Linda!" roared the voice, and then again, "Lin-*da*!" It was only getting closer.

"I don't know, and I'm sorry," offered Terry, but Darryl ignored him and stepped back against the wall just before the door was kicked in.

Big Rick was aptly named. The man stood at least six and a half feet tall, and he was nearly as wide. Terry didn't even look up at him. He was busy washing his hands in the sink, getting as much gore off of them as possible, and Linda's body lay on the floor between them.

"What the fuck?" Big Rick asked, a reasonable response to the distance between the scene before him and the one he'd expected to find.

Darryl stepped from the side of the door, still behind Big Rick, and shoved hard. / *Punish her / Rip her apart for what she did* / Big Rick froze and then fell to the floor and busied himself with the woman. Darryl and Terry both watched the scene for a moment, unable to tear their eyes away, and then Darryl grabbed Terry's arm and the pair of them ran from the bathroom. Behind them came a noise like someone trying to plunge a toilet, but Darryl didn't look back.

"He let you off easy," remarked Mary, the bartender, as the two men staggered for the door.

The alcoholic peanut gallery concurred, giving Darryl and Terry sideways looks that seemed to say, *Been there, done that.*

Darryl shrugged, not sure what to say, only knowing that they needed to leave. The two of them slipped into the night, odd glances chasing them into the moonlight.

There were no sirens as Darryl and Terry walked from the Shipwreck and headed back home, though that was just a matter of time. Darryl didn't think Big Rick would be in any condition to tell the cops what he'd seen when he walked into the bathroom, but there was no way to be sure. Not that it was likely to matter. He couldn't imagine the cops being too interested in anything Big Rick might have to say, given his no doubt colorful past and the bloodbath he'd be discovered playing in. Still, as the North Harbor Apartments came into sight, Darryl shivered violently, despite the warm weather.

"I'm sorry," said Terry again, and Darryl shuddered at the words.

"I know," said Darryl, unable to tell Terry the rest, that while Darryl had been out looking for him, he should have been trying to figure out who had been in his head. *You'll find them*, thought Darryl, *unless they decide to find you first.* Darryl shuddered again, more violently this time, and his teeth chattered like a windup toy. *You should leave right now. Don't even pack, just disappear and try somewhere else. You might even be able to reconnect with Robert. He might still be OK.*

The shuddering ceased, and Darryl turned to Terry. His topknot had gone from lurid purple to pink and blue, and Darryl said, "Let's just get inside."

I'll leave when I find out who it was. Darryl knew it was a mistake, but he also knew that he wouldn't be able to live with himself knowing that he'd never punished the violator or extracted any of the money he'd made with Robert. *Everything is going to be fine,* thought Darryl as he staggered up the steps to the apartment. Sirens were gathering like fireflies in the night, but even though Darryl knew it was a mistake, all he wanted was to lie down. The search for the thief in his head could wait for one more day.

He was wrong about that.

Chapter 62

"Please tell me that you got something that time," said Pat after roaring back into the real world. "I was in forever that time. There had to have been something."

But when Pat spun in his chair, there was no one anywhere near him. Instead, they were all crowded around Brinn's computer. Even Jessica was leaning in over her. This was just the latest insult in what was beginning to feel like a never-ending string of them.

Pat stretched, stood, and then walked over to join them.

"Got him," sang Brinn as he approached. "We fucking got him!"

Jessica pumped her fist in the air while Geoff and Rick high-fived.

Starving and delirious from having those fucking apes in his head, Pat staggered to a halt before them. He couldn't believe what he was hearing. *Got him? How could they get him? I was just there. He was just in me.* None of it made sense. All Pat knew was that after Darryl and that other guy were finished with him, he felt like his grandmother yelling about kids wearing shoes in the house and leaving fingerprints on the walls. Those dudes made his head feel filthy.

"What are you guys yelling about?" Pat asked as he fell into the chair closest to Brinn's desk. "I'm thirsty."

"You got that motherfucker, Pat," shouted Geoff. "You let him do his thing, and we got his IP address. Jessica can find him now!"

The sense of the words finally crashed down on him like a tidal wave. He'd given up on them actually succeeding in leaning on Terry and Darryl. The job had come to feel more like an excruciating academic exercise than a mission that could actually be accomplished. He was just Sisyphus with his damn rock.

"You really got something?"

"Full IP address," said Brinn without turning. "I'm tracking it right now. It won't take long."

Jessica was rubbing her hands together maniacally, Geoff and Rick were slavering at the screen like starving lions who'd spotted wounded prey across the savannah, and Brinn had blue light flashing against her face.

"Are you ready to rumble?" Geoff asked no one, and the group— excluding Pat—burst into peals of laughter.

Pat was shocked to see that even Jessica was busting a gut at the lazy joke. He just sat in silence. All he could think was that he *had* been rumbling, and now he was ready to take the gloves off, slump in his corner, and have a water. His mind ached like a sore muscle. No, more than that—not a headache, but like someone had been working his brain with a melon baller.

"Am I done then?" he asked in a small voice. "Is the weird shit over?"

"Not just yet," said Jessica. "Where are you at, Brinn?"

Pat's stomach dropped sixteen stories. *Why aren't we done? What's left to do? They have the IP address. Mission accomplished.*

"Grand Rapids, Michigan," said Brinn. "I can get closer, I'm just waiting on some—"

"Keep working," said Jessica. "Geoff and Rick, get Pat's computer packed. This show is going on the road."

"What?" Pat asked.

"Do we get to go?" Rick asked, and Jessica shook her head.

"The only people going from here are Pat and me, with one other important guest," said Jessica. "Pat, I wish I could send you home to pack, but we're going to be on a helicopter very soon and I need you ready to go. We can get you whatever you need when you land."

"Wait. Why do I need to go?" Pat whined, hating his voice as it escaped his lips. "Why can't I just stay here and work?"

"Because I need you," said Jessica as she took her phone from her belt, flipped it open, and got dialing. "So get ready. We want these boys busy when we roll in."

Chapter 63

"I want you to tell me everything," said Mrs. Martin as she took her seat at the table across from Cynthia.

Grilled cheese sandwiches and tall glasses of water sat between the two of them, but Cynthia's appetite died with her friend's question. Cynthia hadn't said anything about what she'd seen in the men's apartment.

"Spit it out, my dear. You're harboring something ugly, so let's be rid of it."

"I went exploring last night, on the map," explained Cynthia slowly, and Mrs. Martin nodded. Cynthia knew that she was angry with her—even worse, disappointed. It didn't matter, though. Cynthia wasn't sure of exactly what she'd seen, but she knew it was bad and that Mrs. Martin was the only person who might be able to help. "I saw the men that we saw the other day, from the truck. They live on the other end of the parking lot."

"What were they doing?"

"One of them was mad," explained Cynthia. "He was all purple and black, and he just looked so angry. Dad was really upset, but this was a lot worse. I was going to leave after I saw that, but I went back to see the other man. He'd been at his computer before and he was when I got back, but he was gone, too. He was weaving with the computer. I could see the threads coming from him, and they went into this little box that was hooked to the wall. When I went into him, I could see that he was looking through someone else, and that person was looking at a computer, too. It looked like he was doing something with money, but I couldn't tell for sure."

"Oh my," said Mrs. Martin. She reached for a cigarette, and when she lit it, her hands were shaking.

Cynthia felt like the worst person in the world. "I'm sorry. I know I'm not supposed to do that stuff without you, but I was bored, and I just wanted to explore. Their apartment wasn't marked, and I just thought I'd have a peek, just to see." Cynthia swallowed thickly, and Mrs. Martin exhaled smoke. "I knew it was bad as soon as I was in there," whispered Cynthia.

"Are you sure about what you saw?" Mrs. Martin asked. "You need to be very sure, Cynthia. Are you absolutely positive that you saw him weaving into a computer?"

When Cynthia nodded again, Mrs. Martin nodded, then set her cigarette on the edge of the ashtray and exhaled deeply, smoke and frustration curling over her lips.

"Eat your sandwich," said Mrs. Martin. "I'm going to need to see for myself, and I'm going to need you to come with me."

"Do I have to?"

Mrs. Martin smiled at her sadly. "I have a lot of tricks up my sleeve, dear, but age is not on my side, and I've never been as strong as you. I'll need you to guide me there, and then I'll want your help in case we get into a bind." Mrs. Martin took another drag from her cigarette and said, "Eat up. The sooner it's over, the better."

Cynthia nodded and then tore into her sandwich. She wasn't hungry, but she wanted to do as she was told and for what Mrs. Martin had said to be true. She wanted it to be over.

Chapter 64

Darryl was going through the Roberts's accounts, dumping them all into a single offshore account that only he had the numbers for, but he still felt the intruders. It was like feeling a lover's breath on the back of his neck, and then they were inside.

Darryl had never felt bad about the many, many times he'd violated others in just this way, but he was shocked and wild with hatred for them all the same. He despised them for making his life harder than it already was, for having the nerve to try to see inside of him, yet he forced himself to remain calm. Even though he was positive they were going to try and steal his money, he let them in. There were two of them this time; he was sure of it, just as he'd been sure that there had only been one before.

He'd already seized several hundred thousand dollars, so if this was the beginning of the end, he'd at least made a good start. *They don't know that you know they're here*, Darryl reminded himself, sure that he was mentally strong enough that they wouldn't be able to steal his thoughts, no matter how hard they might try. As far as that went, who the hell cared if they did know they were in him?

Darryl walked to the bathroom, ran his hands over his face, and then stared into the mirror, grinned, and extended a middle finger to himself and to them. They were gone from him as if they'd never been there at all. Darryl spun in the room, looking for them and knowing there would be nothing there to see. He ran to the computer, but everything there was fine, too. There was no way for either of them to have gleaned any information from him or the screen, but Darryl found that even that relief wasn't good enough. He needed to know who they were, and he needed to know why they were fucking with him. He pounded his fist into the wall, and Terry came running.

"Are you OK?"

Darryl shook his head and collapsed to the floor, landing on his ass. "No, I am not," said Darryl. "I feel like I'm going crazy. There was just someone in my head, I know it, but they didn't do anything."

He closed his eyes, and as he tumbled onto his side he heard Terry calling to him. Then there was nothing. Darryl was floating in the air near the ceiling of the apartment, a trick he hadn't tried in years. Indulging in it felt like a step back for him, but then he saw them, and he knew he'd been right to try it. They were floating together, a shimmering form that was both very real and translucent at the same time. Darryl watched them as they sat together in the corner, watching him and Terry and listening like a couple of spies. *How long have they been here? Why are they coming at all? Who are they?* The questions would have to wait. The thieves felt him—he knew it—and just as they'd run from his head, now they ran from the bent world in the apartment and were gone.

Darryl winked back into himself, opened his eyes, and pushed himself to a sitting position.

"We need to leave."

"Now?"

"Yesterday," said Darryl as he stood. "It's probably already too late." *Fuck.*

Chapter 65

"He's clearing it all out," said Pat as he came to, and Jessica grinned.
The game was on. They'd be out in the open soon, and with any luck, in custody very soon after that.

While conditions for Pat had actually improved in some ways here on the road—Jessica was certain they were feeding him better than he fed himself, for instance, and they also took the trouble to keep him hooked to a saline drip to ward off dehydration—it nonetheless had to be terrifying, draining work. Jessica had had decades to get used to Frank, but even she couldn't begin to imagine what it must be like to actually have the slob inside your head.

"It's gone," he said. "All the money is in a new account, and they're going to ground. You need to move now."

Jessica nodded and began to stride from the room. She paused, though, considering her assets and options. She tried to imagine capturing her quarry with just Tesla-helmeted men armed with Tasers but balked at the prospect, forced herself to really consider what was at stake. What happened next could be the tipping point for the United States for the next fifty years. No, she needed Frank on board, too. There was no point in pretending that it could be done any other way.

Frank could still do a shutdown. He was still the alpha in the room, even to a reverse-mute. There could be no shutting him out. Jessica flashed back to that awful last meeting with Howard. He was wrong. Darryl and Terry were exactly what they needed, and she would prove it once she apprehended the TKs and brought the issue to the board.

"I'm leaving," said Jessica, "right now, and I need you to stay here and stay online."

"Done."

"Frank is coming with me," explained Jessica. "He can shut these people off, and he is required for this mission." She shook her head. "I'm sorry, Pat, but this is how it has to be."

"It's fine," said Pat.

What, Jessica was apologizing for taking him off the head-shrinking team? No sweat. He *wanted* to be cut from this weird field team. The initial euphoria had long since faded. He wanted to be back in Hartford and riding a desk amidst his friends. This literally mind-numbing work, with the travel and the risks he was just beginning to realize no one could quantify just yet—not to mention being involved in actually cornering these maniacs—wasn't for him. There was a reason that he didn't watch cop shows, that comedies packed the DVD racks back in his sad old apartment.

"I'm ready to go home."

"Not home," said Jessica. "At least not yet. I need you to do one more thing."

"Oh. OK."

"I need you to log in and be live bait for these assholes," said Jessica. "You know all of the loopholes, all of the stuff that Frank opened up for you and this mission. Darryl or Terry—whoever it is—is already busy dumping assets, gathering stolen money, and he's going to stay that way. He'll be glued to his monitor, so you won't need to do anything but focus on picturing your own computer and making sure he stays that way."

"What? You want me to do this without help?"

"Just enjoy the ride," said Jessica. "You know the scams, the sites, so just follow along. The longer you can keep him occupied, the better our chances. You just need to do your job, and I know you can."

"I don't even know that—how can you?"

"Trust me, the last thing they're going to be thinking of is dumping all of this or getting rid of you. To them it looks like there are still millions of dollars ripe for the plucking, and they're not going to give that up. Just stay calm, and remember, they can't possibly know what we're up to."

"I don't like this."

"We'll be back in Hartford before you know it," said Jessica. "You just need to help us get there."

Chapter 66

Ruth Sherwood walked to her car with a smile on her face. She was tired, even though it was only lunch, but it was a good kind of tired. Working with Nick at the liquor store had been hard, too, but this was different, far more rewarding, and still a little weird. She'd always wondered what kind of place she could've made for herself in the world if she hadn't married so young, and now she was finding out. Since separating from Nick, she'd gulped independence like a rescued swimmer gulps oxygen.

Cheating bastard. There it was, out of nowhere, derailing her pleased, proud train of thought like a dynamited trestle. She hated herself for letting it happen. What made it worse was that she still pined after him like some teenager. When Cynthia was asleep and the world felt dark and dangerous to Ruth, she wanted her man. It couldn't be helped. They'd practically grown up together. Nick had been her soulmate before he'd ever touched her, and when her dreams turned to gripped sheets and a burning itch from what felt like the very center of her, he was the one and only answer to her prayers. She hated him and she loved him, which she knew was the definition of crazy. Now that she was soaring off into a world that still felt more like an excited dream than reality, she also knew she owed it to Cynthia to keep her feet on the ground.

Ruth hated that part. She wanted to be a good mother, but she felt she just had to be more than that as well. She felt like a freed bird, and Cynthia was the loving lanyard holding her back from flying freely. There was nothing for it, though. She'd make it—they both would—and it would be worth it in the end. It was easy to imagine them reminiscing over coffee with tear-streaked faces, Cynthia in her graduation robe and Ruth in a tailored suit, the two of them talking of how proud they were of one another for making it through those tough times together.

Ruth was sticking her key into the car door, thinking not for the first time that if she'd been planning to jump ship she should have waited for a car upgrade, when she felt something press into the side of her head hard.

"Greetings, cunt," said Nick.

Ruth wanted to scream. She hadn't seen him since that awful birthday party—no one had—but she'd never stopped feeling him out there. Still, she'd somehow never expected him to just show up like this—and certainly had never, ever expected to hear him talk to her like that.

She needed to get a grip. Take a breath. *Little boys and petty men hate to let go of their toys, remember?* Nick had been first one and was now the other. She'd tried telling herself that he'd just run, that he'd accepted as she had that the relationship was over and discarded her for that whore, but she'd known deep down she was wrong. She'd known he was always going to be out there—but she'd never imagined the look in his eyes.

"Let me go," said Ruth. "I won't tell anyone I saw you."

Instead of speaking, Nick reached around her and turned the key in the lock, opened the driver's door, and shoved her behind the wheel. There was a moment after he'd slammed the door shut when Ruth thought she could get away. Nick was still reaching for the handle of the back door, and all she needed to do was slide the keys in the ignition, put the car in gear, and slam on the gas, but none of that happened. Ruth fumbled the keys, hit the door lock as a last resort, but then the doors unlocked, and Nick slid into the backseat. *You cheating fucker*, thought Ruth. The gun was pressed against her head again.

"You left the spare keys at home, Ruth," said Nick, his voice cruel but cloyingly familiar. "You thought clearly enough to leave me and take my daughter, you kept it together enough to file divorce papers and get a restraining order, but you left your spare keys at home." Nick sighed, as though he were the one in trouble because of this oversight, and all Ruth could think about was the pepper spray trapped at the bottom of her purse.

"Why don't you drive us home?" said Nick. "Take me to my daughter."

"She's not home," said Ruth.

"So take me to where she is," hissed Nick.

Ruth's mind was reeling, trying to come up with some lie that would placate him, but she knew Nick. He was going to get what he wanted eventually. She did the only thing she could think to. Ruth turned the car on, pulled out of the parking lot, and started driving. Nick wanted to see his daughter, and there was nothing she could do about that—at least not yet. If she was lucky, she'd see a cop or be able to signal another driver that she was in trouble, but Ruth already knew neither of those things was going to happen.

Still, she pleaded with him. "Just leave us alone, Nick. We'll get the charges dropped for what happened at the party. You'll be free then. You'll have Linda and can just leave us alone."

Nick chuckled from the backseat, the gun pressing against her head as she pulled onto the highway.

"You have no idea what I have and what I don't," said Nick. "Just take me to my goddamn daughter."

Chapter 67

"I need to call the police," said Mrs. Martin. She let go of Cynthia's hands and then lit a cigarette. "I need to call the police."

Mrs. Martin had said the same thing twice, but Cynthia didn't know why, nor did she know why Mrs. Martin didn't pick up the phone.

"Need to call the police," repeated Mrs. Martin again, smoke pouring from her mouth. "I can call your mother. We can tell her that we need to run, that we need to go right now. We can tell her where to meet up with us. She has a good head on her shoulders, and we can convince her without telling her about those men in the apartment." Mrs. Martin frowned. "The important thing is to get as far away from them as possible. I can't imagine why they're here, but as long as they are, none of us are safe."

Across the room, Stanley began barking on the couch the dogs were sharing, loud yips to show he was sharing in their distress, and then Libby began to sound off as well. As clear as day, Cynthia heard / *Shut up* / *Shut up* / in her head. The dogs both dropped to the floor, falling from the couch as though they'd been felled by gunfire. Cynthia ran to them, upsetting her chair as she left the table. The dogs were tottering up onto their stubby legs as she got to them, both listing like drunks on the first Friday of the month.

"What did you do?" Cynthia asked. "How could you hurt them?"

"I didn't mean to," said Mrs. Martin.

Cynthia was cowering on the floor with the whining dogs swirling around her.

"We'll go to your apartment," said Mrs. Martin. "We can hide there. No one will think to look there. Your mother gave me a key."

"OK." Cynthia stood, hoisting a dog under each arm.

Mrs. Martin nodded quickly, discharging smoke as her head bobbled up and down. "Now," she said. "We need to leave now."

Grabbing her cordless phone from its charger, she darted to the front door, calling to Cynthia to hurry. Cynthia did as she was told, the placated dogs still under her arms, and followed Mrs. Martin outside.

The sun was shining as they walked into the light, the wind blowing lightly and the temperature a comfortable eighty degrees. Mrs. Martin had already started up the steps to their apartment when Cynthia saw Mom's car pull in front of the building. Cynthia stopped and turned in time to see Mom spill from the driver's side and begin running toward her. A man was following her, a man that Cynthia took a second to realize was Dad.

"Run," said Mom as she charged toward her, but Cynthia's feet were bolted to the ground, just as her eyes were locked to the gun that Dad was holding in his right hand. *Dad hates guns*, she thought, but that didn't seem to matter anymore.

"Not one more step," Dad said.

Mom did as he said, coming to a full, wide-eyed halt, as though she shared Cynthia's view of the gun Dad had now leveled at the back of her head.

"We're going on a little ride," Dad said. "All four of us, including the old bitch on the steps. C'mon, it's time to get in the car, Cynthia."

No one moved. They were frozen like statues where they stood, though Cynthia could hear Mrs. Martin on the phone behind her, whispering something to what Cynthia hoped was the police.

"I said get in the fucking car!" screamed Dad, and then Cynthia was leaping up into the map of North Harbor, the sound of a gunshot chasing her into the tranquility of their place in the sky.

Cynthia had no time to process what the gunshot meant or even that Dad had actually shot the gun at all. She had work to do. She dove from the sky to Dad, lurched to a stop just above him and then buried her hands deep in the black and purple threads flaying the air above him. She began to weave—not as Mrs. Martin had taught her, not for peace or to help him, but to just make him stop. Cynthia could see Mom falling slowly beneath her, a fan of blood still held in the air like a halo around her head, but she kept on—no longer working as a weaver but cutting as a Moirai.

Chapter 68

Darryl completed the last of the transactions and then gave Robert a hard push so that the boy would run. Darryl had left Robert with ten thousand dollars because he thought the kid might have a shot with that much of a stake and granted it to him out of thanks. Of course, their work over the last week had netted Darryl just shy of two million dollars and would be the ruin of Robert's family, and especially his father. Two million. Not bad for a little bit of work. Darryl gave a last look around the apartment. They were leaving everything but the computer. Not that it mattered. They owned nothing but junk and would have replaced it all, anyway.

"Are you sure we have to leave?" Terry asked, and Darryl didn't dignify his question with a response. Terry was still coming to grips with what had happened the night before, and Darryl wasn't surprised that his friend was a mess.

"Yes, I'm sure," said Darryl as he walked to the door. Terry followed him, a sheepish look on his face. "Get in the truck, and let's get the hell out of here. I've had enough of Michigan and enough of this damn apartment to last me a lifetime."

Darryl climbed into the truck and had the engine turned over by the time Terry hopped into the passenger seat. Feeling better by the second, he backed out, then hit the brakes and jammed it into drive to leave North Harbor, sure that he would never see it again. And then he saw them.

Just a few buildings down from their apartment there was a woman facedown on the ground, a growing pool of blood collecting around her head, and a man standing over her and twitching as though he'd stuck his finger into an electrical socket. Darryl didn't care about any of that, and though he could hear Terry speaking next to him, he couldn't understand a word he was saying.

Standing not ten feet from the twitching man was a little girl.

The girl looked as serene as the man looked pained, and Darryl knew that she was bending the poor bastard. Just past her, an old woman was on the phone, and suddenly everything made sense.

Darryl threw the truck into park and ran from it, while behind him Terry screamed, "What are you doing?"

Darryl ignored his friend, his eyes locked on the bitch on her phone as he flew toward the little girl. The old woman knew who he was—he could see that from her popping eyes—and the only way she'd know him would be if she was the one who'd invaded his head along with the girl. Darryl gave her an extra-stiff push for that effrontery. The phone clattered to the concrete stoop before the woman made it, and then they both bounced to the bottom of the stone steps. Darryl figured she was probably dead, given the ugly sounds she made on her trip to the sidewalk, but he could hear her moaning as he walked to the little girl. He guessed her moans would be only temporary.

Darryl wrapped his arms around the girl, hoisted her up like a junior-sized mannequin, and walked past the twitching man to the truck.

"You're driving," he said to Terry as he heaved the girl into the truck, then followed after her. Terry slid over behind the wheel but then fell still, as though he'd come unplugged.

"Drive," growled Darryl, pissed at his stalled-out friend, but also feeling a rising surge of elation. He'd fucking caught one. This would be worlds better than anything that could be done on a computer. North Harbor had offered up a lovely parting gift: his own little monster, right here in their truck.

"Terry, fucking drive," said Darryl again, but Terry remained transfixed by the man dancing on the pavement.

Then both of them were looking past him at the broken old woman, who was somehow trying to rise.

"Drive, Terry!" shouted Darryl, this time smacking him across the head, jolting both Terry and the truck into motion.

Darryl cradled the little girl in his arms, knowing that she'd be back soon. Her topknot was asleep because she was gone, and he began to bend his way into her, already preparing for her to attempt to reject what was happening to her.

Chapter 69

The dogs had been with her. Cynthia remembered feeling the dogs scratching and biting alongside her at the ugly strands above Dad, and then not only could she feel them, she could see them. The dogs were an opaque brown, there but not, and they were digging their teeth in with relish against the black strands. Cynthia urged them on, soothing the dogs as she chopped at her father. It was hard work, awful work, only made worse by the gunshot that was still echoing in his mind and through the strands. Cynthia refused to look over her shoulder, refused to look at the dogs at their work, and refused to look through Dad's eyes. Instead of looking, she cut, and it took very little time to realize that this was what she was born for.

Then the world had begun to swirl as Cynthia worked, and she'd felt like she was being yanked underwater. Dad began to fall away. Cynthia was being torn away from him, the dogs still visible and then gone. She saw the map, and then the world snapped to black. Cynthia couldn't breathe. She was trapped underwater, frozen in a dream that refused to end.

Now Cynthia came to on the bench seat of a truck. She had no idea where she was or what was happening, and then she looked to her left and saw that the man from the apartment, the one with all of the purple, was driving. Turning her head the other way, she saw the other man—the computer man who could weave—staring down at her.

"We need to talk," said the man. "Why don't you start by telling me your name?"

"Cynthia," said Cynthia, her voice felt like it was coming from a million miles away, and she had the beginning stages of a whopper of a headache blooming, but none of that was important. *Dad killed Mom, and I killed him*, thought Cynthia, and the realization was hell. She felt adrift, utterly lost, and suddenly her presence in the truck with the two strangers didn't matter at all. *I may as well be dead, too.*

"Nice to meet you, Cynthia. My name's Darryl. Terry is driving."

Darryl smiled at her, and Cynthia felt tears begin to streak down her cheeks. She hated that she was crying, hated that she was in the truck, and she hated these men. Most of all, she hated herself. If she'd thought more quickly, worked faster, Mom would be OK. If she'd been able to help Dad at Maryanne's birthday party, they might both still be alive.

"No tears," said Darryl, wiping her cheeks with his fingertips.

Cynthia felt a glowing wave pass over her, soothing her headache and making her misery feel like just a passing thing.

"That should help a bit," said Darryl, smiling down at her, and Cynthia realized with a start that he was weaving with her.

"Stop," said Cynthia. She wanted to feel sad—that was what was supposed to happen. She thought about Mom and Dad, about the fight at Nan and Pop's after the stupid trip to Vegas that had started it all, but none of it mattered right now. She felt good, oddly placated in the middle of the front seat.

"More cops going the other way," said Terry.

"Fine with me, as long as they don't turn around," said Darryl as he stroked Cynthia's hair. "That is just fine by me, but we're going to need a new truck very soon." He looked down at Cynthia and said, "Somehow, I don't think that's going to be an issue."

"I won't help you," said Cynthia, smiling despite the pain, her lips pulled back from her teeth in a grin even though she hated these men.

"Well," said Darryl, "you really won't have a choice, but we'll get to all of that later. What I'm really interested in, however, is why in the fuck you and that old woman were watching me."

Cynthia shook her head, not only because she didn't want to tell him, but because she couldn't. She'd had no good reason for looking into their apartment in the first place, except out of curiosity, and it seemed ridiculous now.

"I don't know," said Cynthia, and Darryl nodded.

"I'll expect a better answer later," said Darryl. "I know you're upset, both with us and the situation, but I need you to listen to me. Do not under any circumstances try to bend Terry or myself. If you do, I will kill you, and it will be bad. Do you understand?"

"What's 'bending'?"

"That crap where you broke into my mind," said Darryl. "All that sneaking around you and that old witch were up to, that's bending."

"Mrs. Martin called it weaving."

"Oh, honey, it doesn't deserve a name nearly as pretty as that," said Darryl. "Bending is lying, cheating, and stealing, and nothing else. Your friend might have wanted to paint a big bow on it, but that doesn't make it anything better than what it is." Darryl paused as two more police cars rocketed past them, followed by three black Suburbans and a black cargo van. Darryl shuddered slightly as they passed and then turned to watch them in the back window of the truck. When they were out of sight, he turned back to Cynthia. "Anyways, no bending, no weaving, none of that shit unless I tell you to."

"Or I do," said Terry, and at once Cynthia could hear Darryl in her head. */ You don't listen to him / You listen to me /*

Chapter 70

Mrs. Martin stared at Cynthia's bastard father, at rest at last on the pavement. He was dead, there was no question of that—not that it was going to do her or Ruth much good.

Mrs. Martin could feel that things in her were broken, badly broken, and she knew that she needed to go. They were coming. She'd known they would when she'd used the phone, but she'd thought she and the girl might have been able to hide. Now the girl was gone and the sirens were getting louder and louder, closer and closer, and it was all Mrs. Martin could do to prop herself into a sitting position and pull her clove cigarettes from her pocket. She lit one, stuck the thing in her mouth, and drew off of it, unable to tear her eyes away from the bodies of Cynthia's parents.

"Shit," said Mrs. Martin, blood speckling her cigarette.

The sirens' din was growing in the distance, but there was nothing to do about that but wait—wait and hope that whatever was broken in her could be fixed.

At last Mrs. Martin saw the first responders pulling in, men dressed in blue carrying guns and running about. She drew off of her cigarette and then felt it fall from her lips. It didn't matter. The world was going black, but that was all right; it was her time.

"I've got three over here," cried one of the cops. "Three down!" Mrs. Martin saw him through blurry eyes, watched as he came to her, knelt down. "Help is on the way," he said. "Hold tight."

Mrs. Martin didn't say anything in response; she just released the last of her smoke. Ambulances, more policemen, and a fire truck pulled into the apartment parking lot, and Mrs. Martin watched as EMTs ran to the Robinsons and then to her. The EMTs sounded like they were speaking in code, and then one of them gave her a shot, and Mrs. Martin felt the left side of her body go numb. *That fucker ran a number on you, the verdammter Jude*, thought Mrs. Martin, the old words mixing with the new ones, and memories of the camps coming back through the pain.

Mrs. Martin watched a stretcher pull alongside of her and then felt them lifting her onto it. Her head lolled to the side, the pain coming in diminishing waves now, and she glanced back to the parking lot as she was drawn to the ambulance. Mrs. Martin watched three black SUVs pull into the lot, followed by a van, and she could feel her heart rate quicken. After a moment's discussion with these interlopers, the pilots of her stretcher pulled her past the ambulance and toward the gaping maw of the back of the van. It was full of noisy and festively lit medical equipment, and two men wearing foreign yet terrifyingly familiar visored helmets were hunched over within it, waiting. Mrs. Martin tried to weave one of the men pushing the cart, tried to tell him that she was the wrong one, that the dead woman was who they wanted, but she couldn't do it. She couldn't connect.

The EMTs pushed her stretcher with rather cruel, rattling abruptness into the van, and then the doors slammed shut.

"Please let me go," said Mrs. Martin, but instead of answering her, one of the visored men turned to her with a syringe full of purple liquid. "Please," said Mrs. Martin, and then the man stuck the needle into her arm and pushed the plunger. "Please," said Mrs. Martin again as the world went gray and then faded to black.

Chapter 71

"How long are you going to let her sleep?" Terry asked, and Darryl sighed at the question. Terry had asked this at least three times, and Darryl was tired of hearing it. The little girl had lost her parents, been kidnapped, and been snapped out of a bend by being yanked out of range. Any one of those things could have shut down the most robust adult for a good long time, and Darryl knew firsthand how painful the last of the three could be.

"We're going to let her sleep until she wakes up," said Darryl. "It's not like there's some rush to get her up."

"I know, but we need to switch cars soon. Everybody and their mother is probably on the lookout for us."

Darryl grimaced. Terry was right. They'd only turned on the radio for a minute, but that was long enough to confirm that the wolves were already out, claiming that he and Terry had killed the two people back at the apartments and had taken a little girl hostage. Darryl hadn't expected any less, but it was still troubling to hear. As was the fact that the body count only totaled two. The old woman was completely still—how could she possibly be alive?

Darryl felt sick when he thought about the black trucks and van that had passed them on the way to the apartments. They might as well have crawled directly out of his nightmares. And if they were that secret group he'd imagined snapping at their heels, they had to be pretty happy about seeing their net tightening around their prey.

Twisting away from that vision, Darryl looked out the window, and what he saw flashing past made him want to scream. A parked state trooper was sitting in a speed trap, and even though Terry was watching the limit, Darryl knew the cop was going to pull out.

"Shit," muttered Terry, eyes wide in the rearview.

When Darryl turned, he saw the flashing lights behind them, the siren already starting to wail.

"Pull over," he said, "and don't say a word. I'll do all of the talking." *Oh fuck*, thought Darryl, *you are done.*

Terry did as Darryl said, and Darryl watched the cop roll up behind them and then shut off the sirens, leaving the lights on to alert other drivers. The cop opened his door slowly and began walking toward them, his semiauto visible in his hand.

"He knows it's us, Darryl," said Terry. "He knows who we are, and you need to do something!"

Darryl shoved the cop and the man staggered, and then Darryl hit him again, making his legs march him across the two southbound lanes. The cop made it across both of them but didn't have the same luck with oncoming northbound traffic. A semi whose driver was insufficiently impressed by the cop car's flashers across the median came ripping toward him. The driver tried to turn at the last second, and Darryl watched the scene in what felt like slow motion. Its grill suddenly covered in cop and its driver working the wheel with decidedly limited results, the semi slid hard to the far shoulder before lurching back across the road in a horrible overcorrection and then blowing over the median and into oncoming traffic. Another oncoming truck blared its horn, and then the two trucks collided head-on. Their trailers buckled like massive accordions, the cabs all but disappearing between them. The noise of it was louder than anything Darryl had ever heard, the sound of gods fighting, a world war on the highway. Cars began to pile up behind the wreck, minor accidents resulting from the trucking cataclysm, and then Darryl was pounding Terry on the shoulder, begging him, "Drive, drive!"

Terry did as he was told, and a few seconds later they were the only moving car in sight. Good Samaritans from both sides of the highway ran toward the trucks, while less civic-minded motorists could be seen shouting at one another on the side of the gridlocked road. Darryl looked back to stare at the wreck, the sight of it almost as awe-inspiring as the mess at the docks, and then the twin trucks fireballed in a massive explosion. Even across the hundred or so yards they'd put behind them, he felt the hot wind buffet the car. Darryl could see people in the median begin to stand, lucky folks who had been blown clear of the blast. *I bet there are a lot of them who weren't so lucky*, thought Darryl. When he looked down at Cynthia, he found the little girl somehow still sleeping.

"You just want me to stay southbound?" Terry asked, startling Darryl into breaking his gaze from the slumbering bender next to him.

"Yeah, keep on south," said Darryl. "The sooner we're out of here, the better. At least that mess back there should slow things down."

"It might," said Terry, his eyes locking with Darryl's in the rearview mirror. "They're going to look at that cop's dashboard footage, and they're going to know it was us. I don't think it matters anymore, but they're going to know we're going south."

"We change trucks, head east once we're out of this fucking hellhole, and we're gone."

"They're going to catch us, Darryl," said Terry, sounding somber and oddly calm. "We took it too far when you grabbed that girl. That's the kind of thing that the media will never let go of. Nothing we do can make that go away, especially when they come up with more ways to tie all of this to us. I don't want to turn myself in, but I don't want to die, either."

"We're not going to die, and we're not going to be turning ourselves in." Darryl was stroking Cynthia's hair. She was going to make all of this worth it, he knew it. *If she can get in your head, she can do anything.*

Darryl could see his friend shaking his head, and though he wanted to remind Terry how this whole mess was started, he kept his mouth shut. There had been too much blood spilled since then to worry about old transgressions.

"Yeah, you're right," said Terry. "Just head south. We'll be fine."

Darryl frowned at Terry's bizarre change of heart and then looked at the air between them. He and the girl were bending—*Or weaving, she called it weaving*—Terry without even realizing it. Darryl closed his eyes, relaxed into the seat, and hoped the peace would last for just a few more minutes.

Chapter 72

1945

My dream is impossible, for in it I can see. As I wake, however, I realize that this is no dream. Katarina is kneeling over me, my face grasped in both of her hands, and I can see her as plain as I can see the moonlight through the slats in the timbered walls. I'm frozen there in the hayloft where we have hidden, frozen and waiting for her to say something, to explain my sight the way that she has been able to explain everything else in my life that has never made sense.

"Katarina, what are you doing?" I finally ask her when she doesn't volunteer the information, but she just clamps my head tighter in her hands, and then I feel her thumb wavering over my neck, dancing there over my throat. Fear races through me, a rocket of terror unlike anything I have felt since Dachau, even when the war was raging around us.

"Our journey is done," says Katarina. "Your war is over."

"What do you mean?" I ask, but I know the answer already. The camps have taught me that. Edna Greenberg, my mother, my family—all the dead and nameless, ever-filling pits with their twisted bodies and endless buckets of ash, have taught me never to trust one of these devils. I did, though. I trusted Katarina, and now I am going to suffer for this mistake.

"I mean, I need you, Ora, more than ever before," says Katarina.

I struggle against her, but the woman has an iron grip, and what I'd mistaken for a slim, almost frail body is actually very powerful.

"Hold still, kike. You need to hold still or things will get very bad for you."

/ *They can't be any worse* / I send the words like a missile, my lips never wavering as the thought leaves my mind. Katarina felt it, though. I think she expected little Ora to just roll over, do as she wished and then die, but I still have some fight left in me. I am exhausted, weakened from the years in the camp, starving, and dehydrated from our run from Dachau, but there is one thing I have been practicing every day.

Before Katarina can recover from the shock of my scream in her mind, I blast her as hard as I can, shoving her with my mind exactly as she'd been showing me. The second the wave of energy hits her, I lose my vision—it is as if I never had sight at all. Scrambling to my feet, I use what for most would be a second sight but for me is the only sight I ever really had. Katarina is struggling to stand, and I can see her pain in the pulse of her tendrils. Most of them are purple and red, but there are a few black ones, and some of the black ones are dead looking and limp and hang from her like thick braids. As Katarina works her way to her feet, I hit her again, even harder this time, and she shrieks both in my ears and between them.

I fall to my knees at the noise, willing myself to recover more quickly than she does, but as I look up, Katarina is already closing in on me, her threads filling the space between us with an ugly mass of fear and rage. I suck in air, ready myself to shove her again, hopefully to kill this monster and send her to the hellfire that she so rightfully earned, but before I can do so she is on top of me.

Katarina powers me to the ground with a blow from her fist and then a second from her mind—/ *Down* /—and I drop from the force of the combination. Katarina falls near me, begins battering my face with her hands and my head with her voice, that awful rage that threatened to tear my mind in half. I fight back, lifting my hands up, trying to give her another push to send her into the void, but it is too late. One of her hands is on the side of my head, and the other drags something cool across my throat. Numbness overcomes me, numbness so that I can't feel as much of my own death, but I can still feel my lungs begging for air and hear the screech of my ruined windpipe.

My vision comes back then—the worst time in the world for a blind girl to catch another glimpse of the world—and what I see is far worse than the broken feeling in my mind or the ragged feeling in my throat. Katarina looks like me. No, not good enough: Katarina is me, the exact vision of how I'd always pictured myself as I ran my hands over and over my face. Her eyes are milky white, now she is blind little Ora Rabban, and everything becomes clear. Why she helped me. Why I needed to run with her. Katarina has a special trick. *How many times has she used it?*

"More times than you can imagine," says Katarina. "More times than you want to imagine. Hundreds of times over hundreds of years, but you might have been the sweetest person I've tricked."

I struggle, grabbing for her, but she stands, then unrolls the backpack she's been carrying and pulls out her uniform.

"Don't worry, though. I'll only look like you for a few years, then I'll need to find someone else."

Her fingers go to work on me, and the seconds feel like hours. Above me, I can feel the sunlight through the slats in the barn's worn roof, and I know that she's taking her time with me, doing everything methodically, and unhurried. The light is fading as she begins to strip me, but as she pulls the Nazi jacket over my head, the last of my energy is gone. She has won, and I am just one more dead Jew in a country that is full of them. As she leaves me to my last breaths, I watch her struggle from the hayloft with her lack of sight, and the last thing I see is Katarina descending the ladder, a smile on her face.

Chapter 73

Mrs. Martin woke with a start in a tunnel of a room. The walls were covered in medical equipment, a good deal of it hooked to her and humming, wheezing, and beeping away, all while red dots and lines flashed and flickered. A man wearing the same odd yet familiar helmet and visor worn by the men in the van passed in front of her, and everything came back. Cynthia's father, the gun, the kidnapping, and her own trip in the van. The helmeted man passed out of her peripheral vision, and Mrs. Martin attempted to lift an arm and found that it was strapped to the bed. Attempts to move her other arm, legs, and head proved that it wasn't just the right arm that had been restrained, and Mrs. Martin did the only thing she could think of.

Nothing happened. For the first time since she could remember, Mrs. Martin had tried to leap from her body but nothing happened. The man in the visor and helmet walked in front of her again, a camera dangling from a cord around his neck. He lifted the camera and took a picture, and Mrs. Martin tried to dive into him, an easy task at this proximity, but again nothing happened. The man looked at the back of the camera, then nodded and walked away again. *I'm broken*, thought

Mrs. Martin, and then the door opened at the end of the trailer, and her worst fears were realized.

The raven-haired woman who walked inside was wearing a black jumpsuit and a headset and was unarmed. Mrs. Martin recognized her immediately and was gripped with terror. She had called the police but had never imagined that doing so could bring this upon her.

"Katarina, how have you been?" The woman in the jumpsuit asked the question like she was talking to an old friend, but they weren't friends, not even close. "You remember me, right? Does the name Jessica Hockstetter ring any bells for you?"

"My name is Henrietta Martin, Miss Hockstetter, and I think you must have the wrong person. I was never called Katarina, not even when I was a child. You must have me confused with someone else—"

"Ora Rabban, I know," said Jessica. "We've done this dance before, Katarina, remember?" Jessica walked over to the man wearing the helmet and took a file from the table he was working on. "Ora Rabban before—poor little Ora, who was so lucky to escape the camps, remember? My predecessor, Sam Claussen, wrote up this report, and I know old Sam would recognize you if he were still with the agency. Hell, I know I do, and we met twenty years after the war. Of course, we didn't know then that poor little Ora was dead outside of Dachau and that you were actually Katarina Kaufman. Of course, the Mossad prefers the title you enjoyed at Dachau, don't they?"

"Miss Hockstetter, please. You have me confused with someone else," said Mrs. Martin. "I have never heard of Ora Rabban or this Katarina Kaufman, and you and I have never met. This is all a misunderstanding, and I will be happy to help you clear it up. You must believe me. I'm just an old woman, but the child I was watching was taken. She—"

"The sooner you cut the bullshit, the sooner we can help her," said Jessica in a singsong voice. "I want Cynthia Robinson in safe hands as much as you do, although . . ." Jessica paused and then said, "You probably don't really care all that much that she's safe." Jessica flipped open the folder, skimmed a couple of pages, and then stopped and tapped one of the loose sheets of paper. "If you're back to your old methods—and why change what works?—then she is a TK like you, and you and Cynthia have been using your maps, haven't you? We've worked with a lot of high-level telekinetics, Katarina, but no one can build a map like you. Of course, you had plenty of practice in Dachau and the other camps you were helping to make more efficient, right?"

"My name is not Katarina," said Mrs. Martin, "and nothing that you say makes any sense. Forget all of this. Just try and find the girl, bring her to safety. She is with a pair of monsters right now, and God knows—"

"From one monster to another," said Jessica slowly. "That's the way I see it, and as far as I'm concerned, she's lucky that she ran into Mr. Livingston when she did. We both know what can happen to a child under your watch."

"I have never hurt a child in my life," said Mrs. Martin. "Never. These are lies, all lies, and—"

"Facial recognition software has her at a 99.98999 match," said the man in the helmet. "Still waiting on DNA, but Hartford will have something for us within the hour."

"Lovely," said Jessica. "Do we really need to wait for the DNA, Katarina? You and I both know who and what you are, so let's cut to the chase. Either you're going to help us find Cynthia, or I'm going to have you on the first plane to Israel. I don't think they'd really want to keep you there, but I know they'd love to have you as a guest for at least a little while. Maybe long enough for a trial. That shouldn't take long, though. Your war crimes are well documented."

"You need to get her from those men."

"We will, eventually," said Jessica, "though with your help we could find her faster."

"I've never had that sort of ability," said Mrs. Martin. "I am not who you think I am, and my little parlor tricks will do us no good in finding Cynthia."

"Well, you're wrong about that, Katarina," said Jessica. "We had no idea we'd manage to ensnare you in the middle of the sting we were setting up to trap Darryl and Terry, but sometimes things just work out for the best. Now that we have you, we can use your connection with Cynthia to help locate her, and you must have inadvertently drawn the men here as well. Four of you in one place is a godsend, but not likely to happen without a little prodding. Time is of the essence, of course. I'm sure wherever the three of them are moving, they're headed there as fast as possible."

"I cannot help you. I'm just an old, lonely widow, not this monster that you have invented."

"The problem seems to be," said Jessica, "that you think there's a chance I'm going to believe you. I assure you I don't. I don't need facial-recognition software or a DNA test to know that you're Katarina Kaufman. You killed Ora Rabban once you were far enough away from the camp that you could steal her identity and attempt to defect. You hid in survivor camps for weeks, and then what happened?"

"I have no idea."

"You were recognized," said Jessica. "The Death Angel of Dachau was spotted by some of her former inmates. It took ten years, but eventually you were found, just like so many of the Reich runaways. Oh, they must have been overjoyed to see you carted off, Katarina. But then they would have been sick to learn that the US government wasn't going to execute or even punish you but instead keep you comfortable and put you to work. It wasn't a waste—you were very helpful during the Cold War, after all—but then you ran." Jessica smiled. "You ran, and now we have you again, and if you don't help me find Cynthia, I'll see you in Israel by tomorrow night. This is your last chance."

"What if I help you?" Katarina asked.

"Then you get to live a little longer," said Jessica. "I don't want to sugarcoat things, Katarina. You're a monster, and the US government doesn't need monsters nearly as much as it did forty years ago."

"That girl isn't going to listen to anyone but me," said Katarina. "If you want her to be a good little angel and do your dirty work, you're going to need me." She smiled. "I brought them here to me, the girl and her idiot mother. And the two men, too, though I hadn't intended to. Too bad for them, but more proof of what I can do. You need me."

"I guess we'll have to see about that," said Jessica, before turning to the man in the helmet and saying, "Get her prepped for REC/RES—the sooner the better." Jessica smiled at Katarina. "Just remember, this can end badly for you at any time. You play nice, and I will, too. If we get that girl back and you try and corrupt her, I will see that you suffer. The Jews are still hunting people like you, and they are not in the least bit sick of it. If I called Israel, they'd have agents on a plane before I hung up the phone. Are we clear?"

Katarina nodded. The time for lies was over. She was caught back in the web of the TRC.

Chapter 74

Cynthia woke with a start in the truck. It all came back quickly.
Terry was still driving, his hands on the wheel as he hummed along
with the radio, and Darryl was staring out the window across from
her. All threads connecting the three of them were gone, and Cynthia
was glad for that. She wanted to be sad, and she didn't want to be
happy that she was with these strange men. She wanted things that
were impossible. She wanted to go back home, to Mom or Dad or her
grandparents, even to Mrs. Martin. She just wanted to be with people
who she knew cared about her.

Taking advantage of the moment of peace, she took stock of her
situation. She had been kidnapped by two strange men, and she had
no idea where they might be bringing her. She wasn't even sure if
they knew. Somehow she wasn't scared. Learning the words "divorce"
and "affair" had been a lot scarier than this. She realized she was in a
dangerous place, but still she felt serene. Maybe it was the loss of her
parents—a loss she hadn't been witness to but that she could feel all
the same—but Cynthia felt like nothing really mattered anymore. The
same was not true for her captors, and she knew this put her at an
advantage over them.

Every few songs the DJ on the radio would break into the broadcast and begin talking. These interludes tended to induce moments of under-the-breath swearing from Terry before he violently spun the dial, waited about thirty seconds, and spun it back to the music of his preferred station. Cynthia didn't need her gift to know what was going on. The radio was talking about them, alerting people to look out for them. Cynthia glanced out the window. There didn't seem to be much chance of them being seen. Terry was sticking to the back roads.

You'll need to make your own luck now. The quote had been one of Dad's, and the recollection made her sad, but the thought was no less true.

"I have to pee," said Cynthia after spotting a gas station sign growing above the trees on the horizon. She watched as Terry and Darryl exchanged a long look. "I really do," she said. "I'm going to wet my pants."

"All right," said Terry. "I'll pull off here in a few minutes. Just hold your horses."

Cynthia nodded and smiled thinly. She knew she couldn't weave with either of the men, nor could she invade them completely to see what they were thinking, but she could still vibe off of them very easily, and Terry was nervous. The truck was down to a quarter tank, so there was more reason than just pee to stop, but Terry didn't want to. He wanted to drive and drive and drive.

The gas station sign grew on the horizon and then disappeared behind a wall of timber. Cynthia did have to pee, that wasn't a lie—and with Darryl in the car, was there a point in lying?—but she also wanted to slow them down and maybe even get noticed by someone. As the sign reappeared, Cynthia formulated a plan. *Darryl told you not to bend him or Terry, so don't. Weave like Mrs. Martin taught you.*

"No funny business," said Darryl as Terry parked the truck next to a pair of beater trucks. "I'm serious, Cynthia. We're in a pretty interesting situation right now, and the last thing that any of us need is extra attention. Terry is going to let us off right here, you're going to use the bathroom while he gases up the truck, and then he's going to pick us up. I don't want to regret not making you pee in the woods, is that clear?"

"Yes."

And then she and Darryl slid from the truck. Cynthia could see the back of the clerk's head as he stood behind the register. He was an old man who likely would have enjoyed Mrs. Martin's dogs. Darryl took her around to the unisex bathroom at the back of the station. After knocking on the door and getting no response, he pulled it open for her.

"I'm going to stand right here," said Darryl. "Do not waste any time. Just get in and get out, OK?"

Cynthia nodded again, and Darryl shut the door after her. She sat on the toilet, made her water, and then pulled up her pants before sitting back on the toilet. Cynthia took a deep breath, pictured the gas station, and then roared into the sky above it. The sight from above was not like Mrs. Martin's North Harbor map. The map of the Sunoco was blurry at the edges, and the lines looked as though they'd been drawn by a child. Cynthia wondered at these changes and at the obvious skill that her teacher possessed, and then fired into the gas station.

Cynthia could see Terry on the other side of the counter from her, and she realized with a start that she had landed directly behind the eyes of the old clerk. Knowing that she had only seconds, Cynthia wove her own thoughts around the clerk's, reminding him of the two fugitives on the run he'd heard about on the radio and of the little girl they had taken with them. As she left, she made sure the clerk had two fresh thoughts in his mind: he needed to call the police as soon as Terry left, and then he needed to go around to the back of the building to get a look-see.

Cynthia returned to her body just in time to hear Darryl knock on the door and say, "All right, Cynthia, Terry's going to be pulling the truck back here."

Cynthia stood and opened the door a few seconds later, Darryl giving her an odd look as she left the dingy washroom, likely trying to tell if she'd been up to anything. She knew he might be too busy to keep much of an eye on her for much longer, though, if the clerk did as he was told. Cynthia watched with Darryl from the corner of the building as Terry hung the gas pump up, started the truck, and began to drive back to them.

"All right, get in quick," said Darryl as Terry slid to a stop near them. "I've got the heebie-jeebies."

Cynthia didn't blame him—she did, too—and then the clerk rounded the building and time seemed to slow. Cynthia had her foot on the truck's running board, Darryl was waiting behind her, and Terry was sitting behind the wheel when the clerk appeared with an enormous revolver in one hand and the cordless phone in the other.

"You come here, girl," said the clerk, pulling up short and leveling the gun at Terry. "And you, shut off that truck. Do it quick now—the law's coming, and I'd rather see you leave in cuffs than bags."

Cynthia started toward the man, but Darryl grabbed her forearm and held her in place. She turned to him, a look of fury in her eyes, and then the gas station attendant was talking again.

"Yes, they're still here," he said into the phone. "They're holing themselves up in the gas station, and I think their truck broke down."

None of this made any sense to Cynthia. They weren't "holing up" in the station, and the truck was ready to ride. But then Darryl was dragging Cynthia to the old man, who threw the phone down and then handed his keys to Darryl.

That's when she knew that Darryl was in the man.

"Come on, Terry," shouted Darryl, and Terry left the truck running and followed after them.

The three of them walked around the back of the gas station, where they found an aging Buick. Darryl tossed Terry the keys, and the three of them piled inside, reluctant Cynthia hopping into the backseat with Darryl. The car turned over easily, the bodywork no indication of the care taken for the parts that mattered. Terry pulled around the gas station, and Cynthia stared out of the window at the man. He'd pulled the truck into the road, and gas was leaking everywhere from the pumps. The man gave them a wave as Terry pulled onto the road, and after a short turn the man and the gas station were gone.

"You got him killed. I hope you know that," said Darryl, but Cynthia ignored him. She was well aware of the price of her failure. "I said no funny business, and then you make that poor guy, who was just minding his own business, get involved. Trust me, that guy was better off not interfering, especially with what's going to come next."

Darryl sighed, and Cynthia could tell he was mad enough to hit her. *I don't care, let him*, thought Cynthia. Nothing could have mattered less.

"That's the last time, your last chance. Do you understand?"

Cynthia ignored him, and she could see the fury in Darryl's eyes. He might have swung on her then, but Terry interrupted their bickering.

"Do you guys hear that?"

"Yes," said Darryl. "That's a helicopter. If we're lucky, it's headed to the gas station."

"What if we're not lucky?"

"Just drive, Terry," said Darryl.

Chapter 75

Katarina sat in leg restraints and handcuffs aboard the chopper.
Next to her in the other rear seat was Jessica Hockstetter, and ahead of
them were a pair of pilots dressed in the same headgear that the men in
the van and trailer had worn.

Katarina felt worn to the bone, but this was good—they were going
to find Cynthia and return her little darling to her. Katarina knew all
too well the dangers of being imprisoned by the TRC, but she was
also confident that with the girl she'd be able to escape all over again.
It wouldn't be as easy as the last time, but it would be worth the risk.

The helicopter was flying low to the trees, following the two-lane
road south as it slowly meandered toward Indiana. Guessing that
they would be going south had taken no special intuition. Jessica had
already been sure that was where they would head, and the call from
the gas station had only confirmed it. Now they were just minutes from
getting a visual on the car, assuming they could get a look at the road
for more than a few seconds at a time.

Katarina felt anxious. She hated being locked up like this, hated
flying, and still had a bitter feeling in her stomach that, as soon as
Katarina outweighed her usefulness, that bitch Jessica was going to

send her off to be killed by the Israelites. Katarina had followed the cases of long-missing German officials, and the results were uniformly horrifying. First, a shameful parade for the cameras, next a sham of a trial, and finally the rope. Katarina had read the newspaper religiously following Eichmann's capture, and even though he'd been killed nearly forty years ago, she still had chills at the memory.

I will find a way to live, thought Katarina. That she had once overseen death camps where so many had thought the same thing was not lost on her, but that did not alter the fact that she did not want to die.

The helicopter dipped in closer to the trees, and then Jessica's voice came over the speakers. "Do you feel anything yet? Are they down there?"

Katarina shook her head in answer. She felt nothing. Jessica nodded and turned back to the window, the frustration clear in her eyes.

The helicopter rose and then dipped again as the forest broke into a clean stretch of road. There were three vehicles that could be seen immediately, and Jessica was speaking over their shared comm link, telling the radio operator, "I want cruisers a mile ahead of us and a mile behind us." Katarina smiled to herself at this command. More men with guns weren't going to be much help. They needed someone like her to bring this chase to an end. Katarina sighed to herself, content that the day was likely to end with them still in pursuit, and then in her peripheral vision she saw another helicopter closing on their flank.

The new chopper was unmarked, as was the one Katarina was riding in, and the pilot and radio operator wore helmets identical to those the men in her own ride were crowned with. Why the helmets, unless this new helicopter held another who must be guarded against? A queer thought crossed her mind: *Could that be? No*, she decided, *such a thing simply cannot be possible.* She frowned. *There's no way the old man is still around, but that doesn't mean that there aren't more like him.* Katarina grimaced. *He could be, though, and if he is, he'll be very happy to see you.* This thought was a sickening one, and Katarina only felt worse yet when she turned to Jessica and glimpsed the wry smile crossing the woman's lips.

The helicopter felt as though it was moving faster over the open road, the new perspective beyond the trees allowing them to see much farther than before. Katarina was searching for Cynthia in the three cars they'd spotted but was finding nothing. It was as if the girl had vanished, even though, for all she knew, Cynthia could have been in sight. Roving police cars were visible on the ground as well, some stopped at various crossroads, others patrolling the same stretch of highway they were overseeing.

There was a burst of static from the front of the cockpit, and then the radio operator said, "All right, visual confirmed. All units toward target."

"What's going on?" Jessica asked.

The radioman's voice was clear over the headsets. "There was a suspect at the gas station who engaged in a firefight with police. He's in custody now, shot up but conscious, and he confirmed make, model, and color for us." The radioman pointed below them. "That red sedan right there is our vehicle."

"I want them in custody now," said Jessica, the wry smile replaced by one with a wolfish intensity. "No guns, no bullshit, I want them now. Tell Frank to shut them down immediately."

Frank. Katarina nodded to herself. Frank was alive, they were about to apprehend the others without her help, and Israel was a mere flight away. When they'd taken them all where they were set on taking them, she'd have to make herself useful to them, and in a hurry.

Chapter 76

Darryl had been trying not to think about the helicopters ever since they'd first spotted them, but it was a battle he was losing. It was bad enough seeing all the cops, but the helicopters made him feel like he was in some spy movie, a movie he had never wanted to be a part of. They were going to need to get off of this chunk of road soon, head in any other direction, and try and find some more trees.

Darryl watched in frustration as they passed another parked cop blocking a side road, and then frustration turned to fear as three marked cars behind them turned on lights and sirens. The cop car that had been blocking the side road pulled out after them as well. Four then. Gaining on them. Time to get to work.

Looking through the Buick's back window, Darryl locked eyes with the cop driving the first cruiser and began to bend him. / *Throw on your brakes / Ram them / Shoot them / Kill them* / Darryl shoved hard. The cop should have immediately reacted, but nothing happened. Darryl shoved him again, harder this time, and then Cynthia began to scream. Darryl turned to her in confusion, and then a head-splitting pain tore through him. Darryl heard his own voice added to the wind, and then the car was driving into the median. Darryl caught flickers of Terry trying to maintain control, but he could barely keep his eyes open against the pain.

Darryl felt the world passing by in flashes, the car first bouncing over the lawn, then rolling as the sky became the earth and back again, and finally the car coming to a stop. Terry was working to free himself, right hand on the seat belt release just like Darryl, but Cynthia wasn't moving. *Is she dead?* Darryl had neither the time nor ability to check. Strong arms dragged him from the ruined car and tossed him to the ground like a piece of trash. Darryl tried to push them, but there was nothing there, just a dull spot that felt like a missing tooth.

Darryl screamed as he was cuffed, screamed as they muzzled him, and then someone stuck a needle into his arm. He felt his legs go numb even though he was lying on his belly, and then they were carrying him, then tossing him into the back of a van, where he was strapped to a gurney. Darryl blinked as the last of his consciousness ebbed away. The final thing he saw as his eyes fluttered shut was a man wearing a bizarre helmet leaning over him. Darryl tried one more time to push, to command the man to free him and begin killing, but there was nothing there.

Chapter 77

Two Months Later

Jessica Hockstetter walked from one observation room to the next.
Frank was having a rough day, but that could be expected for a man of
his age. She'd forced herself to check in on him, but what she wanted to
see were the newest acquisitions of the TRC, not some dinosaur. Still,
Frank had proven his usefulness once again, even if using him felt like
asking an elephant to kill a fly.

Jessica took a seat and watched the two men behind the mirror
interact with one another. All of the rooms were recorded twenty-four
hours a day, but she preferred the simplicity of watching her subjects
through one-way glass whenever possible.

Jessica turned as the door behind her slid open and her boss,
Howard Thompson, entered the room and sat down next to her.

"Fascinating, isn't it?" Jessica said, and Howard nodded. He'd been
with the Telekinetic Research Center since just after the war, but even
Howard had to agree that these new acquisitions were special.

Darryl was pacing on the other side of the glass, while Terry sat on
the bottom bunk of a bunk bed. Both of the men looked perturbed,

but Jessica knew that what she was seeing were just the shared emotions of Darryl. Terry, as physically real as he might look, was actually the fantastically corporeal astral projection of a man with multiple personalities who just happened to be a TK. Because he often did bad things, Darryl needed a scapegoat—so he made one for himself. Terry might look, sound, and even feel human to other people, but he was only as real as Darryl allowed him to be.

"Astounding as this trick of his is," explained Jessica, "part of his therapy is going to be convincing him to let go of the ghost. It hampers his abilities and makes it difficult for him to do many of the things that should come to him easily."

"As long as we must keep him, is there no way to retain this ghost of his in some manner? At least, long enough to study it, see if any use can be made—"

Jessica was shaking her head. "That's not a luxury we can afford. We need to be assured of our control of Darryl, and that's going to be challenging enough with just one of him."

Howard sighed. Jessica knew she hadn't told him anything he didn't know but didn't begrudge him making her repeat it, or grieving the loss of this research opportunity. Thinking of the tactical advantages of harnessing the ability to create soldiers or assassins—or, hell, legions of worker bees—Jessica couldn't help but marvel at the possibilities.

"The man needed another set of hands," marveled Howard, "so he created one."

"It's incredible," said Jessica.

"It is that," agreed Howard. "I'm sure you've been over the file every which way. Did the projection do all of the killing?"

"All that we can find, save for the death at the gas station that was caught on the dash cam," said Jessica. "Of course, that doesn't count all of the people that Darryl killed with his mind. He is a very dangerous man."

"You don't say," grumbled Howard.

Even after the intriguing introduction of Darryl's wonder twin to the equation, Howard had continued to argue vehemently for Darryl's immediate termination, but Jessica's argument had managed to overrule him. Howard still felt that a man like Darryl Livingston would be easier to kill than fix, regardless of the little tricks he could pull.

"He has a low probability of success," said Jessica, "but you can you imagine how powerful he'll be if we can get him to cooperate."

"He has nothing on the girl," said Howard. "Even Katarina in her youth has nothing on the girl, not even Frank." Howard's brow furrowed. "How is Frank, by the way?"

"Well enough all things considered," said Jessica. "The fact of the matter is that Frank is very old, and regardless of his mental strength, his body is breaking down."

"This lab is a time bomb if that man dies," said Howard, and Jessica nodded. There was no arguing that. "Without Frank, even if every man and woman in here is wearing a Tesla Helmet we'd still have to worry about one of the TKs turning a guard. Even a temporary lack of control could see the lot of them freed."

Jessica only nodded mildly. The old man never had been able to accept the inherent danger in what they did. *What worth doing comes easily?* There were great rewards to be had with the program—history had shown that time and time again—and those rewards were worth the potential risks.

"Why don't we move on to the girl?" said Howard finally, hoisting himself to his feet.

Jessica stood and walked after him into the hall.

Jessica and Howard swiped key cards at the door to the observation area for Cynthia's room and stepped inside. Even as they took their seats, their eyes were already locked onto the little wunderkind.

Cynthia was sitting with Katarina—still Mrs. Martin to her—and the two of them were talking about something inconsequential. The girl burst into laughter on the other side of the mirror, and Howard turned to Jessica.

"Do you really think that she could be who we've been looking for?"

"We've only done the most minimal testing," said Jessica. "The fear is that we'll push too hard and she'll just shut down, maybe lose the gift entirely. After all, this girl has been through some significant trauma. I'd rather we take it slow and learn about what she can do at a reasonable pace, then drive to compile her full TK score now. She's young, and we have all the time in the world to learn about her."

"You didn't answer my question," said Howard.

"She's the most talented TK we've ever had, including Frank," said Jessica. "If she's not the one, she's the closest we've ever come to it. If we train her right, we're going to have a hell of a thing."

"But what do you think, Jessica?"

"I think this little girl is going to change the world," said Jessica, letting the words slip out like she'd been holding her breath. "I think she might just be the second coming of Frank, but without the psychopathic tendencies. You worry about Darryl because he's done dangerous things, but that little girl in there is going to grow up, and when she does she's going to be unimaginably powerful."

"Thank goodness we have her."

"I cannot imagine what would happen if she were to walk around free in a few years with the power that she has," said Jessica. "She's a loaded gun, there's no doubt about that, but she'll be fine as long as she stays with us."

ACKNOWLEDGMENTS

I'm not sure that I believe in true love. At least, not in the tradi-tional sense of seeing that perfect person across the room and just knowing right then that things are meant to be. I need guts, I guess, something which is no secret to my readers, and in 1998 I found guts by the bucketload.

I was playing a punk rock show in the basement of a music store in front of an audience of about a hundred people. As we finished our set, I did the splits, tearing the entire crotch of my camo shorts in half. No one seemed to notice my plight, except, that is, for the most beautiful girl I have ever seen. Trust me, it wasn't just the broken pants.

In any case, she fixed my shorts with safety pins that she took from a messenger bag she was using as a purse, and we introduced ourselves. Her name was Megan, and that seemed like all that was to come of it. The most wonderful girl in the world had fixed my pants, and I was going to let her slip away. Life is funny that way and even funnier in other ways. Six months later both of us were single and we decided to go on a date. As far as I can tell, that first date is still going.

Of course, things are never perfect. Despite jobs that we both liked, a burgeoning ability to write that I was desperately trying to nurture, and a wonderful daughter, we still had our trials. They were good trials, though—those of you who have done the dance know what I mean. The electric bill that could not be paid but somehow gets handled is a miracle like no other in this world. Finally getting published was another unexpected happening.

A common question that authors get is, "Where do your ideas come from?" Stephen King has written extensively on the subject, and to paraphrase him, basically an idea usually starts out like a little scrap of a bone and if uncovered right, there might just happen to be a T. rex down there underneath all of the dirt. Sometimes, however, ideas come faster, like a hockey puck to the face. *Weavers* is one of the latter.

September 23, 2013, was one of the worst days of my life. Everything felt like it was crashing down around me, and to top it off I was on a work trip in Albany, New York. Things were bleak, they felt like they were getting worse by the second, and after tossing and turning that night, I finally fell asleep. A few hours later I woke up covered in sweat and, in a moment of rare brilliance, grabbed my phone and opened the notes section. I'm not one to believe that authors get ideas from dreams—at least, this one doesn't—but I had just gotten a doozy, and I knew I had to hold on to it. At the time it felt like maybe that idea was all I really had to hold on to.

The note I wrote was simple, and it said, "Carol can see things, p. divorce." Not much to go on, but I had just seen the first Cynthia chapter in my head while I was asleep. Hopefully it was just as vivid for you when you read it a few hundred pages ago. I vowed to myself that no matter what, I was going to get my head on straight, and I was going to write this book. I'm happy to say that right now both things have been accomplished, and neither of them would have been possible without the love and support of my wife.

A little over a year later, it all sort of hit me. I was waking up after having my hip replaced, and my wife was sitting next to me in the hospital. At once it all came crashing down—the book, the recovery, everything I could have lost. I don't deserve someone so wonderful in my life. I'd come to realize that such things are earned—and only then if we're very lucky—and yet there I was in a hospital with the love of my life. It was a hard year—it was a year we earned in a lot of different ways—but I wouldn't trade it for anything. Trust me, if you have surgery and wake up next to the person you love more than anything else in the world, you're in a good place.

Thanks as always to my wife and daughter for their endless support, especially as the reality of just how difficult this book was going to be sort of came to bear on me. I love you guys a ton, and I know that I could not do what I do without your love and support.

Thanks as well to my mom and dad, cheerleaders and first readers as always, and both a huge inspiration for this book as well. I can't say for sure that watching *Dune* with my dad when I was eight allows me to have such weird ideas, but it probably didn't hurt.

Thanks a ton to my editor, Anh, who took a look at an early draft of *Weavers* and gave me a pair of suggestions. Thirty-three thousand words later, the rewrite was done, and if you liked this book, Anh is a big part of the reason—her ideas for changes were utterly instrumental. If you hated it, however, that can all be on me.

Thanks to David for another wonderful edit. Piecing together this weird little story with you the second time around was almost as fun as doing it the first time by myself.

Thanks to Greg for tons of good suggestions as always, and for being a great friend. When this book comes out, you and Maggie will have just passed your second anniversary, so hey, congrats on that.

A big thanks to Jacque, Grace, Kim, and the rest of the Kindle Most Wanted team for putting together an amazing event in NYC. I'm still a little nervous that I'm going to look dorky on camera but am excited to see the results. Plus, it's not every day that you get to have conversations with Blake Crouch, Marcus Sakey, S. G. Redling, and Reed Farrel Coleman like it's the most normal thing in the world.

Thanks to Dr. James Bakeman of Orthopaedic Associates of Michigan and his wonderful staff for getting me safely through surgery and repairing my ruined hip.

Thanks as well to Dr. Dave Thornsen of Fountain Hill Center for being a great friend and a wonderful listener.

Thanks of course to everyone at Thomas & Mercer and Amazon in general. There are so many of you guys, but thanks so much to Jeff, Tiffany, Brooke, Alan, Jon, Sarah, Andrew, Alex, Caroline, Britt, Jodi, Justin, David, Ashley, Luke, and every other darn person that works in those massive buildings. You guys are the best and do so much for your authors that it's really sort of unbelievable.

Finally, thanks to my dear friend and first editor, Terry Goodman, who retired earlier this year. I wish you all the best, Terry, and I will never be able to repay you for what you've done for me and my family, so if you need a body disappeared, keep me in the Rolodex.

One last thing: Cynthia and Darryl and Terry and Jessica and Katarina and everyone else are going to be back sooner rather than later. I can't wait for you guys to see what happens next. Thanks to all of you for reading my work and for giving this writer a chance. You guys are the best, and this world wouldn't be nearly as fun of a place to live in if I couldn't share my stories with you.

ABOUT THE AUTHOR

Aric Davis is married with one daughter and lives in Grand Rapids, Michigan, where he worked for sixteen years as a body piercer. He now writes full-time. He likes weather cold enough to need a sweatshirt but not a coat, and friends who wear their hearts on their sleeves. In addition to reading and writing, he also enjoys roller coasters, hockey, punk rock, and a good cigar.

Davis is the author of eight other books: *From Ashes Rise: A Novel of Michigan*; *Nickel Plated*; *A Good and Useful Hurt*; *The Black Death: A Dead Man Novella*; *Rough Men*; *Breaking Point*; *The Fort*; and *Tunnel Vision*.